Back There in the Grass:
The Horror Tales of Irvin S. Cobb and Gouverneur Morris

The Hippocampus Press Classics of Gothic Horror Series

CLASSICS OF GOTHIC HORROR

Edited by S. T. Joshi

Johnson Looked Back: The Collected Weird Stories of Thomas Burke
The Harbor-Master: Best Weird Stories of Robert W. Chambers
Lost Ghosts: The Complete Weird Stories of Mary E. Wilkins Freeman
Back There in the Grass: The Horror Tales of
Irvin S. Cobb and Gouverneur Morris
The Mummy's Foot and Other Fantastic Tales, Théophile Gautier
Twin Spirits: The Complete Weird Stories of W. W. Jacobs
From the Dead: The Complete Weird Stories of E. Nesbit
Frankenstein and Others: The Complete Weird Fiction of Mary Shelley

Back There in the Grass

The Horror Tales of
Irvin S. Cobb and Gouverneur Morris

Edited by S. T. Joshi

Hippocampus Press

New York

Published by Hippocampus Press
P.O. Box 641, New York, NY 10156.
http://www.hippocampuspress.com

Cover art © 2020 by Aeron Alfrey
Cover design and "Classics of Gothic Horror" logo by Dan Sauer,
dansauerdesign.com
Hippocampus Press logo designed by Anastasia Damianakos.

First Edition
1 3 5 7 9 8 6 4 2

ISBN13: 978-1-61498-292-0

Contents

Introduction

In one sense, Irvin S. Cobb (1876–1944) and Gouverneur Morris (1876–1953) could not be more different. Aside from the commonplace similarity of being American short story writers working at roughly the same time period, their lives were as contrasting as the lives of two popular writers could be. Cobb, a resolute Midwesterner in spite of his long residence in New York, attained immense literary and even media celebrity in the course of his life—a celebrity that culminated in 1935, when he was the master of ceremonies at the Academy Awards in Hollywood, where he was embraced and kissed by Claudette Colbert and Shirley Temple. Morris, a scion of a signer of the Declaration of Independence, did attain success as a writer, but abandoned writing in middle age and became a staid bank president. For our purposes, however, their most significant point in common was the fact that a slim but significant sliver of their literary output consisted of powerful tales of supernatural and psychological terror.

It is also striking that, while virtually nothing is known of Morris's life apart from the mere record of his publications, Cobb left an enormous paper trail that has led to numerous biographies, memoirs, and critical studies. Accordingly, the bulk of this introduction will be devoted to Cobb's life—a life of fascinating twists and turns, and which led him to long residences in widely scattered locales in the United States.

Irvin Shrewsbury Cobb was born on June 23, 1876, in Paducah, Kentucky, a smallish city of 15,000 people located on the Ohio River in the far western part of the state. He was the second of four children of Joshua and Manie (Saunders) Cobb. In his early years his education alternated between local public and private schools; but his formal education came to an abrupt end in 1892, when his family's financial difficulties (chiefly his father's loss of his job and his subsequent descent into alcoholism) compelled the young Cobb to work full-time. In school he had shown great precocity and the ability to learn quickly; and he also learned much from a family friend, "Uncle" Joel Shrewsbury, from whom his middle name derived. Cobb's readings were wide and diverse, ranging from nineteenth-century literary classics to dime novels. He had also hung around the docks where his father worked, gaining a sense of both the commerce and the romance of the river and its steamboat traffic. Other early interests included birds and reptiles as well as the Native American relics found abundantly in the area; and he was fascinated to hear the stories of the old inhabitants of the town as they reminisced about antebellum days. (As a border state, Kentucky had supporters of both the Union and the Confederate cause.)

All these interests seemed to lead inexorably to his working for the local paper, the *Paducah Daily News.* Beginning as a reporter in 1893, he even attained the lofty position of managing editor in 1895, a position he held for two years. Gradually he felt the need to take his journalistic talents to a larger metropolitan paper, and in 1898 he joined the staff of the *Louisville Evening Post,* where he began a humorous column called "Kentucky Sour Mash," a reference to the bootleg liquor of his state. He also worked as a political reporter, being at the state capitol in Frankfort when the Governor-elect, William Goebel, was assassinated on January 30, 1900.

Cobb had met Laura Baker in 1896, and after several years of persistent courting persuaded her to marry him on June 12, 1900. Soon thereafter the *Paducah Daily Democrat* (later the *News Democrat*) lured Cobb back to his hometown with a higher salary (the sum of $30 a week), and he became managing editor. He continued to support his mother and sisters after his marriage, but he also continued to feel the call of the big-city newspaper. In 1904 he went to the biggest city of all, New York, and by a certain brashness managed to secure a job at the *New York Evening Sun,* one of the most distinguished papers of the day. Once established there, he brought his wife and daughter, Elizabeth (born in 1902), to join him. A year later he began an association with the *New York World* that lasted until 1912. Aside from covering such events as the peace conference of the Russo-Japanese War in Portsmouth, N.H., in 1905, he initiated as many as six different humorous columns, most of which ran in the features section on Sunday.

Cobb always maintained that his extensive journalistic writing was good practice for his eventual career as a short-story writer and novelist; but he only undertook the latter around 1908, when a colleague, Samuel Blythe, assured him that the *Saturday Evening Post,* one of the best-paying "slick" magazines of the day, would welcome his contributions. One of his earliest stories, "The Escape of Mr. Trimm," appeared in the *Post* in 1909. Soon Cobb was publishing there and in other magazines, including the Munsey magazines, which catered to a popular audience. Cobb, who had been quite thin in his youth, became a corpulent man in his adulthood, and he poked fun at his girth in one of his earliest volumes, *Cobb's Anatomy* (1912). This book, like many of his others during the first decade or two of his career, was published by George H. Doran Company. Cobb had purchased a small house in Yonkers in 1907, and Doran himself became his neighbor in 1909. His first story collection, *The Escape of Mr. Trimm,* appeared in 1913.

Cobb and other reporters were sent to Europe to cover the outbreak of World War I in the later summer of 1914. He set sail on August 7, 1914, proceeding from Liverpool to Belgium. German shelling of the town of Louvain forced him to take cover there for three days; finally he made it to Brussels. But when the Germans took over that city, he tricked the German officials into allowing him wide latitude to explore the region, and his vivid descriptions of the widespread devastation of Belgium brought him considerable celebrity. Later, he and other reporters were detained by the German Army at Beaumont and then taken to Aix-la-Chapelle, in German-controlled Alsace. Cobb and others wrote a letter directly to the Kaiser, stressing the benefits of having American reporters in Germany (the United States was at this time still officially neutral in the conflict); incredibly, the Kaiser acceded to the argument, allowing the reporters to go behind German lines. After some weeks Cobb managed to get to Vaals, in the Netherlands, and then moved on to London, returning home on November 1. His articles, appearing in the *Saturday Evening Post* and *Philadelphia Public Ledger,* were collected as *Paths of Glory* (1915). He later went on a lecture tour to talk about the war, attracting large audiences.

Cobb wished to return at once to the war front, but illness prevented him: he required an operation for a hernia. He made this unpleasant incident pay immense dividends, for he wrote a long article entitled "Speaking of Operations—," appearing in the *Saturday Evening Post* (November 6, 1915), that proved hugely popular; when it was published as a booklet it sold half a million copies.

Cobb continued to write fiction and other matter in immense quantities. The great majority of this work was humor. He initiated a series of tales featuring Old Judge Priest, a no-nonsense judge in Paducah based on an actual individual, William Sutton Bishop, whom Cobb admired. Subsidiary characters—including a sympathetically portrayed black servant of Priest's, Jefferson Poindexter—were also based on figures in Kentucky. A total of forty-two stories and two short novels about Priest appeared in Cobb's lifetime. Cobb—who seemed to model himself on Mark Twain whenever he could, whether it be his fascination with the great rivers of the Midwest or with comic or travel writing—also wrote a number of humorous travel books, the first being *Europe Revised* (1914), followed by a series of books about individual states as part of "The American Guyed Books Series." He also became a popular after-dinner speaker.

But Cobb's literary reputation never recovered from H. L. Mencken's attack on it in various reviews, which were gathered as "The Heir of Mark Twain" and published in Mencken's *Prejudices: First Series* (1919). The opening of the essay testifies both to Cobb's celebrity and to Mencken's disdain of his writing as second-rate and lowbrow:

> Nothing could be stranger than the current celebrity of Irvin S. Cobb, an author of whom almost as much is heard as if he were a new Thackeray or Molière. One is solemnly told by various extravagant partisans, some of them not otherwise insane, that he is at once the successor to Mark Twain and the heir of Edgar Allan Poe. One hears of public dinners given in devotion to his genius, of public presentations, of learned degrees conferred upon him by universities, of other extraordinary adulations, few of them shared by such relatively puny fellows as Howells and Dreiser. His talents and sagacity pass into popular anecdotes; he has sedulous Boswells; he begins to take on the august importance of an actor-manager. Behind the scenes, of course, a highly dexterous publisher pulls the strings, but much of it is undoubtedly more or less sincere; men pledge their sacred honor to the doctrine that his existence honors the national literature. . . .

In the actual books of the man I can find nothing that seems to justify so much enthusiasm, nor even the hundredth part of it. His serious fiction shows a certain undoubted facility, but there are at least forty other Americans who do the thing quite as well. His public bulls and ukases are no more than clever journalism—superficial and inconsequential, first saying one thing and then quite another thing. And in his humor, which his admirers apparently put first among his products, I can discover, at best, nothing save a somewhat familiar aptitude for grotesque anecdote, and, at worst, only the laborious laugh-squeezing of Bill Nye.[1]

Despite the protestations of Cobb's supporters, Mencken's judgment is fundamentally sound. The fact is that Cobb's brand of writing was, although popular, in no way analogous to the work of Modernists such as Dreiser, Sinclair Lewis, Sherwood Anderson, Willa Cather, William Faulkner, F. Scott Fitzgerald, Ernest Hemingway and others who would dominate the higher reaches of literature in their time. Cobb was relegated to the status of a "funny man" whose very appearance in a popular magazine like the *Saturday Evening Post* confirmed his mediocrity.

But for quite a time Cobb could, while lamenting his lack of critical esteem, pocket the substantial amounts of money he made from his writing. He spent years renovating an abandoned farmhouse in Westchester county, New York, near the town of Ossining, which he named Rebel Ridge; the work was finally finished in 1921. Cobb did return to the war front in early 1918, and his dispatches were later collected in a more obviously patriotic volume, *The Glory of the Coming* (1918). He did considerable writing for films from as early as 1917, although none of these were notable successes. Meanwhile he continued to publish story collections throughout the 1920s. Mencken would at least have appreciated Cobb's vigorous opposition to Prohibition and the rise of the Ku Klux Klan in that decade.

In 1922 Cobb gave up his position as staff contributor to the *Saturday Evening Post* to work for *Cosmopolitan,* then a magazine published by William Randolph Hearst and devoted largely to fiction and articles.

---

1. H. L. Mencken, "The Heir of Mark Twain," *Prejudices: First Series* (New York: Alfred A. Knopf, 1919), 97–98.

For the next decade all his stories appeared there; and in 1926, when he parted ways with George H. Doran, his books appeared under the imprint of the Cosmopolitan Book Corporation. By this time his daughter, who had renamed herself Elisabeth, had become a writer herself, publishing her first novel, *Falling Seeds,* in 1927. Another token of Cobb's celebrity was the building of the 200-room Irvin Cobb Hotel in Paducah: it would be difficult to find a similar establishment of the period named after a living author.

But Cobb's finances took a severe hit with the onset of the Depression in 1929; at the same time, his story-writing inspiration appeared to have dried up. He decided to move his family to Los Angeles to pursue film work; surprisingly, he was actually persuaded to appear in films as an actor himself, since both his large girth and his reputation as a humorist were thought to be tailor-made for the movies. His first film appearance had actually occurred as early as 1915, but from 1932 to 1938 he appeared in eleven more films, including the reasonably notable *Steamboat Round the Bend* (1935), starring his good friend Will Rogers. *Judge Priest* (1934), directed by John Ford and weaving together the narratives of a number of Cobb's tales, also starred Will Rogers in the title role. But after *Our Leading Citizen* (1939), based on one of Cobb's stories, was panned, he retired from the film industry.

By this time Cobb was in failing health, and his wife and daughter moved him back to New York. With his fictional pen in abeyance, Cobb turned to autobiography, writing the immense *Exit Laughing* (1941), a long and engaging account of his varied career as journalist, writer, and family man. Irvin S. Cobb died of dropsy on March 10, 1944. His body was cremated, but his ashes were not interred until some months later, when they were placed in a plot in Oak Park Cemetery in Paducah.

Of Gouverneur Morris, all we know is that he was born in 1876, presumably in New York City, to Gouverneur and Henrietta (Baldwin) Morris. He was the namesake and great-grandson of a Revolutionary War hero and signer of the Declaration of Independence. Graduating from Yale in 1898, he began a literary career that extended to at least a dozen novels and four story collections, published between 1901 and

1934. It is the latter that concern us, for nearly every one of these—*The Footprint and Other Stories* (1908); *The Spread Eagle and Other Stories* (1910); *It and Other Stories* (1912); *The Incandescent Lily and Other Stories* (1914)—contain one or more weird tales. Whereas many of Cobb's stories appeared in the *Saturday Evening Post,* Morris was a fixture at another well-paying "slick" periodical, *Collier's.*

Like Cobb, Morris was extensively involved in the film industry. At least eighteen films from 1914 to 1936 were based on novels or stories by Morris, most notably the silent film *The Penalty* (1920), adapted from his 1915 novel and starring Lon Chaney, Sr., as a deformed mastermind who seeks revenge on the doctor who amputated his legs. Morris also co-wrote the screenplay to two other films.

Morris apparently gave up writing in the mid-1930s and, incongruously, became the president of a bank in Monterey, California. Around 1939 he retired to the small town of Coolidge, in northwestern New Mexico. He died in Gallup, N.M., on August 14, 1953.

Cobb and Morris each seem largely known to the weird community on the basis of a single story—Cobb's "Fishhead" (1913) and Morris's "Back There in the Grass" (1911), both of which were reprinted in various anthologies nominally edited by Alfred Hitchcock (actually edited by Robert Arthur). While these tales may in fact be the summit of each writer's work in weird fiction, both wrote a half-dozen or more additional tales that provide further insights into their writing as a whole and their interest in supernatural or psychological horror.

Late in his career, Cobb made clear that he had written a number of tales of this sort and suggested to the publisher Doubleday, Doran that a volume of them be assembled. He referred to "twelve or fifteen of the so-called 'horror yarns' I've done, including such as 'Darkness,' 'The Escape of Mr. Trimm,' 'An Occurrence up a Side Street,' 'The Exit of Anse Dugmore,' 'The Belled Buzzard,' 'One Block from Fifth Avenue,' 'Fishhead,' 'Snake Doctor,' 'The Gallowsmith,' 'Three Wise Men of the East Side,' etc."[2] This list contains, by today's standards (and even by the standards of Cobb's own day), stories that by no means can be con-

---

2. Letter to Doubleday, Doran (12 May 1941; ms., University of Kentucky), quoted in Wayne Chatterton, *Irvin S. Cobb* (Boston: Twayne, 1986), 108.

sidered "weird" in any meaningful sense, but are largely crime/suspense stories. This volume contains only eight stories, including some of those cited in Cobb's letter; of these, only two or three are actually supernatural, while the others can be regarded as tales of psychological terror or suspense, with a sufficient modicum of fear to warrant inclusion. Even some of these are quite close to mere tales of crime, as in "The Escape of Mr. Trimm," really a kind of *conte cruel* in which a criminal experiences a roller-coaster ride of emotions—first the thrill of escaping from impending imprisonment, then the frustration of being unable to remove the cheap metal handcuffs that prevent his attainment of full freedom. Cobb was particularly fond of this story—perhaps because it was virtually his first story of any kind—and for that reason alone it would be worth including here.

"Fishhead," appearing in a Munsey magazine, the *All-Story Cavalier,* in early 1913, had the distinction of being praised in a brief letter to the editor by the young H. P. Lovecraft: "It is the belief of the writer that very few short stories of equal merit have been published anywhere during recent years. It is easy to imagine with what genuine regret the editors to whom it was submitted declined to print it."[3] That last sentence refers to the fact that the story had been rejected by several editors, including George Horace Lorimer of the *Saturday Evening Post,* who remarked: "It pains me to send back one of the best written stories I have seen in years." Editors at *Everybody's Magazine* ("I don't know when a short story has impressed me more strongly or more unpleasantly") and *Redbook* ("readers aren't educated up to raw beef yet") also praised the story but were apparently afraid to print it, until finally Robert H. Davis of the *Cavalier* accepted it.[4] (For Lovecraft, there were a number of ironies here. First, the repeated rejection of a story because it was too grisly echoes the rejection of such tales as "In the Vault" and "Cool Air" by Farnsworth Wright of *Weird Tales,* who became hesitant to publish

---

3. H. P. Lovecraft, Letter to the Editor, *All-Story Cavalier* (8 February 1913): 361; rpt. in *H. P. Lovecraft in the Argosy,* ed. S. T. Joshi (West Warwick, RI: Necronomicon Press, 1994), 34.

4. See Anita Lawson, *Irvin S. Cobb* (Bowling Green, OH: Bowling Green State University Popular Press, 1984), 89.

such work after the May–June–July 1924 issue of the magazine was banned in the state of Indiana because it had contained "The Loved Dead," a story about a necrophile nominally written by C. M. Eddy, Jr., but extensively revised by Lovecraft. Another such story, "The Rats in the Walls," faced similar rejection as being "too horrible"—and the editor who delivered this opinion was . . . Robert H. Davis.)

It is easy to see why Lovecraft enjoyed the story: it broached the idea of a fish-man hybrid of the sort that he would elaborate upon years later in "The Shadow over Innsmouth" (1931). That story was also probably influenced both by another tale of a fish-man, Robert W. Chambers's "The Harbor-Master" (1897; included as the first five chapters of the episodic novel *In Search of the Unknown* [1904]), and by Algernon Blackwood's "Ancient Sorceries" (in *John Silence—Physician Extraordinary* [1908]), a tale of a small town in southern France all of whose inhabitants turn into cats at night. Lovecraft was also no doubt impressed with the vivid depiction of the almost primitive rural topography, expressly set at a lake on the border between Kentucky and Tennessee, a locale no doubt well known to Cobb. Lovecraft may have gained tips from this story about how to draw upon his own knowledge of the history and topography of New England in his later tales. "Fish-head" was in fact based on a "short descriptive essay for a newspaper column,"[5] but this item has not come to light.

Another story that undoubtedly influenced Lovecraft is Cobb's other overtly supernatural story, "The Unbroken Chain," which appeared in the September 1923 issue of *Cosmopolitan*. Then as now, the issue came out at least a month before its cover date, and Lovecraft received a copy of the issue from Frank Belknap Long in early August, at the very time he was writing "The Rats in the Walls."[6] The tale—dealing with a Frenchman who, because he has an infinitesimal amount of African blood in him, experiences a flash of ancestral memory when he is struck by a train (recalling an ancestor who was killed by an onrushing rhinoc-

---

5. Chatterton, 121.

6. H. P. Lovecraft to J. Vernon Shea (8–22 November 1933), *Letters to J. Vernon Shea, Carl F. Strauch, and Lee McBride White* (New York: Hippocampus Press, 2016), p. 179.

eros) and cries out in an obscure African language—clearly foreshadows Lovecraft's use of the same device when the American businessman Delapore, appalled by the realization that his family practiced cannibalism for centuries, utters words successively in old English, Latin, Gaelic, and a primitive "ape-cry."[7]

If we are repulsed at the apparent racism of Cobb's story,[8] we should be aware that throughout his life Cobb spoke out against racism and championed the achievements of African Americans. We have already seen how he portrayed the black companion of Judge Priest, Jefferson Poindexter, with unfailing sympathy and sensitivity, and how he lamented the rise of the Ku Klux Klan in the 1920s. Upon his return from Europe in 1918, he delivered numerous speeches lauding the bravery of black soldiers on the front.[9] In his newspaper columns he spoke courageously and sarcastically against prejudice against both non-whites and women:

> All men are born free and equal. That immortal statement, you will recall, was penned and adopted by gentlemen largely engaged in owning slaves. Yet nonetheless it is true that all men are born equal unless they happen to be Indians or negroes or Chinamen or Japanese or Hindoos or Mexicans, in which case it would have been much better for them if they had not been born at all. Likewise all men are born free and equal unless they happen to be born women, in which case they rank with the habitual criminals and the congenital idiots.[10]

---

7. H. P. Lovecraft to Frank Belknap Long (8 November 1923); *Selected Letters: 1911-1924,* ed. August Derleth and Donald Wandrei (Sauk City, WI: Arkham House, 1965), 258.

8. It is interesting to note that the avowed racist Lovecraft has actually eliminated the racist element when he adapted the motif in "The Rats in the Walls." Here the protagonist is an unmistakable Caucasian who draws upon his own (white) family heritage when he regresses along the evolutionary scale.

9. Lawson, 164.

10. Cited in Lawson, 71.

Anita Lawson tells of how a black servant of the Cobb family, named Uncle Rufus, told the boy of ghosts and devils:

> When not running errands, he [Rufus] remained inside the one room shack that was all that remained of Dr. Saunders' slave quarters. Like Mandy [another servant], he fed and entertained the children who visited him, offering them sweet potatoes and hoe cakes. But visits to Rufus were most thrilling because of the tales he told of "hoodoos," ghosts, devils and "ha'nts." After an evening visit the children would be afraid to go from his cabin to the main house unless Mandy lighted the way with a lantern from the porch. Rufus' stories were so frightening that Cobb claimed to be a grown man before he could enter a darkened room without tensing in expectation of "Old Raw Haid and Bloody Bones" or some other gruesome phantasm, but the excitement was so enjoyable that the children always went back for more.

This anecdote suggests the source of the story "Darkness," which deals with a man who is so afraid of the dark that he lives for decades with all the lights on in his house, day and night. The story also deals with the perennial issue of blood feuds in rural Kentucky. Cobb addressed the issue on at least one occasion, speaking of feuding families, "not one of those sanguinary feuds of the mountains, involving a whole district, . . . nor yet a feud handed down as a deadly legacy from one generation to another until its origin is forgotten . . . but a shabby, small neighborhood vendetta affecting two families only."[11] This is exactly the sort of feud that leads to death and horror in "Darkness."

Somewhat related to "Fishhead" is "Snake Doctor," which depicts a man who seems to have an uncanny relationship with snakes. But it is very clear that no kind of physical transformation is at play here. Moreover, the story—which tells of a man who suspects the "snake doctor" of having an affair with his wife, and who dies when he thinks he has been bitten by a snake in the snake doctor's house, a snake that proves to be stuffed—is clearly derived from Ambrose Bierce's classic tale of psychological horror, "The Man and the Snake," where a man is terrified to

---

11. Irvin S. Cobb, *Back Home* (New York: George H. Doran, 1912), 70.

death by a toy snake. Nevertheless, Cobb seemed proud that the story won the O. Henry Memorial Award Committee's first prize for best short story of 1922.

Another superb tale of psychological terror, "The Gallowsmith," may have had its inspiration from a hideously botched hanging of a black man in 1896—a man actually known to Cobb.[12] In the story, a seemingly phlegmatic "gallowsmith"—that is, a self-styled expert in the technique and mechanics of hanging—finds himself unwontedly disturbed by the cursing of a condemned man whose execution he mishandles. The conclusion of the story may seem a bit contrived—analogous to those of Cobb's partial contemporary, O. Henry, whose work Cobb admired—but it is a fitting capstone to a narrative of cumulative psychological horror.

The element of contrivance is particularly notable in "Faith, Hope and Charity," the last of Cobb's weird tales included here—a somewhat predictable but still effective tale of comeuppance where three escaped prisoners all suffer the most horrible deaths they can envision. This story in particular reveals the creaking of the short story machinery that justifiably condemned Cobb to second-rate status in American literature.

The one instance where Cobb combined his patented humor with weirdness is "The Second Coming of a First Husband." The humor is perhaps a bit broad and obvious, but succeeds well in its basic purpose.

Gouverneur Morris's weird work largely follows the pattern of Cobb's—predominantly consisting of tales of psychological suspense, with one or two notable tales of supernatural horror. Preeminent among the latter, of course, is "Back There in the Grass" (1911), an incredibly chilling and innovative narrative that broaches the idea of a hideous race of miniature human beings on a remote Polynesian island. Perhaps making a nod to Robert Hichens's classic "How Love Came to Professor Guildea" (1900), which finds terror in the paradoxical notion of a ghost that has fallen in love with a living human, "Back There in the Grass" shows the effects of such unwholesome affection both upon the "womankin" whom a white man has captured and upon the white man

---

12. See Lawson, 24.

himself. The facts that the man keeps his foot-high inamorata as a "kind of pet," and that his (white) fiancée is about to arrive, only augments the terror and pathos of the scenario.

This tale is representative of Morris's work in that it depicts the emotional effects of extraordinary or unusual situations upon the human psyche; most of his other weird tales, however, do so in a generally non-supernatural manner. Hence, "The Crocodile" (1905) presents a powerful portrayal of gloom and depression as a man goes into permanent mourning over the death of his wife, so that his son grows up in an atmosphere of unrelieved melancholy. There is a hint of supernaturalism toward the end, as the ghost of the dead wife seems to make an appearance; but the bulk of the tale focuses on the crippling of both the father's and the son's emotions even as the latter finds some fleeting moments of happiness upon his marriage to a sprightly young woman who unexpectedly enters his life.

"The Footprint" (1907) and "The Bride's Dead" (1908) are Nietzschean tales of survival in remote places. The latter in particular contrasts the physical strength of the brutal Farallone with the psychological strength of the young woman whom he hopes to wrest away from the weak-spirited man she has married; but in the end it is the woman who outlasts him. But although she remains true to her husband, she makes her contempt for him known at the end.

"The Execution" in some ways echoes Cobb's "The Gallowsmith" in focusing on the emotional trauma of state-sanctioned murder. Here the embodiment of almost ruthless courage is the mother of a young man sentenced to death, who escapes and returns to his home, only to suffer an unexpected comeuppance at the hands of his own blind, crippled father.

An uncollected story, "Derrick's Return" (1923), is uncharacteristic in that it is something of a religious (or perhaps anti-religious) fable. The morality of the tale may be a trifle obvious and the element of fantasy may be slight or superficial, but its very anomalousness in Morris's output makes it fully worth reprinting here.

Both Irvin S. Cobb and Gouverneur Morris attained celebrity in their day, but it failed to endure beyond their lifetimes. There is much to be said for the view that, like many other short-story writers of the period (preeminently O. Henry), their tales are at times too artificial and too neatly resolved to be fully realistic; but Cobb's sensitive portrayal of the people and landscape of his native state, and Morris's intense focus on the emotions of people enmeshed in tormenting circumstances, both work well in their weird work, and it is no accident that it is that work that largely causes them to be remembered today. Devotees of weird fiction have always been keen on resurrecting exemplary work from past decades or centuries, and as a result many writers who would otherwise have faded from literary history retain a foothold in public conscious-ness as a result of the scattered weird tales they wrote over a career that may have been devoted to writings of a very different sort. Cobb and Morris fit that paradigm perfectly, and their weird output retains a vitali-ty that allows it to live, while their abundant mainstream work falls into oblivion.

—S. T. JOSHI

Irvin S. Cobb

The Belled Buzzard

There was a swamp known as Little Niggerwool, to distinguish it from Big Niggerwool, which lay across the river. It was traversable only by those who knew it well—an oblong stretch of tawny mud and tawny water, measuring maybe four miles its longest way and two miles roughly at its widest; and it was full of cypress and stunted swamp oak, with edgings of canebrake and rank weeds; and in one place, where a ridge crossed it from side to side, it was snaggled like an old jaw with dead tree trunks, rising close-ranked and thick as teeth. It was untenanted of living things—except, down below, there were snakes and mosquitoes and a few wading and swimming fowl; and up above, those big woodpeckers that the country people called logcocks—larger than pigeons, with flaming crests and spiky tails—swooping in their long, loping flight from snag to snag, always just out of gunshot of the chance invader, and uttering a strident cry which matched those surroundings so fitly that it might well have been the voice of the swamp itself.

On one side Little Niggerwool drained its saffron waters off into a sluggish creek, where summer ducks bred, and on the other it ended abruptly at a natural bank of high ground, along which the county turnpike ran. The swamp came right up to the road and thrust its fringe of reedy, weedy undergrowth forward as though in challenge to the good farm lands that were spread beyond the barrier. At the time I am speaking of it was midsummer, and from these canes and weeds and waterplants there came a smell so rank as almost to be overpowering. They grew thick as a curtain, making a blank green wall taller than a man's head.

Along the dusty stretch of road fronting the swamp nothing living had stirred for half an hour or more. And so at length the weed-stems rustled and parted, and out from among them a man came forth silently and cautiously. He was an old man—an old man who had once been fat, but with age had grown lean again, so that now his skin was by odds too large for him. It lay on the back of his neck in folds. Under the chin he was pouched like a pelican and about the jowls was wattled like a turkey gobbler.

He came out upon the road slowly and stopped there, switching his legs absently with the stalk of a horseweed. He was in his shirtsleeves—a respectable, snuffy old figure; evidently a man deliberate in words and thoughts and actions. There was something about him suggestive of an old staid sheep that had been engaged in a clandestine transaction and was afraid of being found out.

He had made amply sure no one was in sight before he came out of the swamp, but now, to be doubly certain, he watched the empty road first up, then down—for a long half minute, and fetched a sighing breath of satisfaction. His eyes fell upon his feet, and, taken with an idea, he stepped back to the edge of the road and with a wisp of crabgrass wiped his shoes clean of the swamp mud, which was of a different color and texture from the soil of the upland. All his life Squire H. B. Gathers had been a careful, canny man, and he had need to be doubly careful on this summer morning. Having disposed of the mud on his feet, he settled his white straw hat down firmly upon his head, and, crossing the road, he climbed a stake-and-rider fence laboriously and went plodding sedately across a weedfield and up a slight slope toward his house, half a mile away, upon the crest of the little hill.

He felt perfectly natural—not like a man who had just taken a fellowman's life—but natural and safe, and well satisfied with himself and with his morning's work. And he was safe; that was the main thing—absolutely safe. Without hitch or hindrance he had done the thing for which he had been planning and waiting and longing all these months. There had been no slip or mischance; the whole thing had worked out as plainly and simply as two and two make four. No living creature except himself knew of the meeting in the early morning at the head of Little Niggerwool, exactly where the squire had figured they should meet; none knew of the device by which the other man had been lured deeper and deeper in the swamp to the exact spot where the gun was hidden. No one had seen the two of them enter the swamp; no one had seen the squire emerge, three hours later, alone.

The gun, having served its purpose, was hidden again, in a place no mortal eye would ever discover. Face downward, with a hole between his shoulder-blades, the dead man was lying where he might lie undiscovered for months or for years, or forever. His pedler's pack was buried in the mud so deep that not even the probing crawfishes could find it. He would never be missed probably. There was but the slightest likelihood that inquiry would ever be made for him—let alone a search. He was a stranger and a foreigner, the dead man was, whose comings and goings made no great stir in the neighborhood, and whose failure to come again would be taken as a matter of course—just one of those shiftless, wandering Dagoes, here today and gone tomorrow. That was one of the best things about it—these Dagoes never had any people in this country to worry about them or look for them when they disappeared. And so it was all over and done with, and nobody the wiser. The squire clapped his hands together briskly with the air of a man dismissing a subject from his mind for good, and mended his gait.

He felt no stabbings of conscience. On the contrary, a glow of gratification filled him. His house was saved from scandal; his present wife would philander no more before his very eyes—with these young Dagoes, who came from nobody knew where, with packs on their backs and persuasive, wheedling tongues in their heads. At this thought the squire raised his head and considered his homestead. It looked good to him—the small white cottage among the honey locusts, with beehives and flower beds about it; the tidy whitewashed fence; the sound outbuildings at the back, and the well-tilled acres roundabout.

At the fence he halted and turned about, carelessly and casually, and looked back along the way he had come. Everything was as it should be—the weedfield steaming in the heat; the empty road stretching along the crooked ridge like a long gray snake sunning itself; and beyond it, massing up, the dark, cloaking stretch of swamp. Everything was all right, but— The squire's eyes, in their loose sacs of skin, narrowed and squinted. Out of the blue arch away over yonder a small black dot had resolved itself and was swinging to and fro, like a mote. A buzzard— hey? Well, there were always buzzards about on a clear day like this. Buzzards were nothing to worry about—almost any time you could see one buzzard, or a dozen buzzards if you were a mind to look for them.

But this particular buzzard now—wasn't he making for Little Nig-gerwool? The squire did not like the idea of that. He had not thought of the buzzards until this minute. Sometimes when cattle strayed the own-ers had been known to follow the buzzards, knowing mighty well that if the buzzards led the way to where the stray was, the stray would be past the small salvage of hide and hoofs—but the owner's doubts would be set at rest for good and all.

There was a grain of disquiet in this. The squire shook his head to drive the thought away—yet it persisted, coming back like a midge danc-ing before his face. Once at home, however, Squire Gathers deported himself in a perfectly normal manner. With the satisfied proprietorial eye of an elderly husband who has no rivals, he considered his young wife, busied about her household duties. He sat in an easy-chair upon his front gallery and read his yesterday's *Courier-Journal* which the rural carrier had brought him; but he kept stepping out into the yard to peer up into the sky and all about him. To the second Mrs. Gathers he ex-plained that he was looking for weather signs. A day as hot and still as this one was a regular weather breeder; there ought to be rain before night.

"Maybe so," she said; "but looking's not going to bring rain."

Nevertheless the squire continued to look. There was really nothing to worry about; still at midday he did not eat much dinner, and before his wife was half through with hers he was back on the gallery. His paper was cast aside and he was watching. The original buzzard—or, anyhow, he judged it was the first one he had seen—was swinging back and forth in great pendulum swings, but closer down toward the swamp—closer and closer—until it looked from that distance as though the buzzard flew al-most at the level of the tallest snags there. And on beyond this first buz-zard, coursing above him, were other buzzards. Were there four of them? No; there were five—five in all.

Such is the way of the buzzard—that shifting black question mark which punctuates a Southern sky. In the woods a shoat or a sheep or a horse lies down to die. At once, coming seemingly out of nowhere, ap-pears a black spot, up five hundred feet or a thousand in the air. In broad loops and swirls this dot swings round and round and round, coming a little closer to earth at every turn and always with one particular spot upon the earth for the axis of its wheel. Out of space also other moving spots emerge and grow larger as they tack and jibe and drop nearer, coming in their leisurely buzzard way to the feast. There is no haste—the feast will wait. If it is a dumb creature that has fallen stricken the grim coursers will sooner or later be assembled about it and alongside it, scrouging ever closer and closer to the dying thing, with awkward out-thrustings of their naked necks and great dust-raising flaps of the huge, unkempt wings; lifting their feathered shanks high and stiffly like old crippled grave-diggers in overalls that are too tight—but silent and patient all, offering no attack until the last tremor runs through the stiffening carcass and the eyes glaze over. To humans the buzzard pays a deeper meed of respect—he hangs aloft longer; but in the end he comes. No scavenger shark, no carrion crab, ever chambered more grisly secrets in his digestive processes than this big charnel bird. Such is the way of the buzzard.

🐏

The squire missed his afternoon nap, a thing that had not happened in years. He stayed on the front gallery and kept count. Those moving distant black specks typified uneasiness for the squire—not fear exactly, or panic or anything akin to it, but a nibbling, nagging kind of uneasiness. Time and again he said to himself that he would not think about them any more; but he did—unceasingly.

By supper time there were seven of them.

🐏

He slept light and slept badly. It was not the thought of that dead man lying yonder in Little Niggerwool that made him toss and fume while his wife snored gently alongside him. It was something else altogether. Finally his stirrings roused her and she asked him drowsily what ailed him Was he sick? Or bothered about anything?

Irritated, he answered her snappishly. Certainly nothing was bothering him, he told her. It was a hot enough night—wasn't it? And when a man got a little along in life he was apt to be a light sleeper—wasn't that so? Well, then? She turned upon her side and slept again with her light, purring snore. The squire lay awake, thinking hard and waiting for day to come.

At the first, faint pink-and-gray glow he was up and out upon the gallery. He cut a comic figure standing there in his shirt in the half light, with the dewlap at his throat dangling grotesquely in the neck opening of the unbuttoned garment, and his bare bowed legs showing, splotched and varicose. He kept his eyes fixed on the skyline below, to the south. Buzzards are early risers too. Presently, as the heavens shimmered with the miracle of sunrise, he could make them out—six or seven, or maybe eight.

An hour after breakfast the squire was on his way down through the weedfield to the county road. He went half eagerly, half unwillingly. He wanted to make sure about those buzzards. It might be that they were aiming for the old pasture at the head of the swamp. There were sheep grazing there—and it might be that a sheep had died. Buzzards were notoriously fond of sheep, when dead. Or, if they were pointed for the swamp, he must satisfy himself exactly what part of the swamp it was. He was at the stake-and-rider fence when a mare came jogging down the road, drawing a rig with a man in it. At sight of the squire in the field the man pulled up.

"Hi, squire!" he saluted. "Goin' somewheres?"

"No; jest knockin' about," the squire said—"jest sorter lookin' the place over."

"Hot agin—ain't it?" said the other.

The squire allowed that it was, for a fact, mighty hot. Commonplaces of gossip followed this—county politics and a neighbor's wife sick of breakbone fever down the road a piece. The subject of crops succeeded inevitably. The squire spoke of the need of rain. Instantly he regretted it, for the other man, who was by way of being a weather wiseacre, cocked his head aloft to study the sky for any signs of clouds.

"Wonder whut all them buzzards are doin' yonder, squire," he said, pointing upward with his whipstock.

"Whut buzzards—where?" asked the squire with an elaborate note of carelessness in his voice.

"Right yonder, over Little Niggerwool—see 'em there?"

"Oh, yes," the squire made answer. "Now I see 'em. They ain't doin' nothin', I reckin—jest flyin' round same as they always do in clear weather."

"Must be somethin' dead over there!" speculated the man in the buggy.

"A hawg probably," said the squire promptly—almost too promptly. "There's likely to be hawgs usin' in Niggerwool. Bristow, over on the other side from here—he's got a big drove of hawgs."

"Well, mebbe so," said the man; "but hawgs is a heap more apt to be feedin' on high ground, seems like to me. Well, I'll be gittin' along towards town. G'day, squire." And he slapped the lines down on the mare's flank and jogged off through the dust.

He could not have suspected anything—that man couldn't. As the squire turned away from the road and headed for his house he congratulated himself upon that stroke of his in bringing in Bristow's hogs; and yet there remained this disquieting note in the situation, that buzzards flying, and especially buzzards flying over Little Niggerwool, made people curious—made them ask questions.

He was half-way across the weedfield when, above the hum of insect life, above the inward clamor of his own busy speculations, there came to his ear dimly and distantly a sound that made him halt and cant his head to one side the better to hear it. Somewhere, a good way off, there was a thin, thready, broken strain of metallic clinking and clanking—an eery ghost-chime ringing. It came nearer and became plainer—tonk-tonk-tonk; then the tonks all running together briskly.

A sheep bell or a cowbell—that was it; but why did it seem to come from overhead, from up in the sky, like? And why did it shift so abruptly from one quarter to another—from left to right and back again to left? And how was it that the clapper seemed to strike so fast? Not even the breathiest of breachy young heifers could be expected to tinkle a cowbell with such briskness. The squire's eye searched the earth and the sky, his troubled mind giving to his eye a quick and flashing scrutiny. He had it. It was not a cow at all. It was not anything that went on four legs.

One of the loathly flock had left the others. The orbit of his swing had carried him across the road and over Squire Gathers' land. He was sailing right toward and over the squire now. Craning his flabby neck, the squire could make out the unwholesome contour of the huge bird.

He could see the ragged black wings a buzzard's wings are so often rag-ged and uneven—and the naked throat; the slim, naked head; the big feet folded up against the dingy belly. And he could see a bell too—an under-sized cowbell that dangled at the creature's breast and jangled incessantly. All his life nearly Squire Gathers had been hearing about the Belled Buzzard. Now with his own eye he was seeing him.

Once, years and years and years ago, some one trapped a buzzard, and before freeing it clamped about its skinny neck a copper band with a cowbell pendent from it. Since then the bird so ornamented has been seen a hundred times and heard oftener—over an area as wide as half the continent. It has been reported, now in Kentucky, now in Texas, now in North Carolina—now anywhere between the Ohio River and the Gulf. Crossroads correspondents take their pens in hand to write to the country papers that on such and such a date, at such a place, So-and-So saw the Belled Buzzard. Always it is the Belled Buzzard, never a belled buzzard. The Belled Buzzard is an institution.

There must be more than one of them. It seems hard to believe that one bird, even a buzzard in his prime, and protected by law in every Southern state and known to be a bird of great age, could live so long and range so far and wear a clinking cowbell all the time! Probably other jok-ers have emulated the original joker; probably if the truth were known there have been a dozen such; but the country people will have it that there is only one Belled Buzzard—a bird that bears a charmed life and on his neck a never silent bell.

Squire Gathers regarded it a most untoward thing that the Belled Buz-zard should have come just at this time. The movements of ordinary, unmarked buzzards mainly concerned only those whose stock had strayed; but almost anybody with time to spare might follow this rare and famous visitor, this belled and feathered junkman of the sky. Sup-posing now that some one followed it today—maybe followed it even to a certain thick clump of cypress in the middle of Little Niggerwool!

But at this particular moment the Belled Buzzard was heading di-rectly away from that quarter. Could it be following him? Of course not!

It was just by chance that it flew along the course the squire was taking. But, to make sure, he veered off sharply, away from the footpath into the high weeds so that the startled grasshoppers sprayed up in front of him in fan-like flights.

He was right; it was only a chance. The Belled Buzzard swung off too, but in the opposite direction, with a sharp tonking of its bell, and, flapping hard, was in a minute or two out of hearing and sight, past the trees to the westward.

Again the squire skimped his dinner, and again he spent the long drowsy afternoon upon his front gallery. In all the sky there were now no buzzards visible, belled or unbelled—they had settled to earth some-where; and this served somewhat to soothe the squire's pestered mind. This does not mean, though, that he was by any means easy in his thoughts. Outwardly he was calm enough, with the ruminative judicial air befitting the oldest justice of the peace in the county; but, within him, a little something gnawed unceasingly at his nerves like one of those small white worms that are to be found in seemingly sound nuts. About once in so long a tiny spasm of the muscles would contract the dewlap under his chin. The squire had never heard of that play, made famous by a famous player, wherein the murdered victim was a pedler too, and a clamoring bell the voice of unappeasable remorse in the murderer's ear. As a strict churchgoer the squire had no use for players or for play actors, and so was spared that added canker to his conscience. It was bad enough as it was.

That night, as on the night before, the old man's sleep was broken and fitful and disturbed by dreaming, in which he heard a metal clapper striking against a brazen surface. This was one dream that came true. Just after daybreak he heaved himself out of bed, with a flop of his broad bare feet upon the floor, and stepped to the window and peered out. Half seen in the pinkish light, the Belled Buzzard flapped directly over his roof and flew due south, right toward the swamp—drawing a direct line through the air between the slayer and the victim—or, anyway, so it seemed to the watcher, grown suddenly tremulous.

Knee deep in yellow swamp water the squire squatted, with his shotgun cocked and loaded and ready, waiting to kill the bird that now typified for him guilt and danger and an abiding great fear. Gnats plagued him and about him frogs croaked. Almost overhead a logcock clung lengthwise to a snag, watching him. Snake doctors, limber, long insects with bronze bodies and filmy wings, went back and forth like small living shuttles. Other buzzards passed and repassed, but the squire waited, forgetting the cramps in his elderly limbs and the discomfort of the water in his shoes.

At length he heard the bell. It came nearer and nearer, and the Belled Buzzard swung overhead not sixty feet up, its black bulk a fair target against the blue. He aimed and fired, both barrels bellowing at once and a fog of thick powder smoke enveloping him. Through the smoke he saw the bird careen and its bell jangled furiously; then the buzzard righted itself and was gone, fleeing so fast that the sound of its bell was hushed almost instantly. Two long wing feathers drifted slowly down; torn disks of gunwadding and shredded green scraps of leaves descended about the squire in a little shower.

He cast his empty gun from him so that it fell in the water and disappeared; and he hurried out of the swamp as fast as his shaky legs would take him, splashing himself with mire and water to his eyebrows. Mucked with mud, breathing in great gulps, trembling, a suspicious figure to any eye, he burst through the weed curtain and staggered into the open, his caution all gone and a vast desperation fairly choking him—but the gray road was empty and the field beyond the road was empty; and, except for him, the whole world seemed empty and silent.

As he crossed the field Squire Gathers composed himself. With plucked handfuls of grass he cleansed himself of much of the swamp mire that coated him over; but the little white worm that gnawed at his nerves had become a cold snake that was coiled about his heart, squeezing it tighter and tighter!

This episode of the attempt to kill the Belled Buzzard occurred in the afternoon of the third day. In the forenoon of the fourth, the weather being still hot, with cloudless skies and no air stirring, there was a rattle of warped wheels in the squire's lane and a hail at his yard fence. Coming out upon his gallery from the innermost darkened room of his house, where he had been stretched upon a bed, the squire shaded his eyes from the glare and saw the constable of his own magisterial district sitting in a buggy at the gate waiting.

The old man went down the dirtpath slowly, almost reluctantly, with his head twisted up sidewise, listening, watching; but the constable sensed nothing strange about the other's gait and posture; the constable was full of the news he brought. He began to unload the burden of it without preamble.

"Mornin', Squire Gathers. There's been a dead man found in Little Niggerwool—and you're wanted."

He did not notice that the squire was holding on with both hands to the gate; but he did notice that the squire had a sick look out of his eyes and a dead, pasty color in his face; and he noticed—but attached no meaning to it—that when the squire spoke his voice seemed flat and hollow.

"Wanted—fur—whut?" The squire forced the words out of his throat, pumped them out fairly.

"Why, to hold the inquest," explained the constable. "The coroner's sick abed, and he said you bein' the nearest jestice of the peace you should serve."

"Oh," said the squire with more ease. "Well, where is it—the body?"

"They taken it to Bristow's place and put it in his stable for the present. They brought it out over on that side and his place was the nearest. If you'll hop in here with me, squire, I'll ride you right over there now. There's enough men already gathered to make up a jury, I reckin."

"I—I ain't well," demurred the squire. "I've been sleepin' porely these last few nights. It's the heat," he added quickly.

"Well, suh, you don't look very brash, and that's a fact," said the constable; "but this here job ain't goin' to keep you long. You see it's in such shape—the body is—that there ain't no way of makin' out who the feller was nor whut killed him. There ain't nobody reported missin' in this county as we know of, either; so I jedge a verdict of a unknown person dead from unknown causes would be about the correct thing. And we kin git it all over mighty quick and put him underground right away, suh—if you'll go along now."

"I'll go," agreed the squire, almost quivering in his newborn eagerness. "I'll go right now." He did not wait to get his coat or to notify his wife of the errand that was taking him. In his shirtsleeves he climbed into the buggy, and the constable turned his horse and clucked him into a trot. And now the squire asked the question that knocked at his lips demanding to be asked—the question the answer to which he yearned for and yet dreaded.

"How did they come to find—it?"

"Well, suh, that's a funny thing," said the constable. "Early this mornin' Bristow's oldest boy that one they call Buddy—he heared a cowbell over in the swamp and so he went to look; Bristow's got cows, as you know, and one or two of 'em is belled. And he kept on followin' after the sound of it till he got way down in the thickest part of them cypress slashes that's near the middle there; and right there he run acrost it—this body.

"But, suh, squire, it wasn't no cow at all. No, suh; it was a buzzard with a cowbell on his neck—that's whut it was. Yes, suh; that there same old Belled Buzzard he's come back agin and is hangin' round. They tell me he ain't been seen round here since the year of the yellow fever—I don't remember myself, but that's whut they tell me. The niggers over on the other side are right smartly worked up over it. They say—the niggers do—that when the Belled Buzzard comes it's a sign of bad luck for somebody, shore!"

The constable drove on, talking on, garrulous as a guinea hen. The squire didn't heed him. Hunched back in the buggy, he harkened only to those busy inner voices filling his mind with thundering portents. Even so, his ear was first to catch above the rattle of the buggy wheels the faraway, faint tonk-tonk! They were about half-way to Bristow's place then. He gave no sign, and it was perhaps half a minute before his companion heard it too.

The constable jerked the horse to a standstill and craned his neck over his shoulder.

"Well, by doctors!" he cried, "if there ain't the old scoundrel now, right here behind us! I kin see him plain as day—he's got an old cowbell hitched to his neck; and he's shy a couple of feathers out of one wing. By doctors, that's somethin' you won't see every day! In all my born days I ain't never seen the beat of that!"

Squire Gathers did not look; he only cowered back farther under the buggy top. In the pleasing excitement of the moment his companion took no heed, though, of anything except the Belled Buzzard.

"Is he followin' us?" asked the squire in a curiously flat, weighted voice.

"Which—him?" answered the constable, still stretching his neck. "No, he's gone now—gone off to the left jest a-zoonin', like he'd done forgot somethin'."

And Bristow's place was to the left! But there might still be time. To get the inquest over and the body underground those were the main things. Ordinarily humane in his treatment of stock, Squire Gathers urged the constable to greater speed. The horse was lathered and his sides heaved wearily as they pounded across the bridge over the creek which was the outlet to the swamp and emerged from a patch of woods in sight of Bristow's farm buildings.

The house was set on a little hill among cleared fields and was in other respects much like the squire's own house except that it was smaller and not so well painted. There was a wide yard in front with shade trees and a lye hopper and a well-box, and a paling fence with a stile in it instead of a gate. At the rear, behind a clutter of outbuildings—a barn, a smokehouse and a corncrib—was a little peach orchard, and flanking the house on the right there was a good-sized cowyard, empty of stock at this hour, with feedracks ranged in a row against the fence. A two-year-old negro child, bareheaded and barefooted and wearing but a single garment, was grubbing busily in the dirt under one of these feedracks.

To the front fence a dozen or more riding horses were hitched, flicking their tails at the flies; and on the gallery men in their shirtsleeves were grouped. An old negro woman, with her head tied in a bandanna and a man's old slouch hat perched upon the bandanna, peeped out from behind a corner. There were gaunt hound dogs wandering about, sniffing uneasily.

Before the constable had the horse hitched the squire was out of the buggy and on his way up the footpath, going at a brisker step than the squire usually traveled. The men on the porch hailed him gravely and ceremoniously, as befitting an occasion of solemnity. Afterward some of them recalled the look in his eye; but at the moment they noted it—if they noted it at all—subconsciously.

For all his haste the squire, as was also remembered later, was almost the last to enter the door; and before he did enter he halted and searched the flawless sky as though for signs of rain. Then he hurried on after the others, who clumped single file along a narrow little hall, the bare, uncarpeted floor creaking loudly under their heavy farm shoes, and entered a good-sized room that had in it, among other things, a high-piled feather bed and a cottage organ—Bristow's best room, now to be placed at the disposal of the law's representatives for the inquest. The squire took the largest chair and drew it to the very center of the room, in front of a fireplace, where the grate was banked with withering asparagus ferns. The constable took his place formally at one side of the presiding official. The others sat or stood about where they could find room—all but six of them, whom the squire picked for his coroner's jury, and who backed themselves against the wall.

The squire showed haste. He drove the preliminaries forward with a sort of tremulous insistence. Bristow's wife brought a bucket of fresh drinking water and a gourd, and almost before she was out of the room and the door closed behind her the squire had sworn his jurors and was calling the first witness, who it seemed likely would also be the only witness—Bristow's oldest boy. The boy wriggled in confusion as he sat on a cane-bottomed chair facing the old magistrate. All there, barring one or two, had heard his story a dozen times already, but now it was to be repeated under oath; and so they bent their heads, listening as though it were a brand-new tale. All eyes were on him; none were fastened on the squire as he, too, gravely bent his head, listening—listening.

The witness began—but had no more than started when the squire gave a great, screeching howl and sprang from his chair and staggered backward, his eyes popped and the pouch under his chin quivering as though it had a separate life all its own. Startled, the constable made toward him and they struck together heavily and went down—both on their all fours—right in front of the fireplace.

The constable scrambled free and got upon his feet, in a squat of astonishment, with his head craned; but the squire stayed upon the floor, face downward, his feet flopping among the rustling asparagus greens—a picture of slavering animal fear. And now his gagging screech resolved itself into articulate speech.

"I done it!" they made out his shrieked words. "I done it! I own up—I killed him! He aimed fur to break up my home and I tolled him off into Niggerwool and killed him! There's a hole in his back if you'll look fur it. I done it—oh, I done it—and I'll tell everything jest like it happened if you'll jest keep that thing away from me! Oh, my Lawdy! Don't you hear it? It's a-comin' clos'ter and clos'ter—it's a-comin' after me! Keep it away—" His voice gave out and he buried his head in his hands and rolled upon the gaudy carpet.

And now they all heard what he had heard first—they heard the tonk-tonk-tonk of a cowbell, coming near and nearer toward them along the hallway without. It was as though the sound floated along. There was no creak of footsteps upon the loose, bare boards—and the bell jangled faster than it would dangling from a cow's neck. The sound came right to the door and Squire Gathers wallowed among the chair legs.

The door swung open. In the doorway stood a negro child, barefooted and naked except for a single garment, eyeing them with serious, rolling eyes—and, with all the strength of his two puny arms, proudly but solemnly tolling a small rusty cowbell he had found in the cowyard.

Fishhead

It goes past the powers of my pen to try to describe Reelfoot Lake for you so that you, reading this, will get the picture of it in your mind as I have it in mine, For Reelfoot Lake is like no other lake that I know anything about. It is an afterthought of Creation.

The rest of this continent was made and had dried in the sun for thousands of years—for millions of years for all I know—before Reelfoot came to be. It's the newest big thing in nature on this hemisphere probably, for it was formed by the great earthquake of 1811, just a little more than a hundred years ago. That earthquake of 1811 surely altered the face of the earth on the then far frontier of this country. It changed the course of rivers, it converted hills into what are now the sunk lands of three states, and it turned the solid ground to jelly and made it roll in waves like the sea. And in the midst of the retching of the land and the vomiting of the waters it depressed to varying depths a section of the earth crust sixty miles long, taking it down—trees, hills, hollows and all; and a crack broke through the Mississippi River so that for three days the river ran up stream, filling the hole.

The result was the largest lake south of the Ohio, lying mostly in Tennessee, but extending up across what is now the Kentucky line, and taking its name from a fancied resemblance in its outline to the splay, reeled foot of a cornfield negro. Niggerwool Swamp, not so far away, may have got its name from the same man who christened Reelfoot; at least so it sounds.

Reelfoot is, and has always been, a lake of mystery. In places it is bottomless. Other places the skeletons of the cypress trees that went down when the earth sank still stand upright, so that if the sun shines from the right quarter and the water is less muddy than common, a man peering face downward into its depths sees, or thinks he sees, down below him the bare top-limbs upstretching like drowned men's fingers, all coated with the mud of years and bandaged with pennons of the green lake slime. In still other places the lake is shallow for long stretches, no deeper than breast-deep to a man, but dangerous because of the weed growths and the sunken drifts which entangle a swimmer's limbs. Its banks are mainly mud, its waters are muddied too, being a rich coffee color in the spring and a copperish yellow in the summer, and the trees along its shore are mud colored clear up to their lower limbs after the spring floods, when the dried sediment covers their trunks with a thick, scrofulous-looking coat.

There are stretches of unbroken woodland around it and slashes where the cypress trees rise countlessly like headstones and footstones for the dead snags that rot in the soft ooze. There are deadenings with the lowland corn growing high and rank below and the bleached, fire-blackened girdled trees rising above, barren of leaf and limb. There are long, dismal flats where in the spring the clotted frog-spawn clings like patches of white mucus among the weed stalks and at night the turtles crawl out to lay clutches of perfectly round, white eggs with tough, rubbery shells in the sand. There are bayous leading off to nowhere and sloughs that wind aimlessly, like great, blind worms, to finally join the big river that rolls its semi-liquid torrents a few miles to the westward.

So Reelfoot lies there, flat in the bottoms, freezing lightly in the winter, steaming torridly in the summer, swollen in the spring when the woods have turned a vivid green and the buffalo gnats by the million and the billion fill the flooded hollows with their pestilential buzzing, and in the fall ringed about gloriously with all the colors which the first frost brings—gold of hickory, yellow-russet of sycamore, red of dogwood and ash and purple-black of sweet-gum.

But the Reelfoot country has its uses. It is the best game and fish country, natural or artificial, that is left in the South to-day. In their appointed seasons the duck and the geese flock in, and even semi-tropical birds, like the brown pelican and the Florida snake-bird, having been known to come there to nest. Pigs, gone back to wildness, range the ridges, each razor-backed drove captained by a gaunt, savage, slab-sided old boar. By night the bull frogs, inconceivably big and tremendously vocal, bellow under the banks.

It is a wonderful place for fish—bass and crappie and perch and the snouted buffalo fish. How these edible sorts live to spawn and how their spawn in turn live to spawn again is a marvel, seeing how many of the big fish-eating cannibal fish there are in Reelfoot. Here, bigger than anywhere else, you find the garfish, all bones and appetite and horny plates, with a snout like an alligator, the nearest link, naturalists say, between the animal life of to-day and the animal life of the Reptilian Period. The shovel-nose cat, really a deformed kind of freshwater sturgeon, with a great fan-shaped membranous plate jutting out from his nose like a bowsprit, jumps all day in the quiet places with mighty splashing sounds, as though a horse had fallen into the water. On every stranded log the huge snapping turtles lie on sunny days in groups of four and six, baking their shells black in the sun, with their little snaky heads raised watchfully, ready to slip noiselessly off at the first sound of oars grating in the row-locks.

But the biggest of them all are the catfish. These are monstrous creatures, these catfish of Reelfoot—scaleless, slick things, with corpsy, dead eyes and poisonous fins like javelins and long whiskers dangling from the sides of their cavernous heads. Six and seven feet long they grow to be and to weigh two hundred pounds or more, and they have mouths wide enough to take in a man's foot or a man's fist and strong enough to break any hook save the strongest and greedy enough to eat anything, living or dead or putrid, that the horny jaws can master. Oh, but they are wicked things, and they tell wicked tales of them down there. They call them man-eaters and compare them, in certain of their habits, to sharks.

Fishhead was of a piece with this setting. He fitted into it as an acorn fits its cup. All his life he had lived on Reelfoot, always in the one place, at the mouth of a certain slough. He had been born there, of a negro father and a half-breed Indian mother, both of them now dead, and the story was that before his birth his mother was frightened by one of the big fish, so that the child came into the world most hideously marked. Anyhow, Fishhead was a human monstrosity, the veritable embodiment of nightmare. He had the body of a man—a short, stocky, sinewy body—but his face was as near to being the face of a great fish as any face could be and yet retain some trace of human aspect. His skull sloped back so abruptly that he could hardly be said to have a forehead at all; his chin slanted off right into nothing. His eyes were small and round with shallow, glazed, pale-yellow pupils, and they were set wide apart in his head and they were unwinking and staring, like a fish's eyes. His nose was no more than a pair of tiny slits in the middle of the yellow mask. His mouth was the worst of all. It was the awful mouth of a catfish, lipless and almost inconceivably wide, stretching from side to side. Also when Fishhead became a man grown his likeness to a fish increased, for the hair upon his face grew out into two tightly kinked, slender pendants that drooped down either side of the mouth like the beards of a fish.

If he had any other name than Fishhead, none excepting he knew it. As Fishhead he was known and as Fishhead he answered. Because he knew the waters and the woods of Reelfoot better than any other man there, he was valued as a guide by the city men who came every year to hunt or fish; but there were few such jobs that Fishhead would take. Mainly he kept to himself, tending his corn patch, netting the lake, trapping a little and in season pot hunting for the city markets. His neighbors, ague-bitten whites and malaria-proof negroes alike, left him to himself. Indeed for the most part they had a superstitious fear of him. So he lived alone, with no kith nor kin, nor even a friend, shunning his kind and shunned by them.

His cabin stood just below the state line, where Mud Slough runs into the lake. It was a shack of logs, the only human habitation for four miles up or down. Behind it the thick timber came shouldering right up to the edge of Fishhead's small truck patch, enclosing it in thick shade except when the sun stood just overhead. He cooked his food in a primitive fashion, outdoors, over a hole in the soggy earth or upon the rusted red ruin of an old cook stove, and he drank the saffron water of the lake out of a dipper made of a gourd, faring and fending for himself, a master hand at skiff and net, competent with duck gun and fish spear, yet a creature of affliction and loneliness, part savage, almost amphibious, set apart from his fellows, silent and suspicious.

In front of his cabin jutted out a long fallen cottonwood trunk, lying half in and half out of the water, its top side burnt by the sun and worn by the friction of Fishhead's bare feet until it showed countless patterns of tiny scrolled lines, its under side black and rotted and lapped at unceasingly by little waves like tiny licking tongues. Its farther end reached deep water. And it was a part of Fishhead, for no matter how far his fishing and trapping might take him in the daytime, sunset would find him back there, his boat drawn up on the bank and he on the outer end of this log. From a distance men had seen him there many times, sometimes squatted, motionless as the big turtles that would crawl upon its dipping tip in his absence, sometimes erect and vigilant like a creek crane, his misshapen yellow form outlined against the yellow sun, the yellow water, the yellow banks—all of them yellow together.

If the Reelfooters shunned Fishhead by day they feared him by night and avoided him as a plague, dreading even the chance of a casual meeting. For there were ugly stories about Fishhead—stories which all the negroes and some of the whites believed. They said that a cry which had been heard just before dusk and just after, skittering across the darkened waters, was his calling cry to the big cats, and at his bidding they came trooping in, and that in their company he swam in the lake on moonlight nights, sporting with them, diving with them, even feeding with them on what manner of unclean things they fed. The cry had been heard many times, that much was certain, and it was certain also that the big fish were noticeably thick at the mouth of Fishhead's slough. No native Reelfooter, white or black, would willingly wet a leg or an arm there.

Here Fishhead had lived and here he was going to die. The Baxters were going to kill him, and this day in mid-summer was to be the time of the killing. The two Baxters—Jake and Joel—were coming in their dugout to do it. This murder had been a long time in the making. The Baxters had to brew their hate over a slow fire for months before it reached the pitch of action. They were poor whites, poor in everything—repute and worldly goods and standing—a pair of fever-ridden squatters who lived on whisky and tobacco when they could get it, and on fish and cornbread when they couldn't.

The feud itself was of months' standing. Meeting Fishhead one day in the spring on the spindly scaffolding of the skiff landing at Walnut Log, and being themselves far overtaken in liquor and vainglorious with a bogus alcoholic substitute for courage, the brothers had accused him, wantonly and without proof, of running their trot-line and stripping it of the hooked catch—an unforgivable sin among the water dwellers and the shanty boaters of the South. Seeing that he bore this accusation in silence, only eyeing them steadfastly, they had been emboldened then to slap his face, whereupon he turned and gave them both the beating of their lives—bloodying their noses and bruising their lips with hard blows against their front teeth, and finally leaving them, mauled and prone, in the dirt. Moreover, in the onlookers a sense of the everlasting fitness of things had triumphed over race prejudice and allowed them—two free-born, sovereign whites—to be licked by a nigger.

Therefore, they were going to get the nigger. The whole thing had been planned out amply. They were going to kill him on his log at sundown. There would be no witnesses to see it, no retribution to follow after it. The very ease of the undertaking made them forget even their inborn fear of the place of Fishhead's habitation.

For more than an hour now they had been coming from their shack across a deeply indented arm of the lake. Their dugout, fashioned by fire and adz and draw-knife from the bole of a gum tree, moved through the water as noiselessly as a swimming mallard, leaving behind it a long, wavy trail on the stilled waters. Jake, the better oarsman, sat flat in the stern of the round-bottomed craft, paddling with quick, splashless strokes. Joel, the better shot, was squatted forward. There was a heavy, rusted duck gun between his knees.

Though their spying upon the victim had made them certain sure he would not be about the shore for hours, a doubled sense of caution led them to hug closely the weedy banks. They slid along the shore like shadows, moving so swiftly and in such silence that the watchful mud turtles barely turned their snaky heads as they passed. So, a full hour before the time, they came slipping around the mouth of the slough and made for a natural ambuscade which the mixed breed had left within a stone's jerk of his cabin to his own undoing.

Where the slough's flow joined deeper water a partly uprooted tree was stretched, prone from shore, at the top still thick and green with leaves that drew nourishment from the earth in which the half-uncovered roots yet held, and twined about with an exuberance of trumpet vines and wild fox-grapes. All about was a huddle of drift—last year's cornstalks, shreddy strips of bark, chunks of rotted weed, all the riffle and dunnage of a quiet eddy. Straight into this green clump glided the dugout and swung, broadside on, against the protecting trunk of the tree, hidden from the inner side by the intervening curtains of rank growth, just as the Baxters had intended it should be hidden, when days before in their scouting they marked this masked place of waiting and included it, then and there, in the scope of their plans.

There had been no hitch or mishap. No one had been abroad in the late afternoon to mark their movements—and in a little while Fishhead ought to be due. Jake's woodman's eye followed the downward swing of the sun speculatively. The shadows, thrown shoreward, lengthened and slithered on the small ripples. The small noises of the day died out; the small noises of the coming night began to multiply. The green-bodied flies went away and big mosquitoes, with speckled gray legs, came to take the places of the flies. The sleepy lake sucked at the mud banks with small mouthing sounds as though it found the taste of the raw mud agreeable. A monster crawfish, big as a chicken lobster, crawled out of the top of his dried mud chimney and perched himself there, an armored sentinel on the watchtower. Bull bats began to flitter back and forth above the tops of the trees. A pudgy muskrat, swimming with head up, was moved to sidle off briskly as he met a cottonmouth moccasin snake, so fat and swollen with summer poison that it looked almost like a legless lizard as it moved along the surface of the water in a series of slow torpid s's. Directly above the head of either of the waiting assassins a compact little swarm of midges hung, holding to a sort of kite-shaped formation.

A little more time passed and Fishhead came out of the woods at the back, walking swiftly, with a sack over his shoulder. For a few seconds his deformities showed in the clearing, then the black inside of the cabin swallowed him up. By now the sun was almost down. Only the red nub of it showed above the timber line across the lake, and the shadows lay inland a long way. Out beyond, the big cats were stirring, and the great smacking sounds as their twisting bodies leaped clear and fell back in the water came shoreward in a chorus.

But the two brothers in their green covert gave heed to nothing except the one thing upon which their hearts were set and their nerves tensed. Joel gently shoved his gun-barrels across the log, cuddling the stock to his shoulder and slipping two fingers caressingly back and forth upon the triggers. Jake held the narrow dugout steady by a grip upon a fox-grape tendril.

A little wait and then the finish came. Fishhead emerged from the cabin door and came down the narrow footpath to the water and out upon the water on his log. He was barefooted and bareheaded, his cotton shirt open down the front to show his yellow neck and breast, his dungaree trousers held about his waist by a twisted tow string. His broad splay feet, with the prehensile toes outspread, gripped the polished curve of the log as he moved along its swaying, dipping surface until he came to its outer end and stood there erect, his chest filling, his chinless face lifted up and something of mastership and dominion in his poise. And then—his eye caught what another's eyes might have missed—the round, twin ends of the gun barrels, the fixed gleams of Joel's eyes, aimed at him through the green tracery.

In that swift passage of time, too swift almost to be measured by seconds, realization flashed all through him, and he threw his head still higher and opened wide his shapeless trap of a mouth, and out across the lake he sent skittering and rolling his cry. And in his cry was the laugh of a loon, and the croaking bellow of a frog, and the bay of a hound, all the compounded night noises of the lake. And in it, too, was a farewell and a defiance and an appeal. The heavy roar of the duck gun came.

At twenty yards the double charge tore the throat out of him. He came down, face forward, upon the log and clung there, his trunk twisting distortedly, his legs twitching and kicking like the legs of a speared frog, his shoulders hunching and lifting spasmodically as the life ran out of him all in one swift coursing flow. His head canted up between the heaving shoulders, his eyes, looked full on the staring face of his murderer, and then the blood came out of his mouth and Fishhead, in death still as much fish as man, slid flopping, head first, off the end of the log and sank, face downward, slowly, his limbs all extended out. One after another a string of big bubbles came up to burst in the middle of a widening reddish stain on the coffee-colored water.

The brothers watched this, held by the horror of the thing they had done, and the cranky dugout, tipped far over by the recoil of the gun, took water steadily across its gunwale, and now there was a sudden stroke from below upon its careening bottom and it went over and they were in the lake. But shore was only twenty feet away, the trunk of the uprooted tree only five. Joel, still holding fast to his hot gun, made for the log, gaining it with one stroke. He threw his free arm over it and clung there, treading water, as he shook his eyes free. Something gripped him—some great, sinewy, unseen thing gripped him fast by the thigh, crushing down on his flesh.

He uttered no cry, but his eyes popped out and his mouth set in a square shape of agony, and his fingers gripped into the bark of the tree like grapples. He was pulled down and down, by steady jerks, not rapidly but steadily, so steadily, and as he went his fingernails tore four little white strips in the tree bark. His mouth went under, next his popping eyes, then his erect hair, and finally his clawing, clutching hand, and that was the end of him.

Jake's fate was harder still, for he lived longer—long enough to see Joel's finish. He saw it through the water that ran down his face, and with a great surge of his whole body he literally flung himself across the log and jerked his legs up high into the air to save them. He flung himself too far, though, for his face and chest hit the water on the far side. And out of this water rose the head of a great fish, with the lake slime of years on its flat, black head, its whiskers bristling, its corpsy eyes alight. Its horny jaws closed and clamped in the front of Jake's flannel shirt. His hand struck out wildly and was speared on a poisoned fin, and unlike Joel, he went from sight with a great yell and a whirling and a churning of the water that made the cornstalks circle on the edge of a small whirlpool.

But the whirlpool soon thinned away into widening rings of ripples and the cornstalks quit circling and became still again, and only the multiplying night noises sounded about the mouth of the slough.

The bodies of all three came ashore on the same day near the same place. Except for the gaping gunshot wound where the neck met the chest, Fishhead's body was unmarked. But the bodies of the two Baxters were so marred and mauled that the Reelfooters buried them together on the bank without ever knowing which might be Jake's and which might be Joel's.

The Gallowsmith

This man that I have it in mind to write about was, at the time of which I write, an elderly man, getting well along toward sixty-five. He was tall and slightly stooped, with long arms, and big, gnarled, competent-looking hands, which smelled of yellow laundry soap, and had huge, tarnished nails on the fingers. He had mild, pale eyes, a light blue as to colour, with heavy sacs under them, and whitish whiskers, spindly and thin, like some sort of second-growth, which were so cut as to enclose his lower face in a nappy fringe, extending from ear to ear under his chin. He suffered from a chronic heart affection, and this gave to his skin a pronounced and unhealthy pallor. He was neat and prim in his personal habits, kind to dumb animals, and tolerant of small children. He was inclined to be miserly; certainly in money matters he was most prudent and saving. He had the air about him of being lonely. His name was Tobias Dramm. In the town where he lived he was commonly known as Uncle Tobe Dramm. By profession he was a public hangman. You might call him a gallowsmith. He hanged men for hire.

So far as the available records show, this Tobias Dramm was the only man of his calling on this continent. In himself he constituted a specialty and a monopoly. The fact that he had no competition did not make him careless in the pursuit of his calling. On the contrary, it made him precise and painstaking. As one occupying a unique position, he realized that he had a reputation to sustain, and capably he sustained it. In the Western Hemisphere he was, in the trade he followed, the nearest modern approach to the paid executioners of olden times in France who went, each of them, by the name of the city or province wherein he was stationed, to do torturing and maiming and killing in the gracious name of the king.

A generous government, committed to a belief in the efficacy of capital punishment, paid Tobias Dramm at the rate of seventy-five dollars a head for hanging offenders convicted of the hanging crime, which was murder. He averaged about four hangings every three months or, say, about nine hundred dollars a year—all clear money.

The manner of Mr. Dramm's having entered upon the practise of this somewhat grisly trade makes in itself a little tale. He was a lifelong citizen of the town of Chickaloosa, down in the Southwest, where there stood a State penitentiary, and where, during the period of which I am speaking, the Federal authorities sent for confinement and punishment the criminal sweepings of half a score of States and Territories. This was before the government put up prisons of its own, and while still it parcelled out its human liabilities among State-owned institutions, paying so much apiece for their keep. When the government first began shipping a share of its felons to Chickaloosa, there came along, in one clanking caravan of shackled malefactors, a half-breed, part Mexican and the rest of him Indian, who had robbed a territorial postoffice and incidentally murdered the postmaster thereof. Wherefore this half-breed was under sentence to expiate his greater misdeed on a given date, between the hours of sunrise and sunset, and after a duly prescribed manner, namely: by being hanged by the neck until he was dead.

At once a difficulty and a complication arose. The warden of the penitentiary at Chickaloosa was perfectly agreeable to the idea of keeping and caring for those felonious wards of the government who were put in his custody to serve terms of imprisonment, holding that such disciplinary measures fell within the scope of his sworn duty. But when it came to the issue of hanging any one of them, he drew the line most firmly. As he pointed out, he was not a government agent. He derived his authority and drew his salary not from Washington, D. C., but from a State capital several hundreds of miles removed from Washington. Moreover, he was a zealous believer in the principle of State sovereignty. As a soldier of the late Southern Confederacy, he had fought four years to establish that doctrine. Conceded, that the cause for which he fought had been defeated; nevertheless his views upon the subject remained fixed and permanent. He had plenty of disagreeable jobs to do without stringing up bad men for Uncle Sam; such was the attitude the warden took. The sheriff of the county of which Chickaloosa was the county-seat, likewise refused to have a hand in the impending affair, holding it—and perhaps very properly—to be no direct concern of his, either officially or personally.

Now the government very much wanted the hybrid hanged. The government had been put to considerable trouble and no small expense to catch him and try him and convict him and transport him to the place where he was at present confined. Day and date for the execution of the law's judgment having been fixed, a scandal and possibly a legal tangle would ensue were there delay in the premises. It was reported that a full pardon had been offered to a long-term convict on condition that he carry out the court's mandate upon the body of the condemned mongrel, and that he had refused, even though the price were freedom for himself.

In this serious emergency, a volunteer in the person of Tobias Dramm came forward. Until then he had been an inconspicuous unit in the life of the community. He was a live-stock dealer on a small scale, making his headquarters at one of the town livery stables. He was a person of steady habits, with a reputation for sobriety and frugality among his neighbours. The government, so to speak, jumped at the chance. Without delay, his offer was accepted. There was no prolonged haggling over terms, either. He himself fixed the cost of the job at seventy-five dollars; this figure to include supervision of the erection of the gallows, testing of the apparatus, and the actual operation itself.

So, on the appointed day, at a certain hour, to wit, a quarter past six o'clock in the morning, just outside the prison walls, and in the presence of the proper and ordained number of witnesses, Uncle Tobe, with a grave, untroubled face, and hands which neither fumbled nor trembled, tied up the doomed felon and hooded his head in a black-cloth bag, and fitted a noose about his neck. The drop fell at eighteen minutes past the hour. Fourteen minutes later, following brief tests of heart and pulse, the two attending physicians agreed that the half-breed was quite satisfactorily defunct. They likewise coincided in the opinion that the hanging had been conducted with neatness, and with swiftness, and with the least possible amount of physical suffering for the deceased. One of the doctors went so far as to congratulate Mr. Dramm upon the tidiness of his handicraft. He told him that in all his experience he had never seen a hanging pass off more smoothly, and that for an amateur, Dramm had done splendidly. To this compliment Uncle Tobe replied, in his quiet and drawling mode of speech, that he had studied the whole thing out in advance.

"Ef I should keep on with this way of makin' a livin' I don't 'low ever to let no slip-ups occur," he added with simple directness. There was no suggestion of the morbid in his voice or manner as he said this, but instead merely a deep personal satisfaction.

Others present, having been made sick and faint by the shock of seeing a human being summarily jerked into the hereafter, went away hurriedly without saying anything at all. But afterward thinking it over when they were more composed, they decided among themselves that Uncle Tobe had carried it off with an assurance and a skill which qualified him most aptly for future undertakings along the same line; that he was a born hangman, if ever there was one.

This was the common verdict. So, thereafter, by a tacit understanding, the ex-cattle-buyer became the regular government hangman. He had no official title nor any warrant in writing for the place he filled. He worked by the piece, as one might say, and not by the week or month. Some years he hanged more men than in other years, but the average per annum was about twelve. He had been hanging them now for going on ten years.

It was as though he had been designed and created for the work. He hanged villainous men singly, sometimes by pairs, and rarely in groups of threes, always without a fumble or a hitch. Once, on a single morning, he hanged an even half-dozen, these being the chief fruitage of a busy term of the Federal court down in the Indian country where the combination of a crowded docket, an energetic young district attorney with political ambitions, and a businesslike presiding judge had produced what all unprejudiced and fair-minded persons agreed were marvellous results, highly beneficial to the moral atmosphere of the territory and calculated to make potential evil-doers stop and think. Four of the six had been members of an especially desperate gang of train and bank robbers. The remaining two had forfeited their right to keep on living by slaying deputy marshals. Each, with malice aforethought and with his own hands, had actually killed some one or had aided and abetted in killing some one.

This sextuple hanging made a lot of talk, naturally. The size of it alone commanded the popular interest. Besides, the personnel of the group of villains was such as to lend an aspect of picturesqueness to the final proceedings. The sextet included a full-blooded Cherokee; a consumptive ex-dentist out of Kansas, who from killing nerves in teeth had progressed to killing men in cold premeditation; a lank West Virginia mountaineer whose family name was the name of a clan prominent in one of the long-drawn-out hill-feuds of his native State; a plain bad man, whose chief claim to distinction was that he hailed originally from the Bowery in New York City; and one, the worst of them all, who was said to be the son of a pastor in a New England town. One by one, unerringly and swiftly, Uncle Tobe launched them through his scaffold floor to get whatever deserts await those who violate the laws of God and man by the violent shedding of innocent blood. When the sixth and last gunman came out of the prison proper into the prison enclosure—it was the former dentist, and being set, as the phrase runs, upon dying game, he wore a twisted grin upon his bleached face—there were six black boxes under the platform, five of them occupied, with their lids all in place, and one of them yet empty and open. In the act of mounting the steps the condemned craned his head sidewise, and at the sight of those coffins stretching along six in a row on the gravelled courtyard, he made a cheap and sorry gibe. But when he stood beneath the cross-arm to be pinioned, his legs played him traitor. Those craven knees of his gave way under him, so that trusties had to hold the weakening ruffian upright while the executioner snugged the halter about his throat.

On this occasion Uncle Tobe elucidated the creed and the code of his profession for a reporter who had come all the way down from St. Louis to report the big hanging for his paper. Having covered the hanging at length, the reporter stayed over one more day at the Palace Hotel in Chickaloosa to do a special article, which would be in part a character sketch and in part a straight interview, on the subject of the hangman. The article made a full page spread in the Sunday edition of the young man's paper, and thereby a reputation, which until this time had been more or less local, was given what approximated a national notoriety.

Through a somewhat general reprinting of what the young man had written, and what his paper had published, the country at large eventually became acquainted with an ethical view-point which was already fairly familiar to nearly every resident in and about Chickaloosa. Reading the narrative, one living at a distance got an accurate picture of a personality elevated above the commonplace solely by the rôle which its owner filled; a picture of an old man thoroughly sincere and thoroughly conscientious; a man dull, earnest, and capable to his limits; a man who was neither morbid nor imaginative, but filled with rather a stupid gravity; a man canny about the pennies and affectionately inclined toward the dollars; a man honestly imbued with the idea that he was a public servant performing a necessary public service; a man without nerves, but in all other essentials a small-town man with a small-town mind; in short, saw Uncle Tobe as he really was. The reporter did something else which marked him as a craftsman. Without stating the fact in words, he nevertheless contrived to create in the lines which he wrote an atmosphere of self-defence enveloping the old man—or perhaps the better phrase would be self-extenuation. The reader was made to perceive that Dramm, being cognizant and mildly resentful of the attitude in which his own little world held him, by reason of the fatal work of his hands, sought after a semiapologetic fashion to offer a plea in abatement of public judgment, to set up a weight of moral evidence in his own behalf, and behind this in turn, and showing through it, might be sensed the shy pride of a shy man for labour undertaken with good motives and creditably performed. With no more than a pardonable broadening and exaggeration of the other's mode of speech, the reporter succeeded likewise in reproducing not only the language, but the wistful intent of what Uncle Tobe said to him. From this interview I propose now to quote to the extent of a few paragraphs. This is Uncle Tobe addressing the visiting correspondent:

"It stands to reason—don't it?—that these here sinful men have got to be hung, an' that somebody has got to hang 'em. The Good Book says an eye fur an eye an' a tooth fur a tooth an' a life fur a life. That's perzactly whut it says, an' I'm one whut believes the Bible frum kiver to kiver. These here boys that they bring in here have broke the law of Gawd an' the law of the land, an' they jest natchelly got to pay fur their devilment. That's so, ain't it? Well, then, that bein' so, I step forward an' do the job. Ef they was free men, walkin' around like you an' me, I wouldn't lay the weight of my little finger on 'em to harm a single hair in their haids. Ef they hadn't done nothin' ag'in' the law, I'd be the last one to do 'em a hurt. I wisht you could make that p'int plain in the piece you aim to write so's folks would understand jest how I feel—so's they'd understand that I don't bear no gredge ag'inst any livin' creature.

"Ef the job was left to some greenhawn he'd mebbe botch it up an' make them boys suffer more'n there's any call fur. Sech things have happened, a plenty times before now ez you yourself doubtless know full well. But I don't botch it up. I ain't braggin' none whilst I'm sayin' this to you; I'm jest tellin' you. I kin take an oath that I ain't never botched up one of these jobs yit, not frum the very fust. The warden or Dr. Slattery, the prison physician, or anybody round this town that knows the full circumstances kin tell you the same, ef you ast 'em. You see, son, I ain't never nervoused up, like some men would be in my place. I'm always jest ez ca'm like ez whut you are this minute. The way I look at it, I'm jest a chosen instrument of the law. I regard it ez a trust that I'm called on to perform, on account of me havin' a natchel knack in that 'special direction. Some men have gifts fur one thing, an' some men have gifts fur another thing. It would seem this is the perticular thing—hangin' men—that I've got a gift fur. So, sech bein' the case, I don't worry none about it beforehand, nor I don't worry none after it's all over with, neither. With me handlin' the details the whole thing is over an' done with accordin' to the law an' the statutes an' the jedgment of the high court in less time than some people would take fussin' round, gittin' ready. The way I look at it, it's a mercy an' a blessin' to all concerned to have somebody in charge that knows how to hang a man.

"Why, it's come to sech a pass that when there's a hangin' comin' off anywhere in this part of the country they send fur me to be present ez a kind of an expert. I've been to hangin's all over this State, an' down into Louisiana, an' wunst over into Texas in order to give the sheriffs the benefit of my experience an' my advice. I make it a rule not never to take no money fur doin' sech ez that—only my travelin' expenses an' my tavern bills; that's all I ever charge 'em. But here in Chickaloosa the conditions is different, an' the gover'mint pays me seventy-five dollars a hangin'. I figger that it's wuth it, too. The Bible says the labourer is worthy of his hire. I try to be worthy of the hire I git. I certainly aim to earn it—an' I reckin I do earn it, takin' everything into consideration—the responsibility an' all. Ef there's any folks that think I earn my money easy—seventy-five dollars fur whut looks like jest a few minutes' work— I'd like fur 'em to stop an' think ef they'd consider themselves qualified to hang ez many men ez I have without never botchin' up a single job."

That was his chief boast, if boasting it might be called—that he never botched the job. It is the common history of common hangmen, so I've been told, that they come after a while to be possessed of the devils of cruelty, and to take pleasure in the exercise of their most grim calling. If this be true, then surely Uncle Tobe was to all outward appearances an exception to the rule. Never by word or look or act was be caught gloating over his victims; always he exhibited a merciful swiftness in the dread preliminaries and in the act of execution itself. At the outset he had shown deftness. With frequent practise he grew defter still. He contrived various devices for expediting the proceeding. For instance, after prolonged experiments, conducted in privacy, he evolved a harnesslike arrangement of leather belts and straps, made all in one piece, and fitted with buckles and snaffles. With this, in a marvellously brief space, he could bind his man at elbows and wrists, at knees and ankles, so that in less time almost than it would take to describe the process, the latter stood upon the trap, as a shape deprived of motion, fully caparisoned for the end. He fitted the inner side of the cross-piece of the gallows with pegs upon which the rope rested, entirely out of sight of him upon whom it was presently to be used, until the moment when Uncle Tobe, stretching a long arm upward, brought it down, all reeved and ready. He hit upon the expedient of slickening the noose parts with yellow bar soap so that it would run smoothly in the loop and tighten smartly, without undue tugging. He might have used grease or lard, but soap was tidier, and Uncle Tobe, as has been set forth, was a tidy man.

After the first few hangings his system began to follow a regular routine. From somewhere to the west or southwest of Chickaloosa the deputy marshals would bring in a man consigned to die. The prison people, taking their charge over from them, would house him in a cell of a row of cells made doubly tight and doubly strong for such as he; in due season the warden would notify Uncle Tobe of the date fixed for the inflicting of the penalty. Four or five days preceding the day, Uncle Tobe would pay a visit to the prison, timing his arrival so that he reached there just before the exercise hour for the inmates of a certain cell-tier. Being admitted, he would climb sundry flights of narrow iron stairs and pause just outside a crisscrossed door of iron slats while a turnkey, entering that door and locking it behind him, would open a smaller door set flat in the wall of damp-looking grey stones and invite the man caged up inside to come forth for his daily walk. Then, while the captive paced the length and breadth of the narrow corridor back and across, to and fro, up and down, with the futile restlessness of a cat animal in a zoo, his feet clumping on the flagged flooring, and the watchful turnkey standing by, Uncle Tobe, having flattened his lean form in a niche behind the outer lattice, with an appraising eye would consider the shifting figure through a convenient cranny of the wattled metal strips. He took care to keep himself well back out of view, but since he stood in shadow while the one he marked so keenly moved in a flood of daylight filtering down through a skylight in the ceiling of the cell block, the chances were the prisoner could not have made out the indistinct form of the stranger anyhow. Five or ten minutes of such scrutiny of his man was all Uncle Tobe ever desired. In his earlier days before he took up this present employment, he had been an adept at guessing the hoof-weight of the beeves and swine in which he dealt. That early experience stood him in good stead now; he took no credit to himself for his accuracy in estimating the bulk of a living human being.

Downstairs, on the way out of the place, if by chance he encountered the warden in his office, the warden, in all likelihood, would say: "Well, how about it this time, Uncle Tobe?"

And Uncle Tobe would make some such answer as this:

"Well, suh, accordin' to my reckonin' this here one will heft about a hund'ed an' sixty-five pound, ez he stands now. How's he takin' it, warden?"

"Oh, so-so."

"He looks to me like he was broodin' a right smart," the expert might say. "I jedge he ain't relishin' his vittles much, neither. Likely he'll worry three or four pound more off'n his bones 'twixt now an' Friday mornin'. He oughter run about one hund'ed an' sixty or mebbe one-sixty-one by then."

"How much drop do you allow to give him?"

"Don't worry about that, suh," would be the answer given with a contemplative squint of the placid, pale eye. "I reckin my calculations won't be very fur out of the way, ef any."

They never were, either.

On the day before the day, he would be a busy man, what with superintending the fitting together and setting up of the painted lumber pieces upon which to-morrow's capital tragedy would be played; and, when this was done to his liking, trying the drop to see that the boards had not warped, and trying the rope for possible flaws in its fabric or weave, and proving to his own satisfaction that the mechanism of the wooden lever which operated to spring the trap worked with an instantaneous smoothness. To every detail he gave a painstaking supervision, guarding against all possible contingencies. Regarding the trustworthiness of the rope he was especially careful. When this particular hanging was concluded, the scaffold would be taken apart and stored away for subsequent use, but for each hanging the government furnished a brand new rope, especially made at a factory in New Orleans at a cost of eight dollars. The spectators generally cut the rope up into short lengths after it had fulfilled its ordained purpose, and carried the pieces away for souvenirs. So always there was a new rope provided, and its dependability must be ascertained by prolonged and exhaustive tests before Uncle Tobe would approve of it. Seeing him at his task, with his coat and waistcoat off, his sleeves rolled back, and his intent mien, one realised why, as a hangman, he had been a success. He left absolutely nothing to chance. When he was through with his experimenting, the possibility of an exhibition of the proneness of inanimate objects to misbehave in emergencies had been reduced to a minimum.

Before daylight next morning Uncle Tobe, dressed in sober black, like a country undertaker, and with his mid-Victorian whiskers all cleansed and combed, would present himself at his post of duty. He

would linger in the background, an unobtrusive bystander, until the
condemned sinner had gone through the mockery of eating his last
breakfast; and, still making himself inconspicuous during the march to
the gallows, would trail at the very tail of the line, while the short, strag-
gling procession was winding out through gas-lit murky hallways into the
pale dawn-light slanting over the walls of the gravel-paved, high-fenced
compound built against the outer side of the prison close. He would
wait on, always holding himself discreetly aloof from the middle breadth
of the picture, until the officiating clergyman had done with his sacred
offices; would wait until the white-faced wretch on whose account the
government was making all this pother and taking all this trouble, had
mumbled his farewell words this side of eternity; would continue to wait,
very patiently, indeed, until the warden nodded to him. Then, with his
trussing harness tucked under his arm, and the black cap neatly folded
and bestowed in a handy side-pocket of his coat, Uncle Tobe would
advance forward, and laying a kindly, almost a paternal hand upon the
shoulder of the man who must die, would steer him to a certain spot in
the centre of the platform, just beneath a heavy cross-beam. There
would follow a quick shifting of the big, gnarled hands over the unresist-
ing body of the doomed man, and almost instantly, so it seemed to
those who watched, all was in order: the arms of the murderer drawn
rearward and pressed in close against his ribs by a broad girth encircling
his trunk at the elbows, his wrists caught together in buckled leather
cuffs behind his back; his knees and his ankles fast in leathern loops
which joined to the rest of the apparatus by means of a transverse strap
drawn tautly down the length of his legs, at the back; the black-cloth
head-bag with its peaked crown in place; the noose fitted; the hobbled
and hooded shape perhaps swaying a trifle this way and that; and Uncle
Tobe on his tiptoes stepping swiftly over to a tilted wooden lever which
projected out and upward through the planked floor, like the handle of
a steering oar.

It was at this point that the timorous-hearted among the witnesses
turned their heads away. Those who were more resolute—or as the case
might be, more morbid—and who continued to look, were made aware of
a freak of physics which in accord, I suppose, with the laws of horizontals
and parallels decrees that a man cut off short from life by quick and vio-

lent means and fallen prone upon the earth, seems to shrink up within himself and to grow shorter in body and in sprawling limb, whereas one hanged with a rope by the neck has the semblance of stretching lout to unseemly and unhuman length all the while that he dangles.

Having repossessed himself of his leather cinches, Uncle Tobe would presently depart for his home, stopping en route at the Chickaloosa National Bank to deposit the greater part of the seventy-five dollars which the warden, as representative of a satisfied Federal government, had paid him, cash down on the spot. To his credit in the bank the old man had a considerable sum, all earned after this mode, and all drawing interest at the legal rate. On his arrival at his home, Mr. Dramm would first of all have his breakfast. This over, he would open the second drawer of an old black-walnut bureau, and from under a carefully folded pile of spare undergarments would withdraw a small, cheap book, bound in imitation red leather, and bearing the word "Accounts" in faded script upon the cover. On a clean, blue-lined page of the book, in a cramped handwriting, he would write in ink, the name, age, height, and weight of the man he had just despatched out of life; also the hour and minute when the drop fell, the time elapsing before the surgeons pronounced the man dead; the disposition which had been made of the body, and any other data which seemed to him pertinent to the record. Invariably he concluded the entry thus: "Neck was broke by the fall. Everything passed off smooth." From his first time of service he had never failed to make such notations following a hanging, he being in this, as in all things, methodical and exact.

The rest of the day, in all probabilities, would be given to small devices of his own. If the season suited he might work in his little truck garden at the back of the house, or if it were the fall of the year he might go rabbit hunting; then again he might go for a walk. When the evening paper came—Chickaloosa had two papers, a morning paper and an evening paper—he would read through the account given of the event at the prison, and would pencil any material errors which had crept into the reporter's story, and then he would clip out the article and file it away with a sheaf of similar clippings in the same bureau drawer where he kept his account-book and his underclothing. This done he would eat his supper, afterward washing and wiping the supper dishes and, presently bedtime for him having arrived, he would go to bed and sleep very soundly and very peacefully all night. Sometimes his heart trouble brought on smothering spells which woke him up. He rarely had dreams, and never any dreams unpleasantly associated with his avocation. Probably never was there a man blessed with less of an imagination than this same Tobias Dramm. It seemed almost providential, considering the calling he followed, that he altogether lacked the faculty of introspection, so that neither his memory nor his conscience ever troubled him.

Thus far I have made no mention of his household, and for the very good reason that he had none. In his youth he had not married. The forked tongue of town slander had it that he was too stingy to support a wife, and on top of that expense, to run the risk of having children to rear. He had no close kindred excepting a distant cousin or two in Chickaloosa. He kept no servant, and for this there was a double cause. First, his parsimonious instincts; second, the fact that for love or money no negro would minister to him, and in this community negroes were the only household servants to be had. Among the darkies there was current a belief that at dead of night he dug up the bodies of those he had hanged and peddled the cadavers to the "student doctors." They said he was in active partnership with the devil; they said the devil took over the souls of his victims, paying therefor in red-hot dollars, after the hangman was done with their bodies. The belief of the negroes that this unholy traffic existed amounted with them to a profound conviction. They held Mr. Dramm in an awesome and horrified veneration, bowing to him most respectfully when they met him, and then sidling off hurriedly. It would have taken strong horses to drag any black-skinned resident of Chickaloosa to the portals of the little three-roomed frame cottage in the outskirts of the town which Uncle Tobe tenanted. Therefore he lived by himself, doing his own skimpy marketing and his own simple housekeeping. Loneliness was a part of the penalty he paid for following the calling of a gallowsmith.

Among members of his own race he had no close friends. For the most part the white people did not exactly shun him, but, as the saying goes in the Southwest, they let him be. They were well content to enshrine him as a local celebrity, and ready enough to point him out to visitors, but by an unwritten communal law the line was drawn there. He was as one set apart for certain necessary undertakings, and yet denied the intimacy of his kind because he performed them acceptably. If his aloof and solitary state ever distressed him, at least he gave no outward sign of it, but went his uncomplaining way, bearing himself with a homely, silent dignity, and enveloped in those invisible garments of superstition which local prejudice and local ignorance had conjured up.

Ready as he was when occasion suited, to justify his avocation in the terms of that same explanation which he had given to the young reporter from St. Louis that time, and greatly though he may have craved to gain the good-will of his fellow citizens, he was never known openly to rebel against his lot. The nearest he ever came to doing this was once when he met upon the street a woman of his acquaintance who had suffered a recent bereavement in the death of her only daughter. He approached her, offering awkward condolences, and at once was moved to a further expression of his sympathy for her in her great loss by trying to shake her hand. At the touch of his fingers to hers the woman, already in a mood of grief bordering on hysteria, shrank back screaming out that his hand smelled of the soap with which he coated his gallows-nooses. She ran away from him, crying out as she ran, that he was accursed; that he was marked with that awful smell and could not rid himself of it. To those who had witnessed this scene the hangman, with rather an injured and bewildered air, made explanation. The poor woman, he said, was wrong; although in a way of speaking she was right, too. He did, indeed, use the same yellow bar soap for washing his hands that he used for anointing his ropes. It was a good soap, and cheap; he had used the same brand regularly for years in cleansing his hands. Since it answered the first purpose so well, what possible harm could there be in slicking the noose of the rope with it when he was called upon to conduct one of his jobs over up at the prison? Apparently he was at a loss to fathom the looks they cast at him when he had finished with this statement and had asked this question. He began a protest, but broke off quickly and went away shaking his head as though puzzled that ordinarily sane folks should be so squeamish and so unreasonable. But he kept on using the soap, as before.

🐏

Until now this narrative has been largely preamble. The real story follows. It concerns itself with the birth of an imagination.

In his day Uncle Tobe hanged all sorts and conditions of men—men who kept on vainly hoping against hope for an eleventh-hour reprieve long after the last chance of reprieve had vanished, and who on the gallows begged piteously for five minutes, for two minutes, for one minute more of precious grace; negroes gone drunk on religious exhortation who died in a frenzy, sure of salvation, and shouting out halleluiahs; Indians upborne and stayed by a racial stoicism; Chinamen casting stolid, slant-eyed glances over the rim of the void before them and filled with the calmness of the fatalist who believes that whatever is to be, is to be; white men upon whom at the last, when all prospect of intervention was gone, a mental numbness mercifully descended with the result that they came to the rope's embrace like men in a walking coma, with glazed, unseeing eyes, and dragging feet; other white men who summoned up a mockery of bravado and uttered poor jests from between lips drawn back in defiant sneering as they gave themselves over to the hangman, so that only Uncle Tobe, feeling their flesh crawling under their grave-clothes as he tied them up, knew a hideous terror berode their bodies. At length, in the tenth year of his career as a paid executioner he was called upon to visit his professional attentions upon a man different from any of those who had gone down the same dread chute.

The man in question was a train-bandit popularly known as the Lone-Hand Kid, because always he conducted his nefarious operations without confederates. He was a squat, dark ruffian, as malignant as a moccasin snake, and as dangerous as one. He was filthy in speech and vile in habit, being in his person most unpicturesque and most unwholesome, and altogether seemed a creature more viper than he was man. The sheriffs of two border States and the officials of a contiguous reservation sought for him many times, long and diligently, before a posse overcame him in the hills by over-powering odds and took him alive at the cost of two of its members killed outright and a third badly crippled. So soon as surgeons plugged up the holes in his hide which members of the vengeful posse shot into him after they had him surrounded and before his ammunition gave out, be was brought to bar to answer for the unprovoked murder of a postal clerk on a transcontinental limited. No time was wasted in hurrying his trial through to its conclusion; it was felt that there was crying need to make an example of this red-handed desperado. Having been convicted with commendable celerity, the Lone-Hand Kid was transferred to Chickaloosa and strongly confined there against the day of Uncle Tobe's ministrations upon him.

From the very hour that the prosecution was started, the Lone-Hand Kid, whose real name was the prosaic name of Smith, objected strongly to this procedure which in certain circles is known as "railroading." He insisted that he was being legally expedited out of life on his record and not on the evidence. There were plenty of killings for any one of which he might have been tried and very probably found guilty, but he reckoned it a profound injustice that he should be indicted, tried, and condemned for a killing he had not committed. By his code he would not have rebelled strongly against being punished for the evil things he himself had done; he did dislike, though, being hanged for something some rival hold-up man had done. Such was his contention, and he reiterated it with a persistence which went far toward convincing some people that after all there might be something in what he said, although among honest men there was no doubt whatsoever that the world would be a sweeter and a healthier place to live in with the Lone-Hand Kid entirely translated out of it.

Having been dealt with, as he viewed the matter, most unfairly, the condemned killer sullenly refused to make submission to his appointed destiny. On the car journey up to Chickaloosa, although still weak from his wounds and securely ironed besides, he made two separate efforts to assault his guards. In his cell, a few days later, he attacked a turnkey in pure wantonness seemingly, since even with the turnkey eliminated, there still was no earthly prospect for him to escape from the steel strong-box which enclosed him. That was what it truly was, too, a strong-box, for the storing of many living pledges held as surety for the peace and good order of the land. Of all these human collaterals who were penned up there with him, he, for the time being, was most precious in the eyes of the law. Therefore the law took no chance of losing him, and this he must have known when he maimed his keeper.

After this outbreak he was treated as a vicious wild beast, which, undoubtedly, was exactly what he was. He was chained by his ankles to his bed, and his food was shoved in to him through the bars by a man who kept himself at all times well out of reach of the tethered prisoner. Having been rendered helpless, he swore then that when finally they unbarred his cell door and sought to fetch him forth to garb him for his journey to the gallows, he would fight them with his teeth and his bare hands for so long as he had left an ounce of strength with which to fight. Bodily force would then be the only argument remaining to him by means of which he might express his protest, and he told all who cared to listen that most certainly he meant to invoke it.

There was a code of decorum which governed the hangings at Chickaloosa, and the resident authorities dreaded mightily the prospect of having it profaned by spiteful and unmannerly behaviour on the part of the Lone-Hand Kid. There was said to be in all the world just one living creature for whom the rebellious captive entertained love and respect, and this person was his half-sister. With the good name of his prison at heart, the warden put up the money that paid her fare from her home down in the Indian Territory. Two days before the execution she arrived, a slab-sided, shabby drudge of a woman. Having first been primed and prompted for her part, she was sent to him, and in his cell she wept over the fettered prisoner, and with him she pleaded until he promised her, reluctantly, he would make no physical struggle on being led out to die.

He kept his word, too; but it was to develop that the pledge of non-resistance, making his body passive to the will of his jailers, did not, according to the Lone-Hand Kid's sense of honour, include the muscles of his tongue. His hour came at sunup of a clear, crisp, October morning, when a rime of frost made a silver carpet upon the boarded floor of the scaffold, and in the east the heavens glowed an irate red, like the reflections of a distant bale-fire. From his cell door before the head warder summoned him forth, he drove away with terrible oaths the clergyman who had come to offer him religious consolation. At daylight, when the first beams of young sunlight were stealing in at the slitted windows to streak the whitewashed wall behind him with a barred pattern of red, like brush strokes of fresh paint, he ate his last breakfast with foul words between bites, and outside, a little later, in the shadow of the crosstree from which shortly he would dangle in the article of death, a stark offence before the sight of mortal eyes, he halted and stood reviling all who had a hand in furthering and compassing his condemnation. Profaning the name of his Maker with every breath, he cursed the President of the United States who had declined to reprieve him, the justices of the high court who had denied his appeal from the verdict of the lower, the judge who had tried him, the district attorney who had prosecuted him, the grand jurors who had indicted him, the petit jurors who had voted to convict him, the witnesses who had testified against him, the posse men who had trapped him, consigning them all and singly to everlasting damnation. Before this pouring flood of blasphemy the minister, who had followed him up the gallows steps in the vain hope that when the end came some faint sign of contrition might be vouchsafed by this poor lost soul, hid his face in his hands as though fearing an offended Deity would send a bolt from on high to blast all who had been witnesses to such impiety and such impenitence.

The indignant warden moved to cut short this lamentable spectacle. He signed with his hand for Uncle Tobe to make haste, and Uncle Tobe, obeying, stepped forward from where he had been waiting in the rear rank of the shocked spectators. Upon him the defiant ruffian turned the forces of his sulfurous hate, full-gush. First over one shoulder and then over the other as the executioner worked with swift fingers to bind him into a rigid parcel of a man, he uttered what was both a dreadful threat and a yet more dreadful promise.

"I ain't blamin' these other folks here," he proclaimed. "Some of 'em are here because it's their duty to be here, an' ef these others kin git pleasure out of seein' a man croaked that ain't afeared of bein' croaked, they're welcome to enjoy the free show, so fur ez I'm concerned. But you—you stingy, white-whiskered old snake!—you're doin' this fur the little piece of dirty money that's in it fur you.

"Listen to me, you dog: I know I'm headin' straight fur hell, an' I ain't skeered to go, neither. But I ain't goin' to stay there. I'm comin' back fur you! I'm comin' back this very night to git you an' take your old, withered, black soul back down to hell with me. No need fur you to try to hide. Wharever you hide I'll seek you out. You can't git away frum me. You kin lock your door an' you kin lock your winder, an' you kin hide your head under the bedclothes, but I'll find you wharever you are, remember that! An' you're goin' back down there with me!

"Now go ahead an' hang me—I'm all set fur it ef you are!"

Through this harangue Uncle Tobe worked on, outwardly composed. Whatever his innermost emotions may have been, his expression gave no hint that the mouthings of the LoneHand Kid had sunk in. He drew the peaked black sack down across the swollen face, hiding the glaring eyes and the lips that snarled. He brought the rope forward over the cloaked head and drew the noose in tautly, with the knot adjusted to fit snugly just under the left ear, so that the hood took on the semblance of a well-filled, inverted bag with its puckered end fluting out in the effect of a dark ruff upon the hunched shoulders of its wearer. Stepping back, he gripped the handle of the lever-bar, and with all his strength jerked it toward him. A square in the floor opened as the trap was flapped back upon its hinges, and through the opening the haltered form shot straight downward to bring up with a great jerk, and after that to dangle like a plumb-bob on a string. Under the quick strain the gallows-arm creaked and whined; in the silence which followed the hangman was heard to exhale his breath in a vast puff of relief. His hand went up to his forehead to wipe beads of sweat which, for all that the morning was cool almost to coldness, had suddenly popped out through his skin. He for one was mighty glad the thing was done, and, as he in this moment figured, well done.

But for once and once only as those saw who had the hardihood to look, Uncle Tobe had botched up a job. Perhaps it was because of his great haste to make an end of a scandalous scene; perhaps because the tirade of the bound malefactor had discomfited him and made his fingers fumble this one time at their familiar task. Whatever the cause, it was plainly enough to be seen that the heavy knot had not cracked the Lone-Hand Kid's spine. The noose, as was ascertained later, had caught on the edge of the broad jawbone, and the man, instead of dying instantly, was strangling to death by degrees and with much struggling.

In the next half minute a thing even more grievous befell. The broad strap which girthed the murderer's trunk just above the bend of the elbows, held fast, but the rest of the harness, having been improperly snaffled on, loosened and fell away from the twitching limbs so that as the elongated body twisted to and fro in half circles, the lower arms winnowed the air in foreshortened and contorted flappings, and the freed legs drew up and down convulsively.

Very naturally, Uncle Tobe was chagrined; perhaps he had hidden within him emotions deeper than those bred of a personal mortification. At any rate, after a quick, distressed glance through the trap at the writhing shape of agony below, he turned his eyes from it and looked steadfastly at the high wall facing him. It chanced to be the western wall, which was bathed in a ruddy glare where the shafts of the upcoming sun, lifting over the panels at the opposite side of the fenced enclosure, began to fall diagonally upon the whitewashed surface just across. And now, against that glowing plane of background opposite him, there appeared as he looked the slanted shadow of a swaying rope framed in at right and at left by two broader, deeper lines which were the shadows marking the timber uprights that supported the scaffold at its nearer corners; and also there appeared, midway between the framing shadows, down at the lower end of the slender line of the cord, an exaggerated, wriggling manifestation like the reflection of a huge and misshapen jumping-jack, which first would lengthen itself grotesquely, and then abruptly would shorten up, as the tremors running through the dying man's frame altered the silhouette cast by the oblique sunbeams; and along with this stencilled vision, as a part of it, occurred shifting shadow movements of two legs dancing busily on nothing, and of two foreshortened arms, flapping up and down. It was no pretty picture to look upon, yet Uncle Tobe, plucking with a tremulous hand at the ends of his beard, continued to stare at the apparition, daunted and fascinated. To him it must have seemed as though the Lone-Hand Kid, with a malignant pertinacity which lingered on in him after by rights the last breath should have been squeezed out of his wretched carcass, was painting upon those tall planks the picture and the presentiment of his farewell threat.

Nearly half an hour passed before the surgeons consented that the body should be taken down and boxed. His harness which had failed him having been returned to its owner, he made it up into a compact bundle and collected his regular fee and went away very quietly. Ordinarily, following his habitual routine, he would have gone across town to his little house; would have washed his hands with a bar of the yellow laundry soap; would have cooked and eaten his breakfast, and then, after tidying up the kitchen, would have made the customary entry in his red-backed account-book. But this morning he seemed to have no appetite, and besides, he felt an unaccountable distaste for his home, with its silence and its emptiness. Somehow he much preferred the open air, with the skies over him and wide reaches of space about him; which was doubly strange, seeing that he was no lover of nature, but always theretofore had accepted sky and grass and trees as matters of course—things as inevitable and commonplace as the weathers and the winds.

Throughout the day and until well on toward night he was beset by a curious, uncommon restlessness which made it hard for him to linger long in any one spot. He idled about the streets of the town; twice he wandered aimlessly miles out along roads beyond the town. All the while, without cessation, there was a tugging and nagging at his nerve-ends, a constant inward irritation which laid a hold on his thoughts, twitching them off into unpleasant channels. It kept him from centring his interest upon the casual things about him; inevitably it turned his mind back to inner contemplations. The sensation was mental largely, but it seemed so nearly akin to the physical that to himself Uncle Tobe diagnosed it as the after-result of a wrench for his weak heart. You see, never before having experienced the reactions of a suddenly quickened imagination, he, naturally, was at a loss to account for it on any other ground.

Also he was weighted down by an intense depression that his clean record of ten years should have been marred by a mishap; this regret, constantly recurring in his thoughts, served to make him unduly sensitive. He had a feeling that people stared hard at him as they passed and, after he had gone by, that they turned to stare at him some more. Under this scrutiny he gave no sign of displeasure, but inwardly he resented it. Of course these folks had heard of what had happened up at the prison,

and no doubt among themselves would be commenting upon the tragedy and gossiping about it. Well, any man was liable to make a slip once;
nobody was perfect. It would never happen again; he was sure of that
much.

All day he mooned about, a brooding, uneasy figure, speaking to
scarcely any one at all, but followed wherever he went by curious eyes. It
was late in the afternoon before it occurred to him that he had eaten
nothing all day, and that he had failed to deposit the money he had
earned that morning. It would be too late now to get into the bank; the
bank, which opened early, closed at three o'clock. Tomorrow would do
as well. Although he had no zest for food despite his fast, he figured
maybe it was the long abstinence which was filling his head with such
flighty notions, so he entered a small, smelly lunch-room near the railroad station, and made a pretense of eating an order of ham and eggs.
He tried not to notice that the black waiter who served him shrank away
from his proximity, shying off like a breechy colt, from the table where
Uncle Tobe sat, whenever his business brought him into that part of the
place. What difference did a fool darky's fears make, anyway?

Dusk impended when he found himself approaching his three-
room house, looming up as a black oblong, where it stood aloof from its
neighbours, with vacant lands about it. The house faced north and
south. On the nearer edge of the unfenced common, which extended
up to it on the eastern side, he noted as he drew close that somebody—
perhaps a boy, or more probably a group of boys—had made a bonfire
of fallen autumn leaves and brushwood. Going away as evening came,
they had left their bonfire to burn itself out. The smouldering pile was
almost under his bedroom window. He regretted rather that the boys
had gone; an urgent longing for human companionship of some sort,
however remote—a yearning he had never before felt with such acuteness—was upon him. Tormented, as he still was, by strange vagaries, he
had almost to force himself to unlock the front door and cross the
threshold into the gloomy interior of his cottage. But before entering,
and while he yet wrestled with a vague desire to retrace his steps and go
back down the street, he stooped and picked up his copy of the afternoon paper which the carrier, with true carrierlike accuracy, had flung
upon the narrow front porch.

Inside the house, the floor gave off sharp little sounds, the warped floor squeaking and wheezing under the weight of his tread. Subconsciously, this irritated him; a lot of causes were combining to harass him, it seemed; there was a general conspiracy on the part of objects animate and inanimate to make him—well, suspicious. And Uncle Tobe was not given to nervousness, which made it worse. He was ashamed of himself that he should be in such state. Glancing about him in a furtive, almost in an apprehensive way, he crossed the front room to the middle room, which was his bed chamber, the kitchen being the room at the rear. In the middle room he lit a coal-oil lamp which stood upon a small centre table. Alongside the table he opened out the paper and glanced at a caption running half-way across the top of the front page; then, fretfully he crumpled up the printed sheet in his hand and let it fall upon the floor. He had no desire to read the account of his one failure. Why should the editor dwell at such length and with so prodigal a display of black head-line type upon this one bungled job when every other job, of all the jobs that had gone before, had been successful in every detail? Let's see, now, how many men had he hanged with precision and with speed and with never an accident to mar the proceedings? A long, martialed array of names came trooping into his brain, and along with the names the memories of the faces of all those dead men to whom the names had belonged. The faces began to pass before him in a mental procession. This wouldn't do. Since there were no such things as ghosts or haunts; since, as all sensible men agreed, the dead never came back from the grave, it was a foolish thing, for him to be creating those unpleasant images in his mind. He shook his head to clear it of recollections which were the better forgotten. He shook it again and again.

He would get to bed; a good night's rest would make him feel better and more natural. It was an excellent idea—this idea of sleep. So he raised the bottommost half of the curtainless side window for air, drew down the shade by the string suspended from its lower cross breadth, until the lower edge of the shade came even with the window sash, and undressed himself to his undergarments. He was about to blow out the light when he remembered he had left the money that was the price of his morning's work in his trousers which hung, neatly folded, across the back of a chair by the centre table. He was in the act of withdrawing the bills from the bottom of one of the trouser-pockets when right at his feet there was a quick, queer sound of rustling. As he glared down, startled, out from under the crumpled newspaper came timorously creeping a half-grown, sickly looking rat, minus its tail, having lost its tail in a trap, perhaps, or possibly in a battle with other rats.

At best a rat is no pleasant bedroom companion, and besides, Uncle Tobe had been seriously annoyed. He kicked out with one of his bare feet, taking the rat squarely in its side as it scurried for its hole in the wainscoting. He hurt it badly. It landed with a thump ten feet away and sprawled out on the floor kicking and squealing feebly. Holding the wad of bills in his left hand, with his right Uncle Tobe deftly plucked up the crushed vermin by the loose fold of skin at the nape of its neck, and with a quick flirt of his arm tossed it sidewise from him to cast it out of the half-opened window. He returned to the table and bent over and blew down the lamp chimney, and in the darkness felt his way across the room to his bed. He stretched himself full length upon it, drew the cotton comforter up to cover him, and shoved the money under the pillow.

His fingers were relaxing their grip on the bills when he saw something—something which instantly turned him stiff and rigid and deathly cold all over, leaving him without will-power or strength to move his head or shift his gaze. Over the white, plastered wall alongside his bed an unearthly red glow sprang up, turning a deeper, angrier red as it spread and widened. Against this background next stood out two perpendicular masses like the broad shadows of uprights—like the supporting uprights of a gallows, say—and in the squared space of brightness thus marked off, depending midway from the shadow crossing it at right angles at the top, appeared a filmy, fine line, which undoubtedly was the shadow of a cord, and at the end of the cord dangled a veritable jumping-jack of a silhouette, turning and writhing and jerking, with a shape which in one breath grotesquely lengthened and in the next shrank up to half its former dimensions, which kicked out with indistinct movements of its lower extremities, which flapped with foreshortened strokes of the shadowy upper limbs, which altogether so contorted itself as to form the likeness of a thing all out of perspective, all out of proportion, and all most horribly reminiscent.

A heart with valves already weakened by a chronic affection can stand just so many shocks in a given time and no more.

A short time later in this same night, at about eight-forty-five o'clock, to be exact, a man who lived on the opposite side of the unfenced common gave the alarm of fire over the telephone. The Chickaloosa fire engine and hose reels came at once, and with the machines numerous citizens.

In a way of speaking, it turned out to be a false alarm. A bonfire of leaves and brush, abandoned at dusk by the boys who kindled it, had, after smouldering a while, sprung up briskly and, flaming high, was now scorching the clapboarded side of the Dramm house.

There was no need for the firemen to uncouple a line of hose from the reel. While two of them made shift to get retorts of a patent extinguisher from the truck, two more, wondering why Uncle Tobe, even if in bed and asleep at so early an hour, had not been aroused by the noise of the crowd's coming, knocked at his front door. There being no response from within at once, they suspected something must be amiss. With heaves of their shoulders they forced the door off its hinges, and entering in company, they groped their passage through the empty front room into the bedroom behind it, which was lighted after a fashion by the reflection from the mounting flames without.

The tenant was in bed; he lay on his side with his face turned to the wall; he made no answer to their hails. When they bent over him they knew why. No need to touch him, then, with that look on his face and that stare out of his popped eyes. He was dead, all right enough; but plainly had not been dead long; not more than a few minutes, apparently. One of his hands was shoved up under his pillow with the fingers touching a small roll containing seven ten-dollar bills and one five-dollar bill; the other hand still gripped a fold of the coverlet as though the fatal stroke had come upon the old man as he lifted the bedclothing to draw it up over his face. These incidental facts were noted down later after the coroner had been called to take charge; they were the subject of considerable comment next day when the inquest took place. The coroner was of the opinion that the old man had been killed by a heart seizure, and that he had died on the instant the attack came.

However, this speculation had no part in the thoughts of the two startled firemen at the moment of the finding of the body. What most interested them, next only to the discovery of the presence of the dead man there in the same room with them, was a queer combination of shadows which played up and down against the wall beyond the bed, it being plainly visible in the glare, of the small conflagration just outside.

With one accord they turned about, and then they saw the cause of the phenomenon, and realised that it was not very much of a phenomenon after all, although unusual enough to constitute a rather curious circumstance. A crippled, tailless rat had somehow entangled its neck in a loop at the end of the dangling cord of the half-drawn shade at the side window on the opposite side of the room and, being too weak to wriggle free, was still hanging there, jerking and kicking, midway of the window opening. The glow of the pile of burning leaves and brush behind and beyond it, brought out its black outlines with remarkable clearness.

The patterned shadow upon the wall, though, disappeared in the same instant that the men outside began spraying their chemical compound from the two extinguishers upon the ambitious bonfire to douse it out, and one of the firemen slapped the rat down to the floor and killed it with a stamp of his foot.

Darkness

There was a house in this town where always by night lights burned. In one of its rooms many lights burned; in each of the other rooms at least one light. It stood on Clay Street, on a treeless plot among flower beds, a small dull-looking house; and when late on dark nights all the other houses on Clay Street were solid blockings lifting from the lesser blackness of their background, the lights in this house patterned its windows with squares of brilliancy so that it suggested a grid set on edge before hot flames. Once a newcomer to the town, a transient guest at Mrs. Otterbuck's boarding house, spoke about it to old Squire Jonas, who lived next door to where the lights blazed of nights, and the answer he got makes a fitting enough beginning for this account.

This stranger came along Clay Street one morning, and Squire Jonas, who was leaning over his gate contemplating the world as it passed in review, nodded to him and remarked that it was a fine morning; and the stranger was emboldened to stop and pass the time of day, as the saying goes.

"I'm here going over the books of the Bernheimer Distilling Company," he said when they had spoken of this and that, "and, you know, when a chartered accountant gets on a job he's supposed to keep right at it until he's done. Well, my work keeps me busy till pretty late. And the last three nights, passing that place yonder adjoining yours, I've noticed she was all lit up like as if for a wedding or a christening or a party or something. But I didn't see anybody going in or coming out, or hear anybody stirring in there, and it struck me as blamed curious. Last night—or this morning, rather, I should say—it must have been close on to half-past two o'clock when I passed by, and there she was, all as quiet as the tomb and still the lights going from top to bottom. So I got to wondering to myself. Tell me, sir, is there somebody sick over there next door?"

"Yes, suh," stated the squire, "I figure you might say there is somebody sick there. He's been sick a powerful long time too. But it's not his body that's sick; it's his soul."

"I don't know as I get you, sir," said the other man in a puzzled sort of way.

"Son," stated the squire, "I reckin you've been hearin' 'em, haven't you, singin' this here new song that's goin' 'round about, 'I'm Afraid to Go Home in the Dark'? Well, probably the man who wrote that there song never was down here in these parts in his life; probably he just made the idea of it up out of his own head. But he might 'a' had the case of my neighbor in his mind when he done so. Only his song is kind of comical and this case here is about the most uncomic one you'd be likely to run acrost. The man who lives here alongside of me is not only afraid to go home in the dark but he's actually feared to stay in the dark after he gets home. Once he killed a man and he come clear of the killin' all right enough, but seems like he ain't never got over it; and the sayin' in this town is that he's studied it out that ef ever he gets in the dark, either by himself or in company, he'll see the face of that there man he killed. So that's why, son, you've been seein' them lights a-blazin'. I've been seein' 'em myself fur goin' on twenty year or more, I reckin 'tis by now, and I've got used to 'em. But I ain't never got over wonderin' whut kind of thoughts he must have over there all alone by himself at night with everything lit up bright as day around him, when by rights things should be dark. But I ain't ever asted him, and whut's more, I never will. He ain't the kind you could go to him astin' him personal questions about his own private affairs. We-all here in town just accept him fur whut he is and sort of let him be. He's whut you might call a town character. His name is Mr. Dudley Stackpole."

In all respects save one, Squire Jonas, telling the inquiring stranger the tale, had the rights of it. There were town characters aplenty he might have described. A long-settled community with traditions behind it and a reasonable antiquity seems to breed curious types of men and women as a musty closet breeds mice and moths. This town of ours had its town mysteries and its town eccentrics—its freaks, if one wished to put the matter bluntly; and it had its champion story-teller and its champion liar and its champion guesser of the weight of livestock on the hoof.

There was crazy Saul Vance, the butt of cruel small boys, who deported himself as any rational creature might so long as he walked a straight course; but so surely as he came to where the road forked or two streets crossed he could not decide which turning to take and for hours angled back and forth and to and fro, now taking the short cut to regain the path he just had quitted, now retracing his way over the long one, for all the world like a geometric spider spinning its web. There was old Daddy Hannah, the black root-and-yarb doctor, who could throw spells and weave charms and invoke conjures. He wore a pair of shoes which had been worn by a man who was hanged, and these shoes, as is well known, leave no tracks which a dog will nose after or a witch follow, or a ha'nt. Small boys did not gibe at Daddy Hannah, you bet you! There was Major Burnley, who lived for years and years in the same house with the wife with whom he had quarreled and never spoke a word to her or she to him. But the list is overlong for calling. With us, in that day and time, town characters abounded freely. But Mr. Dudley Stackpole was more than a town character. He was that, it is true, but he was something else besides; something which tabbed him a mortal set apart from his fellow mortals. He was the town's chief figure of tragedy.

If you had ever seen him once you could shut your eyes and see him over again. Yet about him there was nothing impressive, nothing in his port or his manner to catch and to hold a stranger's gaze. With him, physically, it was quite the other way about. He was a short spare man, very gentle in his movements, a toneless sort of man of a palish gray cast, who always wore sad-colored clothing. He would make you think of a man molded out of a fog; almost he was like a man made of smoke. His mode of living might testify that a gnawing remorse abode ever with him, but his hair had not turned white in a single night, as the heads of those suddenly stricken by a great shock or a great grief or any greatly upsetting and disordering emotion sometimes are reputed to turn. Neither in his youth nor when age came to him was his hair white. But for so far back as any now remembered it had been a dullish gray, suggesting at a distance dead lichens.

The color of his skin was a color to match in with the rest of him. It was not pale, nor was it pasty. People with a taste for comparisons were hard put to it to describe just what it was the hue of his face did remind them of, until one day a man brought in from the woods the abandoned nest of a brood of black hornets, still clinging to the pendent twig from which the insect artificers had swung it. Darkies used to collect these nests in the fall of the year when the vicious swarms had deserted them. Their shredded parchments made ideal wadding for muzzle-loading scatter-guns, and, sufferers from asthma tore them down, too, and burned them slowly and stooped over the smoldering mass and inhaled the fumes and the smoke which arose, because the country wiseacres preached that no boughten stuff out of a drug store gave such relief from asthma as this hornet's-nest treatment. But it remained for this man to find a third use for such a thing. He brought it into the office of Gafford's wagon yard, where some other men were sitting about the fire, and he held it up before them and he said:

"Who does this here hornet's nest put you fellers in mind of—this gray color all over it, and all these here fine lines runnin' back and forth and every which-a-way like wrinkles? Think, now—it's somebody you all know."

And when they had given it up as a puzzle too hard for them to guess he said:

"Why, ain't it got percisely the same color and the same look about it as Mr. Dudley Stackpole's face? Why, it's a perfect imitation of him! That's whut I said to myself all in a flash when I first seen it bouncin' on the end of this here black birch limb out yonder in the flats."

"By gum, if you ain't right!" exclaimed one of the audience. "Say, come to think about it, I wonder if spendin' all his nights with bright lights burnin' round him is whut's give that old man that gray color he's got, the same as this wasp's nest has got it, and all them puckery lines round his eyes. Pore old devil, with the hags furever ridin' him! Well, they tell me he's toler'ble well fixed in this world's goods, but poor as I am, and him well off, I wouldn't trade places with him fur any amount of money. I've got my peace of mind if I ain't got anything else to speak of. Say, you'd 'a' thought in all these years a man would get over broodin' over havin' killed another feller, and specially havin' killed him in fair fight. Let's see, now, whut was the name of the feller he killed that time out there at Cache Creek Crossin's? I actually disremember. I've heard it a thousand times, too, I reckin, if I've heard it oncet."

For a fact, the memory of the man slain so long before only endured because the slayer walked abroad as a living reminder of the taking off of one who by all accounts had been of small value to mankind in his day and generation. Save for the daily presence of the one, the very identity even of the other might before now have been forgotten. For this very reason, seeking to enlarge the merits of the controversy which had led to the death of one Jesse Tatum at the hands of Dudley Stackpole, people sometimes referred to it as the Tatum-Stackpole feud and sought to liken it to the Faxon-Fleming feud. But that was a real feud with fence-corner ambuscades and a sizable mortality list and nighttime assassinations and all; whereas this lesser thing, which now briefly is to be dealt with on its merits, had been no more than a neighborhood falling out, having but a solitary homicide for its climactic upshot. So far as that went, it really was not so much the death of the victim as the survival of his destroyer—and his fashion of living afterwards—which made warp and woof for the fabric of the tragedy.

With the passage of time the actuating causes were somewhat blurred in perspective. The main facts stood forth clear enough, but the underlying details were misty and uncertain, like some half-obliterated scribble on a badly rubbed slate upon which a more important sum has been overlaid. One rendition had it that the firm of Stackpole Brothers sued the two Tatums—Harve and Jess—for an account long overdue, and won judgment in the courts, but won with it the murderous enmity of the defendant pair. Another account would have it that a dispute over a boundary fence marching between the Tatum homestead on Cache Creek and one of the Stackpole farm holdings ripened into a prime quarrel by reasons of Stackpole stubbornness on the one hand and Tatum malignity on the other. By yet a third account the lawsuit and the line-fence matter were confusingly twisted together to form a cause for disputation.

Never mind that part though. The incontrovertible part was that things came to a decisive pass on a July day in the late 80's when the two Tatums sent word to the two Stackpoles that at or about six o'clock of that evening they would come down the side road from their place a mile away to Stackpole Brothers' gristmill above the big riffle in Cache Creek prepared to fight it out man to man. The warning was explicit enough–the Tatums would shoot on sight. The message was meant for two, but only one brother heard it; for Jeffrey Stackpole, the senior member of the firm, was sick abed with heart disease at the Stackpole house on Clay Street in town, and Dudley, the junior, was running the business and keeping bachelor's hall, as the phrase goes, in the living room of the mill; and it was Dudley who received notice.

Now the younger Stackpole was known for a law-abiding and a well-disposed man, which reputation stood him in stead subsequently; but also he was no coward. He might crave peace, but he would not flee from trouble moving toward him. He would not advance a step to meet it, neither would he give back a step to avoid it. If it occurred to him to hurry in, to the county seat and have his enemies put under bonds to keep the peace he pushed the thought from him. This, in those days, was not the popular course for one threatened with violence by another; nor, generally speaking, was it regarded exactly as the manly one to follow. So he bided that day where he was. Moreover, it was not of record that he told anyone at all of what impended. He knew little of the use of firearms, but there was a loaded pistol in the cash drawer of the mill office. He put it in a pocket of his coat and through the afternoon he waited, outwardly quiet and composed, for the appointed hour when single-handed he would defend his honor and his brother's against the unequal odds of a brace of bullies, both of them quick on the trigger, both smart and clever in the handling of weapons.

But if Stackpole told no one, someone else told someone. Probably the messenger of the Tatums talked. He currently was reputed to have a leaky tongue to go with his jimberjaws; a born trouble maker, doubtless, else he would not have loaned his service to such employment in the first place. Up and down the road ran the report that before night there would be a clash at the Stackpole mill. Peg-Leg Foster, who ran the general store below the bridge and within sight of the big riffle, saw fit to shut up shop early and go to town for the evening. Perhaps he did not want to be a witness, or possibly he desired to be out of the way of stray lead flying about. So the only known witness to what happened, other than the parties engaged in it, was a negro woman. She, at least, was one who had not heard the rumor which since early forenoon had been spreading through the sparsely settled neighborhood. When six o'clock came she was grubbing out a sorghum patch in front of her cabin just north of where the creek cut under the Blandsville gravel pike.

One gets a picture of the scene: The thin and deficient shadows stretching themselves across the parched bottom lands as the sun slid down behind the trees of Eden's swamp lot; the heat waves of a blistering hot day still dancing their devil's dance down the road like wriggling circumflexes to accent a false promise of coolness off there in the distance; the ominous emptiness of the landscape; the brooding quiet, cut through only by the frogs and the dry flies tuning up for their evening concert; the bandannaed negress wrangling at the weeds with her hoe blade inside the rail fence; and, half sheltered within the lintels of the office doorway of his mill, Dudley Stackpole, a slim, still figure, watching up the crossroad for the coming of his adversaries.

But the adversaries did not come from up the road as they had advertised they would. That declaration on their part had been a trick and device, cockered up in the hope of taking the foe by surprise and from the rear. In a canvas-covered wagon—moving wagons, we used to call them in Red Gravel County—they left their house half an hour or so before the time set by them for the meeting, and they cut through by a wood lane which met the pike south of Foster's store; and then very slowly they rode up the pike toward the mill, being minded to attack from behind, with the added advantage of unexpectedness on their side.

Chance, though, spoiled their strategy and made these terms of primitive dueling more equal. Mark how: The woman in the sorghum patch saw it happen. She saw the wagon pass her and saw it brought to a standstill just beyond where she was; saw Jess Tatum slide stealthily down from under the overhanging hood of the wagon and, sheltered behind it, draw a revolver and cock it, all the while peeping out, searching the front and the nearer side of the gristmill with his eager eyes. She saw Harve Tatum, the elder brother, set the wheel chock and wrap the lines about the sheathed whipstock, and then as he swung off the seat catch a boot heel on the rim of the wagon box and fall to the road with a jar which knocked him cold, for he was a gross and heavy man and struck squarely on his head. With popped eyes she saw Jess throw up his pistol and fire once from his ambush behind the wagon, and then—the startled team having snatched the wagon from before him—saw him advance into the open toward the mill, shooting again as he advanced.

All now in the same breath and in a jumble of shock and terror she saw Dudley Stackpole emerge into full sight, and standing clear a pace from his doorway return the fire; saw the thudding frantic hoofs of the nigh horse spurn Harve Tatum's body aside—the kick broke his right leg, it turned out—saw Jess Tatum suddenly halt and stagger back as though jerked by an unseen hand; saw him drop his weapon and straighten again, and with both hands clutched to his throat run forward, head thrown back and feet drumming; heard him give one strange bubbling, strangled scream—it was the blood in his throat made this outcry sound thus—and saw him fall on his face, twitching and heaving, not thirty feet from where Dudley Stackpole stood, his pistol upraised and ready for more firing.

As to how many shots, all told, were fired the woman never could say with certainty. There might have been four or five or six, or even seven, she thought. After the opening shot they rang together in almost a continuous volley, she said. Three empty chambers in Tatum's gun and two in Stackpole's seemed conclusive evidence to the sheriff and the coroner that night and to the coroner's jurors next day that five shots had been fired.

On one point, though, for all her fright, the woman was positive, and to this she stuck in the face of questions and cross-questions. After Tatum stopped as though jolted to a standstill, and dropped his weapon, Stackpole flung the barrel of his revolver upward and did not again offer to fire, either as his disarmed and stricken enemy advanced upon him or after he had fallen. As she put it, he stood there like a man frozen stiff.

Having seen and heard this much, the witness, now all possible peril for her was passed, suddenly became mad with fear. She ran into her cabin and scrouged behind the headboard of a bed. When at length she timorously withdrew from hiding and came trembling forth, already persons out of the neighborhood, drawn by the sounds of the fusillade, were hurrying up. They seemed to spring, as it were, out of the ground. Into the mill these newcomers carried the two Tatums, Jess being stone-dead and Harve still senseless, with a leg dangling where the bones were snapped below the knee, and a great cut in his scalp; and they laid the two of them side by side on the floor in the gritty dust of the meal tailings and the flour grindings. This done, some ran to harness and hitch and to go to fetch doctors and law officers, spreading the news as they went; and some stayed on to work over Harve Tatum and to give such comfort as they might to Dudley Stackpole, he sitting dumb in his little, chittered office awaiting the coming of constable or sheriff or deputy so that he might surrender himself into custody.

While they waited and while they worked to bring Harve Tatum back to his senses, the men marveled at two amazing things. The first wonder was that Jess Tatum, finished marksman as he was, and the main instigator and central figure of sundry violent encounters in the past, should have failed to hit the mark at which he fired with his first shot or with his second or with his third; and the second, a still greater wonder, was that Dudley Stackpole, who perhaps never in his life had had for a target a living thing, should have sped a bullet so squarely into the heart of his victim at twenty yards or more. The first phenomenon might perhaps be explained, they agreed, on the hypothesis that the mishap to his brother coming at the very moment of the fight's beginning, unnerved Jess and threw him out of stride, so to speak. But the second was not in anywise to be explained excepting on the theory of sheer chance. The fact remained that it was so, and the fact remained that it was strange.

By form of law Dudley Stackpole spent two days under arrest; but this was a form, a legal fiction only. Actually he was at liberty from the time he reached the courthouse that night, riding in the sheriff's buggy with the sheriff and carrying poised on his knees a lighted lantern. Afterwards it was to be recalled that when, alongside the sheriff, he came out of his mill technically a prisoner he carried in his hand this lantern, all trimmed of wick and burning, and that he held fast to it through the six-mile ride to town. Afterwards, too, the circumstance was to be coupled with multiplying circumstances to establish a state of facts; but at the moment, in the excited state of mind of those present, it passed unremarked and almost unnoticed. And he still held it in his hand when, having been released under nominal bond and attended by certain sympathizing friends, he walked across town from the county building to his home on Clay Street. That fact, too, was subsequently remembered and added to other details to make a finished sum of deductive reasoning.

Already it was a foregone conclusion that the finding at the coroner's inquest, to be held the next day, would absolve him; foregone, also, that no prosecutor would press for his arraignment on charges and that no grand jury would indict. So, soon all the evidence in hand was conclusively on his side. He had been forced into a fight not of his own choosing; an effort, which had failed, had been made to take him unfairly from behind; he had fired in self-defense after having first been fired upon; save for a quirk of fate operating in his favor, he should have faced odds of two deadly antagonists instead of facing one. What else then than his prompt and honorable discharge? And to top all, the popular verdict was that the killing off of Jess Tatum was so much good riddance of so much sorry rubbish; a pity, though, Harve had escaped his just deserts.

Helpless for the time being, and in the estimation of his fellows even more thoroughly discredited than he had been before, Harve Tatum here vanishes out of our recital. So, too, does Jeffrey Stackpole, heretofore mentioned once by name, for within a week he was dead of the same heart attack which had kept him out of the fight at Cache Creek. The rest of the narrative largely appertains to the one conspicuous survivor, this Dudley Stackpole already described.

Tradition ever afterwards had it that on the night of the killing he slept—if he slept at all—in the full-lighted room of a house which was all aglare with lights from cellar to roof line. From its every opening the house blazed as for a celebration. At the first, so the tale of it ran, people were of two different minds to account for this. This one rather thought Stackpole feared punitive reprisals under cover of night by vengeful kinsmen of the Tatums, they being, root and branch, sprout and limb, a belligerent and an ill-conditioned breed. That one suggested that maybe he took this method of letting all and sundry know he felt no regret for having gunned the life out of a dangerous brawler; that perhaps thereby he sought to advertise his satisfaction at the outcome of that day's affair. But this latter theory was not to be credited. For so sensitive and so well-disposed a man as Dudley Stackpole to joy in his own deadly act, however justifiable in the sight of law and man that act might have been—why, the bare notion of it was preposterous! The repute and the prior conduct of the man robbed the suggestion of all plausibility. And then soon, when night after night the lights still flared in his house, and when on top of this evidence accumulated to confirm a belief already crystallizing in the public mind, the town came to sense the truth, which was that Mr. Dudley Stackpole now feared the dark as a timid child might fear it. It was not authentically chronicled that he confessed his fears to any living creature. But his fellow townsmen knew the state of his mind as though he bad shouted of it from the housetops. They had heard, most of them, of such cases before. They agreed among themselves that he shunned darkness because he feared that out of that darkness might return the vision of his deed, bloodied and shocking and hideous. And they were right. He did so fear, and he feared mightily, constantly and unendingly.

That fear, along with the behavior which became from that night thenceforward part and parcel of him, made Dudley Stackpole as one set over and put apart from his fellows. Neither by daytime nor by nighttime was he thereafter to know darkness. Never again was he to see the twilight fall or face the blackness which comes before the dawning or take his rest in the cloaking, kindly void and nothingness of the midnight. Before the dusk of evening came, in midafternoon sometimes, of stormy and briefened winter days, or in the full radiance of the sun's sinking in the summertime, he was within doors lighting the lights which would keep the darkness beyond his portals and hold at bay a gathering gloom into which from window or door he would not look and dared not look.

There were trees about his house, cottonwoods and sycamores and one noble elm branching like a lyre. He chopped them all down and had the roots grubbed out. The vines which covered his porch were shorn away. To these things many were witnesses. What transformations he worked within the walls were largely known by hearsay through the medium of Aunt Kassie, the old negress who served him as cook and chambermaid and was his only house servant. To half-fearsome, half-fascinated audiences of her own color, whose members in time communicated what she told to their white employers, she related how with his own hands, bringing a crude carpentry into play, her master ripped out certain dark closets and abolished a secluded and gloomy recess beneath a hall staircase, and how privily he called in men who strung his ceilings with electric lights, although already the building was piped for gas; and how, for final touches, he placed in various parts of his bedroom tallow dips and oil lamps to be lit before twilight and to burn all night, so that though the gas sometime should fail and the electric bulbs blink out, there still would be abundant lighting about him. His became the house which harbored no single shadow save only the shadow of morbid dread which lived within its owner's bosom. An orthodox haunted house should by rights be deserted and dark. This house, haunted if ever one was, differed from the orthodox conception. It was tenanted and it shone with lights.

The man's abiding obsession—if we may call his besetment thus— changed in practically all essential regards the manners and the practices of his daily life. After the shooting he never returned to his mill. He could not bring himself to endure the ordeal of revisiting the scene of the killing. So the mill stood empty and silent, just as he left it that night when he rode to town with the sheriff, until after his brother's death; and then with all possible dispatch he sold it, its fixtures, contents and goodwill, for what the property would fetch at quick sale, and he gave up business. He had sufficient to stay him in his needs. The Stackpoles had the name of being a canny and a provident family, living quietly and saving of their substance. The homestead where he lived, which his father before him had built, was free of debt. He had funds in the bank and money out at interest. He had not been one to make close friends. Now those who had counted themselves his friends became rather his distant acquaintances, among whom he neither received nor bestowed confidences.

In the broader hours of daylight his ways were such as any man of reserved and diffident ways, having no fixed employment, might follow in a smallish community. He sat upon his porch and read in books. He worked in his flower beds. With flowers he had a cunning touch, almost like a woman's. He loved them, and they responded to his love and bloomed and bore for him. He walked downtown to the business district, always alone, a shy and unimpressive figure, and sat brooding and aloof in one of the tilted-back cane chairs under the portico of the old Richland House, facing the river. He took long solitary walks on side streets and byways; but it was noted that, reaching the farther outskirts, he invariably turned back. In all those dragging years it is doubtful if once he set foot past the corporate limits into the open country. Dun hued, unobtrusive, withdrawn, he aged slowly, almost imperceptibly. Men and women of his own generation used to say that save for the wrinkles ever multiplying in close cross-hatchings about his puckered eyes, and save for the enhancing of that dead gray pallor—the wasp's-nest overcasting of his skin—he still looked to them exactly as he had looked when he was a much younger man.

It was not so much the appearance or the customary demeanor of the recluse that made strangers turn about to stare at him as he passed, and that made them remember how he looked when he was gone from their sight. The one was commonplace enough—I mean his appearance— and his conduct, unless one knew the underlying motives, was merely that of an unobtrusive, rather melancholy seeming gentleman of quiet tastes and habits. It was the feeling and the sense of a dismal exhalation from him, an unhealthy and unnatural mental effluvium that served so indelibly to fix the bodily image of him in the brainpans of casual and uninformed passers-by. The brand of Cain was not on his brow. By every local standard of human morality it did not belong there. But built up of morbid elements within his own conscience, it looked out from his eyes and breathed out from his person.

So year by year, until the tally of the years rolled up to more than thirty, he went his lone unhappy way. He was in the life of the town, to an extent, but not of it. Always, though, it was the daylit life of the town which knew him. Excepting once only. Of this exceptional instance a story was so often repeated that in time it became permanently embalmed in the unwritten history of the place.

On a summer's afternoon, sultry and close, the heavens suddenly went all black, and quick gusts smote the earth with threats of a great windstorm. The sun vanished magically; a close thick gloaming fell out of the clouds. It was as though nightfall had descended hours before its ordained time. At the city power house the city electrician turned on the street lights. As the first great fat drops of rain fell, splashing in the dust like veritable clots, citizens scurrying indoors and citizens seeing to flapping awnings and slamming window blinds halted where they were to peer through the murk at the sight of Mr. Dudley Stackpole fleeing to the shelter of home like a man hunted by a terrible pursuer. But with all his desperate need for haste he ran no straightaway course. The manner of his flight was what gave added strangeness to the spectacle of him. He would dart headlong, on a sharp oblique from the right-hand corner of a street intersection to a point midway of the block—or square, to give it its local name—then go slanting back again to the right-hand corner of the next street crossing, so that his path was in the pattern of one acutely slanted zigzag after another. He was keeping, as well as he could, within the circles of radiance thrown out by the municipal arc lights as he made for his house, there in his bedchamber to fortify himself about, like one beset and besieged, with the ample and protecting rays of all the methods of artificial illumination at his command—with incandescent bulbs thrown on by switches, with the flare of lighted gas jets, with the tallow dip's slim digit of flame, and with the kerosene's wick three-finger breadth of greasy brilliance. As he fumbled, in a very panic and spasm of fear, with the latchets of his front gate Squire Jonas' wife heard him screaming to Aunt Kassie, his servant, to turn on the lights—all of them.

That once was all, though—the only time he found the dark taking him unawares and threatening to envelop him in thirty years and more than thirty. Then a time came when in a hospital in Oklahoma an elderly man named A. Hamilton Bledsoe lay on his deathbed and on the day before he died told the physician who attended him and the clergyman who had called to pray for him that he had a confession to make. He desired that it be taken down by a stenographer just as he uttered it, and transcribed; then he would sign it as his solemn dying declaration, and when he had died they were to send the signed copy back to the town from whence he had in the year 1889 moved West, and there it was to be published broadcast. All of which, in due course of time and in accordance with the signatory's wishes, was done.

With the beginning of the statement as it appeared in the *Daily Evening News,* as with Editor Tompkins' introductory paragraphs preceding it, we need have no interest. That which really matters began two-thirds of the way down the first column and ran as follows:

"How I came to know there was likely to be trouble that evening at the big-riffle crossing was this way"—it is the dying Bledsoe, of course, who is being quoted. "The man they sent to the mill with the message did a lot of loose talking on his way back after he gave in the message, and in this roundabout way the word got to me at my house on the Eden's Swamp road soon after dinnertime. Now I had always got along fine with both of the Stackpoles, and had only friendly feelings toward them; but maybe there's some people still alive back there in that county who can remember what the reason was why I should naturally hate and despise both the Tatums, and especially this Jess Tatum, him being if anything the more low-down one of the two, although the youngest. At this late day I don't aim to drag the name of anyone else into this, especially a woman's name, and her now dead and gone and in her grave; but I will just say that if ever a man had a just cause for craving to see Jess Tatum stretched out in his blood it was me. At the same time I will state that it was not good judgment for a man who expected to go on living to start out after one of the Tatums without he kept on till he had cleaned up the both of them, and maybe some of their cousins as well. I will not admit that I acted cowardly, but I will state that I used my best judgment.

"Therefore and accordingly, no sooner did I hear the news about the dare which the Tatums had sent to the Stackpoles than I said to myself that it looked like here was my fitting chance to even up my grudge with Jess Tatum and yet at the same time not run the prospect of being known to be mixed up in the matter and maybe getting arrested, or waylaid afterwards by members of the Tatum family or things of such a nature. Likewise I figured that with a general amount of shooting going on, as seemed likely to be the case, one shot more or less would not be noticed, especially as I aimed to keep out of sight at all times and do my work from under safe cover, which it all of it turned out practically exactly as I had expected. So I took a rifle which I owned and which I was a good shot with and I privately went down through the bottoms and came out on the creek bank in the deep cut right behind Stackpole Brothers' gristmill. I should say offhand this was then about three o'clock in the evening. I was ahead of time, but I wished to be there and get everything fixed up the way I had mapped it out in my mind, without being hurried or rushed.

"The back door of the mill was not locked, and I got in without being seen, and I went upstairs to the loft over the mill and I went to a window just above the front door, which was where they hoisted up grain when brought in wagons, and I propped the wooden shutter of the window open a little ways. But I only propped it open about two or three inches; just enough for me to see out of it up the road good. And I made me a kind of pallet out of meal sacks and I laid down there and I waited. I knew the mill had shut down for the week, and I didn't figure on any of the hands being round the mill or anybody finding out I was up there. So I waited, not hearing anybody stirring about downstairs at all, until just about three minutes past six, when all of a sudden came the first shot.

"What threw me off was expecting the Tatums to come afoot from up the road, but when they did come it was in a wagon from down the main Blandsville pike clear round in the other direction. So at this first shot I swung and peeped out and I seen Harve Tatum down in the dust seemingly right under the wheels of his wagon, and I seen Jess Tatum jump out from behind the wagon and shoot, and I seen Dudley Stackpole come out of the mill door right directly under me and start shooting back at him. There was no sign of his brother Jeffrey. I did not know then that Jeffrey was home sick in bed.

"Being thrown off the way I had been, it took me maybe one or two seconds to draw myself around and get the barrel of my rifle swung round to where I wanted it, and while I was doing this the shooting was going on. All in a flash it had come to me that it would be fairer than ever for me to take part in this thing, because in the first place the Tatums would be two against one if Harve should get back upon his feet and get into the fight; and in the second place Dudley Stackpole didn't know the first thing about shooting a pistol. Why, all in that same second, while I was righting myself and getting the bead onto Jess Tatum's breast, I seen his first shot—Stackpole's, I mean—kick up the dust not twenty feet in front of him and less than halfway to where Tatum was. I was as cool as I am now, and I seen this quite plain.

"So with that, just as Stackpole fired wild again, I let Jess Tatum have it right through the chest, and as I did so I knew from the way he acted that he was done and through. He let loose of his pistol and acted like he was going to fall, and then he sort of rallied up and did a strange thing. He ran straight on ahead toward the mill, with his neck craned back and him running on tiptoe; and he ran this way quite a little ways before he dropped flat, face down. Somebody else, seeing him do that, might have thought he had the idea to tear into Dudley Stackpole with his bare hands, but I had done enough shooting at wild game in my time to know that he was acting like a partridge sometimes does, or a wild duck when it is shot through the heart or in the head; only in such a case a bird flies straight up in the air. Towering is what you call it when done by a partridge. I do not know what you would call it when done by a man.

"So then I closed the window shutter and I waited for quite a little while to make sure everything was all right for me, and then I hid my rifle under the meal sacks, where it stayed until I got it privately two days later; and then I slipped downstairs and went out by the back door and came round in front, running and breathing hard as though I had just heard the shooting whilst up in the swamp. By that time there were several others had arrived, and there was also a negro woman crying round and carrying on and saying she seen Jess Tatum fire the first shot and seen Dudley Stackpole shoot back and seen Tatum fall. But she could not say for sure how many shots there were fired in all. So I saw that everything was all right so far as I was concerned, and that nobody, not even Stackpole, suspicioned but that he himself had killed Jess Tatum; and as I knew he would have no trouble with the law to amount to anything on account of it, I felt that there was no need for me to worry, and I did not—not worry then nor later. But for some time past I had been figuring on moving out here on account of this new country opening up. So I hurried up things, and inside of a week I had sold out my place and had shipped my household plunder on ahead; and I moved out here with my family, which they have all died off since, leaving only me. And now I am about to die, and so I wish to make this statement before I do so.

"But if they had thought to cut into Jess Tatum's body after he was dead, or to probe for the bullet in him, they would have known that it was not Dudley Stackpole who really shot him, but somebody else; and then I suppose suspicion might have fell upon me, although I doubt it.

Because they would have found that the bullet which killed him was fired out of a forty-five-seventy shell, and Dudley Stackpole had done all of the shooting he done with a thirty-eight caliber pistol, which would throw a different-sized bullet. But they never thought to do so."

Question by the physician, Doctor Davis: "You mean to say that no autopsy was performed upon the body of the deceased?"

Answer by Bledsoe: "If you mean by performing an autopsy that they probed into him or cut in to find the bullet I will answer no, sir, they did not. They did not seem to think to do so, because it seemed to everybody such a plain open-and-shut case that Dudley Stackpole had killed him."

Question by the Reverend Mr. Hewlitt: "I take it that you are making this confession of your own free will and in order to clear the name of an innocent party from blame and to purge your own soul?"

Answer: "In reply to that I will say yes and no. If Dudley Stackpole is still alive, which I doubt, he is by now getting to be an old man; but if alive yet I would like for him to know that he did not fire the shot which killed Jess Tatum on that occasion. He was not a bloodthirsty man, and doubtless the matter may have preyed upon his mind. So on the bare chance of him being still alive is why I make this dying statement to you gentlemen in the presence of witnesses. But I am not ashamed, and never was, at having done what I did do. I killed Jess Tatum with my own hands, and I have never regretted it. I would not regard killing him as a crime any more than you gentlemen here would regard it as a crime killing a rattlesnake or a moccasin snake. Only, until now, I did not think it advisable for me to admit it; which, on Dudley Stackpole's account solely, is the only reason why I am now making this statement."

And so on and so forth for the better part of a second column, with a brief summary in Editor Tompkins' best style—which was a very dramatic and moving style indeed—of the circumstances, as recalled by old residents, of the ancient tragedy, and a short sketch of the deceased Bledsoe, the facts regarding him being drawn from the same veracious sources; and at the end of the article was a somewhat guarded but altogether sympathetic reference to the distressful recollections borne for so long and so patiently by an esteemed townsman, with a concluding paragraph to the effect that though the gentleman in question had declined to make a public statement touching on the remarkable disclosures now added thus strangely as a final chapter to the annals of an event long since occurred, the writer felt no hesitancy in saying that appreciating, as they must, the motives which prompted him to silence, his fellow citizens would one and all join the editor of the *Daily Evening News* in congratulating him upon the lifting of this cloud from his life.

"I only wish I had the language to express the way that old man looked when I showed him the galley proofs of Bledsoe's confession," said Editor Tompkins to a little interested group gathered in his sanctum after the paper was on the streets that evening. "If I had such a power I'd have this Frenchman Balzac backed clear off the boards when it came to describing things. Gentlemen, let me tell you—I've been in this business all my life, and I've seen lots of things, but I never saw anything that was the beat of this thing.

"Just as soon as this statement came to me in the mails this morning from that place out in Oklahoma I rushed it into type, and I had a set of galley proofs pulled and I stuck 'em in my pocket and I put out for the Stackpole place out on Clay Street. I didn't want to trust either of the reporters with this job. They're both good, smart, likely boys; but, at that, they're only boys, and I didn't know how they'd go at this thing; and, anyway, it looked like it, was my job.

"He was sitting on his porch reading, just a little old gray shell of a man, all hunched up, and I walked up to him and I says: 'You'll pardon me, Mr. Stackpole, but I've come to ask you a question and then to show you something. Did you,' I says, 'ever know a man named A. Hamilton Bledsoe?'

"He sort of winced. He got up and made as if to go into the house without answering me. I suppose it'd been so long since he had anybody calling on him he hardly knew how to act. And then that question coming out of a clear sky, as you might say, and rousing up bitter memories—not probably that his bitter memories needed any rousing, being always with him, anyway—may have jolted him pretty hard. But if he aimed to go inside he changed his mind when he got to the door. He turned round and came back.

"'Yes,' he says, as though the words were being dragged out of him against his will, 'I did once know a man of that name. He was commonly called Ham Bledsoe. He lived near where'—he checked himself up, here—'he lived,' he says, 'in this county at one time. I knew him then.'

"'That being so,' I says, 'I judge the proper thing to do is to ask you to read these galley proofs,' and I handed them over and he read them through without a word. Without a word, mind you, and yet if he'd spoken a volume he couldn't have told me any clearer what was passing through his mind when he came to the main facts than the way he did tell me just by the look that came into his face. Gentlemen, when you sit and watch a man sixty-odd years old being born again; when you see hope and life come back to him all in a minute; when you see his soul being remade in a flash, you'll find you can't describe it afterwards, but you're never going to forget it. And another thing you'll find is that there is nothing for you to say to him, nothing that you can say, nor nothing that you want to say.

"I did manage, when he was through, to ask him whether or not he wished to make a statement. That was all from me, mind you, and yet I'd gone out there with the idea in my head of getting material for a long newsy piece out of him—what we call in this business heart-interest stuff. All he said, though, as he handed me back the slips was, 'No, sir; but I thank you—from the bottom of my heart I thank you.' And then he shook hands with me—shook hands with me like a man who'd forgotten almost how 'twas done—and he walked in his house and shut the door behind him, and I came on away feeling exactly as though I had seen a funeral turned into a resurrection."

Editor Tompkins thought he had that day written the final chapter, but he hadn't. The final chapter he was to write the next day, following hard upon a dénouement which to Mr. Tompkins, he with his own eyes having seen what he had seen, was so profound a puzzle that ever thereafter he mentally catalogued it under one of his favorite headlining phrases: "Deplorable Affair Shrouded in Mystery."

Let us go back a few hours. For a fact, Mr. Tompkins had been witness to a spirit's resurrection. It was as he had borne testimony—a life had been reborn before his eyes. Even so, he, the sole spectator to and chronicler of the glory of it, could not know the depth and the sweep and the swing of the great heartening swell of joyous relief which uplifted Dudley Stackpole at the reading of the dead Bledsoe's words. None save Dudley Stackpole himself was ever to have a true appreciation of the utter sweetness of that cleansing flood, nor he for long.

As he closed his door upon the editor, plans, aspirations, ambitions already were flowing to his brain, borne there upon that ground swell of sudden happiness. Into the back spaces of his mind long-buried desires went riding like chips upon a torrent. The substance of his patiently endured self-martyrdom was lifted all in a second, and with it the shadow of it. He would be thenceforth as other men, living as they lived, taking, as they did, an active share and hand in communal life. He was getting old. The good news had come late, but not too late. That day would mark the total disappearance of the morbid lonely recluse and the rejuvenation of the normal-thinking, normal-habited citizen. That very day he would make a beginning of the new order of things.

And that very day he did; at least he tried. He put on his hat and he took his cane in his hand and as he started down the street he sought to put smartness and springiness into his gait. If the attempt was a sorry failure he, for one, did not appreciate the completeness of the failure. He meant, anyhow, that his step no longer should be purposeless and mechanical; that his walk should hereafter have intent in it. And as he came down the porch steps he looked about him, not dully, with sick and uninforming eyes, but with a livened interest in all familiar homely things.

Coming to his gate he saw, near at hand, Squire Jonas, now a gnarled but still sprightly octogenarian, leaning upon a fence post surveying the universe at large, as was the squire's daily custom. He called out a good morning and waved his stick in greeting toward the squire with a gesture which he endeavored to make natural. His aging muscles, staled by thirty-odd years of lack of practice at such tricks, merely made it jerky and forced. Still, the friendly design was there, plainly to be divined; and the neighborly tone of his voice. But the squire, ordinarily the most courteous of persons, and certainly one of the most talkative, did not return the salutation. Astonishment congealed his faculties, tied his tongue and paralyzed his biceps. He stared dumbly a moment, and then, having regained coherent powers, he jammed his brown-varnished straw hat firmly upon his ancient poll and went scrambling up his gravel walk as fast as two rheumatic underpinnings would take him, and on into his house like a man bearing incredible and unbelievable tidings.

Mr. Stackpole opened his gate and passed out and started down the sidewalk. Midway of the next square he overtook a man he knew—an elderly watchmaker, a Swiss by birth, who worked at Nagel's jewelry store. Hundreds, perhaps thousands of times he had passed this man upon the street. Always before he had passed him with averted eyes and a stiff nod of recognition. Now, coming up behind the other, Mr. Stackpole bade him a cheerful good day. At the sound of the words the Swiss spun on his heel, then gulped audibly and backed away, flinching almost as though a blow had been aimed at him. He muttered some meaningless something, confusedly: he stared at Mr. Stackpole with widened eyes like one who beholds an apparition in the broad of the day; he stepped on his own feet and got in his own way as he shrank to the outer edge of the narrow pavement. Mr. Stackpole was minded to fall into step alongside the Swiss, but the latter would not have it so. He stumbled along for a few yards, mute and plainly terribly embarrassed at finding himself in this unexpected company, and then with a muttered sound which might be interpreted as an apology or an explanation, or as a token of profound surprise on his part, or as combination of them all, he turned abruptly off into a grassed side lane which ran up into the old Enders orchard and ended nowhere at all in particular. Once his back was turned to Mr. Stackpole, he blessed himself fervently. On his face was the look of one who would fend off what is evil and supernatural.

Mr. Stackpole continued on his way. On a vacant lot at Franklin and Clay Streets four small boys were playing one-eyed-cat. Switching his cane at the weed tops with strokes which he strove to make casual, he stopped to watch them, a half smile of approbation on his face. Pose and expression showed that he desired their approval for his approval of their skill. They stopped, too, when they saw him—stopped short. With one accord they ceased their play, staring at him. Nervously the batsman withdrew to the farther side of the common, dragging his bat behind him. The three others followed, casting furtive looks backward over their shoulders. Under a tree at the back of the lot they conferred together, all the while shooting quick diffident glances toward where he stood. It was plain something had put a blight upon their spirits; also, even at this distance, they radiated a sort of inarticulate suspicion—a suspicion of which plainly he was the object.

For long years Mr. Stackpole's faculties for observation of the motives and actions of his fellows had been sheathed. Still, disuse had not altogether dulled them. Constant introspection had not destroyed his gift for speculation. It was rusted, but still workable. He had read aright Squire Jonas' stupefaction, the watchmaker's ludicrous alarm. He now read aright the chill which the very sight of his altered mien—cheerful and sprightly where they had expected grim aloofness—had thrown upon the spirits of the ball players. Well, he could understand it all. The alteration in him, coming without prior warning, had startled them, frightened them, really. Well, that might have been expected. The way had not been paved properly for the transformation. It would be different when the *Daily Evening News* came out. He would go back home—he would wait. When they had read what was in the paper people would not avoid him or flee from him. They would be coming into his house to wish him well, to reëstablish old relations with him. Why, it would be almost like holding a reception. He would be to those of his own age as a friend of their youth, returning after a long absence to his people, with the dour stranger who had lived in his house while he was away now driven out and gone forever.

He turned about and he went back home and he waited. But for a while nothing happened, except that in the middle of the afternoon Aunt Kassie unaccountably disappeared. She was gone when he left his seat on the front porch and went back to the kitchen to give her some instruction touching on supper. At dinnertime, entering his dining room, he had without conscious intent whistled the bars of an old air, and at that she had dropped a plate of hot egg bread and vanished into the pantry, leaving the split fragments upon the floor. Nor had she returned. He had made his meal unattended. Now, while he looked for her, she was hurrying down the alley, bound for the home of her preacher. She felt the need of his holy counsels and the reading of scriptural passages. She was used to queerness in her master, but if he were going crazy all of a sudden, why that would be a different matter altogether. So, presently, she was confiding to her spiritual adviser.

Mr. Stackpole returned to the porch and sat down again and waited for what was to be. Through the heat of the waning afternoon Clay Street was almost deserted; but toward sunset the thickening tides of pedestrian travel began flowing by his house as men returned homeward from work. He had a bowing acquaintance with most of those who passed.

Two or three elderly men and women among them he had known fairly well in years past. But no single one of those who came along turned in at his gate to offer him the congratulation he so egerly desired; no single one, at sight of him, all poised and expectant, paused to call out kindly words across the palings of his fence. Yet they must have heard the news. He knew that they had heard it—all of them—knew it by the stares they cast toward the house front as they went by. There was more, though, in the staring than a quickened interest or a sharpened curiosity.

Was he wrong, or was there also a sort of subtle resentment in it? Was there a sense vaguely conveyed that even these old acquaintances of his felt almost personally aggrieved that a town character should have ceased thus abruptly to be a town character—that they somehow felt a subtle injustice had been done to public opinion, an affront offered to civic tradition, through this unexpected sloughing off by him of the rôle he for so long had worn?

He was not wrong. There was an essence of a floating, formless resentment there. Over the invisible tendons of mental telepathy it came to him, registering emphatically.

As he shrank back in his chair he summoned his philosophy to give him balm and consolation for his disappointment. It would take time, of course, for people to grow accustomed to the change in him—that was only natural. In a few days, now, when the shock of the sensation had worn off, things would be different. They would forgive him for breaking a sort of unuttered communal law, but one hallowed, as it were, by rote and custom. He vaguely comprehended that there might be such a law for his case—a canon of procedure which, unnatural in itself, had come with the passage of the passing years to be quite naturally accepted.

Well, perhaps the man who broke such a law, even though it were originally of his own fashioning, must abide the consequences. Even so, though, things must be different when the minds of people had read-justed. This he told himself over and over again, seeking in its steady repetition salve for his hurt, overwrought feelings.

And his nights—surely they would be different! Therein, after all, lay the roots of the peace and the surcease which henceforth would be his portion. At thought of this prospect, now imminent, he uplifted his soul in a silent pæan of thanksgiving.

Having no one in whom he ever had confided, it followed naturally that no one else knew what torture he had suffered through all the nights of all these years stretching behind him in so terribly long a per-spective. No one else knew how he had craved for the darkness which all the time he had both feared and shunned. No one else knew how miserable a travesty on sleep his sleep had been, he reading until a heavy physical weariness came, then lying in his bed through the latter hours of the night, fitfully dozing, often rousing, while from either side of his bed, from the ceiling above, from the headboard behind him, and from the footboard, strong lights played full and flary upon his twitching, aching eyelids; and finally, towards dawn, with every nerve behind his eyes taut with pain and strain, awakening unrefreshed to consciousness of that nimbus of unrelieved false glare which encircled him, and the stench of melted tallow and the stale reek of burned kerosene foul in his nose. That, now, had been the hardest of all to endure. Endured un-ceasingly, it had been because of his dread of a thing infinitely worse—the agonized, twisted, dying face of Jess Tatum leaping at him out of shadows. But now, thank God, that ghost of his own conjuring, that wraith never seen but always feared, was laid to rest forever. Never again would conscience put him, soul and body, upon the rack. This night he would sleep—sleep as little children do in the all-enveloping, friendly, comforting dark.

Scarcely could he wait till a proper bedtime hour came. He forgot that he had had no supper; forgot in that delectable anticipation the dis-illusionizing experiences of the day. Mechanically he had, as dusk came on, turned on the lights throughout the house, and force of habit still operating, he left them all on when at eleven o'clock he quitted the bril-liantly illuminated porch and went to his bedroom on the second floor. He undressed and he put on him his night wear, becoming a grotesque shrunken figure, what with his meager naked legs and his ashen eager face and thin dust-colored throat rising above the collarless neckband of the garment. He blew out the flame of the oil lamp which burned on a reading stand at the left side of his bed and extinguished the two candles which stood on a table at the right side.

Then he got in the bed and stretched out his arms, one aloft, the other behind him, finding with the fingers of this hand the turncock of the gas burner which swung low from the ceiling at the end of a goose-necked iron pipe, finding with the fingers of that hand the wall switch which controlled the battery of electric lights roundabout, and with a long-drawn sigh of happy deliverance he turned off both gas and electricity simultaneously and sank his head toward the pillow.

The pæaned sigh turned to a shriek of mortal terror. Quaking in every limb, crying out in a continuous frenzy of fright, he was up again on his knees seeking with quivering hands for the switch; pawing about then for matches with which to relight the gas. For the blackness—that blackness to which he had been stranger for more than half his life—had come upon him as an enemy smothering him, muffling his head in its terrible black folds, stopping his nostrils with its black fingers, gripping his windpipe with black cords, so that his breathing stopped.

That blackness for which he had craved with an unappeasable hopeless craving through thirty years and more was become a horror and a devil. He had driven it from him. When he bade it return it returned not as a friend and a comforter but as a mocking fiend.

For months and years past he had realized that his optic nerves, punished and preyed upon by constant and unwholesome brilliancy, were nearing the point of collapse, and that all the other nerves in his body, frayed and fretted, too, were all askew and jangled. Cognizant of this he still could see no hope of relief, since his fears were greater than his reasoning powers or his strength of will. With the fear lifted and eternally dissipated in a breath, he had thought to find solace and soothing and restoration in the darkness. But now the darkness, for which his soul in its longing and his body in its stress had cried out unceasingly and vainly, was denied him too. He could face neither the one thing nor the other.

Squatted there in the huddle of the bed coverings, he reasoned it all out, and presently he found the answer. And the answer was this: Nature for a while forgets and forgives offenses against her, but there comes a time when Nature ceases to forgive the mistreatment of the body and the mind, and sends then her law of atonement, to be visited upon the transgressor with interest compounded a hundredfold. The user of narcotics knows it; the drunkard knows it; and this poor self-crucified victim of his own imagination—he knew it too. The hint of it had that day been reflected in the attitude of his neighbors, for they merely had obeyed, without conscious realization or analysis on their part, a law of the natural scheme of things. The direct proof of it was, by this nighttime thing, revealed and made yet plainer. He stood convicted, a chronic violator of the immutable rule. And he knew, likewise, there was but one way out of the coil—and took it, there in his bedroom, vividly ringed about by the obscene and indecent circlet of his lights which kept away the blessed, cursed darkness while the suicide's soul was passing.

Snake Doctor

In the North they call them devil's darning needles. But in the South they are snake doctors, and for a reason. These harmless and decorative dragon-flies with their slim arrow-like bodies, their quick darting flight and their filmy wings, as though the arrows had been fletched with bits of drawn lace, are clothed, down there, with a curious fetish. When a cotton-mouth is sick—and if his feelings match his disposition he must be sick most of the time—the snake doctor comes hurrying to him with the medication for what ails him. Perhaps seventy-five or a hundred years ago some slave newly in from Africa saw a cotton-mouth moccasin sunning its flat, heart-shaped head on top of the yellow creek water, and along the creek came flashing one of these swift creatures seeking a perch upon which to leave its eggs, and the black man saw it suddenly check and hover and stand at poise in the air an inch above the snake's still head, and from that figured this strange bug was a voo-doo bug, ministering to the ailing reptile. In such a matter any man's theory is as good as the next one's. The provable thing is that a good many of the whites and more than a good many of the negroes believe in the fable for a fact; and nearly all of them, regardless of color, know the libeled insect as snake doctor.

Now, one of the men I have intent to write about here was known as Snake Doctor, too; and for this, also, there were reasons. To begin with, he was very long and thin, a mere rack of bones held together under the casing of a taut yellow skin; and he had popped, staring eyes, and was amazingly fast in his bodily movements. See him slipping through the willows, so furtive and quick and diffident, with his inadequately small head, his sloped shoulders, his erratic side-steppings this way or that, and thereby inevitably you were reminded of his namesake. You were bound to think of the one when you thought of the other; just naturally you couldn't help it. To top the analogy, he lived right among the moc-casins, taking no harm from them and having no fear of them, seemingly.

Along Cashier Creek, where they throve in a wicked abundance, was his regular ranging ground. His cabin stood in the bottoms near a place notorious for its snakes. They were his friends, so to speak. He caught them and with his bare hands he handled them as a butcher might handle links of sausage. He sold them, once in a while, to natural-ists or showmen or zoological collectors: there was a taxidermist in Memphis who was an occasional customer of his. In the season he ren-dered down their soft fat and drew it off in bottles and retailed it; snake oil being held a sovereign remedy for rheumatism.

By such traffickings he was locally reputed to have made large sums of money. But he rarely spent any of this money; so he went by the name of miser, also. Well, in a way of speaking, he was a miser; he zealously coveted what he got and kept it hidden away in the chinking of his log shack. But he was nowhere near so well-off as the community gave him credit for being. The snake business is a confined and an uncertain busi-ness and restricted, moreover, to its special markets. A dealer's stock in trade may be plentiful, as in this case, but his patrons must be sought. To be exact, Snake Doctor had ninety-seven dollars in his cache.

But swearing to the truth of this on a stack of Bibles a mile high wouldn't have made the people in the Cashier Creek country have it so. Popular opinion insisted on multiplying his means and then adding naughts. Nor could you, by any argument, have won over his neighbors, white or black, to a fair estimate of the man's real self, which was that here merely was a poor, shy, lonely eccentric touched in the head by hot suns and perhaps by spells of recurrent swamp fevers.

They had contempt for him but mixed in with the contempt was fear. To them he was to be shunned as one having commerce on famil-iar footing with the most loathly and the most hated of all the creatures that crawl. There was a solitary exception to the current rule of preju-dice; a single individual among them who had compassion for him and a measure of understanding and right appraisal of him. This individual, curiously enough, was a woman. She was a minority of one. We'll come to her presently. The rest had forgotten his proper name or else had never heard it. By their majority voice he was Ole Snake Doctor. They knew he was familiar with the ways of the cotton-mouth; they half be-lieved he spoke its language.

In this particular region ordinary folks believed many things that weren't so. Superstition, growing out of ignorance, had twisted honest nature into a myriad of perverted and detractive shapes. The innocent little blue-streaked lizard was a "scorpyun" and its sting killed. A porous white stone found in the bellies of rutting deer was the only known cure for a mad dog's bite; clap it on the wound and it clung fast like a leech and sucked the poison out. You never saw many jay-birds in the woods between dinner-time and dusk on a Friday because then nearly all the jay-birds had gone below to tell the news of a malicious world to their master, the devil. You rarely could hit a rain crow with a rifle bullet because this slim, brown, nervous bird enjoyed the special protection of old Nick. If a snapping-turtle clamped his jaws down on your flesh he wouldn't let go till it thundered. A breath of warm air blowing across your path on a cool night in the woods meant a "witch-hag" had passed that way.

Or take snakes: The Prophet of Old put the curse on them forever after when in his story of the Garden he typified evil as a serpent; man-kind has been enlarging the slander ever since. Moreover, in these parts, Caucasian ingenuity as regards snakes and their ways had overlaid a deep embroidery of ill-repute upon an already rich background of Afri-can folklore. There was the hoop snake, which is mischievous and very deadly, and wears a deadly horn in its head, and there was the joint snake, which is a freak; both fabulous but both accepted as verities. All well-meaning snakes lay under the scandalous ban. Milk snakes, garter snakes, chicken snakes, puff adders, blue racers and coach-whips were to be destroyed on sight; for their licking, forked tongues were "stingers" and dripped venom. If you were bitten by any snake your hope was first to drink all the raw whisky you could get hold of. Or if, within ten minutes after being bitten, you clamped upon the wound the still quiver-ing halves of a young chicken which, while alive, had been split open with a hatchet or a knife, there yet was a chance for you. Lacking either of these cures or both of them, you must expire in torment. The bitten part would swell enormously; the poison spreading and magnifying in your blood would rack you with hideous pains; then swiftly it would reach your heart and you were gone.

Every sort of snake was tricky and guileful but the moccasin of the low grounds the most so of all. Kill a moccasin and spare its mate, and the mate would track you for miles, set on vengeance. It was the habit of the moccasin when meat was scarce to lie beneath the yonkerpads—pond lilies, a Northerner would call them—with its head shoved up among the broad green leaves and its mouth stretched wide and gaping, a living lure for such luckless birds and bees as mistook the snare of the parted jaws with their white linings for a half-opened lily bud.

It was in accord with a quite natural law that the moccasin should be singled out for these special calumnies. Of the four venomous snakes of Temperate North America he is the least personable in looks and behavior. He lacks the grace of his upland cousin, the copperhead, and he lacks the chivalry of his more distant kinsman, the rattler, which gives the enemy due warning before he strikes. He has none of the slimness of form nor patterned beauty of that streak of fanged lightning which lives in the palmetto scrubs, the coral snake. He is mournfully colored and miserably shaped. The tones of dull creek mud and of stale creek slime mingle in his scrofulous mottlings. There is leprosy in the pale foxings of his lips, and dropsy in his bloat amidships. Take him in the dead of summer when, with stored-up meanness his belly is monstrous and heavy, and see him then making loopy S's in the torpid water, as he swims, or stretched out, baking himself on the blistered creek-bed and, with his skinny neck and stumpy, inadequate tail joined to that lumpy body, he'll suggest to you a sort of legless malignant lizard rather than a true snake. Only in the eyes of the taxidermist does he redeem himself for these manifold shortcomings. Being without bright tints to fade in the mounting, his stuffed skin needs no special varnishing to make it seem authentic. It is a poor compliment, perhaps, but his only one. Of all other counts and for all other qualities he is copiously defamed and folks generally are prone to believe the worst of him.

Japhet Morner did for one. For him, swamp-water athrive with typhoid germs, or rancid corn pones in which the active seeds of pelagra lived, or mosquitoes carrying malaria and ague in their bills, conveyed no sense of peril. The mosquitoes were to be endured, the water was to be drunk. And biliousness was the common lot of man, anyway. At least, in this neck of the woods it was. But snakes, now, were different;

any snake and all snakes whatsoever. He accepted for truth all the hard things that might be said of a snake. Certain other things he likewise believed, namely, that first, his nearest neighbor, Snake Doctor, held unwholesome communion with the cotton-mouths; that second, Snake Doctor had a treasure in money hid away in his shack—on this point he was very sure; and that third, the same Snake Doctor was entirely too fond of his, Japhet's wife, Kizzie, and she of him.

So it would appear he had a triplet of reasons for holding the other in disfavor—envy of him for his stored wealth, a gnawing suspicion from seeing in him a potential philanderer, and finally, that emotion of fearsome distrust bred out of stupidity and credulity, which his kind were likely to have for any fellow-man fashioned in different likeness from the run of them. That the shambling, soft-brained Snake Doctor was as sexless as a dirt-clod would have been apparent to any straight-seeing observer; and it should have been as plainly visible even to this husband of hers that Kizzie Morner was a good woman and an honest one. But the jaundiced eye sees everything as yellow, and yellow is the color for jealousy, too, and it suited Japhet Morner's mood to brew jealousy in his mind. Brewing it steadily there was strengthening his will for the putting-through of a private project which for a long time he had been conning over in his thoughts. The issue came to a head on a certain day.

It was a day in that drear season of the year when the birds have quit singing in the daytime and the locusts have started. Summer had sagged as though from the sheer exhaustion of its own wasted fervor. The lowland woods had lost that poisonous green sprightliness which came to them in early April and lasted until the August hot spell set in. Even the weeds, which in the bottoms grew rank and high and close-set, almost as canes in a canebrake, were wilted and weary-looking. The sun had come up that morning behind clouds. In the middle of the forenoon the clouds still banked together to hide the heavens but the heat seemed intensified, and pressed the unstirring air close down to the burnt earth. As Japhet Morner came out of the timber into the scorched clearing behind his house the sweat dripped from him and he panted in the close still humidity. His two dogs trailed him, their tongues lolling. One of them brushed against his leg. He hauled off and fetched the dog a sound kick in the ribs. He was not in a happy humor.

At sunup, after a breakfast of cold scraps left from the night before, he had gone down to Cashier Creek to get a bait of sunfish. If he were lucky he might catch a catfish for his string. He had no luck, though. The creek was shrunken; it was lower than he ever remembered seeing it. The drought had sucked up its strength. At the shallows it was no more than a thin sluggish trickle. In deeper places there scarcely was current enough to keep twigs and dropped leaves moving on the unrippled coffee-colored surface. Along the edges, wide bare strips of the stream's customary bottom showed. Cooked hard and dry by the sun, the mud here was cracked into irregular squares and parallelograms—the dividing seams always running at rough right angles—and the corners of each crusted segment had crinkled up so that the general effect suggested a bad job of flagged pavement, scamped in the original contract and now warping apart at all joints. Beyond, right and left, rose sharply the walls of the stream. Cashier Creek was a creek without a valley to it. There was no dip in the ground toward it. The flats came right up to its verges, and then, without warning, the earth was shorn straight away to the scoured-out bed, so that its course ran in what resembled an artificial cutting. In this part of the country many creeks are like that—with abrupt sides that sheer down steep and smooth except where water erosion has scored and runneled the soft earth. Only here and there some glacier has left its autograph in a scour of red gravel to remind parched mankind that once upon a time there was an Age of Ice in the world.

Japhet fished and fished and was rewarded with no nibbles whatsoever; seemingly, even the littlest fishes were too languid to bite at worms he dangled for them in likely spots. He came down stream to the Big Hole, so called, where, an eighth of a mile up from Snake Doctor's shanty, the creek widened to thrice its usual breadth. Here a tight wedge of driftwood blocked the waters. Each successive freshet had added flotsam to the rude dam, lost cross-ties, uprooted trees, corn stalks, chips, fence-rails, sticks. Ordinarily this lesser riffle would cover the pool so thickly that, with the top dressing of cream-colored foam, there was created the simulation of a solid footing; a stranger might have been pardoned for believing he could walk across and keep dry-shod. But now all here was clear of gently eddying debris. The consumed stream, instead of slapping against the spanning driftage, ran under it with an oozy, guzzling sound. Directly in the middle there was a busy little whirlpool, funneling downward.

On one of the lowermost of the bared logs a cotton-mouth was twisted up, taking his ease in the congenial fever-warmth. He was a big fat one—fully two feet long and as thick through his girth as a boy's arm. From the bank edge above, Japhet saw him and looked about for something to throw at him. In a section where gravel is rare and all rock formations are buried a hundred feet down under the silt the verb "to stone" neither is used nor known. Your weapon invariably is a "chunk" and with it—a hard clod or a lump of wood or whatever it is—you "chunk" away at your target.

The man found a sizable missile, a heavy, half-rotted sycamore bough, and he snapped it off to suitable length and flung it, twirling, at the motionless mark. His aim was good. The stricken snake flapped out of coil and dragged its broken loops from sight into an interlacing of naked limbs on the farther side of its log. The stick bounced hard and splashed in the pool. Japhet saw how that it swirled around and around and then, briskly, was sucked beneath the jam. With a quickened curiosity he moved downstream a rod or two and waited. Although the jam was now, so to speak, a suspension bridge, and in places stood inches clear of the water, the stick did not emerge into view below it. No drift showed there, either; the creek for a space flowed clear of rubbish. Evidently, objects caught in that small whirlpool above were carried in and under to lodge and be held fast by some submerged trapwork of soaked and sunken limbs. Probably they would stay there for months, perhaps stay there always. Turning the matter of the phenomenon over in his mind, he flung away his bait can, spun his fishing cane so that the line wrapped around it, and made off through the woods for his home, nearly a mile away. The two dogs racked along at his heels. Coming out of the woods one of them made the mistake of nudging him.

Having disciplined the scrooging dog with his boot toe he slouched out into the six-acre "dead'nin'." His puny patch of corn, for lack of the hoe, was smothering in weeds. In bare spots where the thin soil was washed so close down to the underlying clay-pan that here not even weeds would sprout, the crawfish had pushed up their conical watchtowers of dried mud. Tall ash boles, girdled and dead, threw foreshortened shadows across the clearing—shadows such as gallows trees might cast. His house, of two rooms and built of unpainted up-and-down plank-ing, squatted in the inadequate shade of a stunted hackberry tree. A well was at one corner: a slim pole with a cross-piece, bearing pendent gourds for the martins to nest in, poked above the roof of curled gray shingles. Martins were harbored because they kept the mosquitoes down. There was no flower bed, no truck patch, no fencing. Across the open space, with the heat waves dancing before him, the outlines of the house seemed to waver and twist like an object seen through smoke. It stood a foot from the earth, on log props. Because of seepage there were no cellars in this neighborhood. The inevitable dogs lived under the houses and bred their fleas there, and the hogs, too, if so be a house owner had any hogs.

It was nearly noon now. His wife, barefooted and in a skimpy blue frock open at the throat, was cooking the midday meal, the principal meal of the three. He came up to the door and she, looking up from the cook stove where she was turning the strips of sizzling meat in the skillet, saw the look on his face. Her mouth twitched apprehensively. By the signs she knew when he was in one of his tantrums.

"Ketch anything, Jafe?" she asked, nervously.

"Ketch anything this weather?—whut'd you expect I'd ketch?" From his voice it might be figured that, vicariously, he blamed her for the fail-ure of the expedition.

He hunkered down on the doorstep, his fishing pole still in his hands, and shook his head to free it of the drops which trickled over his face and into his eyes.

"That pore old Mist' Rives come by here a spell ago, mighty nigh shook to pieces with a chill," she said, after a bit.

"Oh, he come by, did he?" His tone, purposely, was disarming. "Well, did he come in?"

"Jes' fur a minute."

"Jes' fur a minute, heh? And whut did he want?"

"He wanted could I give him somethin' fur his ailmint. He jes' about could drag one sorry foot before the other—barely could make it up here frum his place. I reckon he must be down in bed with the fever by now; I could tell by the t'ech it wuz risin' in him when he left here and started back home ag'in. It'll be mighty pitiful, him down flat of his back and nobody there to do nothin' fur his comfort. I give him a dost out of our Butler's Ager Drops. I would a-give him a little smidgin' of licker only—only—" She left the sentence unfinished. "That pore shackly Mist' Rives, he— *Oh,* please don't, Jafe!"

Turning, he had cut viciously at her with the long cane. She shrank back as it whipped through the air, and took the lashing stroke on her forearm, thrown up to fend off the blow.

"Mist' Rives! Mist' Rives!" He mimicked her, furiously. "How many times I got to tell you that there old hoodoo's name is Snake Doctor? Him that'd skin a louse fur its hide and taller and you callin' him 'Mist' Rives'! You'll be callin' him 'Honey' and 'Sugar' next without I learn you better. Pet names, huh? Well, I aim to learn you."

She flinched at the threat, rubbing the welt on her skin; but he made no effort to strike her again. He sat glowering, saying nothing at all as she made hurry to dish up the food and put it before him; she hoped the weight of victuals in his stomach might dull the edge of his temper. For her part, she had the wisdom to keep silent, too. She ate on her feet, serving him between bites and sups, as was the rule in this household.

After dinner he stretched himself on the floor of the inner room. But he did not sleep. He was busy with his thoughts. One thing he had seen that day, and another thing he had heard—he was adding them together, as the first sum in a squalid equation. She drew a cane-bottom chair outdoors and sat under the hackberry tree, fanning herself, and "dipping" snuff with a peach-twig which she scoured back and forth on her gums. After a little while she was driven into the kitchen. It began to rain in sharp violent showers. The rain made the house inside no cooler; merely changed it from a bake-oven to a steam-box.

It was getting along toward four o'clock before Japhet emerged from the front room. He drew on his heavy knee-length boots, which he had removed before lying down, and laced them up. This done, he spoke to her for the first time since noon.

"Where's that there vi'l of licker?" he said. "Fetch it here to me."

They kept a small store of whisky by them—all in that district did the same—for chills and possible snake bites. She brought him a pint flask nearly full and he shoved it into his hip pocket. Then immediately, as though moved by a fresh idea, he hauled it out again and put it down on the kitchen table.

"Come to think about it," he said, "I won't be needin' to tote no sperrits along with me where I'm goin'. Cotton-mouths is all down in the slashes or else along the creek, and where I'll be all this evenin' is up on Bailey's Ridge on the high ground."

He was not given to favoring her with explanations of his motives or accounts of his movements. This departure from fixed habit emboldened his wife to put a question.

"Fixin' to go shootin', Jafe?" she asked, timidly.

"I aim to gun me a mess of young squirrels 'twixt now and dusktime. I heard 'em barkin' all 'round me this mornin'. Ef they're that plenty in the low ground they'll be out thicker'n hops after the mulberries and the young hikk'ry nuts up Bailey's Ridge."

He took up his single-shot rifle where it stood in a corner, and from an opened box on a shelf scooped a handful of brass shells. Then he went outside and tied up both his dogs. One was a hound, good for hunting rabbits. It was proper that he should be left behind. But the smaller dog, a black mongrel, was a trained squirrel dog. As his wife stood in the doorway, Japhet read the dumb curiosity which her face expressed.

"With the leaves ez thick ez the way they air, still huntin' is best this time o' year," he explained. "So I won't be needin' Gyp. Don't let neither one of 'em gnaw hisself loose and follow after me. Set me up a snack of cold supper on a shelf. Likely I won't git back till it's plum' night-time-gunnin' fur them squirrels is best jes' before dark, and I'll be away off yonder at the fur end of the Ridge, three miles frum here, when I git ready to start back. 'Tain't ez ef I wuz rangin' in the low ground."

He turned north through the struggling corn rows and in a minute was gone from her sight into the dripping woods. He kept on going north for nearly a mile until he came to where a wild red mulberry tree stood in a small natural opening. Some of the overripe fruit, blackened and shrivelled, still clung to the boughs; and where there are mulberries in the summer woods, there squirrels almost certainly will likewise be. Very neatly he shot two young grays through their heads. Japhet was a master marksman. It was his one gentlemanly accomplishment. In all other regards he was just plain poor white trash, as one of his negro neighbors would have phrased it—behind Japhet's back. But unsuspected by any who knew him, he had a quality of mind which is denied many of his class—an imagination. It was in excellent working order this day. He now was proving that it was.

He tied the brained squirrels together and swung them, tails downward, over a strap of his suspenders. If needed, they were to be evidence in his behalf—part of his alibi. Next he sat down under a tree awhile with his pipe going, partly for solace and partly to keep away the midges and gnats and the ever present plague of mosquitoes. He sat out two brisk showers with the intervals between them. Then, getting up he set off, keeping always to the deeper woodlands, in a swing which would bring him down Bailey's Branch, now wasted to a succession of mere puddles, and along the skirts of Little Cypress Slash to the sunken flats edging Cashier Creek. The are of his swing was wide. It took him all of two hours, traveling carefully and without haste through the steamy coverts, to reach the point he aimed for.

He came to halt, cautiously and well sheltered, behind the farthermost fringes of a little jungle of haw bushes where the diminishing woods frayed out in a sort of green promontory fifty yards or so back of Snake Doctor's cabin. This was his chosen destination, so here he squatted himself down in a nest of sodden leaves and grass to wait. It had begun to shower again, good and hard. He was drenched. No matter, though; he figured he would not have so very long to wait. As it turned out he didn't.

There was no house dog to come nosing him out and barking an alarm. That Snake Doctor owned no dog would have marked him, in this part of the land, as a person totally different from his fellows, even had there been lacking other points of variance. What Snake Doctor did own was a mare, or the ruins of one. A wag at the county seat had said once Ole Snake Doctor's nag put him in mind, every time he saw her, of a string band; she had xylophone ribs and a fiddle-shaped head and legs like bass drum sticks. She was housed in a log crib a few rods behind the only slightly larger log cabin of her owner. Where he stooped in his point of woods, Japhet could hear her stirring restlessly in her stall. He might have seen her through the cracks between the logs of her shelter except for a brush fence which bounded the small weed-grown clearing.

His plan was simple enough and yet, as he saw it, fault-proof. Feeding time was at hand; soon Snake Doctor, ailing though he was, surely would

be coming out from his cabin to bait the old rack-of-bones. Japhet counted on this. He'd get him then, first pop. He'd teach him what the costs
were of colleaguing with another man's lawful wedded wife, and the lesson would be the death of him. At a half crouch in his ambush, Japhet
told himself that his motive was jealousy; that he was here as a white man
and an injured husband for the satisfaction of his personal honor and in
the defense of his threatened thresholds. By a conscious effort of his will
he kept in the background of his mind the other purpose that had
brought him on this errand. In such moments as he let his thoughts dwell
on it he strove to regard it as a side-issue, a thing incidental to the main
intent. It had to do with money—with Snake Doctor's hoarded money.

The next step after the principal act would be to dispose of the body.
That should be easy. He could carry the meager frame over his shoulder
for a mile, if needs be. And he wouldn't have to carry it for a mile either—
only as far as the Big Hole; then lower the burden into the water and let it
slip in under the log jam. The chunk he had killed the moccasin with had
stayed under there; skinny old Snake Doctor would stay too. This done,
he would come back here to the cabin and hunt out the hidden treasure.
He figured it shouldn't take him a great while to find it; he already had a
sort of notion as to its whereabouts, a strong clew to start on. Having
found it he would circle back up through the woods, reentering his field
from the upper or northern side, with two squirrels flapping his flank for
proof that he had been hunting on Bailey's Ridge. Suspicion never could
touch him. Why should it?

He counted on the rain which was now falling to wipe out his tracks
in Snake Doctor's horse lot. Anyhow, it probably would be days or
weeks before any one missed the hermit and made search for him; in
that time the tracks would have vanished, rain or no. It was greatly in his
favor that when Snake Doctor was away from home, or supposed to be,
folks religiously refrained from setting foot on the premises. They
mightily feared the cotton-mouths with which the recluse was reputed to
consort. There was even a story that Snake Doctor kept for a watchman
in his house the granddaddy of all created cotton-mouths and set this
monster on guard when he stirred abroad. So he needed no locks on
his doors nor bar for his single window, the legend amply protecting his
belongings in his absences.

Ten minutes passed, fifteen, and Japhet was eyes up on his knees, his rifle at poise, his eyes watching through the tops of the weeds which fringed the ambuscade. Something or other—something quick and furtive—stirred behind him. Startled, he turned his head, saw that the disturber was a belated catbird, and looked front again. In that brief space of time the victim had come into sight. Through the rain and the slackening daylight he could see, above the ragged top of the intervening brush fence, the white patch of Snake Doctor's loppy old straw hat and below the hat the folds of a dark coat drawn over a pair of hunched narrow shoulders as the wearer of these garments came briskly toward the stable, which meant also toward him. At this distance he couldn't miss.

Nor did he. At the shot, the figure jerked backward, then went over face forward. The killer rose upright, exultation contending with tautened nerves within him. He stole up to the fence, set a foot in the tangled brushwood with intent to climb it and then, at what he saw, froze into a poised shape of terror, his eyes bulging, his mouth opened in a square shape, and his rifle dropping from his twitching fingers.

He had just killed Snake Doctor—killed him dead with a 32-caliber slug through the head. And here on his door-sill stood Snake Doctor, whole and sound, and staring at him! And now, Snake Doctor, dead by all rights and rules, yet living, was uttering a cry and starting out of the doorway toward him.

Japhet Morner had sucked in superstitions with his mother's milk. He believed in "ha'nts" and "witch-hags" and "sperrits," believed in "conjures" and "charms" and ghosts and hoop-snakes; believed that those under the favor of infernal forces might only be killed with a bullet molded from virgin silver. And his mistake was, he had used lead out of a brass shell.

Power of motion returned to him. He threw himself backward and whirled and ran into the deeps of the darkening woods, making whimpering whining sounds like a thrashed puppy as he went.

Terror rode him into the steamy woodlands. Exhaustion, dizziness, the feeling that he must get under the shelter of a sound roof, must have the protection of four walls about him, brought Japhet Morner out again along toward midnight. The rain had ceased; the moon was trying to come forth. A short distance southeast of his place he struck a dirt road which would lead him there. Beyond the next bend he would be in sight of home.

Around the turn he saw coming toward him a joggling light—a lantern hung on a buggy or light wagon, he figured—and heard the creak of wheels turning in the muddied softness. Nameless horrors had made a fugitive of him; the fugitive instinct still possessed him. Anyway, all shocked and shaken and shivering as he was, hatless and wet and dripping with muck, it would be better for him if no prying eyes beheld his present state. He flattened down in a clump of wayside bushes to bide until the approaching traveler passed.

Moving briskly, the rig was almost opposite him when, from the other direction—the same direction he had been following—came a call:

"Hello there!—who's joggin'?" The voice seemed to spring out of the darkness.

"Whoa!—Stiddy, boy!" Whoever was driving, pulled up his horse, which had shied at the sudden hail. "Me—Davis Ware," he answered back. "That you, Tip Bailey?"

"Yep, hoofin' it out from the Junction, and tolerable tired, if anybody should ask you. What's bringin' you out this hour of night, Davis—somebody sick?"

"Sick nothin'! There's been hell poppin' in these bottoms tonight."

Behind the weed screen ten feet away the listener stiffened, his blood drumming in him. He knew the speakers, both neighbors of his, one of them a local leader. The foot passenger hurried up alongside the buggy; his face, inquisitive and alarmed, showed in the dim circlet of lantern light.

"What do you mean?"

"A killin'—that's whut I mean. An abominable, cold-blooded killin' ef ever there wuz one."

"God! Who's been killed?"

"I'm fixin' to tell you, man. It happened jes' shortly before dusk at ole Snake Doctor's place."

"Was it him was killed?"

"Gimme time, can't you?" This Ware was one who must tell his tale

his own way or not at all. "It seems like Snake Doctor's been chillin'
lately. He wuz purty bad off to-day—I mean yistiddy. And so, right after
supper-time when the rain wuz lullin' a little, Mizz Kizzie Morner she
footed it down frum her place to hisn, fetchin' some physic with her and
a plate of hot vittles fur him. It seems like she wuzn't feared to go there.
I'd 'a' been, I'll own up, but she wuzn't. Well, purty soon after she got
there it seems like he tried to git up out of his bed to go feed that old
crow-bait sorrel of his'n. It had started in ag'in by then, pourin' down
hard and so she made him stay where he wuz. And she put on his old hat
and throwed his old coat 'round her to keep off the wust of the wet, and
she started out of the back door to do the feedin'. And no more'n she'd
got outside in the lot than a shot come frum the aidge of the woods right
over the fence and down she went with a bullet through her brains."

"God's sake! Dead?"

"No, not dead, but same ez dead. She barely wuz breathin' here not
ten minutes ago when I left her house. Old Doctor Bradshaw, he's there
with her now and he says it's a miracle she's lasted this long. Well, it
seems like Snake Doctor jumped up at the shot and run out to see whut
had happened and there she lay a-welterin'. And him,—well, he's been
takin' on like all possessed ever since. I wouldn't 'a' believed he could
'a' had so much feelin' in him ef I hadn't seen him with my own eyes. It
wuz him run for help, though—he did have sense enough left to do that.
He found me in my tobacco patch and I dropped everything and took
out for there, and a bunch of us picked her up and toted her home on a
wagon bed. She's shot in the left side of the head just over the temples;
the bullet went clean through and come out on the right side."

"But who did it?"

"I'm comin' to that. 'Twuz that low-flung husband of hers done it—
that's who. It seems like he must 'a' followed her down to Snake Doctor's and laid in wait fur her and felled her ez she come out. Gawd
knows why, onless 'twuz jes' pyure pizen meanness."

"The murderin' dog! They're certain 'twas him, then?"

"Shore ez gun's iron 'twuz him. Snake Doctor ketched a quick look
at him over the fence ez he darted off. And right there they found his
rifle where he'd dropped it before he whirl't and run—fool thing fur him
to do—and I seen his tracks, myself, in the soft ground, goin' and comin'

and where he must 'a' stood when he fired. I seen 'em by lantern light after I got there—and fully half a dozen others seen 'em, too. There's a long red streak on her arm where he must 'a' been whuppin' her sometime durin' the day."

"Hangin's a sight too good! Did they catch him?"

"No, but they will. Some thinks he's made fur the slashes and hid out there—his tracks led off that way. There'll be a line of men throwed all the way 'round Little Cypress before sunup. They're organizin' the posse at the Morner place."

"Sheriff got there yet?"

"No, but he's due by daylight or sooner. They telephoned in from Gallup's Mills to him and he's already started with his pack of dogs. The trail ought to lay good, ground bein' damp the way it is. Ole Snake Doctor he's carryin' on and ravin' 'round, sayin' the Lord's goin' to strike the murderer down in his tracks. But I'm puttin' my main dependence on them bloodhounds—on them, first, and then mebbe on a good stout plow line and the limb of a tree. Oh, they'll ketch him, and when they do, I 'low to be there. I'm jes' puttin' out fur my place to roust out my oldest boy and fetch him back with me. There's a good-size crowd mustered already but we'll need every able-bodied hand we can git."

"Don't let me hold you up any longer, then," said the pedestrian, a deadly grimness in his tone. "I'm ready now—got a pistol here in my hip pocket. That poor thing! She always was a good-hearted, hard-workin' woman and mightily put-upon. As for Jafe Morner—well, if I should be so lucky as to be the one to jump him out of the sticks, I'm goin' shoot first and ask questions afterwards. I'll be waitin' there at Morner's when you get back, Davis."

He broke into a half-run.

In the patchy moonlight which sifted through the shredding rain-clouds, Snake Doctor's house made a black square against the lesser blackness of its background. To it, panting in his haste, came the assassin, running. He feared the place—to the bottom of his desperate soul he feared it—but a fear yet greater was driving him hither. Previously it has been stated that this man had a powerful imagination. To a literate person it might have been a gift. To him, in this emergency, it was a curse. It set his already sore and smitten nerves on end; still, it honed his wits to a sharper edge.

What he overheard back there on the dirt road had remodeled his formless flight into a shaped intent. Now he had to deal, not with phantoms and daunting apparitions, but with tangible dangers; dangers not less frightful than those others perhaps, but to be coped with—if his luck held—and outwitted by physical devices. There was no remorse in him. After all he was fairly well suited by the outcome of his mistake; getting safely away was what concerned him. In his present plight, weaponless, without a cent in his pocket, with the countryside rousing to hunt him, escape was out of prospect. But with money to buy his way along he'd have a good chance. Let the Sheriff come on with his dogs, then, let the mob form, with their talk of a rope and cold lead! Given any sort of break he'd best them. He would strike through the deep timber for the river; in six hours of steady traveling he could make it. At the river he would hire a shanty-boater to ferry him across to the Arkansas side; in some town over there buy clothes and get his hair cut; then catch a train and travel as far west or as far south as the steam-cars would take him. And it was Snake Doctor's cash that would buy the way for him! Getting this money had been in the angles of his original plan; a seemingly unearthly intervention had diverted him from it. Now he was returning to it, with a tremendous motive, self-preservation, urging him to speed. He had little time, though.

Mighty little. He knew the interior arrangements of Snake Doctor's one room—the pallet in this corner, the fireplace in that, the chair and the table drawn out on the sagging floor. In the one spying visit he ever had paid Snake Doctor two weeks before when this shooting scheme first formed in his mind, he had noted these things in detail. He had marked also the very spot where he was certain the place of concealment for the money was. All through his stay, Snake Doctor, tremulous and plainly apprehensive, had maneuvered to keep between the unbidden, unwelcome caller and the corner where the comforters and blankets were placed. Also, the recluse's eyes had helped to betray him; time and time again they had turned nervously to the wall just beyond and above the bedding, a point, say, five or six feet above it. Just about there, probably in a concealed gap between or behind the logs, the loot surely must be.

He thrust through the planked door, sagging on its leather hinges, and crossed directly to the fireplace. There was no fire in it, but, on stooping and fumbling with his hands, he found chips there ready to be kindled, and under the chips scraps of paper—good! He needed a light of sorts to search by. He had matches in his pocket, corked in a bottle, water-tight. He got them out as quickly as his shaking fingers would let him. There were only four of them. One after another he struck them, applying their points of flame to the paper. But the paper was damp from rain coming down the mud chimney, and no fire caught until the fourth and last match had been struck. Then it merely flickered; it ran slowly along the edge of the charring paper, smoking and threatening to go out.

Alright, then, let it go out, if it wanted to. He could see in the dark as well as the next one, and had hands to feel with. He made for the corner diagonally across the cabin and ran his hands swiftly along the exposed upper surface of a certain log, probing for any deep depressions in the rotted bark adhering to it, nicking the dried clay mortar with his nails. He tried that log without result, started on the log above it—and sucked in his breath as loose scraps of bark fell away at his touch from where they covered a niche in the joining. The cavity thus exposed was roughly circular in shape, the diameter about of a man's arm; he could tell that by fingering its edges. This must be the hole. Greedily he thrust his right hand in. It touched something—something slick and round and firm and smooth—and there came a quick darting sting as pointed things, sharp and keen, jabbed his thumb, tearing the skin as he jerked his hand out.

In that same breath the feeble flame in the fireplace caught well and flared up, its blaze filling the cabin with a wavery, unreliable radiance. Japhet Morner, flinging his hand up before his face, saw by that red brightness that on the inner side of his thumb were two tiny torn punctures, half an inch apart, from which drops of blood had started; and then, on beyond, two feet away, at the level of his stricken eyes he saw the forepart of a thick snake, its hideous dull-marked head lifted and thrust back just within the round of the orifice, its mouth wide open, with the cottony linings revealed, its neck taut and curved as though ready to strike again.

He gave a strangled slobbering howl and leaped to the other side of the room, sobbing, gasping, uttering fragments of wordless sound. The blood jumped and spurted from his flirted thumb to prove the wounds though minute were deep.

He must have whisky to drink or the cloven, hot carcass of a freshly-killed chicken to bind fast to the bite, or he was done for. At his house half a mile away was whisky and there were chickens asleep on their roost. He might make it. He whirled about, then recoiled as though a hard blow had stopped him. He couldn't go where men were assembling, ready and anxious to stretch his neck for him.

Now then, his brain told him that, already and thus soon, quick pangs were leaping down his thumb, through his hand, flaming along his wrist and up his arm. The poison must be racing in his veins, mounting and growing, as he had heard it would. He had a feeling that his hand was swelling, making the skin tighter and tighter. There was no help, and even did help come now it would come too late. He howled and dropped and rolled on the floor, his head knocking against the rough boards.

Up in the creviced wall the forward length of the snake showed, its head still guardingly reared on its slim neck, its lidless pale eyes, like twin crumbs of blurred glass, aglow in the shifting firelight.

He got upon his feet, and a terrific pain struck at his heart, squeezing and wringing it. His throat closed and he choked. A second pain twisted his heart.

With a drunken leap he cleared the sill of the rear doorway, ran in a wavering course a few strides out across the horse lot and then, as his knees gave way under him, he pitched forward on his face, his lolled mouth full of weeds and muddy grass stems. The drumming fingers of his outstretched right hand almost touched a reddish-black smear where the earth was trampled and the grass flattened down.

"Good reddance, by Gravy! I'd call it that; wouldn't you, Doc?"

The speaker was driving Dr. Bradshaw back to his home near Gallup's Mills. The other raised his head wearily. He had been up all night and he was an old man. The rocking motion of the buggy was soothing to him, even though the newly-risen sun did put its slanted rays right into his eyes.

"Well," he said, "I'd not have wished the death he died on any man, no matter what he'd done to deserve it. Yet I reckon there was a sort of rough justice in it, too. Anyway, we've been saved a lynching or else a regular hanging. And one would have been a scandal on the county and the other an expense to the tax-payers. Maybe you have got the right idea about it, Jim Meloan.

"I'm looking at it more from the professional point of view. I've had two strange experiences this past night, Jim. I've seen an undernourished sickly woman, after being shot through the brain, linger for nearly seven hours before she died, and I've examined the body of a man who'd been killed by a snake bite—killed good and quick, too, judging by the evidences."

"Well, Doc, ain't that the way a cotton-mouth always does kill a man—sudden like?" asked Meloan. "I've always heared tell—"

"Never mind what you've heard," said the old doctor; he was cross because he was sleepy. "I'm going by the facts, not by fairy-tales. I was born and raised down here and I've been practicing medicine in this county for going on forty-six years and as a country doctor I ought to know something about these things if anybody does. And I tell you that in all my life I've never known of but two or three people actually being bitten by water moccasins, and until this morning I never had personal knowledge of anybody at all dying from the bite of any kind of snake. Horses?—well, yes. Dogs?—maybe so. But not a human being until now.

"Still, the proof is clear enough in this case. I think I'll have to write a paper about it for the next meeting of the State Medical Society. The places where the fangs nipped him were right there in the ball of his thumb—two bloody deep little scratches, side by side. And then there was that look on his face—*ugh!* I'm fairly hardened but I'm not going to forget Jafe Morner's face in a hurry. He died quick, I'd say offhand, but he died hard, too; I'll swear to that part of it. Well, he was the kind who likely would flicker out pretty brisk under certain circumstances. Ever notice the color of his skin and those heavy pouches under his eyes? Bad whisky and bad food and swamp fevers didn't put those signs on him. The late Japhet had a rotten bad heart, Jimmy."

"He shorely did," agreed Meloan fervently. "Yistiddy proved that."

"I don't mean exactly in that sense," explained the physician. "I mean he had an organic weakness. Curious thing, though, there was no swelling 'round the wounds nor any swelling in his hand or arm; no noticeable blotching of the skin, either. And yet, if there's anything in the accepted theories of the toxic effects of a snake's bite, those conditions should have been marked. Oh, I'll have quite a paper to read before the Society!"

"Mebbe the swellin' had done went down before you got to him?" suggested the morbidly interested farmer.

"No, he couldn't have been dead more than a short while when they went down there to set the dogs on the trail and found him; Sheriff Gill tells me he was still warm. And I was there not ten minutes after that. It's a mighty unusual case—several features about it that puzzles me. F'rinstance, now what about the snake that gashed him? Which-a-way did it come from beforehand and where did it head for afterwards? I didn't see any snake tracks in the ground close to where he was laying—I looked for 'em, too. Still, the lot was pretty well trompled. Now, that poor forlorn old creature that you people in this neighborhood call Snake Doctor, he's got his own pet theory about it. He keeps on saying it was the Vengeance of the Lord falling upon a red-handed murderer. He thinks the fellow was drawn back to the seat of his crime—well, that might be so; I've heard of such things before—and that the Divine Wrath lit on him. But if I was him I'd be poking under the stable or the cabin for a whopping big snake.

"He tells me, though—and he ought to be an authority on the subject if anybody is—he tells me that a water moccasin never travels many yards away from the water and that night-times they always den up somewhere, being cold-blooded creatures that love the sunshine. And on top of that he swears to me that there never have been any moccasins close about his diggin's unless he'd brought 'em there dead or else as prisoners in a sack."

"Why, looky here, Doc," broke in Meloan; "he lied to you, then. There's always been a sayin' 'round here that Snake Doctor kept a hugeous big cotton-mouth right with him in his house all the time!"

"Yes, that's true. I saw it, myself, not an hour ago," said the doctor, smiling a little. "I reckon the old fellow's smarter than some folks give him credit for being. He took me in his shack and showed it to me."

"But I thought you jes' now said that—"

"Wait till I finish. He took me in and showed it to me, just as I'm telling you. But it was deader than Hector. It was a stuffed snake—with glass eyes and all. It seems a professional taxidermist who was up here from Memphis some years ago mounted it for our eccentric friend. Well, I'll tell the world he made a good job of it. Life-like?—you bet you! See it in a poor light and you'd almost be ready to swear you saw it move its head. I wouldn't have the thing 'round me for any amount of cash. But it seems this old fellow had a purpose in keeping it.

"That point came out in a sort of a peculiar way, too. It's been common gossip, I understand, that Snake Doctor had a store of money laid by. No doubt you've heard exaggerated stories about the size of his wad; but I'm prepared to tell you it wasn't much—just under a hundred dollars, all told. After he'd ca'mmed down he told me he didn't crave to keep it any more. He said he wanted it spent, paying for a proper funeral for that poor woman—said she was the only friend he'd had in the world: the only one that ever gave him a kind look or a kind word. So he asked me and Tip Bailey to take charge of it and then he took us in his shanty and got it out from the secret place where he'd kept it hid. It was tucked down in behind a break in the chinking between two of the side logs. And—listen to this, Jim—right in front of it, just back inside the mouth of the opening, he'd set that stuffed cotton-mouth of his, figuring that the bare sight of it, with its neck all bent like as if it was fixing to lunge and its jaws wide open, would kind of discourage anybody who might take a notion to start exploring in there.

"And, then for a further precaution—oh, he's got plenty of sense in his way—he'd gone and lined the inside of the hole all 'round the edges and half-way down to the bottom with coils of barbed wire, with the points sticking up every which way. Anybody who rammed his hand in there suddenly would certainly get gaffed. Not that anybody would, who'd seen the snake first."

The old doctor yawned heavily. "Purty smart little notion, I'd call it."

The Second Coming of a First Husband

If only Mrs. Thomas Bain had been content to compare Mr. Thomas Bain with men about him he, for his counter-arguments, would not have been put to a serious disadvantage. Out of her ammunition locker he might have borrowed shells to be fired in his own defense. Did she, for instance, cite the polished beauty of Mr. So-and-So's drawing-room behavior, speaking with that subtle inflection which as good as said that his own society manners left much to be desired, Mr. Bain's rebuttal would have been prompt and ready: He would have spoken right up to point out the fact that So-and-So notoriously neglected his family or that he drank entirely too much for his own good or that he habitually failed to pay his just debts. Mr. Bain was no scandal-monger, understand, still a man must fight back with such weapons as he may command.

But Mrs. Bain's method of attack was entirely too subtle for him; it left him practically weaponless. Out in the world he amply was competent to fend for himself. Beneath the domestic roof-tree, when his wife sat in judgment on him, and his ways, on his small shortcomings or his larger faults, he completely was at a loss for proper rebuttal. It gave him such a helpless feeling! It would have given any normal man a helpless feeling. And Mr. Bain was in all essential regards a normal man—a good citizen, a good provider and, as husbands go, an average fair husband.

I would do Mrs. Bain no injustice. She was a normal woman, too. But it is only natural when destiny has fashioned an advantage to fit one's hands that one employs it. Her advantage was a very great one. Her criticisms of Mr. Bain took the form of measuring him off against the mental picture of her first husband.

And her first husband was dead. Now, in common decency, an honorable man—and Mr. Bain was an honorable man—may not speak ill of the dead. What is more, had he, under stress of provocation, been minded to retort that after all Mrs. Bain's first husband was not exactly perfection either, he could have produced no proof in support of the assertion. For he had never seen his predecessor. He knew nobody who had known the deceased. The present Mrs. Bain had been for three years a widow when first he set eyes on her. She had lately returned then from Honolulu; it was in Honolulu that she had been bereft, as the saying is, by the hand of death. And Honolulu is a long distance from Brockway, Mass., where Tom Bain's people, a stay-at-home stock, had lived these five generations past.

So, on those frequently recurring occasions when Mrs. Bain, with a saddened, almost a wistful, air was moved to remind herself of her first husband's marvelous qualities—his temperament, his flawless disposition, his tact, his amiability or what not—there was for her second husband nothing to do except to suffer on in an impotent silence. It is not well that anyone on this earth—and more especially a husband—should be required to suffer discomforts in silence. Suffering calls for vocal expression.

Otherwise, as human beings go, Mr. and Mrs. Bain were well suited, one for the other. It was that dead first husband of hers, who, invoked by her, kept rising up to mar the reasonable happiness which might have been theirs. The thing was getting on his nerves. Indeed, at the time this account begins, it already had got upon his nerves. He had come to the point where frequently he wished there had never been such a thing as a first husband.

There were times when he almost permitted himself the wish that there never had been such things as second husbands, either.

With the acute vividness of a war-scarred veteran remembering the time he was shot, he could recall the occasion when Mrs. Bain's first husband first came into his life. They had been married only a few weeks; the honeymoon was over; he who always had traveled singly was adjusting himself to the feel of double harness. This was an easier job for the lady than for her mate; she had been through the process once before. But while Tom Bain might be a green hand at this business of being married, still subconsciously he already was beginning to adjust himself in his ordained and proper place in the matrimonial scheme as it related to him and this very charming lady. In other words, he had reached the period where he was slipping out of the bridegroom pose into the less studied and more matter-of-fact status of a husband. He was ready to quit acting a part and be his own self again always, though with regard for the limitations and restrictions imposed by the new estate upon which he had entered.

The campaign against him—we may as well call it a campaign—opened on the evening following their return from the trip to White Sulphur. That first day at his desk had been a hard one; so much which seemed to require his personal attention had accumulated while he was away. He left the office pretty well fagged out. On his way home he built up a pleasant vision of a nice quiet little dinner and then a peaceful hour or so in the living-room in slippers and an old smoking jacket.

Mrs. Bain met him at the door with a greeting that put him in thorough good humor. This, he decided, was the best of all possible worlds to live in and his, undoubtedly, was the best of all possible ways of living.

"You're late, dearest," she said. "You've just time to run upstairs and slip on your evening clothes. I've laid them out for you."

"Why, there's nobody coming in for dinner, is there?" he asked.

She drew away from him slightly.

"No, there's no one coming," she said. "What difference does that make?"

"Well," he said, "I'm rather tired and so I sort of thought that, seeing there'd be only the two of us, I'd come to the table just as I am."

"Very well, dear," she said, "suit yourself."

But he took note that she had briefened the superlative "dearest" to the shorter word "dear." Also she slipped herself out of the circlet of his encircling arm. Suddenly there was a suggestion—a bare hint—of an autumnal chill in the air.

"Suit yourself," she repeated.

But, as a newly married man, how could be suit himself? He clad himself in the starchy shirt, the high tight collar that nipped his throat, the pinchy patent leathers and all the rest of the funereal regalia in which civilized man encases himself on any supposedly festal occasion. She gave him an approving look when ten minutes later he presented himself before her.

"Tom," she said as they sat down, "I think you always should dress for dinner. Arthur always said that a gentleman should dress for dinner."

He stared at her, puzzled for a moment.

"Arthur?" he echoed.

"My first husband," she explained. "Arthur looked so well in his evening clothes."

"Oh," he said, like that. That was all he said for a minute or so. He was thinking.

She was thinking, too. Practically all women are popularly supposed to have intuition, and certainly this particular woman had her share of it. Probably it was in that very moment of reflection that the lady decided on a future plan of action.

At any rate, this was the beginning. Eventually, Mr. Bain awoke to a realization that he was the victim of a gentle tyranny—that he had fallen captive to an enemy force made up of an affectionate but somewhat masterful lady and the memory of a dead and gone personality. Mrs. Bain's first husband was persistently dogging Mrs. Bain's second husband. Daily, after one fashion or another, he was reminded of Arthur. Arthur, it seemed, had never lost his temper. What made the comparison hurt the more was the indubitable fact that Mr. Bain occasionally did lose his. Arthur had never raised his voice above a well low-pitched key of innate refinement—no matter how irritated he might be. Arthur had been so tidy; Arthur never left his clothes lying about where he dropped them. Arthur had never given her a cross word in all the seven years of their life together. Arthur invariably had been so considerate of her feelings. It was Arthur this and it was Arthur that; she realized her power and she used it. Mrs. Bain's first husband was ever, so to speak, at the elbow of Mrs. Bain's second husband, by proxy chiding him, admonishing him, correcting him, scolding him, even. And for all that he was a naturally sunny-natured and most companionable person, Mrs. Bain's second husband, at the end of the first year of his married life, was in a fair way to become a most unhappy person. Their matrimonial craft was sliding down the rapids toward a thundering Niagara and she didn't realize it and he, thoroughly under the dominion of forces with which he found himself somehow powerless to cope, only dimly and dully appreciated the peril. He wanted above all things to have and to hold his wife until death did them part. But always there was Arthur tagging along, making a crowd of three out of what might have been a congenial company of two.

But, as someone has most aptly said, it's always darkest just before the dawn. In this instance, though, deliverance came to the oppressed, not with the graduations of the spreading dawn but rather with the solid emphasis of a bolt from the blue. There was an evening of bridge with the Tuckers and Bain, who played well, had for a partner Mrs. Tucker who didn't. It is barely possible that he had betrayed a passing emotion of testiness once or twice. At midnight as they were entering their house Mrs. Bain renewed her remarks on an issue to which reference already had been made on the way home in the cab.

"My dear," she was saying, "I really must repeat again that, to my way of thinking, no amount of exasperation could have justified you in showing your feelings as you did show them at least twice at that card-table. Now, Arthur would never—"

At this instant Mr. Bain's finger found the push-button just inside the jamb of the livingroom door and the lights flashed on. What next ensued—the vocal part of it, I mean—might have suggested to an eavesdropper, had there been one, that the vowel sounds were being repeated by two persons laboring under a strong excitement.

"Ay?" That was his startled ejaculation.

"E-e-e-e!" A shrill outcry, part scream, part squeal, from her.

"I—I—" Mr. Bain again.

"Oh!" Mrs. Bain's turn.

"You!" Her startled gasp of recognition.

"Yes, Evelyn, that's who it is." This, in matter-of-fact tones, was a third voice speaking.

After this for a moment the spell of a terrific stupefaction held both Mr. and Mrs. Bain silent.

Standing in the middle of the floor facing them, was a shadow. I use the language advisedly. With equal propriety I might write down "apparition" or "wraith" or "shape" or "spirit" to describe that which confronted them. I prefer the word "shadow."

It had the outline, somewhat wavery and uncertain, of a man. It had the voice of a man—a voice calm, assured, almost casual. It had the garb of a man or at least it had the nebulous faint suggestion of garbing. But it had no substance to it, none whatsoever. It had no definable color, either. It had rather the aspect of a figure of man done in lines of very thin smoke. You could look right through it and distinguish, as through a patch of haze, the pattern of the wall-paper behind it. And now, as it spoke again, you could in some indefinable sort of way see its voice starting from down in its chest and traveling on up and up and so out at its lips. It was no more than a patch of fog, modeled by some unearthly magic into the semblance of a human form. It was inconceivable, impossible, an incredible figment of the imagination, and yet there it was.

Its second speech was addressed to Mr. Bain, who had frozen where he was, his finger still touching the push-button, his eyes enlarged to twice their size and his lower jaw sagged.

"You are astonished? Permit me to introduce myself. I am Arthur—Mrs. Bain's first husband. I am glad to meet you."

Mr. Bain came to himself all of a sudden. The shackles of twelve months of bottled-in restraint fell from him.

"Are you?" he answered. "Well, I'm damned if I'm glad to meet you."

"I understand." The voice was gentle, almost compassionate. "But you will be glad later on, I think—very glad. Shall we sit down, all of us?"

The Thing took a chair. And the back of the chair cloudily revealed itself as a sub-motif for the half-materialized torso of its occupant. Mechanically, moving jerkily, Mr. Bain followed suit; he also took a chair. Mrs. Bain, uttering whimpering sounds down in her throat, already had fallen upon a couch and was huddled there. It was just as well the couch had been handily near by, for her legs would no longer support her.

Her first husband—we may as well call him that—turned to her.

"Control yourself, Evelyn," he bade her. "There is no occasion for any excitement. Besides, those curious sounds which you are now emitting annoy me. I haven't long to stay and I have much to say."

He cleared his throat—the process might be followed by the eye as well as with the ear—and proceeded:

"I have been endeavoring for months past to bring about this meeting. In fact, ever since shortly after your second marriage to this gentleman. I have sought to return to earth for the one purpose which brings me tonight. But it was difficult—very difficult." He sighed a visible sigh. "It is not permitted that I should explain the nature of the obstacles. I merely say that they were very great. As you will notice, I am not able to even yet attain the seeming solidity—the weight and specific density which I craved to take on. So I just came along in the somewhat sketchy and incomplete guise in which you now see me.

"My reason for coming is simple. I desire to see justice done. Where I was, I could not rest in peace knowing that you, Evelyn, were lying so outrageously and, what was worse, making me an unwitting accomplice, as it were, to your lying.

"Evelyn, you have been a wicked woman. You have done this gentleman here—" including Mr. Bain with a wave of a spectral arm—"a cruel wrong. But what, from my point of view, is even worse, you have done me a grave wrong as well. I may be only a memory—I may say that that precisely is what I am—but even a memory has its feelings, its sense of responsibility, its obligations to itself.

"Very well, having made that point clear, I shall proceed: Sir, for nearly a year past you have been intimidated by the constantly presented image of a paragon. Am I not right? Your peace of mind has been seriously affected. And I resent the slander on my name. It has been an insult which no self-respecting memory should be compelled to stand. Sir, I wish you to know the truth: I was not a paragon, and I thank God for it. I was not the perfect husband this woman would have you believe. I was fussy, faulty, crotchety—and I am proud of it!"

"Oh, Arthur!" Mrs. Bain, under attack, was reviving, rallying to her own defense as powers of coherent speech returned to her.

"Don't 'Oh, Arthur' me—but listen. And you, too, sir, if you will be so good? We quarreled frequently in those years of our married life. She complained of my brusque ways, of my fits of irritability, of my refusal to like many of the people that she persisted in liking, of my tastes and my habits and inclinations. She didn't care for some of my friends; I didn't care for many of hers. I objected to any number of things about her—and rarely refrained from saying so. She has told you that between us there was never a cross word. *Bah!*—there were tens of thousands of cross words. When we got on each other's nerves, which was often, neither of us hesitated to let it be known. When we disagreed over something—or anything—we argued it out—quarreled it out, frequently. We loved each other, it is true, but merely loving did not make either of us angelic. We fell out and made up and fell out again. There were times when we were like a pair of cooing doves and again there were times when the proverbial monkey and parrot had little, if anything, on us. In short, and in fine, sir, we behaved just as the average reasonably well-mated married couple do behave. And for my own sake, and incidentally for yours, sir, I would not have you believe differently.

"That, I believe, is practically all I had to say to you. Having said it, I wish to add a final word to our wife, here. Evelyn, speaking with such authority as is befitting a first husband, I wish to state that, so far as my observations from another sphere have gone, your present husband is a first-rate fellow. I like to think of him as my successor. And I intend to see that he has a fair deal from you. I trust this visit from me has been a lesson to you. Hereafter, in your dealings with him you will please be so good as to stand on your own merits. You will kindly refrain from dragging me into your arguments as an advocate on your side. My stock of patience is no greater than it was before I became a memory—remember that. I sincerely trust it will not be necessary for me to admonish you personally a second time. Because I warn you here and now that next time I shall return under circumstances that may be most embarrassing to you. Next time there will be no privacy about my appearance; I shall appear to you in public. You'll be a talked-about woman, Evelyn. There'll be pieces about you in the paper and spiritualists and trance mediums and delvers into the occult—a meddlesome nosey lot, too, I may add—will make your life a burden for you. So have a care, Evelyn!

"Sir, to you I extend my best wishes. I'm sorry we didn't meet before. Well, some of these days we'll make up for lost time—when you join me on the plane where I am at present residing. Well, I guess that will be about all. . . . Oh, if you don't mind, I'll just dissipate into air and float up the chimney—it's more convenient." Out of a nothingness near the fireplace came a voice growing thinner and fainter: "Good-bye, Bain, old chap; good-bye, Evelyn—and don't forget."

It was at this juncture that Mrs. Bain went off into a swoon. It also should be noted down that even as he sprang to her side to revive her

Mr. Bain wore on his face a look of husbandly solicitude and concern, but his feet twittered in a dance measure.

Personally, I do not believe in ghosts. I assume, reader, that you do not believe in ghosts, either. But Mrs. Bain does, and as for Mr. Bain he does, too, firmly—and as a happily married man is each day renewing and strengthening his belief in them.

The Unbroken Chain

In the year 1819 a string of twenty-one black slaves was passing along an African game trail bound for Mombasa. In this connection the word *string* advisedly is used. These twenty-one blacks were hitched in a tether, one after another, like a mess of fish on a stringer. Only, in the case of the fish the cord would have been threaded through the gills; this lot were yoked together.

They were chained, neck by neck. Each one of them wore an iron collar, clamped on. A four-foot length of iron chain, springing from this collar in front, teamed him with the fellow going before him; a similar chain joined him fast to the slave following next in order. This left his legs free for the march and his hands for carrying a burden—if one were given him to carry—or for scratching himself or for beating himself on the breast in lamentation for his captivity; yet in all respects held him well secured.

If there were any places of favor they belonged to the pair who traveled at the far ends of the leash. The file leader had no chain dragging under his chin but only a chain at his back. The one at the extreme rear likewise had to support just half the burden of metal which each of the nineteen intermediates bore.

The gang lived and ate and slept in their chain. At nighttime they lay down in a ring, their feet pointing to a common focus where a fire burned to keep off the leopards and the lions. By day they moved along to the accompaniment of a constant grating and clanking, each using his free hand, if he had one, to ease the pressure of the neck ring upon the base of his throat or where its rivets irked the top jointings of his chine behind. They were naked excepting for monkey skin breech-clouts about their loins. They were all adult males and therefore, in the eyes of their present proprietors, rather more to be prized than the run of a mixed assortment would have been. They were members of a tribe living well back in the country, in the foothills of the mountains; their tribal mark was the filing of their upper front teeth to sharp points. They had been taken in a night raid of the valorous Masai. Formerly they would have been massacred on the spot by the light of the blazing huts or reserved for sacrificial torture on the return of the victors to their own village. But lately the Masai had found a more profitable if less congenial way for disposing of all able-bodied prisoners.

Now they bound them and brought them out to a place called Kilwa and lodged them in a barracoon. To this place the Arabs came up from the sea—and once in a while the Portuguese—and these exporters bargained with the Masai for their human spoils and carried them away. On this side of Africa the trade had not attained the proportions which made the trade on the Guinea Coast so enormously profitable. Indeed, on the Indian Ocean the traffic never amounted to a fifth of what it did where the Congo ran down to the Atlantic; but at this time it was growing fast—thanks to a steadily rising market and a steady demand for prime and prize offerings in certain parts of the world, notably Persia and Turkey in the East, and Cuba, Brazil and the more southerly states of the new North American republic on the other side of the world.

This especial group of slaves was in herd to six Arabs who bore weapons for defense and heavy hippo-pelt whips for disciplining their purchases. If the subchief who strode on ahead to set the pace wished to halt the procession, he cut backward at the nearest pair of bare legs; if his squad sought to stimulate the train to brisker speed they made general play with their lashes on the limbs and bodies most convenient to them. Thus it was that without words the commands and the desires of the owners were made manifest—and obeyed—by the newly bought. In any tongue, or lacking any, a rawhide speaks a parable which the dullest wit may comprehend.

Of a morning when the Arabs and their yoked commodities still were ten days from salt water, an adventure and a disaster befell the little caravan. On this day they were moving east by south across a high plateau. We who have never been there are accustomed to think of interior Africa as one great jungle, dark, miasmic, knotted with poisonous tropic growths. But here stretched a vast upland plain lying some thousands of feet above sea level. It was clothed in a rich pasturage through which game trails crossed and crisscrossed like the wrinkles in the palm of a washwoman's hand. It was parked with fine trees in an effect of studied and ordained landscaping. It was fairly well watered, and it literally rippled with game both great and small—birds and beasts and some reptiles; grass-eaters and flesh-eaters and bug-eaters. Wild animals—and not so very wild, either, some of them—abounded in a plenitude which those of us who know only the temperate zones are accustomed to associate with our ideas of insect life in midsummer, but not with four-legged or with two-legged creatures. Where the antelope and zebra fed they filled the scope of the eye, multiplying themselves by thousands and uncountable thousands. When, taking panic from real or fancied dangers they fled to other grazing grounds, they streaked away interminably in a suggestion of driven rain slanting across the earth; and the noise of their hoofs made suitable thunder for the living storm-burst that they were.

At a point where the herbage grew rank and high a bull rhino charged the travelers. There were no elephants in this part; here the rhino was the largest of all the brutes as, indeed, next only to the elephant, he is the largest quadruped to be found anywhere in the world and, for his bulk and his swiftness and his malignant disposition, almost the most dreaded and the most dreadful. He may stand six feet and more at the shoulder, may, in the instance of a full-grown male specimen, weigh up to six thousand pounds—the strength of a three-ton truck, the sheathing of an armored tank, the power and speed of a runaway switch engine; and with all this, the snout of a unicorn, the eyes of a mole, the brain of a very stupid boar pig, but a scent and a hearing as keen as any and keener than most, and as quick on his feet, to check and to pivot, as a toe dancer.

In the British Protectorate and farther south, toward the tip of the continent, they kill them today up to this size and heft. A hundred years ago, away back yonder in 1819, they certainly ran, by average, no smaller than they run today, and their tempers probably were just as uncertain. A century, more or less, works no material change in a rhino's mood. His mood, like his shape, has come down unimpaired and substantially unaltered since the day when he emerged, all plated and scaly and dripping, from the primordial mists.

The rhino which assailed the passing troop was as big as they grew and as mean natured. Probably the sound made by the convoy as it drew near him—the *pat-pat* of naked feet padding upon the hard trodden path, the clangor of all that jouncing metal ware, perhaps the crack of a well-aimed whiplash and the agonized screech of its mark as his flesh flinched and wealed under the stroke—was an irritation to him. From Cummings and Speke on down to this present time the game hunters have told us that about the sulky bull rhino you never can be sure. He may take it into his horned and leathery head to run away from a single stalker, or in a sudden fit of purblind rage may elect to attack a whole *safari*. But whatsoever he takes it into his head to do, that he does, bulging straight ahead at a gait which is incredibly fast for a thing so lumbersome and, while at rest, apparently so awkward. Forward on he rushes, an irresistible, crushing, ripping, rending projectile; vicious, fearless, devilish; seeming more a machine than a mammal, more the spectacle of a monstrous woundup mechanism than an affair of blood and bones.

It was so with this particular rhino which on this particular bygone time charged down upon the slave squad. He heaved himself up into sight from a trampled wallow some two hundred yards distant, at the left-hand side of the trail, just as these invaders on the privacy of his bedchamber were abreast of him. He squealed once or twice, sniffed at the taint in the air, and then, lowering his front until the slobbery lower tip almost touched the earth, he came at right angles thundering down upon the travelers, uttering sharp, furious snorts, that were like the blasts of a steam whistle, as he came.

For the Arabs the tooted danger signal was ample. They scattered, leaping spraddle legged into the high grass and making for some trees which rose near-by. From personal experience and from hearsay they knew that, once they cleared out of the direct way of the brute, he probably would not swerve from his course to pursue a single fugitive unless possibly the wind, blowing from one of them to him, informed his nose of what his poor eyes could not tell him. Even so, they veered off frantically toward the trees with intent to climb them.

Brief as the time was, the slaves likewise had full warning of what was upon them. All in a frenzied half-minute or so they did many futile, purposeless things. They gibbered and shrieked, they fought at their fetters, they dragged the line out to its full length, trying, all of them, to flee from the point of greatest peril; they huddled in together next, tangling themselves in the chain, then once more swung away from the common center, so that for an instant there was presented this tragic grotesquerie—it was like a figment from a nightmare—of ten joined black shapes straining to move in one direction and ten more striving to move in the opposite direction; but each batch, by its own crazed efforts, defeating the intent of the other; and in between, as the connecting link for this foolish and antic tug-of-war, a dancing and dangling puppet figure of a black man, his head half twisted off his shoulders, his distorted body writhing and capering, his toes lifted bodily off the earth, his eyes bulging from his skull as he glared full-face upon the misshapen deadly mass which bore him down.

The rhino struck this fairest of all possible targets a perfect bull's-eye, impaling it on the longer of his two horns. For an instant the Arabs, looking back from among the tree trunks, beheld an even more fantastical japery than the one of a moment before. In the middle space of their vision they saw the armed prow of the beast, with the spitted wretch held high up on the great head which now was upraised; and from this clumped apex there stretched out to right and left a slanted, rigid, V-formation—a prong forty feet long from tip to tip, formed on either plane of naked forms, ten this side and ten that, regularly spaced apart, the necks lengthened inordinately, the heads aiming all the same way, the poised taut bodies pulled straight out behind, the arms set and trailing aft, the legs drawn back horizontally and kept so by the might which had lifted and now carried them forward—for all the world like a wedge of black geese in ordered geometric flight along the flanks of a swift craft that had shoved her bow into their alignment.

For the briefest of timable spaces this triangled phenomenon endured. Then the hurtling phalanx lost shape, flapped down, folded in on itself and collapsed in the grass when the rhino, freeing his head of that which cumbered it, whirled about to slash and trample the confused litter underfoot and then was gone from sight, puffing out the last of his vented spleen as he vanished.

Cautiously the dispersed Arabs tracked back to the trail. The damage to them in property values was greater than they feared it would be. Indeed, the loss well-nigh was a total loss. The middle slave practically was in bits; his breast was little more than a great hole, and where the gross brute, turning back, had sideswiped at him, the flesh was sheared away froin his ribs like fillets from a dressed cod; some such casualty as this they had expected, naturally. But from this chief victim's chain-mates they found the life gone, also. No hangman's noose ever had cracked a single spine more expeditiously than those iron necklets under that terrific jolt had cracked the spines of the hapless bondsmen. Broken-necked, they lay in the coil of their own heaped bodies.

At first look it seemed the entire twenty-one were dead. But as it turned out there was an item for possible reclamation. A slave whose station had been at the extreme rear of the string was found to be breathing. His chest was battered and his chin torn and his shoulders were all roweled by the tough grass blades through which he had been ploughed and dragged; but his neck lay straight in its collar band, not twisted about as were the necks of the twenty; and soon he groaned and moved and threshed with his body.

His escape from the common fate might reasonably be accounted for. By virtue of his having been at the tail end of the tether, the colliding jerk which killed the rest had come to him from one way only—from in front; also, in the instant following the impact, there had been no pendent weight of dragged forms behind to help snap his vertebræ for him. Moreover, just before the rhino struck, he either had the wit to seize the chain in his two hands arid hold it fast, with a few precious inches of slack between him and his grip, or else involuntarily he had done this. At any rate, it had been his salvation; his fingers still were cramped in the links. Under prodding he presently sat up.

He hardly seemed worth saving, though. He was idiotic from fright. He continued to tug at his coupling, trying to drag himself farther from the dead pile which anchored him. In his blubbering, bubbly speech repeatedly he shrieked out words which the Arabs took to be his name for a bull rhinoceros. Nevertheless, they elected to take him along with them; better a scrap of salvage from the calamity than none at all.

By a species of butchers' work which need not here be described, but it was done with knives and spear blades, they redeemed their hampered ironmongery and they lashed the jarred imbecile to his feet and resumed the interrupted trek, going now seven all told where before there had been twenty-seven. Since they traveled light they also traveled fast. That night they overtook at its camping place a larger convoy under command of their sheik and accompanied by a Portuguese factor. Having told their story they incorporated their remaining chattel with the main stock and drove him on down to Mombasa. There a dhow took him and his new companions aboard and carried them to an appointed rendezvous offshore. Being young and able-bodied and in good case, save for his abiding fright, he was bartered at current rates to a lanky Yankee skipper who, at home in the state of Maine, was a church deacon and a citizen walking in most mindful ways.

Chained now at wrist and ankle instead of neckwise, the solitary survivor of the rhino's pettishness was stowed, with sundry hundreds of his kind, in the 'tween decks of a smart, fast, American-built clipper ship. This being done, Captain Hosea Plummer and his crew of good men and true had up the mudhook and headed away for a far distant place of entry, on the soil of their own, their native land of freedom.

The Middle Voyage, as they called it then, was without mishap and with no more than the average percentage of mortality among the live freightage. Having successfully eluded the British and the American men-of-war which popularly were supposed to keep watch for such as he, the master in due time dropped anchor in a certain estuary well sheltered behind a certain island lying between Charleston and Savannah. Here he smuggled to shore his cargo—or what part of it had lived out the trip—and then, having dealt for cash with his consignees and with a fine jag of money in his pockets, went up the coast to the godly Down-East town of Portland for a period of vacation and sober thanksgiving.

For, mind you, Captain Hosea Plummer not only was a pious soul but was a grateful one.

♈

In the year 1920 a Mr. G. Claybourne Brissot was living the life of a gentleman in retirement near Smithtown, Long Island. He was known to be by birth Southerner, but he spoke with scarcely a trace of Southern accent. Judging by his speaking voice, you would have said he came of some cultured New England stock; only when he spoke rapidly or under stress did there slur into his tone a suggestion—a trace, as a chemist might say—of the softening of the consonant *r* and the slovenly treatment of the final *g*. This, though, might easily be accounted for. It would appear that in his early youth he had been sent North to be educated. Up here he had been tutored; later he went through Harvard and thereafter remained in the North, living first, for a while in New York City and now on this estate which he owned north of Smithtown village, on a site half a mile back from the Sound.

He seemed to have no ties in the section where he had been born. He never visited the South although his wealth, which was considerable, had been created there; and he rarely spoke of it. Nor did he make mention, ever of any kinspeople, living or dead, that he might have down there. He did not belong to the Southern Society in New York or to any of the state societies. It was almost inevitable that as a child he must have had black playfellows or, at the least, a black nurse, but in his household staff there were no negroes whatsoever; a rather unusual thing when you remember that most transplanted Southerners like to have colored domestics about them. His valet was a Frenchman; his cook an Armenian—Mr. Brissot liked his foods highly spiced and well oiled—his chauffeur a second generation Italian, his head gardener a Scot, and his maidservants usually were Irish girls or Swedish.

He lived very much to himself; really, you might call him a recluse. When he traveled he traveled alone excepting that he took along his valet and occasionally his chauffeur. I mean to say he had no traveling companion of his own sort. He knew Europe thoroughly and especially southern Europe, where he had motored extensively, but of his own country all he now saw was a narrow strip along the Eastern seaboard. As a young man he had married, but it would appear that within a year or two after his marriage he and his wife, who since was dead, had separated and thereafter had lived apart. There had been one child and, according to a more or less vague hearsay, the child still lived, although the father was not known ever to have spoken of it. By one report, the child had been born with a deformity on it or a blemish of some sort and had been put away elsewhere by the father. This was only gossip; proofs to back it were lacking.

Mr. Brissot was not a member of any club. Apparently he had no intimate, no confidant whatsoever, unless his lawyer in New York, Mr. Cyrus H. Tyree, might be termed such. The acquaintance he had with his neighbors on Long Island, many of them persons of refinement and property, was little more than a bowing acquaintance. Not one, speaking with truth, could say he was a friend to this reserved and secluded gentleman. For such associates as he had he mainly preferred foreigners, and notably Frenchmen. Once in a while he had some visiting foreigner for his guest. Otherwise he did no entertaining; accepting very few invitations and extending practically none at all. Perhaps the typical educated Frenchman's tolerance, his racial freedom from so many of the prejudices which bind so many of us—perhaps these appealed to him. Or perhaps his preference might be explained on the ground—since he had a French name and presumably was, on one side at least, of Latin descent—that some handed-down sentiment in his nature inclined him to seek the company of men of a Latin strain.

He loved music, being himself a fair pianist and better than a fair singer. In his singing and his playing invariably he favored French and German and Italian music. For our native folk-songs and for our more ambitious work he seemed not to care at all. As for the rest, he was a plump man of middle age and medium height, with straight, dark hair, rather sensitive features, brooding brown eyes and an aloof, almost a shrinking manner. It was as though, having a distinct personality of his own, he nevertheless strove to subdue it, to hide it away from people as he hid himself away. Always he wore plain, dark, well-cut garb, but always, too, he wore a bright colored necktie and on his fingers heavy jeweled rings; and these stipplings of florid color, taken with his otherwise somber garments and his air, seemed odd, out of place.

Naturally, Mr. Brissot was an object of interest to his neighbors. People discussed him in the terms of a mild and restrained curiosity; they wondered about him; some probably built up mythical and more or less fantastic theories of their own to account for him and his ways.

So there was a distinct stir of polite surprise one afternoon when he came to an amateur race meet on a private half-mile track at the Blackburn estate, which adjoined his own.

Staying at the Blackburn place at this time was Judge Martin Sylvester, who before his elevation to the federal bench had been a member of the lower house of Congress and before that lieutenant-governor of one of the South Atlantic states. That same night, meaning by that the night following the racing, Mr. George Blackburn sat with his distinguished visitor on the terrace of the house overlooking the Sound. It was after midnight; the other members of the household had gone off to bed. The two men, both of them elderly, were having the last of a last smoke before they turned in. There befell between them one of those small silences which come sometimes when a pair of men in excellent accord with each other and reasonably well content smoke good cigars together. It was the guest who broke the spell of it.

"Blackburn," he said, "what's the greatest tragedy, almost, that our American civilization has to offer?" Without pausing he went on, answering his own question: "I'm going to tell you what I think it is. I think that about the cruelest tragedy we've got in this country today is the man with a tincture of negro blood in his veins—the infinitesimal trace which according to our laws of consanguinity nevertheless brands him a negro—and who still has education, good taste, refinement, even may have in him sometimes the seed of genius which makes him an artist or a creator. But in our national scheme of things, North or South, there's no place for him at all.

"Life must be hell for such a man—it's bound to be. Think of it—he goes through his days despising his enforced contact with the run of his own race—the race to which we arbitrarily and, as I hold, properly assign him—and yet denied association on equal terms with white people of his own cultural rating. Oh, yes, yes, I know you Northerners sometimes make a pretence of according him companionship of a sort, but it's only a pretence—a shadow and not the substance of the social equality for which he must crave, world without end. Mind you, I'm not arguing in favor of any other convention for treating him. I have the orthodox convictions of an orthodox Southerner—prejudices you'd call 'em, some of 'em—but even so I can't help from seeing the pitiable side of it.

"And the most pitiable part of it is that there's nothing he can do or you or I can do, or would do, to better things for him. We've got to keep our own stock clean and undefiled if we can—got to sacrifice the exceptional individual for the sake of ourselves and our race. One drop of black ink in a pint of clear water discolors the whole cupful—the stain goes all the way through from top to bottom. That's true in chemistry; it's true in biology; true of all creation and all procreation. And you can't get away from it. You can't buck against the everlasting laws. You're only a fool and a criminal if you try. But that don't keep you from being sorry sometimes, does it?

"I can think of just one other tragedy to equal it—a kindred tragedy, this is, and maybe it's a greater one. And that's the case of a man who, let us say, has in him only a sixteenth or a thirty-second or even a sixty-fourth degree of the negroid admixture, a man who passes for a pure Caucasian, who goes unsuspected and yet must go always with a curse hanging over him—the curse of the fear that some day, somehow, somewhere, some word from him, some involuntary spasmodic act of his, some throw-back manifestation of motive or thought that's been hiding in his breed for generation after generation, will betray his secret and utterly undo him. Call it by what scientific jargon or popular term you please—hereditary instinct, reversion to type, transmitted impulse, dormant primitivism, elemental recurrence—still the haunting dread of it must be walking with him in every waking minute. It must be there always, poisoning his private thoughts and warping his nature. *Ugh!*"

"Say, Judge," asked Blackburn, "conceded that all you say is true—and I guess it is, every word—what on earth set you off at that unhappy tangent upon such a night as this?"

"Oh, I don't know," said the Southerner. He laughed a cryptic little laugh. "The moonlight, I reckon. It's the sort of moon which Private John Allen of Mississippi liked to say we used to have down South before the War. It's set me to thinking of things I've seen and heard down in my country—distressing things mainly. Now, I remember once—" He broke off, considering his shriveled peak of cigar ash as though this were a thing immensely important.

Presently he spoke again, making his tone casual: "Blackburn, this next door neighbor of yours—this Mr. Brissot who was over here this afternoon for a little while—he interested me."

"He must have—judging by the questions you've been asking about him ever since he left. Well, there's not much I can tell you that I haven't already told you, and that's precious little; Brissot is by way of being our one small neighborhood mystery. He's a puzzle to you, I take it. Well, I'm not surprised at that—he's been a puzzle to us these last four or five years since he moved in."

"Yes," said the Judge, "he is a puzzle. Or, at any rate, I'd say he was a rarity. I only saw him for a few minutes—only talked with him a few minutes, I mean—but I've had him on my mind ever since. There were certain things about the man—" Again he left a sentence unfinished before it was well begun. For his next words he lowered his voice and before uttering them glanced behind him as though to make sure no servant was within hearing.

"Blackburn, I might as well get it off my chest. But remember what I'm going to say is said in the strictest confidence—on the square." He stressed the last word with a special intonation.

"I get you," said his host, putting the same ritualistic emphasis into his answer. "We're in Lodge; the door's locked and the Tyler on guard. But why all this secrecy?"

"Because, lacking proof, I commit an indiscretion when I even hint at what's been working inside my brain. It's the sort of thing that a man down my way doesn't even whisper unless he's prepared, in case of a show-down, to back up his insinuation with sworn evidence or a gun or both. Even then compassion might make him hesitate. But that's enough for a preamble. I reckon we understand each other.

"Now, this Mr. Brissot—while we were being introduced I felt sort of drawn to him. Someway, in all that big crowd of fine, clever, kindly people, he seemed so terribly alone. And when you happened to mention that he also was from the South, I decided right off that at least we'd have one congenial topic to talk over together—one thing in common. But, as it turned out, we didn't. Because when I spoke of families and said I had a sister-in-law whose mother had been a Claybourne—you remember you called him by his full name in introducing us—he shied away from the subject like a galled colt that's been flicked on a raw place. And he didn't have any state pride about him, either—not a particle—and that's a blamed peculiar thing, too, in a Southerner born.

"To have been born in certain states of this union is an incident. But to have been born in certain others is, to the man who was born there, a profession. Take a man, let's say, from Ohio. Unless he happens to be a Republican candidate for President he makes no capital out of the circumstance that his parents chose to set up housekeeping in Ohio instead of Illinois or Iowa or Michigan. Ask him where he was born and he says 'Ohio,' like that, and lets it go at that. But it's apt to be different with a man who hailed originally from Indiana or with one from California—being a Native Son is a thing for him to advertise—and to a degree the same thing applies up here in the North, to a Massachusetts man, if he came from Boston, or to a Philadelphian or to one of your old Knickerbocker line in New York.

"As for the South—well, go anywhere below Mason and Dixon's Line and see what happens. Especially if you take a Virginian or a Marylander or a Kentuckian or a Louisiana man or a Carolinian—above all a South Carolinian. He may be modest enough in most regards but just mention his home state and he'll start bragging as though a special virtue resided in it and a special virtue in him for having had the forethought and the good taste to have been born there. He never forgets it and he's not likely to let you forget it, either. Ninety-nine times out of a hundred, family means a lot to him. Probably he had a Confederate daddy or a Revolutionary great-granddaddy that he's proud of. Or maybe an ambassador for a cousin or somebody for a great-uncle who was in Buchanan's cabinet.

"I know how it is because I'm a victim of the habit myself. I come from a stock that boasts the loudest. One of my grandfathers came from Richmond and my mother was a Charleston woman—born in one of those old houses down on the Battery, a house that has been in her family for more than a hundred years. See there—I'm beginning to take credit to myself for my forbears even while I'm describing how the other fellow behaves. It's in us—we just naturally can't get away from it.

"But your hermit friend over here next door—why, he actually flinched when I tried to talk family with him. And yet, if his name counts for anything, he's of that old Huguenot stock down there in the tidewater country who're vainer than Lucifer of their breed—vainer even, as a rule, than the rest of us are. Funny—very funny! It's as though he had something to conceal, as if—well, what would you say about it yourself?"

"But surely just because of that you wouldn't suspect the—the other thing?" said Blackburn. "The man is sallow, I admit—dark-skinned, in fact, but—"

"That has nothing to do with it," said Judge Sylvester. "In my time I've known a hundred men of the so-called Nordic strain—clean-bred Anglo-Saxon or straight Celtic—who were darker by ten shades than he is. I'm right smart of a brunette myself, if it comes to that, or anyhow I used to be before my hair turned white. And his finger nails would pass muster—I looked closely at them, and the little half-moons at their bases were as clear as yours are or mine—no suggestion there of the tell-tale dark blush that's like a bruise. Nor any chalk, as we say, in his eyeballs, either; they had the right bluish-white cast. But as he turned away from me—I was studying him closely—I don't know why, but I was—there suddenly came into his face as I saw it in profile a sort of—well, I won't say a cast; I don't know how to put it in words—but a something or other as if another face under the skin were fitting itself into the contour of his face, a face that—oh, thunder, I can't express it and yet I sensed it, felt it, recognized it intuitively! I don't want to be morbid but just to satisfy my own curiosity I'd certainly like to have a look at the man stripped."

"Why stripped, of all things in the world?"

"I'll tell you why—it's the final test for the negroid smudge. Or at least that's what the people down in my country all firmly believe. I don't know what ethnologists would say about it, but we believe that if a human being has in him the smallest possible tincture of African blood it will reveal itself in a sort of stain or streak or smear right down the middle of his back. The eyes, the nails, the arches of the insteps—they may all be above suspicion; the features may be as Caucasian as George Washington's were, or Lord Byron's—but along the line of the spine, thicker and darker at the base of the column and growing fainter and lighter as the vertebræ grow smaller at the top, where the nape is, will run that faint unmistakable smear that's like the stroke of a tar brush. Like a stroke of the Tar Brush—to put it brutally!

"I repeat—I don't want to be morbid, Blackburn, but I surely would like to have a look at your neighbor's spine. Mind you, though, no living soul is ever to know what I've just said. Maybe I'm wrong—the Lord knows I hope I am."

But of course Judge Sylvester never had his curious wish. Two days later he finished out his visit and went back to his home near Augusta, and two weeks later, to the day, Mr. Brissot was dead at a grade-crossing of the Long Island railroad after an electric locomotive ran into his automobile.

He instantly was killed and so was his chauffeur. The third occupant of the car was the famous explorer and big game hunter, Colonel Bate-Farnaro, who had licked the desert and bested the jungle only, by this ironic trick of destiny, to be smashed up while riding on a paved avenue through a modern real estate development in a suburban addition to one of Greater New York's outlying suburbs.

This noted man, who was English by birth and of mixed English and Italian ancestry, had been staying a couple of days with his friend, Mr. Brissot. The two men had known each other abroad, and when the Colonel came over here to lecture, Mr. Brissot invited him down to his place for a quiet week-end in the country before the beginning of the tour. On a Monday morning they started back for town in Brissot' s closed car, bringing with them the visitor's luggage. Being mainly British, the Colonel might travel across Thibet with a tooth brush for equipment—if he had to—but by that same token could not bring himself to go Friday-to-Mondaying without taking along at least one very large, very English looking kit bag and a suitcase or so.

Where the collision occurred, one of the electrified branches of the railway bisected the highroad at acute angles. The junction for the moment and for some reason or other was untended; there were no guard gates and the watchman was away from his post. It was a bad time, as it proved, for him to be absent from his duties. For a high-powered locomotive was moving west at high speed, carrying a single flat with an emergency crew aboard and bound for the scene of a small freight derailment a few miles farther down the line. Word of the tie-up had been flashed to division headquarters a few minutes earlier; the engineer of the wrecker had orders to make time, for traffic temporarily was tied up, and he was making it—giving his motor all the juice she would take.

Two hundred yards distant the locomotive tore out of a shallow cut into view of the crossing just as the Brissot car came up a slight elevation approaching the right-of-way. The engineer did what he could which was mighty little, seeing he could not materially check his gait in so short a distance. He sounded his whistle in warning and he shut off his power and braked down hard.

The chauffeur did his best, too; but it would seem the trouble with him—a fatal trouble, as it turned out—was that in the imminent and impending face of the whizzing menace which so suddenly had come upon him, he altogether lost his head. Subsequent inquiry tended to develop the fact—or rather the theory—that first he tried to get over the track before the onrushing locomotive reached there and then that he changed his mind and tried to halt his car on the nearer side and that the upshot was he killed his motor. Be that as it may, the outstanding circumstance was this: The automobile, at a dead stop, stood squarely straddling the rails for an appreciable period of time before the squatty locomotive, bleating in sharp staccato blasts, struck it broadside and flung it sixty feet in a scrapheap of crumpled metal and broken parts.

Mr. Brissot and Luigi, his chauffeur, were both of them dead when they were picked up. The latter terribly was mutilated; he was scrodded like a fish where he had been hurled through his windshield. By some freak of physics or of fate, Colonel Bate-Farnaro had been spared his life. He had a broken leg though, and several of his ribs were caved in. He was carried, unconscious, to Jamaica and thence to a hospital in the city. At first it was feared his skull might be fractured. As it proved, he was suffering from a considerable concussion of the brain; that, mainly, was what kept him unconscious so long. It was two days later when he came to his senses and a day after that before the surgeons allowed him to see visitors.

The first to see him then was the late Mr. Brissot's lawyer. Mr. Cyrus Tyree had come hurrying from town immediately on hearing of the lamentable thing that had happened; he had returned that night and had been waiting, ever since, for this opportunity to get from the injured Englishman his version of the affair. Mr. Tyree anticipated, since Colonel Bate-Farnaro was an adventure-seeker of acknowledged repute and therefore probably accustomed to tragedy and quick danger, that the latter had kept his head and should be able to give a reasonably coherent account of what passed in those few dreadful seconds between the appearance of the wrecker and its collision with the stalled automobile. Nor was the lawyer disappointed in this hope. But almost the first extended remark by the bandaged-up Englishman, after Mr. Tyree had been presented to him and the nurse had left the room, seemed profoundly to disturb the caller.

"Ever since I got my wits back I've been lying here puzzling over a most extraordinary circumstance connected with this distressing occurrence," said the invalid. "In the midst of my regret for the shocking death of my host and my reflections on my own close squeak, I've not been able to put it out of my mind. Poor dear Brissot, God rest him, always struck me as being a remarkably close-mouthed person—not in the least given to idle talk about this and that, I mean to say. But why he should have been so secretive regarding his African experiences—I mean to say, why to me, of all persons, he should have been so secretive—well—"

"Pardon me," interrupted Mr. Tyree, in a suddenly concerned way; "did you say his African experiences?"

"Yes, yes"—the Britisher moved his swathed head impatiently. "He had knowledge, naturally, of the years I'd spent in interior Africa. If only he'd chosen to tell me that he'd been there too we'd have had something in common, something that would have been most confoundedly interesting for both of us to talk about."

"But Mr. Brissot was never in Africa," said Mr. Tyree, still in that strained tone; "I can positively assure you of that."

"My dear sir, I can't possibly be mistaken." The Colonel spoke emphatically.

"I can only repeat that you must be mistaken," stated Mr. Tyree gravely. "My late client had traveled extensively, as you probably know. But he never visited Africa. There were reasons why, of all the places in the world, he would never have gone—" He broke off and started afresh: "I give you my word of honor, Colonel, that Claybourne Brissot never in all his life set foot on African soil."

"Your pardon again, my dear fellow, but surely you are the one who is wrong. We practically are strangers; even so, I assume that as Brissot's solicitor and presumably as his friend, you enjoyed his confidence?"

"I did, to a greater extent than any living being did."

"Well then, in that case, there was a chapter in his life he could not have told you of. I may be a bit knocked about and I confess to a nasty headache, but, in view of past experiences I myself have had, there are certain matters regarding which I could not possibly be deceived. Why, from my recollection of that horrid disaster on Monday there stands out above all the rest of the details a certain phase of it which absolutely convinced me of this: Brissot, at some time or another, must have had intimate acquaintance with African wild life—with the language of a certain very remote tribe—with matters that one could learn only at first hand, out there, on the spot."

Mr. Tyree bent forward where he sat alongside the bed. There was a curious intent look, almost a startled look, on his face, and his eyelids lowered until his eyes were mere slits.

"Colonel," he said, "would you please tell me in detail exactly what happened—with particular reference to these—these disclosures which, you say, aroused your—*hum*—suspicion?"

"There isn't so much to tell. There we were and yonder was that cursed engine coming down upon us. Here I sat, penned up in that confounded coop of a car, and here just alongside me was Brissot, and there, just directly in front of us, was the chauffeur, who all at once seemed to have gone quite mad from fright and was screaming out most horribly. You see, we all three of us had sufficient time for apprehending what was about to happen. In a time like that things may pass in a flash—but you see them all, and if you live through it you remember them afterwards.

"We even had opportunity for making a move to get out of the car. I don't say we could have succeeded, any of us, but at least there was an appreciable time for trying.

"No use, though! The chauffeur seemed to be entangled in his steering wheel—quite a stoutish chap he was, and a snug fit for his seat, I should say. And the car door on my side of the car was caught. We'd noticed that morning before we left Brissot's place that the lock was jammed and wouldn't work. On the running board upon the other side—the side from which the locomotive was coming—my luggage had been piled up and tied on after we got in. So there we were, you see, all three of us practically prisoners and quite helpless.

"Poor Brissot did his best. He seized the door handle on his side and he turned it and tried to shove his way out. But his head was all he succeeded in getting entirely out. I figure my larger kit bag—it was quite heavy, really—must have slumped down or slipped forward in some way just at that instant—possibly his sudden push at the door shifted it—for the door was forced directly back again, pinching Brissot by the throat so that he stuck fast, as though his neck were locked in a vise; and there he stayed, poor chap, like one set in a pillory, unable to move either way and directly facing his doom until the blow came.

"I recall the entire thing very clearly, even though it all happened in much less time than I require now to tell you of it. It was as though I had one eye for Brissot's hideous plight and one for the chauffeur's state and an extra one for watching that engine approach and for calculating, by its speed, how long it would be before we were struck. Somehow my interest in myself was semi-detached, as you might say—I'd made up my mind already that I, for one, had no earthly chance to escape. I've noticed the same thing before in emergencies that might be called comparable to this one—once with a Cape buffalo when my gun-bearer deserted me after I'd fired and missed, and once again in a bit of a mess with a wounded tiger out in India.

"And it was just then, at that precise moment, while poor Brissot's head was held so tightly, that he cried out the words which made me know he had been where, in my time, I have been—away up the interior, well on toward the Uganda district. As he uttered them I too, in spite of all else, was struck by the same paralleling fact which, through some abnormal spasmodic trick of memory, must have driven itself then and there right into his brain. It was a curious freak; probably one of these psychological sharps could explain it. I can't. I only know that I also was impressed, even in the one brief instant and under those circumstances, by the graphic resemblance which that locomotive, rushing straight at us, snorting and grinding and tooting, bore to a bull rhino charging, as the brute always does, with its head down and its belly hugging the earth."

"Do you actually mean to say he called out the word rhinoceros?"

"Yes and no; the thing was more remarkable even than if he had used the English word. What he exclaimed—shrieked, rather—was a phrase of two native words. The very looks of that approaching monster must vividly have brought those words back to him now, years and years perhaps after he first heard them used, no doubt under somewhat similar conditions.

"He cried out—not once but three times—*'Niama tumba! Niama tumba! Niama tumba!'* just so. And that is from the language of the Mbama, a tribe now almost extinct, who lived beyond the country of the Masai on the inner side of our British Protectorate in what was formerly Portuguese East Africa. There are only a few of them left—the slave trade first, and the white man's diseases afterwards, long ago decimated them. The words, literally translated, mean 'great animal'—and that's the Mbamas' only name for the bull rhino. Extraordinary coincidence, I call it—if one may speak in such a sense of such a thing being coincidence?"

Mr. Tyree made no answer. For a bit he sat like a man stunned by an incredible tale of an incredible manifestation.

Faith, Hope and Charity

Just outside a sizable New Mexico town the second section of the fast through train coming from the Coast made a short halt. Entering the stretch leading into the yards, the engineer found the signal set against him, indicating the track on ahead was temporarily blocked.

It was a small delay though. Almost at once the semaphore, like the finger of a mechanical wizard, made the warning red light to vanish and a green light to appear instead; so, at that, the Limited got under way and rolled on into the station for her regular stop.

But before she started up, four travelers quitted her. They got out on the off side, the side farthest away from the town, and that probably explains why none of the crew and none of the other passengers saw them getting out. It helps also to explain why they were not missed until quite some time later.

Their manner of leaving her was decidedly unusual. First, one of the vestibule doors between the third sleeping car and the fourth sleeping car opened and the trap in the floor flipped up briskly under the pressure of an impatient foot on the operating lever. A brace of the departing ones came swiftly into view, one behind the other. True, there was nothing unusual about that. But as they stepped down on the earth they faced about and received the figure of a third person whose limbs dangled and whose head lolled back as they took the dead weight of him into their arms. Next there emerged the fourth and last member of the group, he being the one who had eased the limp figure of Number Three down the car steps into the grasp of his associates.

For a fractional space their shapes made a little huddle in the lee of the vestibule. Looking on, you might have guessed that among them there was a momentary period of indecision touching on the next step to be taken.

However, this muddle—if that was what it was—right away straightened itself out. Acting with movements which somehow seemed a bit difficult and awkward, as though their very haste hampered them, the two burden-bearers carried their unconscious load down the short embankment and deposited it on the cindery under-footing close against the flank of the slightly built-up right of way.

Number Four bent over the sprawled form and fumbled at it, shoving his hands into first one pocket and then another. In half a minute or less he straightened up and spoke to the remaining pair, at the same time using both hands to shove some article inside the vent of his waistcoat.

"I have got them," he said, speaking in English with a foreign accent.

They pressed toward him, their hands extended.

"Not here and not yet, Señors," he said sharply. "First we make sure of the rest. First you do, please, as I do."

Thereupon he hopped nimbly up the shoulder of the road-bed and headed toward the rear of the halted train, slinking well in under the overhang of the Pullmans; in fact, brushing against them as he went. His mates obeyed his example. They kept on until they had passed the tail coach, which was a combination coach, and then they stepped inward between the rails and continued on westward, still maintaining their single-file formation.

Immediately the dusk swallowed them up. It was only for a space of instants that their diminishing outlines against the paling afterglow of the sunset were revealed to anybody who might be sitting or standing on the observation end of the club car. So far as could be learned afterward, nobody there took note of them.

Yet there was something peculiar about the way each one of these three plodding pedestrians bore himself. The peculiarity was this: He bore himself like a person engaged in prayer—in a silent perambulating act of piety. His head was tucked in, his face turning neither to the right nor left; his eyes were set steadfastly forward as though upon some invisible goal, his hands clasped primly in front of him.

Thus and so the marching three plodded on until the train, having got in motion, was out of sight beyond a curve in the approach to the station. Then they checked and came together in a clump, and then, had you been there, you would have understood the reason for their devotional pose. All three of them were wearing handcuffs.

The man who had spoken before unpalmed a key ring which he was carrying. Working swiftly even in the half-darkness, he made tests of the keys on the ring until he found the proper keys. He freed the wrists of his two fellows. Then one of them took the keys and unlocked his set of bracelets for him.

He, it would seem, was the most forethoughted of the trio. With his heel he kicked shallow gouges in the gritty soil beside the track and buried the handcuffs therein. After that they briefly confabbed together, and the upshot of the confab was that, having matched for the possession of some object evidently held to be of great value, they separated forces.

One man set off alone on a detour to the southeast, which would carry him around the town. His late companions kept on in a general westerly direction, heading toward the desert which all that day they had been traversing. They footed it fast, as men might foot it who were fleeing for their lives and yet must conserve their strength. As a matter of fact, they were fleeing for their lives. So likewise the one from whom they had just parted was fleeing for his life.

It was partly by chance that these three had been making the transcontinental journey in company. Two of them, Lafitte the Frenchman, and Verdi the Italian who had Anglicized his name and called himself Green, met while lying in jail at San Francisco awaiting deportation to their respective countries. Within a space of a month each had been arrested as a refugee from justice; within the space of one week the formalities for extraditing the pair of them were completed.

So, to save trouble and expense: to kill, as it were, two birds with one stone, the authorities decided to send them together across to the Eastern seaboard where, according to arrangements made by cable, they would be surrendered over to police representatives coming from abroad to receive them and transport them back overseas. For the long trip to New York a couple of city detectives had them in custody.

When the train bearing the officers and their charges reached the junction in lower California where the main line connected with a branch line running south to the Mexican border, there came aboard a special agent of the Department of Justice who had with him a prisoner.

This prisoner was one Manuel Gaza, a Spaniard. He also recently had been captured and identified; and he also was destined for return to his own land. It was not by prior agreement that he had been retransferred at this junction point to the same train which carried the Italian and the Frenchman. It just happened so.

It having happened so, the man who had Gaza in tow lost no time in getting acquainted with his San Francisco brethren. For a number of reasons it seemed expedient to all the officers that from here on they should travel as a unit. Accordingly the special agent talked with the Pullman conductor and exchanged the reservations he previously had booked, getting instead a compartment adjoining the drawing-room in which the four from the city were riding.

It was on a Friday afternoon that the parties united. Friday evening, at the first call for dinner, the three officers herded their three prisoners forward to the dining car, the passage of the sextet through the aisles of the intervening sleepers causing some small commotion. Their advent into the diner created another little sensation.

Since it was difficult for the handcuffed aliens to handle knife and fork, they were given such food as might readily be eaten with a spoon or with the fingers—soups and omelets and soft vegetables and pie or rice pudding. The detectives ate fish. They shared between them a double order of imported kippers—a dish not on the typewritten menu for this meal but selected from the printed list of staple edibles.

Presumably they were the only persons on the train who that day had chosen the kippered herrings. Shortly, the special agent was giving private thanks that his church prescribed no dietetic regulations for Friday, because within an hour or two after leaving the table, the San Francisco men were suffering from acute and violent cramps—ptomaine poison had them helpless.

One seemed to be dangerously ill. That night at a town near the border between California and Arizona, he was taken off the train and carried to a hospital. During the wait at the station, a local physician dosed the second and lesser sufferer, whose name was McAvoy, and when he had been somewhat relieved of what ailed him, the doctor gave him a shot of something in the arm and said he ought to be up and about within twenty-four hours or some much matter.

During the night McAvoy slept in the lower berth of the compartment and the secret agent sat up, with the communicating door open, to guard the aliens, who were bedded in the so-called drawing-room.

Their irons stayed on their wrists; their lone warden was accepting no foolish odds against him. He had taken the precaution to transfer the keys of the Frenchman's handcuffs and the Italian's handcuffs from McAvoy's keeping to his own, slipping them on his key ring, but this had been done in case McAvoy should become seriously ill en route and it should devolve upon him to make at least a lap of the journey single-handed.

Next morning McAvoy's tortured stomach was much easier but he felt weak, he said, and drowsy. Given a full twelve hours of rest, though, he thought he would be able to go on guard when the nightfall came.

So through the day while the Limited rocked across the dusty desert he lay in his berth, and the special agent occupied the camp stool or an end of the drawing-room sofa. The trapped fugitives sat in the drawing-room seats, smoking cigarettes, and when the officer was not too near, talking among themselves.

Mainly they talked in English, a language which Gaza the Spaniard and Lafitte the Frenchman spoke fairly well. Verdi or Green, as the case might be, had little English at his command but Gaza, who had spent three years in Naples, spoke Italian; and so when Verdi used his own tongue, Gaza could interpret for the Frenchman's benefit. They were allowed to quit the drawing-room only for meals.

When dinner hour came on that second evening of their trip, McAvoy was in a doze. So the Department of Justice man did not disturb him.

"Come on, boys," he said to the three aliens; "time to eat again."

He lined them up in front of him in the corridor and they started the regular processional. It was just at that moment that the train broke its rhythmic refrain and began to clack and creak and slow for that unscheduled stop outside that New Mexico town. By the time they had reached the second car on ahead, she'd almost stopped and was lurching and jerking.

In the vestibule beyond that second car the special agent was in the act of stepping across the iron floor lip of the connection when a particularly brisk joggle caused him to lose his hat. He gave a small exclamation and bent to recover it. Doing so, he jostled against Gaza, the third man in the line, and therefore the next and nearmost man to him.

The agile Spaniard was quick to seize on his chance. He half turned and, bringing his chained wrists aloft, sent them down with all his might on the poll of the officer's unprotected skull. The victim of the assault never made a sound—just spraddled on his face and was dead to the world.

No outsider had been witness to the assault. No outsider came along during the few seconds which were required by the late prisoners to open an off-side car door and make their escape after the fashion which already has been described for you. Nobody missed them—for quite a while nobody did.

It wasn't until nearly nine o'clock, when McAvoy had roused up and got uneasy and rung for the porter and begun to ask questions, that a search was made and an alarm was raised.

Penned up together through that day, the aliens had matched stories, one story against another. A common plight made them communicative; a common peril caused each to turn with morbid reiteration to his own fatal predicament. It was as though he took a melancholy pride in painting his prospect as the most desperate.

There was no doubt that each looked upon the penalty which awaited him on the farther side of the Atlantic Ocean as a more dreadful thing than the things which these, his brother murderers, would suffer. He shrank from the frightful prospect of it but nevertheless kept dwelling upon it.

Said the Frenchman to the Spaniard: "He"—indicating his recent cellmate, the Italian—"he knows how with me it stands. With him, I have talked. He speaks not so well the English but sometimes he understands it. Now you shall hear and judge for yourself how bad my situation is."

Rapidly, graphically, with working features, with foreshortened gestures of his linked hands, this criminal sketched his past. He had been a Marseilles dock hand. He had killed a woman. She deserved killing, so he killed her. He had been caught, tried, convicted, condemned. While lying in prison, with execution day only a few weeks distant, he had made a getaway.

In disguise he had reached America and here had stayed three years. Then another woman, in a fit of jealousy, betrayed him to the police. He had been living with that woman. She also was French. To her he had given his confidence. It would appear that women had been his undoing. He went on:

"Me, I am as good as dead already. And what a death!" A spasm of shuddering possessed him. "For me the guillotine is waiting. The devil invented it. It is so they go at you with that machine: They strap you flat upon a board. Face downward you are, but you can look up, you can see—that is the worst part. They fit your throat into a grooved shutter; they make it fast. You crane your neck; you bring your head back; your eyes are drawn upward, fascinated. Above you, waiting, ready, poised, your eyes see the—the knife."

"But only for a moment do you see it, my friend," said the Spaniard, in a tone of one offering comfort. "Only a moment and then—pouff—all over!"

"A moment! I tell you it is an eternity. It must be an eternity. Lying there, you must live a hundred lives, you must die a hundred deaths. And then to have your head taken off your body, to be all at once in two pieces. Me, I am not afraid of most deaths. But that death by the guillotine—ah-h!"

The Spaniard bent forward. He was sitting alone facing the other two, who shared a seat.

"Listen, Señor," he stated. "Compared with me, you are the lucky one. True, I have not yet been tried—before they could try me I fled away out of that many-times accursed Spain of mine."

"Not tried, eh?" broke in the Frenchman. "Then you have yet a loophole—a chance for escape; and I have none. My trial, as I told you, is behind me."

"You do not know the Spanish courts. It is plain you do not, since you say that," declared the Spaniard. "Those courts—they are greedy for blood. With them, to my kind, there is not mercy; there is only punishment.

"And such a punishment! Wait until you hear. To me when they get me before them they will say: 'The proof is clear against you; the evidence has been thus and so. You are adjudged guilty. You took a life, so your life must be taken. It is the law.'

"Perhaps I say: 'Yes, but that life I took swiftly and in passion and for cause. For that one the end came in an instant, without pain, without lingering, yes, without warning. Since I must pay for it, why can not I also be made to die very quickly without pain?'

"Will they listen? No, they send me to the garrote. To a great strong chair they tie you—your hands, your feet, your trunk. Your head is against a post, an upright. In that post is a collar—an iron band. They fit that collar about your neck. Then from behind you the executioner—may he forever fry in hell!—he turns a screw.

"If he chooses he turns it slowly. The collar tightens, tightens; a knob presses into you behind. You begin to strangle. Your tongue comes forth from your mouth and swells. Your eyes pop from their sockets. Your face turns black. Oh, I have seen it myself! I know. You expire by inches! I am a brave man, Señors. When one's time comes, one dies. But oh, Señors, if it were any death but that! Better the guillotine than that! Better anything than that!"

He slumped back against the cushions, and rigors passed through him.

It was the Italian's turn. "I was tried in my absence," he explained to the Spaniard. "I was not even there to make my defense—I had thought it expedient to depart. Such is the custom of the courts in my country. They try you behind your back when you perhaps are thousands of miles away, as I was.

"They found me guilty, those judges. In Italy there is no capital punishment, so they sentenced me to life imprisonment. It is to that—that—I now return."

The Spaniard lifted his shoulders; the lifting was eloquent of his meaning.

"Not so fast," said the Italian. "You tell me you lived once in Italy. Have you forgotten what life imprisonment for certain acts means in Italy? It means solitary confinement. It means you are buried alive. They shut you away from every one in a tight cell. It is a tomb, that is all. You see no one ever, you hear no voice ever. If you cry out, no one answers. Silence, darkness, darkness, silence, until you go mad or until you die.

"Can you picture what that means to one of my race, to an Italian who must have music, sunshine, talk with his fellows, sight of his fellows? It is in his nature—he must have these things or he is in torture, in constant and everlasting torment. Every hour becomes to him a year, every day a century, until his brain bursts asunder inside his skull.

"Oh, they knew—those fiends who devised this thing—what to an Italian is a million times worse than death—any death. I am the most unfortunate one of the three of us. My penalty is the most dreadful by far."

The others would not have it so. They argued the point with him and with each other. It was a strange triangular debate that they carried on. They renewed it at intervals all through the day, and twilight found their beliefs all unshaken.

Then, under the Spaniard's leadership, came their deliverance out of captivity. It was he who, on the toss-up, won the revolver which they had taken from the person of the senseless special agent. Also it was he who suggested to the Italian that for the time being, at least, they stick together. To this the Italian had agreed, the Marseilles man Lafitte already having elected to go on his own.

After the latter, heading east by south, had left them, the Spaniard said reflectively:

"Did you hear what he said at the last? He is optimistic, that one, for all that he seemed so gloomy and down-hearted to-day when speaking of that guillotine of his. He said he now had faith that he would yet dodge his fate. Five minutes after he is off that train he speaks of faith!"

"I can not go quite that far," answered the Italian "We are free, but for us there will be still a thousand dangers. So I have not much faith, but I have hope. And you, my friend?"

The Spaniard shrugged his shoulders. His shrug might mean yes or it might mean no. Perhaps he needed his breath. He was going at a jog-trot down the tracks, the Italian alongside him.

Take the man who had faith. Set down as he was in a country utterly strange to him, this one of the fugitives nevertheless made steady and unmolested progress. He got safely around and by the New Mexico town. He hid in the chaparral until daybreak, then took to a highway running parallel with the railroad.

A "tin-canner," which is what they were beginning to call an itinerant motor tourist in those parts, overtook him soon after sun-up and gave him a lift to a small way station some forty miles down the line. There he boarded a local train—he had some money on him; not much money but enough—and undetected and, so far as he might judge, unsuspected, he rode that train clear on through to its destination a hundred miles or so farther along.

Other local trains carried him across a corner of Colorado and clear across Kansas. Forty-eight hours later or thereabouts, he was a guest in a third-rate hotel on a back street in Kansas City, Missouri.

He stayed in that hotel for two days and two nights, hiding most of the time in his room on the top floor of the six-story building, going down only for his meals and for newspapers. The food he had to have; the newspapers gave him information, of a sort, of the hunt which the authorities in several interior states were supposed to be making for the three fugitives. It was repeatedly stated that all three were believed to be fleeing together. That cheered Lafitte very much. It strengthened his faith of ultimately escaping.

But on the morning of his third day in that cheap hotel, when he came out of his room and went down the hall to ring for the elevator— there was only one passenger elevator in this hotel—he saw something. Passing the head of the stairs, which ended approximately midway of the stretch between the door of his room and the wattled iron door opening on the elevator well, he saw, out of the corner of one watchful eye, two men in civilian garb on the steps below him, their faces being just about at the level of the floor.

They had halted there. Whether they were coming up or going down there was no way of telling. It seemed to him that at sight of him they ducked slightly and made as if to flatten themselves back against the side wall. That, though, might have been only his imagination play-ing him a little trick. There was just one quick flash for him and then he was past them.

He gave no sign of having seen them. He stilled an impulse to make a dash for it. Where was he to dash for, with the stairs cut off? He fol-lowed the only course open to him. Anyhow he told himself he might be wrong. Perhaps his nerves were misbehaving. Perhaps those two who seemed to be lurking just there behind him on those steps were not in-terested in him at all. He kept telling himself that, while he was ringing the bell, while he was waiting for the car to come up for him.

The car did come up and, for a wonder, promptly: an old-fashioned car, creaky, musty. Except for its shirt-sleeved attendant, it was empty. As Lafitte stepped in, he glanced sidewise over his shoulder, making the movement casual—no sight of those two fellows.

He rode down, the only passenger for that trip so there were no stops on the descent. They reached the ground floor, which was the of-fice floor. The elevator came to a standstill, then moved up a foot or so, then joltingly down six inches or so, as the attendant, who was not ex-pert, being an early-morning substitute for the regular elevator man, maneuvered to bring the sill of the car flush with the tiling of the lobby.

The delay was sufficiently prolonged for Lafitte to realize, all in a flash, he had not been wrong. Through the intervening grille of the shaft door he saw two more men who pressed close up to that door, who stared in at him, whose looks and poses were watchful, eager, prepared. Besides, Lafitte, having spent three years in this country in intimacy with members of the resident criminal class, knew plain-clothes men when be saw them.

Up above and here below, he was cut off. There still was a chance for him, a poor one but the only one. If he could shoot the elevator aloft quickly enough, check it at the third floor or the fourth, say, and hop out, he might make a successful dart for the fire escape at the rear of the ho-tel—provided the fire escape was not guarded. In the space of time that the elevator boy was jockeying the car, he thought of this, and having thought it, acted on it.

Swinging his fist from behind with all his might, he hit that helpless substitute on the point of the jaw and deposited him, stunned and temporarily helpless, on his knees in a corner of the cage. Lafitte grabbed the lever, shoved it over hard, and up the shaft shot the car. Before he could get control of it, being unfamiliar with such mechanism and in a panic besides, it was at the top of the house. But then he mastered it and made it reverse its course, and returning downward he pulled the lever, bringing it toward him.

That was the proper notion, that gentler manipulation, for now the car, more obedient, was crawling abreast of the third-floor level. It crept earthward, inch by inch, and without bringing it to a dead stop he jerked up the latch of the collapsible safety gate, telescoped the metal outer door back into its folded-up self, and stooping low, because the gap was diminishing all the while, he lunged forward.

Now that elevator boy was a quick-witted, a high-tempered Irish boy. He might be half-dazed but his instincts of belligerency were not asleep. He told afterward how, automatically and indignantly functioning, he grabbed at the departing assailant and caught him by one leg and for a fleeing moment, before the other kicked free, detained or at least retarded him.

But by all that was good and holy he swore he did not touch the lever. Being down on all-fours at the rear side of the slowly sinking car, how could he touch it? Why, just at that precise fraction of a second, the elevator should pick up full speed was a mystery to him—to everybody else, for that matter.

But pick up full speed it did. And the Irish boy cowered down and screamed an echo to a still louder scream than his, and hid his eyes from the sight of Lafitte with his head outside and his body inside the elevator, being decapitated as completely and almost as neatly—if you could use the latter word in such connection—as though a great weighted knife had sheared him off at the neck.

Take the Spaniard and the Italian: Steadily they traveled westward for nearly all of that night which followed their evacuation from the Limited. It put desirable distance between them and the spot where they had dumped the special agent down. Also it kept them warm. This was summertime but on the desert even summer nights are chilly and some-times they are downright cold. Before dawn, they came on a freight train waiting in a siding for more important traffic to pass. Its locomotive faced west. That suited their book.

They climbed nimbly aboard a flat and snuggled themselves down behind a barrier of farm implements. Here, breakfastless but otherwise comfortable, they rode until nearly midday. Then a brakeman ap-peared, swinging himself from car to car, and found them. He harshly ordered them to get themselves up out of there and off of there.

Immediately though, looking at them where they squatted half-hidden, his tone softened, taking on a more friendly note, and he told them he'd changed his mind about it and they could stay aboard as long as they pleased. On top of this, he hurried forward as though he might have important news for the engine crew or somebody. He kept glanc-ing back toward where they were crowded.

They chose to get off. They had noted the quick start as of recogni-tion which the brakeman had given. They figured—and figured rightly—that by now the chase for them was on and that their descriptions had been telegraphed back and forth along the line. The train was traveling at least twenty miles an hour but as soon as the brakeman was out of sight, they jumped for it, tumbling like shot rabbits down the slope of the right of way and bringing up all jarred and shaken in the dry ditch at the bottom.

Barring bruises and scratches, Green had taken no hurt, but Gaza landed with a badly sprained ankle. He gathered himself up, and with Green to give him a helping arm, hobbled away from the railroad.

To get away from that railroad was their prime aim now. Choosing a course at random, they went north over the undulating waste lands and through the shimmering heat, toward a range of mottled high buttes ris-ing on beyond.

It took them until deep into the afternoon to cover a matter roughly of five miles. By now, Gaza's lower left leg was elephantine in its pro-portions and every forced step he took meant a fresh stab of agony. He knew he could not go much farther. Green knew it too, and in his brain began shaping tentative plans. The law of self-preservation was one of the few laws for which he had respect. They panted from heat and from thirst and from weariness.

At the end of those five miles, having toiled laboriously up over a fold in the land, they saw close at hand and almost directly below them, a 'dobe hut, and not quite so near at hand, a big flock of sheep looking like woolly white larvæ against the slope where they grazed on the scanty and astringent herbage. At the door of the cabin, a man in overalls was stripping the hide from a swollen dead cow.

Before they could dodge back below the sky-line, he straightened his back and looked and saw them and stood expectantly. There was nothing for them to do except to go toward him. At their slow approach, an expression of curiosity crept over his brown face and stayed there. He looked like a Mexican or possibly a half-breed Indian. He wore no beard, which would be a rare thing for a sheep herder, but not so rare a thing if he were part Indian.

When Gaza, stumbling nearer, hailed him in English, he merely shook his head dumbly. Then Gaza tried him in Spanish and to that he replied volubly. For minutes they palavered back and forth, then the stranger served them with deep drafts from a water-bottle swinging in the doorway with a damp sack over it. The water was lukewarm and bitterish-tasting but it was grateful to their parched throats. Then he withdrew inside the little house and Gaza, for Green's benefit, translated into Italian what talk had passed.

"He says he is quite alone here, which is the better for us," explained the Spaniard, speaking swiftly. "He says that a week ago he came up from Old Mexico, seeking work. A gringo—a white man—gave him work. The white man is a sheep man. His home ranch is miles away. In a sheep wagon he brought this Mexican here and left him here in charge of that flock yonder, with provisions for a month.

"It will be three weeks then before the white man, his employer, comes again. Except for that white man he knows nobody hereabouts. Until we came just now, he had seen no one at all. So he is glad to see us."

"And accounting for ourselves you told him what?" asked Green.

"I told him we were traveling across country in a car and that going down a steepness last night the car overturned and was wrecked and I crippled myself. I told him that, traveling light because of my leg, we started out to find some town, some house, and that, hoping to make a short-cut, we left the road, but that since morning and until we blundered upon this camp, we had been quite lost in this ugly country. He believes me. He is simple, that one, an ignorant credulous peon.

"But kind-hearted, that also is plain. For proof of it observe this." He pointed to the bloated, half-flayed carcass. "He says three days ago just over that red hill behind us, he found this beast—a stray from somewhere he knows not where. So far as he knows there are no cattle droves in these parts—only sheep.

"She was sick, she staggered, she was dizzy and turned in circles as if blind, and froth ran from her mouth. There is a weed that does that to animals which eat it, he says. So, hoping to make her well again, he put a scrap of rope on her horns and led her here. But last night she died. So to-day, with his big sharp knife, he has been peeling her.

"Now he goes to make ready some food for us. He is very hospitable, also, that one."

"And when we have eaten, then what? We can't linger here."

"Wait, please, Señor. To my mind already an idea comes." His tone was authoritative, confident, and under his heavy mustache a smile showed. "First we fill our empty stomachs to give us strength, and then we smoke a cigarette, and while we smoke, I think. And then—we see."

On *frijoles* and rancid bacon and thin corn cakes and bad coffee, which the herder brought them on tin platters and in tin cups, they did fill their empty stomachs, squatting meanwhile in the skimpy shade of an improvised arbor of thin brush set on poles which fronted the 'dobe. Then they smoked together, all three of them, smoking cigarettes rolled in corn-husk wrappers.

The Mexican was hunkered on his heels, making smoke rings in the still hot air, when Gaza, getting on his feet with difficulty, limped toward the doorway, gesturing to show that he craved another swig from the water-bottle. When he was behind the other two, almost touching them, he drew the special agent's pistol and fired once and their host tumbled forward on his face and spraddled his limbs and quivered a bit and was still, with a bullet hole in the back of his head. There was very little blood; there was only a slight oozing from the wound.

This killing gave the Italian, seasoned killer as he was, a profound shock. It seemed so unnecessary unless—? He started up, his features twitching, and backed away, fearing the next bullet would be for him.

"Remain tranquil, Señor," said the Spaniard, almost gaily. "For you, my comrade, there is no danger. There is for you hope of deliverance, you, who professed last night to have hope in your soul.

"Now me, I have charity in my soul—charity for you, charity for myself, charity also for this one lying here. Behold, he is now out of his troubles. He was a dolt, a clod of the earth, a creature of no refinement. He lived a hermit's life, lonely, miserable, in filth. He knew only sheep—and sheep are poor company even for a clod. Now he has been dispatched to a better and a brighter world. That was but kindness." With his foot he touched the sprawled corpse.

"But in dispatching him I had thought also for you—for both of us. I elucidate: First we bury him under the dirt floor of this house, taking care to leave no telltale traces of our work. Then you make a pack for your back of the food that is here. You take also the water-bottle, filled. Furthermore you take with you this pistol which is mine and which I give to you.

"Then, stepping lightly on rocky ground or on hard ground so that you make no tracks, you go swiftly hence and hide yourself in those mountains until—who can tell?—until those who will come presently here have ceased to search for you. With me along, lamed as I am, me to hamper you, to hold you back, there would be no chance for either of us. But you, going alone—you armed, provisioned, quick of foot—you have a hope."

"But—but you? What then becomes of you? You—you sacrifice yourself?" In his bewilderment the Italian stammered over the words.

"Me, I stay here to greet the pursuers. It is quite simple. In peaceful solitude I await their coming. It can not be long until they come. That man of the freight train will be guiding them back to pick up our trail. By to-night at latest, and probably sooner, I expect them."

At sight of the Italian's more deeply mystified face he broke now into a laugh.

"Still you are puzzled, eh? You think that I am magnanimous, that I am generous? Well, all that I am. But you think me also a fool and there you err. I save you perhaps but likewise perhaps I save myself. Observe, Señor."

He stooped and lifted the dead face of his victim. "See now what I myself saw the moment I beheld this herder of ours: This man is much my shape, my height, my coloring. He spoke a corrupt Spanish such as I can speak. Put upon me the clothes which he wears, and remove from my lip this mustache which I wear, and I would pass for him even before the very eyes of that white man who hired him.

"Well, very soon I shall be wearing his clothes, my own being hidden in the same grave with him. Within ten minutes I shall be removing this mustache. He being newly shaven, as you see for yourself, it must be that in this hovel we will find a razor. I shall pass for him. I shall be this mongrel dull-wit."

A light broke on the Italian. He ran and kissed the Spaniard, on both cheeks and on the mouth.

"Ah, my brother!" he cried out delightfully. "Forgive me that for a moment I thought you hard-hearted for having in seeming wantonness killed the man who fed us. I see you are brilliant—a great thinker, a great genius. But, my beloved"—and here doubt once more assailed him—"what explanation do you make when they do come?"

"That is the best of all," said Gaza. "Before you leave me you take a cord and you bind me most securely—my hands crossed behind my back—so; my feet fastened together—so. It will not be for very long that I remain so. I can endure it. Coming then, they find me thus. That I am bound makes more plausible, more convincing the tale I shall tell them.

"And this is the tale that I shall tell: To them I shall say that as I sat under this shelter skinning my dead cow, there appeared suddenly two men who fell upon me without warning; that in the struggle they hurt my poor leg most grievously, then, having choked me into quietude, they tied my limbs, despoiled me of my provender, and hurriedly departed, leaving me helpless. I shall describe these two brutal men—oh, most minutely I shall describe them. And my description will be accurate, for you I shall be describing as you stand now; myself I shall describe as I now am.

"The man from the train will say: 'Yes, yes, that is true; those are surely the two I saw.' He will believe me at once; that will help. Then they will inquire to know in which direction fled this pair of scoundrels and I will tell them they went that way yonder to the south across the desert, and they will set off it that direction seeking two who flee together, when all the while you will be gone this way, north into those mountains which will shelter you. And that, Señor, will be a rich part of the whole joke.

"Perhaps, though, they question me further. Then I say: 'Take me before this gringo who within a week hired me to watch his sheep. Confront me with him. He will identify me, he will confirm my story.' And if they do that and he does that—as most surely he will—why, then they must turn me loose to go about my business and that, Señor, will be the very crown and peak of the joke."

In the excess of his admiration and his gratitude, the Italian just naturally had to kiss him again.

They worked fast and they worked scientifically, carefully, overlooking nothing, providing against every contingency. But at the last minute, when the Italian was ready to resume his flight and the Spaniard, smoothly shaven and effectually disguised in the soiled shirt and messy overalls of the dead man, had turned around and submitted his wrists to be pinioned, it was discovered that there was no rope available with which to bind his legs. The one short scrap of rope about the spot had been used for tying his hands.

The Spaniard said this was just as well. Any binding that was drawn snugly enough to fetter his feet securely would certainly increase the pain in the inflamed and grossly swollen ankle joint.

However, it was apparent that he must be securely anchored, lest suspicion arise in the minds of his rescuers when they arrived. Here the Italian made a contribution to the plot. He was proud of his inspiration.

With the Mexican's butcher knife he cut long narrow strips from the fresh slick cowhide. Then the Spaniard sat down on the earth with his back against one of the slim tree trunks supporting the arbor, and the Italian took numerous turns about his waist and his arms and the upper part of his body, and tightly knotted the various ends of the skin ribbons behind the post. Unaided, no human being could escape out of that mesh. To the pressure and the wriggle of the prisoner's trunk, the moist, pliant lashings would give slightly but it was certain they neither would work loose nor snap apart.

So he settled himself in his bonds, and the Italian, having shouldered his pack, put a lighted cigarette between his benefactor's lips and once more fervently kissed him in token of gratitude and wished him success and made off with many wavings of the arm and shouted farewells.

So far as this empty country was concerned, the Italian was a greenhorn, a tenderfoot. Nevertheless, and considering his fatigue and everything, he made excellent progress. He marched northward until dark, lay that night under a murdered man's smelly blanket behind a many-colored butte and next morning struck deeper into the broken lands. He entered what he hoped might be a gap through the mountains, treading cautiously along a narrow natural trail half-way up the face of a dauntingly steep cliff side.

He was well into it when his foot dislodged a scrap of shaly rock which in sliding over the verge set other rocks to cascading down the slope. From above, yet larger boulders began toppling over into the scoured-out passageway thus provided, and during the next five minutes the walled-in declivity was alive and roaring with tumbling huge stones, with dislodged earth running fluid like a stream, with uprooted stunty piñons, with choking acrid dust clouds.

The Italian ran for dear life; he managed to get out of the avalanche's path. When at length he reached a safe place and looked back, he saw behind him how the landslide had choked the gorge almost to its brim. No human being—no, not even a goat, could from his side scale that jagged and overhanging parapet. It was reasonable to presume that it could not be mounted from the other side. Between him and pursuit was a perfect barrier.

Well content, he went on. But presently he made a discovery, a distressing discovery, which took the good cheer right out of him. This was no gateway into which he had entered. It was a dead-end leading nowhere—what westerners call a box canyon. On three sides of him, right, left and on ahead, rose tremendously high walls, sheer and unclimbable. They threatened him; they seemed to be closing in on him to pinch him flat. And, of course, back of him retreat was cut off. There he was, bottled up like a fly in a corked jug, like a frog at the bottom of a well.

Frantically he explored as best he could the confines of this vast prison cell of his. He stumbled upon a spring and its waters, while tainted lightly with alkali, were drinkable. So he had water and he had food, some food. By paring his daily portions down almost to starvation point, he might make these rations last for months. But then, what? And in the meantime, what? Why, until hunger destroyed him, he was faced with that doom which he so dreaded—the doom of solitary confinement.

He thought it all out and then he knelt down and took out his pistol and he killed himself.

In one of his calculations that smart malefactor, the Spaniard, had been wrong. By his system of deductions, the searchers should reach the 'dobe hut where he was tethered within four hours, or, at most, five. But it was nearer thirty hours before they appeared.

The trouble had been that the brakeman wasn't quite sure of the particular stretch where he had seen the fugitives nestled beneath a reaping machine on that flat car. Besides, it took time to spread the word; to summon county officials; to organize an armed searching party. When at length the posse did strike the five-mile trail leading from the railroad tracks to the camp of the late sheep herder, considerably more than a day had elapsed.

The track was fairly plain—two sets of heavy footprints bearing north and only lacking where rocky outcrops broke through the surface of the desert. Having found it, they followed it fast, and when they mounted the fold in the earth above the cabin, they saw the figure of a man seated in front of it, bound snugly to one of the supports of the meager arbor.

Hurrying toward him they saw that he was dead—his face was blackened and horribly distorted; that his glazed eyes goggled at them and his tongue protruded; that his stiffened legs were drawn up in sharp angles of agony.

They looked closer and they saw the manner of his death and were very sorry for him. He had been bound with strands of fresh rawhide, and all through that day he had been sitting there exposed to the baking heat of the sun, and heat, operating on damp new rawhide, has an immediate effect. Heat causes certain substances to expand but green rawhide it causes to contract very fast to an ironlike stiffness and rigidity.

So in this case the sun glare had drawn tighter and tighter the lashings about this poor devil's body, squeezing him in at the stomach and the breast and the shoulders, pressing his arms tighter and tighter and yet tighter against his sides. That for him would have been a highly unpleasant procedure—impeding his circulation, hampering his breathing, bruising his flesh—but it would not have killed him.

Something else had done that. One loop of the rawhide had been twisted about his neck and made fast at the back of the post. At first it might have been no more than a loosely fitting circlet but hour by hour it had hardened and shrunken into a choking collar, a diminishing noose, a terrible deadly yoke. Veritably it had garroted him by inches.

Gouverneur Morris

The Crocodile

I

The first locality of which I have any recollection was my father's library—a tall, melancholy room devoted to books and illusions. Three sides were of books, sombrely bound, reaching from the floor to within three feet of the ceiling. Along the shelf, which was erroneously supposed to protect the tops of the top row of books from the dust with which our house abounded, were stationed, at precise intervals, busts done in plaster after the antique and death-masks. Beginning on the left was the fury-haunted face of Orestes; next him the lachrymose features of Niobe; followed her Medusa, crowned with serpents. The rest were death-masks—Napoleon, Washington, Voltaire, and my father's father. The prevailing dust, settled thick upon the heads of these grim images, lent them the venerable illusion of gray hair. The three walls of books were each pierced by a long, narrow window, for the room was an extension from the main block of the house, but over two of these the shutters were opaquely closed in winter and summer. The third window, however, was allowed to extend whatever beneficence of light it could to the dismal and musty interior. A person of sharp sight, sitting at the black oak table in the middle of the room, might, on a fine day, have seen clearly enough to write on very white paper with very black ink, or to read out of a large-typed book. Through the fourth wall a door, nearly always closed, led into the main hall, which, like the library itself, was a tall and melancholy place of twilight and illusions. When my poor mother died, in giving me birth, she was laid out in the library and buried from the hall. Consequently, according to old-fashioned custom, these apartments were held sacred to her memory rather than other portions of the house in which she had enjoyed the more fortunate phases of life and happiness. The room in which my mother had actually died was never entered by any one save my father. Its door was double locked, like that of our family vault in the damp hollow among the sycamores.

The first thing that I remember was that I had had a mother who had died and been buried. The second, that I had a father with a white face and black clothes and noiseless feet, whose duty in life was to shut doors, pull down window shades, and mourn for my mother. The third was a carved wooden box, situated in the exact centre of the oak table in the library, which contained a scroll of stained paper covered with curious characters, and a small but miraculously preserved crocodile. I was never allowed to touch the scroll or the crocodile, but in his lenient moods, which were few and touched with heartrending melancholy, my father would set the box open upon a convenient chair and allow me to peer my heart out at its mysterious contents. The crocodile, my father sometimes told me, was an Egyptian charm which was supposed to bring misfortune upon its possessor. "But I let it stay on my table," he would say, "because in the first place I am without superstition, and in the second because I am far distant from the longest and wildest reach of misfortune. When I lost your mother I lost all. Ay! but she was bonny, my boy—bonny!" It was very sad to hear him run on about the bonniness of my mother, and old Ann, my quondam nurse, has told me how at the funeral he stood for a long time by the casket, saying over and over, "Wasn't she bonny? Wasn't she bonny?" and followed her to the vault among the sycamores with the same iteration upon his lips.

It was not until I was near eight years old that my father could bear the sight of me, so much had we been divided by the innocent share which I had had in my mother's death. But I was not allowed to pass those eight years in ignorance of the results of my being, or of the constant mourning to which my father had devoted the balance of his days. I was brought up, so to speak, on my mother's death and burial. Another child might have been nurtured thus into a vivid contrast, but I ran fluidly into the mould sober, and came very near to solidifying. Death and its ancientry have a horrible fascination for children. And for me, wherever I turned, there was a plenitude of morbid suggestion. Indeed, our plantation—held by the family from the earliest colonization of

Georgia, spread along the low shore of a turbid river tributary to the Savannah, and dwindled, partly by mismanagement and partly by the non-success of the rebellion, into a sad fulfilment of its bright colonial promise—was itself moribund. In the swamps, still showing traces of the dikes, which had once divided it into quadrilaterals, the rice which had been our chief source of income no longer flourished. The slave quarters, a long double row of diminutive brick cubes, each with one chimney, one door, and one window at the side of the door—such dwellings as children draw painfully on slates—still standing, for the most part, damp and silent, showed that the labor which had made the rice profitable was also a thing of other days. The house itself, a vastly tall block of burned bricks, laid side by side instead of end to end, as in modern building, stood on a slight rise of ground with its back to the river, among lofty and rugged red oaks, rotten throughout their tops with mistletoe. An avenue, roughened by disuse into a going worse than that of a lumber road, nearly a mile long, straight as justice, shaded by a double row of enormous live oaks, choked and strangled with plumes and beards of gray moss, led from the county road through the scant cotton fields and strawberry fields to the circle in front of the house. I used to fancy, and I think Bluebeard's closet lent me the notion, that the moss in the live oaks was the hair of unfortunate princesses turned gray by suffering and hung among the trees in wanton and cruel ostentation by their enemies.

Nothing but a happy and cheerful woman, a good housewife, ready-tongued and loving, could have lent a touch of home to our melancholy disestablishment. Women we had in the house, two black and ancient negresses, rheumatic and complaining, one to cook and one to make the beds, and old Ann, my mother's Scotch nurse, a hard, rickety female, whose mind, voice, and memory were pitched in the minor key. We had a horse, no mean animal, for my father had known and loved horses before his misfortune, but ugly and unkempt, and it was the duty of an old negro named Ecclesiastes, the one lively influence about the place, to look after the interests of this little-used creature. My father and myself completed the disquieting group of living things. Concerning things inanimate, we had enough to eat, enough to wear, and enough to read. And the clothes of all of us were black. Until I was twelve years old I believed fervently that to mourn all his life long for dead wives and mothers was the whole end and destiny of man. In my twelfth year, however, my uncle Richard, a florid, affectionate, and testy sportsman, paid us a visit on matters connected with the mismanagement of the estate. He stayed three days. On the first he shot duck, on the second quail; on the morning of the third he talked with my father in the library; in the afternoon he took me for a walk. In the evening he went away and I never saw him again.

"Richard," he had said, for I had been given his name, "I want to see the vault before I go. I haven't seen it since your mother was buried."

It was a warm, bright, still December day, the day before Christmas, and my uncle seated himself nonchalantly on the low wall which surrounded the vault, his knees crossed, his mouth closed on a big cigar, and his eyes fixed on the "legended door."

"People who go into that place in boxes," he said, "never come out. Has that ever occurred to you, Richard?"

I said that it had.

"You never saw your mother, my boy," he went on, "but you wear mourning for her."

"It seems to me almost as if I had known her," I said, "because—"

"Yes," cut in my uncle, "your father has kept her memory alive. He has neglected everything else in order to do that. Now tell—what was your mother like?"

I hesitated, and said finally, "She was very tall and beautiful."

My uncle smiled grimly.

"You would know her then," he said, "if you saw her? Answer me truthfully, and remember that other women are sometimes tall and beautiful."

I admitted a little ruefully, that I should not know my mother if I saw her.

"No, you wouldn't," said my uncle, "and for this reason, too; your mother had an amusing little face, but she was neither beautiful nor tall."

"But—" I began.

"Your father," my uncle interrupted, "has come to believe that his wife was tall and beautiful because he thinks that the idea of lifelong devotion to a memory is tall and beautiful. He is a little hipped about himself, my boy, and it makes me rather sick. I will tell you an anecdote. Once there was a man. He met a girl. For three weeks they talked foolishly about foolish things. Then they were married. Nine months later a son was born to them, and the girl died. The man mourned for her. At first he mourned because he missed her. Then because he respected her memory. Then because he liked to pose as one everlastingly unhappy and faithful till death. He made everybody about him mourn, including the little child, his son, and finally he died and was put in the vault with the girl, and no one in the world was the better by one jot for any act of the man's life. . . . Let me hear you laugh. . . ."

I looked up at him, much puzzled.

"Not at the anecdote," he said, "which isn't funny—but just laugh."

I delivered myself of a soulless and conventional ha-ha. My uncle put back his head and roared. At first I thought he must be sick, for until that moment I had never heard any one laugh. I had read of it in books. And as a dog must have a first lesson in digging, so a child must have a first lesson in laughing. My uncle never stopped. He roared harder and louder. Tears ran down his cheeks. Something shook me, I did not know what. I heard a sound like that which my uncle was making, but nearer me and more shrill. I felt pain in my sides. My eyes became blurred and stinging wet. With these new sounds and symptoms came strange mental changes—a sudden knowledge that blue was the best color for the sky, heat the best attribute of the sun, and the act of living delightful. We roared with laughter, my uncle and I, and the legended door of the tomb gave us back hearty echoes. In the desert of my childhood I look back upon that oasis of laughter as the only spot in which I really lived. When my uncle went away he said: "For God's sake, Dickie, try to be cheerful from now on. I wish I could take you with me. But your father says, no. Remember that the business of living is with Life. And let Death mind his own business."

The door closed behind that ruddy, cheerful man, and left us mourners facing each other across the supper table.

"Papa," said I presently, "haven't we a picture of mamma?"

"I had them all destroyed," said my father. "They were not like her. The last picture of her—" here he tapped his forehead—"will perish when I am gone. Ay, but laddie," he said, "she is vivid to me."

"Tell me about her, please, papa," I said.

"She was a tall, stately woman, laddie," he said, "and bonny—ay, bonny. Life without her has neither breadth nor thickness—only length."

"What color was her hair?" I asked.

"Boy," he said, "you will choke me with your questions. Her hair was black like the wing of a raven. Her eyes were black. She moved in beauty like the night."

Here my father buried his white face in his white hands, and remained so, his supper untasted, for a long time. Presently he looked up and said with pitiful effort:

"And what did you with your uncle Richard?"

"We sat on the wall of the vault," I answered, "and laughed."

It was a part of my father's melancholy pose to renounce anger together with all the other passions, but at the close of my thoughtless words he sprang to his feet, livid.

"For that word," he cried, "ye shall suffer hellish."

And he dragged me, more dead than alive, to the library. But what form of punishment he would have inflicted me with I do not know. For a circumstance met with in the library—a circumstance trivial in itself and, to my mind, sufficiently explicable—shook my father into a new mood. The circumstance was this: that one of the servants (doubtless) had opened the carved box in the centre of the table, taken out the crocodile, probably to gratify curiosity by a close inspection, and forgotten to put it back. But I must admit that at first sight it looked as if the inanimate and horrible little creature had of its own locomotion thrust open the box and crawled to the edge of the table. To instant and searching inquiry the servants denied all knowledge of the matter, and it remained a mystery. My father dismissed the servants from the library, returned the crocodile to its box, and remained for some moments in thought. Then he said, very gravely and earnestly:

"The possession of this dead reptile is supposed to bring misfortune upon a man. For me that is impossible, for I am beyond its longest and wildest reach. But with you it is different. Life has in store for you the possibility of many misfortunes. Take care that you do not bring them upon yourself. Pray that you have not already done so by giving vent to ghoulish laughter in the presence of your dead mother. Now take yourself off—and leave me with my memories."

That night there was an avenue of moss-shrouded live oaks in dreamland, down which I fled before the onrush of a mighty and ominous crocodile.

The next day was Christmas, and we resumed the monotony of our stolid and gloomy lives.

II

At eighteen I was a very serious and colorless youth. It may be that I contained the seeds of a rational outlook upon life, but so far they had not sprouted. My father's pervading melancholy was more strong in me than red blood and ambition. With him I looked forward to an indefinite extension of the past, enlivened, if I may use the paradox, by two demises, his and my own. I had much sober literature at my tongue tips, a condescending fondness for the great poets, a normal appetite, two suits of black, and a mouth stiff from never having learned to smile. I stood in stark ignorance of life, and had but the vaguest notion as to how babies are made. My father, preserved in melancholy as a bitter pickle in vinegar, had not aged or changed an iota from my earliest memory of him—a very white man dressed in very black cloth.

One morning my father sent from the library for me, and when I had presented myself said shortly:

"Your Uncle Richard is dead. He has left nothing. He was guardian, as you may know, of Virginia Richmond, the daughter of his intimate friend. She is coming to live with us. Let us hope that she is sedate and reasonable. You have never seen anything of women. It may be that you will fall in love with her. You may consult with me if you do, though I am no longer in touch with youth. She is to have the south spare room. You may tell Ann. She will be here this evening (my father always spoke of the afternoon as the evening). You may tell her our ways, and our hatred of noise and frivolity. If she is a lady that will be sufficient. I think that is all."

My father sighed and turned away his face.

"To a large extent," he said, "she has been educated abroad. I hope that she will not bore you. But even if she should, try to be kind to her. I know you will be civil."

"Shall you be here to welcome her?" I asked.

"I shall hope to be," said my father. "But I have proposed to myself to gather some of the early jasmine to— If I am urgently needed for anything I shall be in the immediate vicinity of the vault."

Virginia Richmond arrived in an express wagon, together with her three trunks and two portmanteaus. She sat by the driver, a young negro, with whom she had evidently established the most talkative terms, and did not wait for me to help her deferentially to the ground, but put a slender a foot on the wheel, and jumped.

"It's good to get here," she said. "Are you Richard?"

"Yes, Virginia," I said, and felt that I was smiling.

"Where's Uncle John?" she said. "I call him Uncle John because his brother was my adopted uncle Richard always. And you're my cousin Richard. And I'm your cousin Virginia, going on seventeen, very talkative, affectionate and hungry. How old are you?"

"I shall be nineteen in April," I said, "and my father is somewhere about the grounds"—I did not like to say *vault*—"and I will try to find you something edible. Are you tired?"

"Do I look tired?"

"No," I said.

"How do I look?"

"Why," I said, "I think you look very well. I—I like your look."

A better judge than I might have liked it. She had a rosy face of curves and dimples, unruly hair of many browns, eyes that were deep wonders of blue, a mouth of pearl and pomegranate.

"You," she said, "look very grave—and—yes, hungry. But you have nice eyes and a good skin, though it ought to be browner in this climate, and if you don't smile this minute I shall scream."

So I smiled, and we went into the house.

"My God! cousin," she cried, to my mind most irreverently, "can't you open something and let in the light?"

"My father," I said, "prefers the house dark."

"Then let it be dark when he's in it," she cried, "and bright when he's out of it." And she ran to a window and struggled with the shutter. When she had flung that open she braced herself for an attack upon the next; but I bowed to the inevitable, and saved her from the trouble of consummating it. The floods of light let thus into the hall and dining-room seemed to my mind, sophisticated only in dark things, a kind of orgy. But Virginia was the more cheered.

"Now a body can eat," she said. "Ham—hoe-cake—Sally Lunn—is that Sally Lunn? Oh, Richard, I have heard of these things—and now—" wherewith she assaulted the viands.

"Don't you have ham in Europe, Virginia?" I asked.

"Ham!" she cried. "No, Richard, we have quarters of pig cut in thick slices—but meat like this was never grown on a pig. This," and she rapped the ham with her fork, and laughed to hear the solid thump, "was once part of an angel—a very fat angel."

"And you are a cannibal," I said. It was my first gallantry.

She gave me a grateful look.

"I had not hoped for it," she said. And for twenty minutes she ate like a hungry man and talked like a running brook.

"And now," she said, "for the house. First the library. Uncle Richard told me about all the death heads with dusty brows."

"Did he tell you about the crocodile?" I asked.

"Which crocodile?" said Virginia gravely.

"We have one only," I answered. "And I'm afraid it won't interest you very much. . . . This is the library."

She was for having the shutters open.

"My father wouldn't like it," I said.

"This once," said she, and I served the whim.

"Yes," she said, after examination, "it *is* dreadful. Show me the crocodile, and then let's go."

But she was more interested in the scroll.

"It's Arabic," she said; "I can read it."

"You can read Arabic?"

"Indeed, yes. When papa's lungs went bad we lived in Cairo. He died in Egypt, you know. . . . Listen. . . . It says: *'That man who holds me* (it's the crocodile talking) *in both hands, and cries thrice the name of Allah, shall see the face of his beloved though she were dead.'"*

"That's not our version," I said. "We believe that the possession of that beast invites misfortune."

"But you don't read Arabic," said Virginia. "Quick, Richard, take this thing in your two hands and call 'Allah' three times—loud, because it's a long way to Egypt—why, the man doesn't want to play—"

I had taken the crocodile in my hands, but balked, and I believe blushed, at the idea of raising my voice above the conversational pitch to further so absurd an experiment.

"Don't you want to see the face of your beloved?"

"I have none," said I.

"Then I'd cry 'Allah' till I had," said she. "Please—only three times."

So I held the crocodile, looking very foolish, and called three times upon the prophet. Then I turned to Virginia and met her eyes. The same thought occurred to us both, for we looked away. It was then that my father entered.

"Richard," he said, "the shutters—"

I made haste to close them, for I was blushing.

"This is Virginia!" said my father. "Welcome to our sad and lonely house. I thought just now that I heard some one calling aloud."

"It was Richard," said Virginia. "This scroll—" and she translated to my father.

"Oh, for faith to believe," said he. He took the crocodile in his hands and examined it with sad interest. "I have just come from her tomb, Virginia," he said. "I have been laying jasmine about it."

"Oh, the dear jasmine!" cried Virginia. "It's splendidly out, and to-morrow I shall fill the house with it."

"The house—" said my father hazily.

"Don't you like flowers, Uncle John?"

"I neither like nor dislike them," said my father.

"Then why, for heaven's sake—" but she stopped herself. "And you, Richard, don't you like them?"

"I have grown to think of them," said I, "if at all, as something odorous and sad, vaguely connected with funerals."

"Oh, no!" cried Virginia. "They are beautiful and gay, and they are connected with weddings—"

"Don't," said my father quickly. He was still holding the crocodile. "But I do not blame you, child. You will soon learn our ways. Since our great loss we have kept very quiet. . . . Ay, my dear, but you should have seen Richard's mother—was she not bonny, Richard?"

I bowed.

"I could fain look upon her again," he said. "And the scroll—does it not say *'even though she were dead?'*... Who was it called 'Allah'? ... You, Richard? ... And what face did you see? ..."

"Tell him," said Virginia.

"Ay, tell me," said my father.

"I saw Virginia's face," said I.

Then we left him. But in the hall Virginia laid her hand on my shoulder.

"Haven't you noticed?" said she.

"What?" said I.

"Your father," said she.

"No," said I; "what ails him?"

Virginia tapped her forehead.

"Mildewed here," said she.

"I don't understand," said I.

"Never mind then, Richard," said she; "I'll take care of you."

That night I dreamed that I heard my father calling the name of Allah. But in the morning I rose early, and, going to the woods, gathered an armful of jasmine for Virginia.

She received it cheerfully.

"Is this—er—in *memory* of any one?" she asked.

"Yes," I said boldly, "it's in memory of me."

"Then I will keep it, Richard," she said. "Flowers are for the living."

"Yes," I said.

"And crocodiles," said she, "are for the dead."

III

For a long time I looked upon the innocent gayness and frivolity of Virginia with blinking eyes, as a person blinks at the sudden match lighted in the middle of the night. I had been pledged to darkness from my earliest years, and now, while my character, still happily plastic, was receiving its definite stamps, I blinked hankeringly at the light that I might have loved, and at the same time steeled myself to go through with the prearranged marriage. As in the Yankee States children are brought up to believe that it is wicked to be joyous on Sunday so I had been taught to believe of every twenty-four hours in the week.

I cannot think peacefully of that unhappy period in Virginia's life forced on her by us two moribunds. She was the sun, soaring in bright, beneficent career, brought suddenly to impotence by a London fog. And I take it that to be bright and happy, and to fail in making others so, is the most grievous chapter in life. But Virginia's glowing nature had its effect on mine, and in the end she set my spirits dancing. With my father, however, the effect of a madcap sunbeam in the house was altogether different. For it served only to plunge him deeper into gloom and regret. If we came to dinner with him fresh from the joyous morning and in love with laughter, the misery into which he was too palpably thrown reacted so that for all three of us the afternoon became clouded. Sometimes his sorrow would take the form of mocking at all things peaceful and pleasant. In particular the institution of marriage aroused in him hostility.

"Ay, marry," he would say, "Richard, and beget death. It may be hereditary in our family. Exchange your wife, who is your soul, for a red and puling inconsequence, that shall serve down the tiresome years to remind you day and night of the sunshine which has been extinguished for you."

And I remember once retorting on him sharply to the effect that if he threw me so constantly in my own face I would leave his roof, and in the intemperance of the moment I fully purposed to do so. "I will do no worse among strangers," I said, "or in hell, for that matter."

My father fairly shrivelled before the unfilial words, and retreated so pathetically from his foolish position that my attack melted clean away.

"But why," I said afterward to Virginia, "wouldn't he let me go? Why did he say that he could not live without me? And why, in God's name, when it was all over, did he cry?"

And Virginia thought for a few moments, which was unusual with her, and said presently: "Richard, either your father is the greatest lover that ever lived, or else he is a tiresome egomaniac. Frankly, I believe the latter. You are an accessory, a dismal carving on the mouldy frame in which he pictures himself. When I first came I used to tell him how terribly sorry I was that he had lost his wife. But I've given that up. Between you and me, it made him a little peevish. Now I say to him, 'Uncle Richard, you're the unhappiest man I ever saw,' and that comforts him tremendously. Sometimes he asks me if I really think so, and when I say that I do he almost smiles. And I have caught him, immediately after a scene like that, looking at himself in the mirror and pulling his face even longer than usual. . . . There, I've shocked you."

"No, Virginia," I said, "but I should hate to believe of any man what you believe of my father. His grief must be sincere."

"It may be," said Virginia, "or it may have been once. I believe it isn't now. I believe that if your mother came to life your father would—"

Virginia did not finish. We were seated in the cool hall, for the porch was piping hot, and our conversation was interrupted by a loud cry emanating from the library.

"Allah—Allah—Allah!"

"If I weren't charitable, which I am," said Virginia, "I would say that that was done for effect. He knows we're here. Bet you, he's looking at himself in the glass."

"Virginia," I began angrily, and I was for telling her that she was ill-natured, when the library door opened and my father came out.

"Oh!" said he, with a fine start, "I did not know you were there. . . ."

Virginia gave me one look, at once hurt and amused. Then she turned to my father and said gravely: "Did anything happen, Uncle Richard, when you called? Did you see the—the face—of—"

"No, child," said my father sadly. "I was so foolish, I may say undignified, as to try a childish and foolish experiment. It is unnecessary to say that the tall and stately form and classic face of Richard's dear mother did not appear to me. But I caught a glimpse of another face, Virginia—a face white and broken by sorrow and regret, a face that it was not pleasant to see. . . . How it all comes back to me," he went on. "Here I stood by her casket, ignorant of time and place—ignorant of all earthly things but loss—and for the last time looked upon her beauty. No, not for the last time,

> "'For all my daily trances
> And all my nightly dreams
> Are where thy bright eye glances
> And where thy footstep gleams.'

"Ay, child, but she was bonny! Was she not bonny, Richard?"

I do not know what prompted Virginia to ask the sudden question which turned my father's face for a moment into a painful blank, and placed him in a position from which he extricated himself, I am forced to believe, only by a real and searching act of memory.

"What was her name?" said Virginia quickly.

It was a full half minute before my father managed to stammer my mother's name. But during the ensuing days it was constantly on his lips, as if he wished to make up to it for the oblivion into which it had been allowed to drop.

That afternoon it rained violently, and Virginia persuaded me to explore with her the mysteries of the ancient and cobwebby attic which occupied the whole upper floor of our house. It was a place in whose slatted window-blinds sparrows built their nests, and in which a period, that of my mother's brief mistressship, had been perfectly preserved. It was the most cheerful part of the house.

Among other things we found in a trunk of old fashion my mother's wedding regalia. A dress of apple-green silk embroidered about the neck and wrists with tiny forget-me-nots, faded to the palest shade of lilac; a pair of tiny shoes of the same apple-green silk, with square toes and dark jade buttons; a veil of Venetian point, from which a large square had been cut, and the brittle remnants of a wreath—my mother's wedding wreath, which old Ann had often told me was combined of apple and orange flowers. When Virginia stood up and held the neck of my mother's dress level with the neck of her own it did not reach to her ankles, and she smiled at me.

"Richard," she said, "I could not get into this dress. Your tall and stately mother was no bigger than I."

"And no sweeter, I fancy," said I. For the being together with Virginia over my mother's things had suddenly opened my heart to her.

"Oh, Virginia," I went on, "it makes me sick to think of your living on in this dead house. I want you to be happy. I want to make you happy. You arez the only good thing that was ever in my life. I know it now. And I—I want to be happy, too. . . ."

We explored the attic no more that day, and after supper we told my father.

IV

From the very announcement to him of our engagement a marked change came over my father. Hitherto his influence had been for darkness, but of a silent and quiet character, like that which clouds spread through a wood at noon; but now he had become baleful and pointed in his efforts to make us unhappy.

To set in motion any machinery of escape was too impracticable and tedious to be thought of. Had I been for myself alone, I would have left him at this period and endeavored to support myself. But with Virginia to care for—and I could not leave her while I made my own way—the impulse was empty. He made attacks on our happiness with tongue and contrivance. He descended to raillery and sneers, even to coarseness. Yet when the confines of endurance had been approached too closely, and I threatened to cross them, he clung to me with such a seeming of feeling and patheticalness that I was forced to hold back. Through these harsh times Virginia was all sweetness and patience, but her cheeks lost their color and her body the delicious fulness of its lines.

My father was at times so eccentric in his behavior that I had it often in mind to ask the investigations of a physician. But as often the horror of a son prying after madness in his father withheld me. As always, his actions centred around the observance of his private grief. And to that great mental structure which he had made of my mother's beauties and virtues, he added incessantly wings and superstructures, until we had portrayed for us a woman in no way human or possible. To draw odious comparisons between Virginia and my mother, between his capacity for loving and my own, were his constant and indelicate exercises.

"Do you think you love, Richard?" he would say. "If she were to die this night, where would your love be at the end of the year? Is she bonny enough to hold a man's heart till death shall seek him out too? She's well enough in her way, your Virginia, I'll not deny that. But does a man remember what was only well enough? Does a man remember the first peach he ate? Nay, he will not remember that. But will he forget the first

194 GOUVERNEUR MORRIS

time that he heard Beethoven? Your mother, she was that—rich, strong music, she was—the bonny one—the unforgetable. Ah, the majesty of her, Richard, that was only for me to approach!"

And such like, till the heart sickened in you. Often he made us go with him to the vault and listen to his speeches, and kneel with him in the wet. Finally he played on us a trick that had in it something of the truly devilish, and was the beginning of the end. He began by insisting that we should be married and appointing a day. There was to be a minister, ourselves, and the servants. We were glad enough to be married, even on such scanty terms; and I well remember with what eagerness I arose on the glad morning, and slipped into my better suit of black, for I had no gayer clothes. Virginia did not come down to breakfast, but toward the close of that meal, at which my father was the nearest he ever came to being cheerful, I heard her calling to me from the upper story. When I knocked at her door she opened it a little and showed me a teary face. "Richard," she said, "they've taken away my clothes and left only a black dress. I *won't* be married in black."

"Does it matter, dear?" I said. "Put it on and we will ransack the attic for something gayer."

But we found the attic locked. My father had provided against resistance.

"Does it matter, dear?" I said. "It's not your clothes I'm marrying—it's my darling herself."

So she smiled bravely and we went downstairs. The ceremony was appointed for eleven in the morning. But at that hour neither the minister, nor my father, nor the servants were to be found. We waited until twelve. Then I went out to look for my father. I went first to the vault and there found him. He was kneeling in the wet, facing the door, and holding in his hands the stuffed crocodile. He had, I suppose, been calling the name of Allah in the wild hope of seeing my mother's face.

"Have you forgotten that we are to be married today?" I said.

He rose, hiding the crocodile beneath his coat.

"No," he said, "I had not forgotten that. Why should I be forgetting that? But the minister, he could not come—at the last minute he could not come."

"Then you should have told us," I said sternly.

"Would you be angry with me, Richard, my son?" he answered gently.

"Why couldn't the minister come?" I said, giving no heed to his question.

The gentleness, which must have been play-acting, went out of my father's voice.

"The minister," he said sneeringly: "faith, the minister, he had a more important funeral to attend."

My gorge rose and fell.

"What have you done with Virginia's trunk?" I said.

"It will be back in her room by now," said my father.

"Thank you," said I, "and good-day to you."

"Good-day, Richard? Good-day?"

"Yes," said I. "I am going to take her away."

"You'll not go far without money," said he.

"With heart," said I, "we shall go to the ends of the earth."

My father turned to the vault and addressed the shade of my mother. "Hear him," cried he, "hear him that took you from me. He's going to the ends of the earth. He turns his back upon your hallowed bones. . . ." His words became unintelligible.

🐏

During the packing of my trunk I left off again and again to go to Virginia's door to ask if all were well with her. For there had been a look in my father's face which haunted me like a hint of coming evil. And although nothing but good came of that afternoon, still its events were so strange as to make me believe that men are often forewarned of the unusual. It was about three o'clock that suddenly I heard my father shrieking aloud in his library. Thinking that sickness must have seized him, I bounded down the stairs to offer assistance or search for it if necessary. But except for a pallor unusual even with him, he was not apparently sick. The crocodile lay belly up on the table, as if it had been hastily laid down.

"What's the matter?" I asked.

"Richard," said my father, in great excitement, "the door of the vault is open. But now I heard it creaking upon its hinges—"

Virginia, who had heard the shrieks, now joined us, her face white with alarm.

"What is it?" she cried.

"The resurrection of the dead!" cried my father, and, thrusting my detaining arm suddenly aside, he literally burst out of the house. I followed at my best speed, and Virginia brought up the rear. In this order we raced through the woods, brightly mottled with sunshine and shadows, in the direction of the vault. Run as I would, I could not gain on my father, who seemed to possess the speed of a pestilence. As he ran he kept crying: "God is merciful! I shall see the face of my beloved."

I cannot account for what happened. A little lady, dressed in apple-green silk, with a wreath of flowers upon her head, appeared suddenly in the path, ahead of and facing my father. She held out her arms as if to detain him. But he bore down upon her at full speed, and I cried out to warn her. Then they met. But there was no visible or audible sign of collision. My father literally seemed to pass through her. He ran on, always at top speed, and the little lady in the apple-green silk was no longer to be seen in any direction. Yet she seemed to have left an influence in the bright forest, gentle and serene, and I could swear that there lingered in the air a faint smell of apple blossoms and orange blossoms. And it may be the echo of a cry of pain—the ghost of a cry.

When I came to the vault its door was wide open, and I found my father within, breaking with his thin hands the lid from my mother's coffin. I was not in time to prevent him from completing his mad outrage. The lid came clean away with a ripping noise, and my father gazed eagerly at the face thus rudely revealed to the light of day. But what horrible alchemy of the grave had brought into shape the face upon which my father looked so eagerly is not for mortal man to know. For the face was not my mother's, but his own.

Gently he laid his hand on the forehead, and gently he said: "Was she not bonny, Richard? . . . Was she not bonny?"

V

Our honeymoon was nearly a week old, when one morning Virginia and I were taking breakfast in the glass dining-room of the old Hygeia Hotel. The waiters, the other guests, the cups, saucers, knives, and spoons all made eyes at us, but we were wonderfully happy. An old gentleman approached our table with a kind of a sad tiptoe gait. Tears were in his eyes.

"My dear boy," he said, "I have not the heart to congratulate you on your happiness, for I cannot help remembering what a good father you have so recently lost. I was present at his wedding, and I have not seen him since. But as you see—" and the old gentleman drew attention to the tears in his eyes.

"Aren't you mistaken, sir?" said I. "Aren't you thinking of somebody else's father?"

"Why, no," said he, "your father was —— ——. Don't tell me he wasn't."

"I shall have to," I said, "for he wasn't. My father was a crocodile."

The Footprint

I. BETWEEN TWO BAYS

We were waiting for the tide to ebb before resuming work on the schooner's bottom. There was nothing the matter with her planks; but she had become so foul by months of cruising in the warm, fertile waters of the Gulf of California that she could not come about in anything less than a whole-sail breeze. From the water-line down she had grown a yard-long beard of sea-greens that must have weighed several tons. This growth, teeming with marine life—diminutive abalones, crabs, spiders, baby squids, and enormous barnacles that looked like extinct volcanoes filled with marrow—made the work of cleaning her difficult and repulsive. With the least exposure to the tropic sun she stank like a rotten fish; the weeds clung to her planks as hair clings to the head, and we were forever slicing our hands and forearms on the barnacles. We had warped her into one of two small shallow bays, divided from each other by a high promontory of drifted sand; and as the tide receded, and left her drying and stinking, we worked against time and a slender larder to get her clean. When the unfinished work had been covered by the rising tide, and further barbering become impossible, we would retire to the sands that divided the two bays, to grumble and to smoke.

The sand of which the promontory was composed, though dry as dust, had a kind of inherent cohesiveness that caused it to maintain itself in hillocks and pinnacles and curious monumental forms, among which it was possible to find shade. Our favorite place to smoke and grumble was a hollow, round like a bird's nest, with one beetling elevation of sand to the west of it and another to the east. Except at high noon there was always shade in the hollow, and sometimes a kind of draught (less

199

than the least breeze) was imagined to pass over it. Looking south or north from this nest the views were very much the same, except that in the foreground, or forewater of the south exposure, was the grounded schooner and the schooner's boat moored to the beach by a staked oar. To the eyes of instruments there may have been a calculable difference between the two bays of which we had the prospect, but to the human eye there was none; nor was there between the white desert shores, blotched with pale-blue shadows, that semicircled them. The two bays were like the upper-half of a vast pair of blue spectacles, of which the promontory dividing them was the nosepiece; the semicircling beaches, the silver rims; the blue shadows, tarnishes. It was a prospect with which one soon sickened and soon grew angry. Of vegetation there was not so much as one dead stem.

During our periods of enforced idleness the prevailing atmosphere was one of pessimism. Our expedition had been a failure from the beginning. We were even ashamed to recall what we had once conceived to be its purpose. We said only: "Let us once get back to San Francisco and somebody will smart for his smartness." We had long since consigned the map, with its alluring directions in red ink, its infinity of plausible detail, and its general and particular verisimilitude, to the reddest devils of the deep sea. "Let Arundel get the rubies himself," we said. "Rubies—hell!"

There were five of us: four young fools, Crisp, Hawes, Meff and myself, and Morgridge, who was an old fool. We formed, together with Arundel, sick in a San Francisco hospital with tuberculosis of the bone (and lucky to be so well off, we thought), a stock company with a jointly paid-in capital of twenty-five hundred dollars. The company had paid Arundel two hundred dollars for his map, chartered the schooner (renamed her the *Ruby*), found her in water, provisions, and firearms, and, with Morgridge in command, set sail for the Gulf of California.

Arrived without mishap in those sharky, blistering waters, we cruised week after week, month after month, seeking the key to Arundel's map. "I can only tell you," he had said, "that there are two bays, very much alike, separated by high sand-dunes. The bay to the north is marked, where it bites deepest into the desert, by a kind of granite monolith that you can see for miles. It must be fifty feet high, and looks like an obelisk in the making. The trail starts a little to the north of this, and then you can apply the map, and it will tell you more than I can."

We happened to be seated, grumbling and smoking, between two such bays as Arundel had described. But they were not the first pair we had found, nor the second. The whole coast was pitted with semicircular bays, and it had been no great trick to discover pair after pair as like as the eyes in a man's head. The trick was to find one single, solitary needle of granite. And in that we had dismally failed. Indeed, in the course of a hundred landings at various points we had not found so much as one pebble bigger than a robin's egg. There was nothing but sand; there wasn't even sandstone. The only big, hard things were abalone shells that had been washed ashore. To have continued so long to hunt for a granite monolith in a region which emphatically denied the possibility of its containing one was a reflection upon the intelligence of all concerned.

Morgridge, who was near-sighted and never without his binoculars, lay on his belly and elbows, listlessly following the gambols of a porpoise-school in the waters of the northern bay. He remarked that the sight cooled him. Meff, with his eye on the tide, said that he was sorry to say we could get back to work in about twenty minutes; Hawes and Crisp were quarrelling desultorily over a game of piquet, in which was involved the filthiest, most dog's-eared pack of cards I ever saw. "I *said* you had point," said Crisp; "shut up and go on." "Tierce to the king, twice," said Hawes, not with any great hope. "You saw the discard," said Crisp, "I only took one card; you *must* know that I've got the knave quint in diamonds. It's awfully damn dull playing with you. I have to tell you everything." "Yes, you're the whole show," said Hawes. "Everybody knows that." The voices of the two, if sarcastic, were listless, and neither seemed capable of raising more than a shadow of resentment in the other. "Lead, fool," said Hawes quietly. "Twenty-one, Pinhead," retorted Crisp, and he led with the king of spades.

"Boys," said Morgridge suddenly, " there's a junk heading into the bay."

II. THE MAN WITH THE YELLOW UMBRELLA

The waters of the Gulf of California are rarely sailed; the shores more rarely tramped. Of the region's shadows not one is cast by the hand of the law. Diogenes would find there no honest face in which to shine his lantern. There men with itching palms, and pasts that clamor of unsuccess, voyage now and then in ill-formed craft, drawn by rumors. To some the inland mountains have yielded metals; now and then a lucky crew are enticed along a wake of ambrosial sweetness, to find in the waters a lump of ambergris that floats in the rainbow colors of its self-exuded oil, and is more precious than gold. From beneath the waters now and then are fished up bright and heavy pearls, orient, and abalone. But of the crews that go there is one that comes back with treasure, the mother of rumors, there are two that come back with nothing but scurvy, and there are seven that do not come back at all.

Only Chinamen, light of appetite and clean to the last nail, can long endure the climate, and only the Chinese expeditions strike an average of success. But in those unpoliced waters a junk of Chinamen is a thing for white men to avoid. It is a devil, sea-buffeting, and, before the wind, swift. It is filled with cheap lives, it is full of greed, full of rifles, and formidable in patience and surprise.

That the crew of the junk now rounding the northern horn of the northern bay, perhaps a half-mile distant, would not soon discover us among the shadows and hollows of the dunes, was probable; and, of course, the schooner was completely screened from the most alert eye by the whole mass of the promontory which divided one bay from the other. But it was also probable that in the course of time the junk would round that screen and become unpreventably interested in our private affairs: interested surely, and perhaps involved. For if the junk's captain thought that we had anything that he wanted, he would try to take it. But not at once.

There would pass between the junk and the schooner very ceremonious and courteous greetings, and the junk would lumber away as if intent upon some far-off destiny. But she would not go very far; just out of sight around the next corner, and she would come back; not the same night, when all of us would be watching, nor the night after, when half of us would be still nervous enough to keep awake, but later by several nights, and at her own well-chosen and sudden time. She had a crew, probably of at least twenty-five, with a rifle, knife, and revolver apiece; she had a little machine-gun, probably. Surely she had no morals.

To the naked eye the junk presented little but a color scheme, and it needed a turn at the binoculars to see faces and details. The color scheme, like that of all junks, was a sincere if misguided effort to achieve the beautiful. Her body was painted indigo blue; the square sail by which she was drawn slowly into the bay was pure vermilion. And aft some one had spread, to keep off the sun, a bright yellow umbrella.

From a brazier in the bow of the junk rose a tottering thread of bluish smoke, and beside the brazier (all this through the glass) stood a lofty Chinaman. He was nearly naked, and absolutely expressionless; a splendidly moulded, utterly lifeless statue of brownish-yellow clay. An enormous brass cymbal dangled by a thong from each of his wrists. The inanimate cymbals were the only things about him that moved. Amidships was a circle of half-naked men, squatting, gesticulating, and articulating, who seemed intent upon something in their midst. We hazarded that it was a game of fan-tan. In the stern, only a little less statuesque (because of more drapery) than the man in the bow, stood the helmsman, his hands clasped about the grip of a twelve-foot indigo oar, whose blade, half immersed, followed in the junk's wake like the dorsal fin of a shark. A little in front, and to one side of the helmsman, was spread the yellow umbrella. Under it was seated, cross-legged, a Chinaman, mountainous with robes and fat. He was more than a detail and, except for his umbrella, less than a complete tone of the junk's color scheme. His voluminous robes, mauvely and greenly brocaded with indistinguishable patterns, were of the richest and darkest blue imaginable. He exuded an atmosphere of riches. You knew at once that he was many times a millionaire. You knew, too, that he had lived well, and revolved among pleasant episodes and people. There was an expression upon his face that I have never before seen upon the face of an Oriental—jollity. Through the glass we could see that from time to time he smiled, a broad appreciative smile, begotten doubtless of some sudden, transient thought. And whenever he smiled he twirled the handle of the yellow umbrella with his fat fingers. On his head was a little blue cap terminated by a large green button. Occasionally he fanned himself with a little round fan.

The junk's course was a long curve, parallel to that of the shore, and as close to it as the shelving nature of the beach would safely allow. As she was steered more and more to the starboard her big vermilion sail began to shut off our view of the stern and to cast its shadow over the fan-tan players. The helmsman and the man with the yellow umbrella disappeared, and as the junk veered more and more a funny fat little vermilion dinghy came into sight, trailed by a rope off her port quarter. The breeze had now sunk to a series of mild, unconnected puffs, and the junk's progress was very slow. She had covered half of the bay's curve, and was distant from us perhaps a quarter of a mile, when suddenly the man in the bow raised his cymbals and brought them together. As the cymbals separated for a second stroke, the clanging, brassy crash of the first concussion reached our ears; and with it a chorus of piercing minor falsetto notes from the fan-tan players, who had risen to their feet.

The junk swung more and more, and the yellow umbrella began to detach itself from the lower port corner of the vermilion sail. Two men ran forward to the anchor, and as the junk came into the wind and to the end of her momentum let it go with a fine splash. The junk's stern now faced the shore, and the man with the yellow umbrella rose and waddled to the rail. The little round fan disappeared up one of his voluminous sleeves, and from the same receptacle he drew what appeared to be a double-ended purse, well filled. This he flung into the water—a golden sacrifice, we learned later, to the gods who had given him leave to pass across their sea. Then he waddled forward, and, seating himself on the rail, swung his legs and the skirt of his robe outboard, dropped heavily into the dinghy, and precipitately seated himself. He was followed by the junk's helmsman, who, having cast loose, dipped with a long paddle, and directed the overladen craft toward the shore. The clashing of the cymbals and the chorus of falsetto wails, which had never ceased, now redoubled in ardor and tempo, and as suddenly stopped,when the dinghy bumped against the beach, and the man with the yellow umbrella clambered heavily over her bow and stood upon the shore.

He turned and watched the greatly lightened dinghy as she returned, powerfully driven, to the junk, and was swung aboard. He stood, a rotund, mauve, and blue glory under his yellow umbrella, and watched the lowering of the junk's sail. He did not move a muscle, only when the junk's anchor was raised and she, under the impulse of long sweeps that appeared mysteriously from her sides, began to crawl forward like a huge blue spider with legs, and turning to return upon her course, he produced his little round fan and fanned himself. But until the junk disappeared behind the northern horn of the bay he did not make any other motion, or take his eyes from her.

Then, however, he pivoted heavily and, waddling in a slow but determined manner, crossed the beach, his gorgeous brocades blazing and sparkling in the sun as their folds and surfaces shifted and rippled with his motion, and his right hand working the little round fan, and his left supporting the yellow umbrella, he began to mount, slow and determined, the tumbling desert dunes of sand that stood behind the beach. Up these and into them bobbed the yellow umbrella until, after one last bobbing, it disappeared from view.

"I'm going to find out where he's going," said Morgridge.

We fetched our rifles from the schooner and, reclimbing the promontory, in a body descended to the beach on the other side, and followed it to the point where its smooth surface was broken at right angles by the deeply marked footprints of the fat Chinaman.

III. RENEWED FAITH

We followed the track up into the dunes, with Morgridge leading by twenty feet and Hawes bringing up the rear. Meff and I, making jocular efforts to burrow aids to ascending locomotion from each other, "scrapped" along in the middle. I had hooked a surreptitious finger into Meff's belt, and thereby lightened myself during one entire step, when (it was just as Meff secured his release by planting an elbow in the pit of my stomach) suddenly Morgridge, who had reached to the higher levels of the dunes, ejaculated sharply and sprang out of sight. We scrambled briskly, all four of us, to be in the know, and found him, his thumbs in his armpits, a smile on his face (a jocosely assumed attitude of low comedy), and his right foot planted high upon the curve of a gigantic weather-worn pillar of granite that lay in and out of the sand.

"Morgridge," said he, "that great leader in the act of discovering Arundel's landmark, and proving to a sceptical world that Arundel was not a liar. My God! boys," he cried, his expression shifting from one of low comedy to one of uncontainable greed and excitement. "My God! boys, we've as good as got 'em."

"The damn thing," said Crisp, "has fallen down, and that's why we couldn't see it. Kick it; somebody with stout shoes."

"Don't kick it," said Meff, "it's a good landmark to get itself found." He stooped and patted the monolith as one pats a good dog.

"Now this is where it stood," said Morgridge, "and Arundel's map says the course is due east from the pedestal."

"Direction due east," said Hawes, "and distance forty miles."

Attached to my watch-guard was a very accurate little compass set in striped tiger's eyes, a boyhood relic from Petoskey, Michigan. I looked from this to the tracks made by the fat Chinaman, and found that, having approached the fallen monolith from a little south of west, he had, on reaching its former base, veered a little and pointed his steps due east. Running my eyes along the line indicated, I had presently a glimpse, very far off, of the yellow umbrella bobbing deeper and deeper into the arid, scorching desert.

"Surely," I said, "our fat friend is going where we are going, but he won't do any forty miles in one clip. There must be stopping-places that Arundel missed."

"I believe you," said Morgridge. "We've only to follow the yellow umbrella."

"And when night comes?" objected Crisp.

"Stars," said Hawes, "stars enough to find *this* trail."

We laughed, because the very depth of the fat Chinaman's footprints recalled his humorous rotundity and the waddling, self-satisfied dignity of his gait.

"He will know where to find food and water," said Morgridge.

"Seriously, though," said Meff, "is it possible that he should really be entering upon a forty-mile walk in this heat—at his size?"

"Come along," said Morgridge.

"His food shall be my food," said Meff; "where he rests will I rest, his drink shall be my drink, and his rubies—"

"Shall be divided by lot," said Crisp.

We took up the trail, floundering heavily, and making slow way of it. We were unused to walking; the atmosphere at the surface of the desert fumed and gyrated in the heat. The sun, now west of the zenith, lay upon the back like a garment of fire. Our sweat laved the unfertile sand. We had not, after the first quarter of a mile, a single joke or happy thought left among us.

At first we gained upon the yellow umbrella, and had the fat Chinaman looked over his shoulder there were times when he must have seen us; but he was intent upon his journey, and waddled eastward at a rate which was unpleasant to equal, and so difficult to exceed that we were soon content not to.

He preceded us by half a mile; in that atmosphere it had the effect of less; and he never swerved from his course, nor glanced to the right or the left. If my sweat-stung eyes had been keen for beauty, I should have admired inordinately the gorgeousness of color made against the silver desert by the blue robes and yellow umbrella of our celestial friend. But I was beneath admiring, and noticed only, and I do not know why, that, as the sun descended lower from the zenith, the umbrella was tilted further and further to interrupt its scorching rays, so that first the Chinaman's head disappeared behind its lower rim, then his shoulders, and then his trunk to the waist.

Thus passed a number of hours, but not the limits of that fat Chinaman's endurance and patience. Momentarily I expected to see the yellow umbrella turn to right or left and halt at some cache of water and food. But we were destined to enjoy no such blessed nepenthe that day.

Serenely and indomitably bobbed the yellow umbrella, carrying its oval of shadow over innumerable desert miles. From a slender crescent it became a full orbit that flamed in the rays of the setting sun.

"We must get nearer before dark," said Morgridge, and he set up a herculean example of progress. But the fat Chinaman, whom we had laughed at for his labored waddling, began now to stand in our jaded minds for the very acme and poetry of motion. By dusk we respected him; but by dark, though we had gained a quarter of a mile and wished ourselves dead, we pronounced him, petticoats and fat considered, the most wonderful walker that the world had ever known.

At dark he lowered his umbrella, and for a time we lost sight of him. But as the stars brightened we could follow his deep steps, and had presently a sight of him, his robes silvery in the starlight, and perceived that he had faced about and was coming toward us.

Breathing quickly, but utterly fearless, he waddled into our midst.

"I come all the way back," he said, "to say I go altogether forty miles without no stop. I think it very fine courteous action to take all this trouble for strange gentlemen. You like to come all the way, I say nothing, none of my damn business. Only stop to tell you very far away, all the way nasty sand. I very fine rich China merchant, and know how to give very fine courteous advices. You rest little while and go back. I go on now, and wish you very fine pleasant evening and return journey."

He turned and waddled away.

"Hold on," said Morgridge, "we're going with you."

The fat Chinaman paused and considered.

"Very well," he said, "we all travel together, more or less pleasant way to travel. Only I very clever, experienced fine traveller, and not put up with no complaints and damn swearing—Like pleasant conversation and all good friends. We go along two miles in an hour, and by and by finish journey. You walk along by me"—he pointed to me with his fat finger. "You got very fine respectable face."

"My friends," I said with a bow, "have not had my advantages."

"Rascals?" asked the fat Chinaman. "Introduce their names."

I presented the four, and said my own name.

"My name Sang Ti—very fine, revered, damn name," said the merchant. "But like fine poet says of time, 'she flies.'"

I walked forward beside him, not knowing whether to laugh at the jovial absurdity of the gentleman who had given me a character, or to cry because his indefatigable waddle was so hard to breast.

"You sweat much?" he asked in a friendly, interested tone.

IV. SANG TI

"Do you often go where you are going?" I asked.

"Go now for first time," said Sang Ti. "Chen Chan very fine old sacred holy place to end days in."

"You don't expect to end your days at Ch—Chen—Chan?" I asked. "Do you?"

"Oh, yes, before long. You see, I am dedicate from little boy to the High Gods. I am requested to have very fine high successful happy life, through intercession of parents and promises to the High Gods. All is accomplish. I go high up; lead a very fine benevolent life; accumulate very large fortune; do everything just right; and now must pay up promises made for me to the High Gods by parents."

The moon had risen, and the desert was as if flooded with quicksilver and ink. Sang Ti turned his fat, jolly face, beaded with sweat, and beamed at me. He thrust a hand under the silk cord that girdled him at the waist.

"On forty-fifth day of birth," he said, "I hand over this cord to priest of the High Gods; and he hand over to me to hold the ruby box and holy shark tooth; and I think a little while of the insignificance of life, and am soon strangled by priest. Then I have paid up."

"Do you mean to say," I exclaimed, "that you are taking all this trouble to get yourself strangled?"

"The promises of parents," said he, "now dead, is very fine holy sort of thing, not to be broken. I will arrange to have you and your friends see the strangling. It will be very interesting, dignified occurrence."

Though Sang Ti enjoyed, for a Chinaman, a very large command of the English language, I was concluding that he either could not possibly know what he was talking about, or that he was making an elaborate effort to "string" me, when, with the tail of my eye, I caught him in the act of feeling his throat, very tenderly, with a fat thumb and forefinger. His face for the moment wore an expression of wonder mixed with panic. But in a moment it passed, and with a sudden laugh he lowered his hand.

"You are considering me very practical joker," he said, "but I give you very honest man's word that being strangled at forty-five is very damn miserable joke. I am, however, a very fine philosopher."

"What's the holy shark tooth?" I asked.

"Him not too good to touch," said Sang Ti. "He take care of ruby box."

We labored on in silence, and the moon sailed higher and higher in the heavens. A faint, hot breeze arose and blew in our faces.

"The night," said Sang Ti, "is a Nubian empress; her robes are sewed with diamonds; the moon is a gong of silver; the sand is the ashes of broken words."

"Are you making that up, or translating?" I asked.

"The wind," he said, "is some very fine high god sighing. I fancy Liang Tsang."

"Who is he?"

"Liang Tsang a yellow elephant by daylight, but by night-time a very potent, strong god that blows around the world. He a breeze when he sigh, and a wind when he groan."

"Isn't he happy?" I asked. "Why does he sigh and groan?"

"Because he an exile. He can blow everywhere but not over China. But when the end of the world approaches it is promised him that for one day in the spring of year he shall be a violet, with roots in fertile soil of Shan-tung. It a saying of us, 'Keep your promises, for the day approaches when Liang Tsang shall be a violet in the fields of Shan-tung, and the perverted shall be divided among a thousand thousand hells.'"

"Does your creed embrace so many hells?" I asked.

"Oh, yes," he said simply, "or what could be done with all Caucasian and European races? In Chinaman's creed there is very satisfactory place provided for everybody."

"The policy of the open door?" I suggested.

"Open to go in," he said, "and shut to go out."

I looked over my shoulder and saw that our company had begun to straggle badly. Only Meff and Morgridge were in easy speaking distance; Crisp was two hundred yards behind them, and another hundred yards separated Hawes and Crisp. As I looked, Morgridge called to me to stop.

He came up, followed by Meff, exhausted, angry, and completely blown.

"This not a proper time to stop," said Sang Ti. "I tell you before, too long a walk for you gentlemen. I see at once you not well bred for travelling. With me it very different matter. I come of very fine old stock; I am descended in straight recorded line from a camel and a shark. Must get a long way before morning; cooler now."

"We'll halt now," said Morgridge in an arrant, angry, bullying voice. "See?"

"I got no time," said Sang Ti. "You not able to come, I go alone, wishing you first very pleasant halt and subsequent journey."

"No you don't," said Morgridge, "you don't lose this crowd—not in this desert. You'll rest, yourself, till we're ready to go on."

Sang Ti stood his umbrella into the sand, and turned back the borders of his sleeves.

"You," he said to Morgridge, "are very uncivil, lazy, selfish damn rascal, and you, too."

He stood between Morgridge and Meff, looking quickly from one to the other.

"You interfere with Chinese gentleman, he teach you more respectable damn manners." So saying, and just as Crisp was coming up, he seized Morgridge and Meff by the backs of their necks and began to knock their heads together. He finished the lesson of courtesy by suddenly jerking in opposite directions and letting go. Meff fell in his tracks, but Morgridge, dropping his rifle, staggered for a long distance before he came to ground.

With a silvery laugh Sang Ti regained his umbrella and waddled away.

"I'll kill the dog," yelled Morgridge, springing with blazing eyes for the rifle which had been shaken from his hand.

"No," said Crisp. And as Morgridge sprang for the rifle he hooked his foot and threw him heavily. Then he sat on him.

Morgridge, with all the strength thrashed and pressed out of him, could only wriggle and swear obscurely in a whining voice. He was on the verge of tears.

I am far from suspecting Sang Ti of the fear of death, but he reserved to himself the choice of its manner, and had dropped in conversation the hint that he was very earnest to be strangled. Anyway, though the desert was flooded with light from the setting moon, he disappeared from view in a wonderfully short time; and we (who were five fools) slept in our tracks while the night waned, and woke to see the dawn stream up behind the eastern rim of the desert like a conflagration.

I shall not soon forget the horrible march that then began, straight into the molten furnace eye of the sun. Whatever of moisture was in us was sucked out through the pores of our scorching hides and turned into dust.

We felt ourselves grow light. All the constituents which had made human beings of us began to diminish except two: pain swelled in our brains, and in our mouths, our tongues. The heat that we had endured on the coast was temperate compared to the blasts of that inland desert.

We would have laid down and died, or some of us would (Meff was forever suggesting it) if very early in the morning we had not been led by the Chinaman's tracks to the top of a long rise, from which could be seen, far in the distance, what looked like purple feathers stuck into the sand on the further length of a piece of broken mirror, and which we knew to be trees growing by a lake. Indeed, specks of scarlet gleamed among the feathers, and we guessed that they were roofs upon the habitations of men.

Forward we went, and downward for an hour, and then upward, until once more we could see the trees and the lake and the roofs. But they seemed no nearer than before. And all day it was so.

We began what was to be our last long ascent. During it the sun sank so low that our shadows reached the top an hour before our bodies. But the trees then and the lake had been drawn wonderfully nearer.

At our feet was spread the lake, shaped roughly like a vast human foot, and beyond it among the trees we could see pagoda-shaped buildings and, going and coming, long-robed Chinamen, and little children and dogs. We could hear the dogs. And as the dusk deepened, braziers began to twinkle palely here and there. It was dark when we reached the lake, and, casting aside our weapons and watches, plunged into it, and felt the water rush in through our pores and begin to rebuild our wasted tissues and make rounded men of us once more. After a while, chin-deep immersed in deliciousness, with the rapture of hooked fish that have been returned to their element, we began to drink.

V. CHEN CHAN

We walked, dripping, around the end of the lake, and in close order, with weapons handy, for we did not know what reception to expect, passed down an avenue of ragged travellers' palms, and reached the first house of the single-streeted settlement. In the doorway of the house, smoking a long thick-stemmed pipe, sat Sang Ti. The water still running from our clothes, we drew up before him.

"Everybody gone to bed except me," was his greeting. "I of opinion that life too short now for sleep. Now suppose you look about a bit, and go back home. Priest say this very unhealthy place for white men. Only other white visitor name Arundel; some low damn thieving rascal. Priest say, if you come up, to say better go way again."

"How many people live here?" asked Morgridge in a voice which he strove to make civil.

"Maybe about thirty," said Sang Ti.

"Thirty men?" I asked.

"Oh, no," he said, "all kinds."

"You see," I said, "we couldn't go back right off. We couldn't walk a mile more to save our souls. We'll have to rest a bit."

"Priest not like that," said Sang Ti; "but never mind. Suppose all stay except that old rascal." He indicated Morgridge with his pipe stem.

"I guess we'll all stay," said Crisp firmly.

"All that contrary to rules," objected Sang Ti. "But all same contrary to rules to use force; so what can do? Why you come, anyhow? Maybe you come to steal very fine High God's ruby box?"

His eyes twinkled from one guilt-confessing face to the next, and he chuckled.

"Suppose, yes," he said, "and suppose you make off with ruby box, and suppose you go a little way and that uncivil rascal"—again he pointed to Morgridge—"feel sudden pain and die, and then that man—"

"My name is Crisp," said Crisp.

"Suppose then that man Crisp feel sudden pain and die, and so on, You think not very nice? Ruby box have live in Chen Chan for maybe two, thousand years. Chen Chan oldest settlement in America. Very High God Liang Tsang cross desert one time, and have to put foot down once. That make very fine lake. All same time he drop ruby box and holy shark's tooth, and pretty soon he cross ocean, and see junk of China fishermen. And he blow into junk's sail, and she go ashore and break to pieces; and all the China fishermen and wives crosses desert, and stops at lake and builds temple for ruby box and shark's tooth, and then makes one man priest, and builds little holy village and call her Chen Chan. That mean in English 'The Footprint.'"

"Do many people come here?" I asked.

"Arundel," said he, "and he get away. That because he drop ruby box. Others have come never get away. First come Mexicans, five hundred years ago; then some Spanish men, and then Arundel, and then you. And I tell you better go back, and leave very High Holy God's ruby box alone."

"Could we go to-morrow?" I asked. "We've got to have food and rest."

"Well, suppose you stop in house"—he pointed into the dark doorway—"and not disturb meditation any longer. Maybe you find some food," he went on. "And by and by, in the morning, you go away."

"Couldn't we wait till night?" I asked. "It's cooler going at night."

"I tell you," he said, "you wait till after strangulation, which takes place ten o'clock sharp. Then you go."

"If you are going to be strangled to-morrow," I said, "you are the calmest-minded man in this world."

"Between you and me," he said, "I think one very damn miserable business; but parents make promise, and what can do?"

He made himself as small as he could in the doorway, so that we could squeeze past him into the dark house. It had but one room; and by good luck and much feeling we found in one corner a vast bowl of cold-boiled rice. Crisp dragged it into the middle of the room, and, dipping with our hands, we gorged ourselves, and one by one toppled over and slept.

I was wakened by Crisp. It was broad daylight.

"What," said Crisp, "is all this talk about strangling? Is he using a word that he thinks means something else? I've been having dreams about it all night."

"The whole thing's like a dream," I said; "but I believe, as I believe in—well, in hell—that Sang Ti expects to be put to death this morning. What time is it?"

"Nine o'clock," said Crisp. We waked the others, and among us finished the boiled rice. We had scarcely done so when, from outside, came suddenly the sound of persistent pounding on a brass gong.

We crowded out of the house to find the twenty-five or thirty inhabitants of the village—men, women, and children—in a group in the street, intent upon something that was approaching from its further end. We stood aloof from the little crowd, who, if they were aware of our presence, gave no sign, and craned our necks, to see what was coming.

It was Sang Ti, waddling along under his yellow umbrella and fanning himself. Behind him followed an emaciated Chinaman in flowing gray silk. It was the latter who was pounding on the gong.

As the procession passed the inhabitants of the village, all the inhabitants turned as if on one pivot to follow it. And a moment later our beads turned in the same way.

Sang Ti, with a jolly, contented expression, and looking neither to the right nor the left, having reached a point a little beyond where we were standing, turned and came back, always followed by the man in gray with the persistently pounded gong. This passage of the two up and down the village street was repeated many times without variation. But it was not till the third trip that we noticed anything further about the man in gray. Then we noticed, all of us at the same moment, that his little green cap suddenly loosened about his head, rose, perhaps half an inch, made a fraction of a revolution, and settled back.

Hitherto the procession had struck me as grotesque if not precisely humorous, believing, as I did, that Sang Ti's contented expression was muscular and not mental, but the sudden moving, without apparent agency, of the green cap, was horrible. It gave me the idea, I do not know why, that the cap concealed something that was alive and unclean.

The procession and the gong-beating was continued until nearly ten o'clock. Then, as Sang Ti made his usual turn just below where we were standing, the gong ceased and was followed by a silence peculiarly accented. Sang Ti passed up the street, followed by the man in gray, whose cap suddenly moved again, and by the whole population of the village, even the chow dogs.

And we, as unnoticed as if we had been invisible, made haste to follow in the wake.

The yellow umbrella halted in front of a dark-red pagoda of stained and carved wood. Sang Ti furled it and thrust it, point down, into the sand at one side of the steps that led into the pagoda. Then he passed through the door, and we could see, as the steps elevated him, that with his hands he was unfastening the silk cord which girdled his waist.

Inside the pagoda, or temple, there was not much light. We found ourselves in a high-ceilinged red room about forty by thirty. At the upper end, on a high granite pedestal, sat a hideous bronze god, blurred by smoke which rose from a blue-and-white bowl on his knees. Against the walls of the place were ranged long poles of polished teak, finished at their tops with enormous images, scroll-sawed out of shining brass; masks, roosters, turtles, scorpions, dragons, and strange fruits.

Immediately in front of the pedestalled god, and facing us, sat Sang Ti in a vast teakwood chair. He continued to wear his jolly, contented expression, but allowed his eyes to rest on no one.

The chair in which he sat had the central panel of its back prolonged, so that its top extended several inches above his head and projected on either side. This back piece was pierced to the top with two series of holes, each about an inch in diameter, parallel to each other and perhaps six inches apart. It looked like an enormous cribbage board.

Sang Ti handed his silk cord to the man in gray, and the latter, thrusting its ends through two convenient and opposite holes, and stepping behind the chair, drew them until the half loop of the cord lay loosely across Sang Ti's throat.

Then he knotted the loose ends, and, producing in some sleight-of-hand manner a golden casket incrusted with rubies of all qualities, from pigeon blood to pale pink, placed it in Sang Ti's hands. Sang Ti lowered his eyes and examined the casket. A very slight shiver passed through his fat frame, and he shifted his feet uneasily.

The priest now thrust under the knot at the back of the loop a long, heavy rod of stained ivory, and gave it a quick twist from left to right. The loose loop became tight across Sang Ti's throat, and at a second twist half disappeared in his flesh.

A horrid choking noise was forced from his half-open mouth, and he shot at me a sudden look of heart-breaking appeal that brought my rifle to my shoulder.

But I was not so quick as Morgridge. In that confined place the crack of his rifle was like the detonation of a small cannon. The place filled with smoke and the sound of scurrying feet.

We gathered about Sang Ti when the smoke enveloping him had lifted, and found that the bullet meant for the strangler had been aimed too low. The top of Sang Ti's skull was split down the middle, and only the loosened cords kept him from failing forward. But the bullet, nevertheless, had done its appointed work, for the priest lay behind the chair, shot through the diaphragm, and a great red stain was spreading over the front of his gray robes.

And now a very horrid thing happened. From under the priest's cap, loosened by the fall, crawled a little dust-colored snake with a venomous head, and ran at Morgridge. Morgridge struck at the reptile with the butt of his rifle, but not quickly enough. He screamed as its fang pierced his boot, and fell to the floor as if struck by a thunderbolt.

The snake, turning, darted for the pedestal on which the god sat, but not in time wholly to escape the butt of Crisp's rifle. Dragging a broken tail it disappeared into a crack between the pedestal and the floor.

We looked at Morgridge. He was purple, horrible. He might have been dead for a week. Then we ran—God, how we ran—through the village and out into the desert. We ran until Meff began to call from far in the rear that he could run no more. We waited till he came up, and hated him for delaying us. But when we found that even in the first burst of panic he had had the presence of mind to snatch the ruby box, we began to praise him and clap him on the back.

We passed it from hand to hand and wondered what the rubies would bring.

"I think Arundel overrated them," I said.

"Yes," said Meff. "But aren't some of them corkers? Look at that fellow."

"The light-pink ones," said Hawes, "aren't worth much more than glass."

"It ought to bring fifty thousand," I said. "See what's inside."

Hawes found the catch, and, as he raised the lid, suddenly screamed and flung the box high into the air. Over and over it turned, and there whirled free from it a little snake, and the two fell at a distance from each other. But the fate of that snake was sudden; turn and dart as he would, bullet after bullet grazed him and toss him on spurts of sand. He was torn to pieces in five seconds, and we turned to Hawes. He had found the time to thrust his bitten finger into his mouth, and that was all. He was dead as a stone.

VI. CRISP AND MEFF

The first impulse of us three survivors was once more to bolt. But where, or to what purpose? About and about were the scorching undulations of desert. Behind the ill-omened visage of Chen Chan, where death lurked under men's caps and in the reliquaries of their gods. Ahead, but so far that it could not be reached by any sudden panic-born effort, lay the ocean and escape. If we were to get away at all it could only be by slow-sustained exertion, directed by the quiet mind. I think Meff was the first to realize this.

"I think," he said, "that we had better rest for a few minutes."

"We ought to bury poor Hawes," said Crisp. But one glance at the violet bloated corpse was enough. No man with a stomach could have handled it. There was left upon it no trace of a comrade through many vicissitudes. Personality, that so often lingers after death and so long resists the chemistry of the grave, was gone from it, and had left nothing of the friend. The eyes were repelled, and the muscles, that might have scraped a hollow in the sands, were turned to water.

The ruby casket lay at a distance. Meff caught it up (not before a cautious examination with the muzzle of his rifle), and we did not sit down to rest until we had placed a long undulation of the desert between us and the corpse of Hawes.

Our situation called for discussion. Whether to strike circuitously for the broad track which we had made in coming, or directly for the sea; whether to push through in one frantic march, so as to keep the start already made over possible pursuit; or to rest betimes, one to watch while two slept, and to trust to our rifles in case of attack by the looted villagers. We agreed, finally, to find our way to the schooner by compass rather than waste time by tedious indirections, and if we had the endurance, as we surely had the impulse, to make one march of it. We thought by so doing to have suffered less in the end. These matters being ordered, we got to our feet and set our faces to the west.

For the first hour Meff carried the ruby casket; but after that, for it was heavy and, having no handles, an awkward package, we took turns. It was wonderful, and turn by turn we noticed it, what a handicap that small lump of treasure proved to the locomotion of the individual who carried it. Invariably he fell behind, with lagging legs, and at heart a petulance that undermined his resolution to go on. Had the carrier of it alone been to consult it would soon have been abandoned by the way. Its value was problematical. In the ultimate distribution of the gems incrusting it we were sure to be cheated, and meanwhile it was awkward to hold, heavy to carry, and a diminisher of speed.

Of our subsequent march that day there is nothing to record but weariness, until about an hour before sundown there was formed, by those agencies of nature which play tricks with the eyes of men, far to the north, a mirage. We beheld against the sky a range of the desert across which, his grass-green robes girded about his loins, there moved upon a course parallel with our own the wavering, yet distinct and gigantically magnified, image of a Chinaman. We had but a minute's view of him, vast and shadowy, like a storm cloud, or some vengeful and evil genius out of a dream, and then, presto, the desert refractions altered and the image vanished. For the first time in our desert wanderings, either going in or coming out, we felt cold—cold to the marrow. That the vast size of the Chinaman was an hallucination we knew, but we knew also that an actual man must have been the basis for the magnification, that his course was parallel to our own, and his sudden appearance in the heavens an illegible but disquieting portent. Had but one man of Chen Chan had the hatred to dog our steps? Or had a council decreed that to wrest the casket and perhaps our lives from us but one man was necessary? If the latter, and a certain fateful significance in the mirage impelled us to adopt it, what occult power could he possess to hold our vigilance and our rifle practice so cheap? And might we not with certainty look for him to strike in that hour of darkness which would precede the rising of the moon? In one presumption only was there any grain of comfort: that, forebodings notwithstanding, he might be, like Sang Ti, a solitary desert voyager intent upon a destiny in no way commingled with our own. But conscience told us that this was far-fetched presumption, and we moved uneasily forward, with roving and scared eyes.

To have been witness to, and part of, so many shocking deaths; to be bearing the fruits of an unjustifiable theft; and to have for accompaniment to our march a fateful and constant, although invisible, presence, was a torture to the mind and conscience. But it had, too, the effect of compelling a rate of progress that had otherwise been impossible, and casting a certain reticence into the demands made upon us by hunger and thirst.

Well, the dark hour before moonrise came and passed. Nothing happened. The moon rose, dripping light, and sailed toward the zenith. Nothing happened. And we began to believe in such slender promises of security; to go forward with less determination, and to suffer acutely from emptiness, parchedness, and fatigue. So that when Meff made the proposition to rest, and himself offered to keep the first watch, Crisp and I were only too willing. A man is seldom permitted to remember at just what advance of weariness his mind ceases to act, and he goes to sleep. But of the present occasion I seem to remember the exact point. I saw, with an eye of the mind, the unfortunate Sang Ti sitting in the temple to be strangled; I heard from Meff a kind of contented grunt; I shifted my right arm the better to sustain my head, and at that instant fell asleep.

I was awakened, I think, by the moonlight stealing under the brim of my hat and shining upon my closed eyes. I woke, I know, with a kind of dread catching at my heart. I sat up and saw that his promise of vigilance had been beyond Meff's strength to keep. He lay upon his back with his face completely covered by his hat. The fingers of his right hand were clasped tightly about one end of the ruby casket. There were no grounds for the feeling of dread with which I had waked. Yet the feeling abode. It was the feeling that a guilty man has who believes rather than knows that he is being watched. I looked beyond Meff, across the desert, and my heart froze. I had seen—I could swear it—for one fleeting instant, a yellow face that ducked away behind a near-by ridge of sand.

I seized my rifle and rushed to the point at which it had vanished. From there I obtained an expansive view of the desert. But there was no form to show that a man had been lying in the sand, nor any tracks of feet. I was mentally staggered, and, after rushing a few purposeless steps this way and that, returned, thoroughly dazed, to my companions. The noise of my sudden upspringing had not disturbed them. They continued heavily asleep, and had not moved a muscle. Only it seemed to me that Meff's hat had slipped a little from his face; and as I looked it actually shifted a little more, and then—to my horror—it rose a little and settled back. It was preposterous to think that Meff's quiet breathing could so move the heavy felt. Then, as if to settle once for all the agency of the motion, Meff's hand, that had been clasped about the ruby casket, went up to his hat in a kind of petulant way, and removed it.

Whether it was Meff's scream or mine that broke the silence I shall never know. I only know that I was on my feet, wildly firing at a streak of gray that hissed as it ran and dodged the spurts of sand tossed by the bullets.

Crisp was on his feet, rifle in hand, staring wildly about him.

"What is it?" he cried.

"It was under Meff's hat all the time," I shouted back. "It's the one with the broken tail—that hid under the altar. That Chinaman is hunting us down with it," I shouted on; "I tell you he is. Damn him! We're goners—goners. Look at Meff!"

But it was not good to look at Meff.

"Which way did it go?" said Crisp in a sombre voice.

"That way," I said. "You can see the track; see how the broken tail had to drag."

"You missed it—of course."

"Yes," I said, "of course. I nearly got it once. But I didn't, and that's all there is to it. Except it will come back. It's following us. It and that Chinaman. We must hurry now. We must hurry. We mustn't stop again, and we must look back all the time."

Crisp stopped and picked up the ruby casket.

"We must leave that," I said, "it isn't ours, you know, Crisp. You'll leave it, won't you, Crisp?"

"No," said he. "By God!"

VII. CRISP

But the sun, rising hot upon our backs, found me in a saner condition than Crisp. For hours he had been cursing and swearing because he was thirsty; but now he began to talk with a kind of crazy boastfulness, saying that he was not the man to go without water when there was plenty of it to be had for the mere seeking. He knew the signs, he said, and as soon as he saw them would lead me to a spring hole. I needn't be afraid; he would see to it that I had a good drink. He even warned me against drinking too fast. "When we strike water," he said, "you'll be for rushing in and swigging a bucket, but mind what your uncle says, and don't. First you want to moisten a rag and suck it, and when you get used to that you can swallow a few drops, and then after you begin to swell a bit you can negotiate your bucket." And so on all the long hours. His eyes, wide and glassy, roamed the horizon in search of signs, and toward noon he began to mistake hillocks of sand for vegetation, and I was obliged to join with him in long zigzags that ended in disillusion and wasted precious time. To have gone against him in his craziness might have ended murderously. There was no good in his eye. After a while he began to visit his disappointments upon me; to curse me because the green bushes were sand, and to say that I ought to have told him so in the first place. Several times, too, for he would not suffer me to carry it, he dropped (impelled, I think, by a kind of insane mischievousness) the ruby casket, and we had to go back for it. It was beyond patience. But I was not man enough to cross him, or to say what I thought.

Suddenly he stopped and pointed to the right.

"Well, my boy," he began, "what did I tell you? Are those green bushes or not?"

I could see none, but before I could say so he broke out violently:

"Don't lie to me. Say 'yes' or 'no,' but don't lie. If you lie," he went on with a very horrid expression, "I will kill you. Now, then, which is it, bushes or not?"

It entered my mind to shoot him down, and perhaps I made a threatening motion. Anyway he sprang at me, wrenched the rifle from my hands and retreated warily.

"You're gone crazy," he said, and, rather kindly, "a drop of water'll fix you up. Now you watch out for that"—here he flung the ruby casket at my feet—"and I'll go fetch you a drop of water. Sorry you're crazy."

He turned and, like Robinson Crusoe, a gun under each arm, started away toward his imaginary patch of green. But was it imaginary—this last patch? Or was my mind, too, going? It seemed to me at one moment that there was a patch of green, at the next that there was not. I stood irresolute, and rubbed my swollen eyes, blinked, and then made a step or two after Crisp. But he had developed a wonderful acuteness of ear, and heard me.

"You stay there," he shouted, "or I'll fix you."

I stood and watched his slow course toward—yes, it was a patch of green. Of the color I was now as sure as Crisp had been, but of the substance, no. If it was vegetation—a sudden fear gagged me for a moment, and then I shouted to Crisp.

"Look out!" I yelled. "It's silk!"

I saw his head turn and be called to me.

"Water," he called, "it's water."

But it was not water, and Crisp, blinded by his infatuation, walked straight up to the Chinaman of the mirage, who, in a girt-up green robe, had risen in his path. It seemed to me that the Chinaman made a gesture with his hand, as of a man casting something quietly on the ground, and then I saw that Crisp had flung the rifles from him, and was running toward me with frantic leaps and bounds. He was sane enough now, poor fellow, and no less aware than I of the gray death that struck at his heels. I had one moment of clear vision. The Chinaman had vanished. With a scream, that still rings in my ears, and in a shower of sand, poor Crisp went down, and then there was darkness in my eyes, and I was running, running desperately, and clasping something heavy to my breast.

In my frenzied panic I must have snatched up the ruby casket, for when I came to my senses, how much later I do not know, but soon, for I was still desperately running, I had it clutched with one aching hand to my breast. I had been running up a long incline of the desert, but the impulse of terror came to an end, and I stopped short. There was no sweat in me to run out; but I glowed and burned like a furnace, and for a long time my only vision was a kaleidoscope of crazily swirling white dots. I looked behind me when my vision had cleared, but there was nothing to be seen but sand, blazing in the sun.

I climbed then very slowly a few inches to the step, to the top of the rise, and saw before me, very far, between hills of sand, segments of the blue and tranquil sea.

VIII. THE CHINAMAN IN GREEN

Had I been alone in the desert I would have had eyes for nothing but those placid and refreshing stretches of blue; but it was peopled for me and haunted: by the ghosts of comrades, and by the Chinaman in green who hunted me, and by the broken-tailed snake that he could loose against me when he conceived that the hour of his opportunity had struck. I must have cut a grotesque and horrible figure of fear and caution; halting to look behind with wild eyes; starting, stopping; sucking at the hot desert air, now breaking for a few yards into a lumbering run; and now dragging my feet as if to each there had been riveted a ball and chain. So a guilty man, and one hounded by fear, might act in the nighttime or the dusk, in a city street, convinced that in each dark doorway, or behind each corner, the fearful lurked to spring upon him. But here was I so acting in broad sunlight, in a region that for miles in every direction was open to the eye like a book; levelish and free of cover toward every point of the compass, and still I advanced, starting, cowering, running, halting like an actor of melodrama rehearsing a rôle of terror.

The direction that I followed thus stageily intersected at last the broad trail that our little company had made on its march to Chen Chan. Here were the deep footprints of Sang Ti; the shuffled marks of Morgridge's big feet; Crisp's firm and even tread; Meff's small and neat impress; the long stride of Hawes; and here I had gone on well-arched, buoyant feet. Of all that company I only could now write my progress in the sands; I only lived on for a time.

At another time that broad and tragic spoor and turned me aside to break a fresh and unsuggestive path; but now I had a sense of companionship with it, and followed it feeling no longer so utterly lonely, afraid, and alone.

I passed the fallen monolith, and saw in the bay, half full of tide, the schooner, riding in safety, and the schooner's boat moored to the beach of the promontory by a staked oar. On board that schooner was water—food—home. I had an exhilaration of escaped danger that lent me wings. I ran along the hard beach toward the boat and my feet splashed in the advancing rim of the tide. There was a breeze in my face, and my fears were blown from me and fell behind. I shouted as I ran.

It was but half a dozen strong strokes to the schooner. I snatched up the ruby casket from the seat where I had lain it, and sprang aboard, and found myself face to face with the Chinaman in green. His robes were dripping sea water, and there was a kind of smile on his lips. In one hand, held tenderly as a girl holds a pet bird, was the little gray snake. White lids covered its eyes, and its broken tail hung from between his fingers and dangled listlessly like a bit of string. The smile on the Chinaman's face wavered and broadened. There was a kind of friendliness in it. I smiled back at him. And when he held out his other hand, open, I placed in it the ruby casket. And he, gently and quietly as a girl might slide a necklace into a jewel-box, slid into it the little gray snake, dead now, for what reason I know not, and closed the cover with a faint snap.

I ferried him to the shore, and stood watching him until he had disappeared over the brow of the desert with his face toward Chen Chan.

The Execution

I

The room was dark as the pit and its midnight silence was accentuated rather than disturbed by the soft, steady, grating sound of a rat gnawing in the wall, and by the loud metallic ticking of a clock. Suddenly upon one of the walls appeared a perpendicular thread of pale gray. This widened by gradations that were almost imperceptible, and which were accompanied by faint creaking noises like those made by iron hinges that have not been oiled. The thread widened to a rope, to a broad ribbon, after a while to the width of a broad window. Through the rectangles of the sash appeared a swirling gray vista of falling snow, half shrouded by the dark figure of a man, his cap and shoulders thatched with snow. A pane of glass fell to the floor with a sharp *pang*. The rat in the wall ceased his gnawing; and only the clock continued to break the silence. Presently the lower half of the sash began to move upward, until there was a sufficient opening for the man to pass through. Before entering he shook the snow from his cap and shoulders, and, seated on the window-sill, his body in and his legs out, brushed the snow from his feet. Then he swung his legs into the room, one after the other, and, turning, reached out his arms and drew to the shutters. The room was again dark as the pit. A faint sound, between a crunch and a squeak, told that the man had closed the sash.

Presently the man struck a match. The spurt of blue and yellow flame showed a thin, white, shaking hand and a thin, white face—a young face aged by care, by premature cleverness, by suffering and by sin. It had a hunted look. The match went out. The man lighted another and moved about the room as if looking for something. He lighted match after match, moving about the room as he did so, so that its disposition and its effects were gradually disclosed: a great fireplace with big logs laid upon split shingles and newspapers, the dark hollow of an old, high-shouldered leather chair, a grandfather's clock, doors leading to other parts of the house, four windows, a table covered with an oil-cloth, a big mirror in a cheap veneered frame.

From time to time during his stealthy peregrinations the man felt of his throat with his left hand. The gesture had the effect of a something characteristic and habitual; it was as if the man had once been afraid for his throat and had got into the habit of feeling to see if all was still well with it. When he came before the mirror with a lighted match in one hand, the other, which went again to his throat, instead of being quickly withdrawn, remained, and its thin nervous fingers clasped and pressed here and there, as one clasps and presses one's throat when it is sore to locate the exact area of inflammation. With the last flicker of the match (still feeling of his throat) the man leered at his reflected image, and nodded to it. And his lips seemed to form and give out, without any actual utterance, the words, "you'll do."

His next move, which was to the deep leather chair in which he seated himself, proved that, whatever his ultimate motive in entering the house might be, he had no immediate intentions to the burglarious or murderous. Indeed, his loud, steady breathing betokened that he was on the point of falling asleep. But at the very moment when his senses were passing heavily into oblivion the grandfather's clock, after a kind of mechanical throat clearing, struck twice. The man roused himself, drew off his heavy boots, lighted a match, and, yawning again and again, walked quietly to one of the doors leading out of the room, opened it, struck another match, stepped over the threshold, and closed the door behind him.

The whole house creaked and groaned in a sudden gust of wind; a dribble of soot and old mortar fell rattling into the fireplace. The ticking of the clock sounded louder after the extraneous noises had ceased. The rat began once more to gnaw in the wall; guardedly at first, but soon with a rasping steadiness that made it seem as if his whole heart were in the act. The rat might have been likened to a prisoner who was trying to work his way out of jail.

Presently the man could be heard moving about in the room immediately above that which he had just quitted. But not for long. The sound of his steps soon ceased.

II

Hours later, in the same doorway by which the young man had left the room, there appeared, palely illumined by the candle which she carried, the emaciated figure of an old woman. Her thin, bony face, with its deep sunken eyes and high-bridged nose, suggested the face of a hawk; the thin, harsh lips and the harsh, protruding jaw gave her a look of strong will and inflexibility, but the snow-white hair, drawn tightly to a knot at the back of her head, suggested, it is hard to say why, a gentleness and motherliness which the hawk face belied. She was shabbily dressed in black; her skirt did not reach below her ankles, and disclosed a pair of bony feet encased in coarse white stockings and broken-down slippers. Her movements, though brisk and sure, were those of a person who does not see clearly; and she seemed to be laboring under an almost irrepressible agitation. Her first action on entering the room was to hold the candle very close to the face of the clock, and to advance her eyes equally close to it, so as to ascertain beyond doubt the exact position of the hands. The hands indicated that the hour was exactly a quarter to six. The old woman pressed her hand nervously against her lean breast, and groaned. Then she set the candle on the table, and kneeling on the cold board floor, her face in her hands, began to mumble and mutter as if in prayer, prayer in which there were a thousand things to pray and only seconds in which to pray them. Tears came through her fingers and trickled down her bony wrists.

In the doorway there now appeared a young woman, also illumined by a candle which she carried. Her face, thin and white, had a kind of gentle prettiness about it and was crowned by glories of dark hair. The young woman was also dressed in black, but her gown, though of an old fashion, hung gracefully and was of a decent fit. The young woman had evidently been crying, but had composed herself. With a pitying glance at the old woman who knelt, and prayed and wept, she crossed to the fireplace and thrust her candle among the papers and kindlings laid to start the big logs. Having assured herself that the fire had caught, she set the candle on the table, slipped her hands under the old woman's shoulders, and raised her to her feet.

"Mother!" she said, "I hoped you'd sleep through it."

"No, dear—no, dear," said the old woman. She wiped at her eyes with the backs of her hands.

"Come by the fire, mother, the cold is terrible."

The old woman suffered herself to be led to the fire, where she spread her lean hands to the blaze that was beginning to leap among the logs. She had managed to stop her tears (it is easy for the old both to begin tears and to stop them) and to regain a certain composure.

"Yes, it is terribly cold," she said. "I don't remember such another storm as we've had. On the north side of the house the snow is almost up to the second story windows."

Her eyes sought the face of the clock, but at that distance she could not see the hands.

"What time is it?" she asked.

"It is just five minutes to six, mother."

"Are you sure the clock is right?"

"Yes, mother."

The old woman began to nod her head repeatedly, as old people are prone to do when their minds are far away.

"Sunrise," she said, "is just at six o'clock to-day."

"Yes, mother."

"But we shan't see the sun to-day, even if the clouds pass. We must keep the shutters closed all to-day."

"Yes, mother."

"They always say 'at sunrise,'" said the old woman querulously, "but they mean the time when it rises, not the sight of it. In the eyes of the law sunrise means a certain time."

"Yes, mother."

"What time is it now?"

"It is nearly four minutes to six, mother."

"You'll keep an eye on the clock, won't you, dear?" said the old woman. She rocked before the fire, her hands still spread to the warmth. "Just at sunrise we must go on our knees and pray to God."

"Yes, mother. You are trembling with cold; let me get your shawl for you."

"I don't want my shawl," said the old woman. "I would have put it on if I'd wanted it."

The young woman knelt by the fire, and readjusted the logs with quick, dexterous movements. Combustion answered to the bettered draught and began to roar up the chimney.

"Beyond the grave," said the old woman, as if answering a question, "there are no clouds." She went on, still as if questions were being put to her: "Beyond the grave there is mercy; the Governor of Heaven will have mercy on those who have sinned."

"Yes, mother."

"I tell you," cried the old woman in a kind of prophetic ecstacy, "we shall all meet beyond the grave."

If further questions arose in her soul she answered them by mutterings that were not words. The young woman crossed to the door by which she had entered, closed it and returned to the fire.

"What time is it now?" asked the old woman.

"It is three and a half minutes to six."

"He has finished his breakfast now," said the old woman, "and they are leading him out."

There came faintly from some inner and upper portion of the house a sound as of a floor creaking.

"Do you hear anything?" said the old woman, a kind of awful expectancy in her face. "I thought I heard the creaking of boards. I thought I heard the scaffold creaking."

The sound was repeated.

"It's in the house," said the young woman, "upstairs somewhere. Some one is moving about. Listen."

There came now a distinct sound of slow, heavy steps.

"There is no one in the house but ourselves that *can* move," said the old woman.

"Could it be father?"

"He hasn't moved for three months; you know he can't move; he's crippled with his rheumatism. He'll die of it."

The young woman's eyes widened with terror.

"It's coming down the stairs," she said.

The old woman, erect, courageous, full of fight, stepped briskly between her daughter and the door. It opened, and in the frame appeared the bent figure of a gigantic old man. He was clad in a rough heavy overcoat, the collar turned up; below the skirt of the coat showed a foot of coarse white nightgown. His hairy shanks were bare, and his feet were thrust into a pair of enormous carpet slippers. A Jove-like head and face, streaming with white hair and beard, crowned the motley figure. But the face had, instead of eyes, sockets, and, held to its left ear by an immense, sinewy, hairy hand, was a long, old-fashioned ear-trumpet of japanned tin.

"What is wrong?" said the old man, in a voice that sounded like a heavy wagon crossing a wooden bridge.

The old woman seized him by the shoulders and began to shake him.

"You will kill yourself!" she said. "There is nothing wrong."

"Stop shaking me," said the old man fiercely.

The old woman's hands dropped from his shoulders, but she continued to scold him.

"You had no business to get up," she said. "You must go right back to bed. Do you want to kill yourself?"

"Something is wrong," persisted the old man. He pushed his wife aside as if she had been a feather, and groped toward the fireplace, talking as he went.

"Do you think I could have got up and walked if there hadn't been something wrong," he said. "Why are you all up?"

The old woman hovered, so to speak, on the flank of his advance, anxious, frightened, between scolding and tears.

"There is nothing wrong," she said.

"You lie," said the old man. "Is it about my son?"

He turned his head heavily from his wife to his daughter, as if he could see them with his empty sockets and read in their faces the truth.

His daughter advanced and took him by the arm.

"Nothing has happened, father." She spoke briskly and cheerfully. "Come to the fire. How good it is to see you walking about, just as natural as life. Isn't it good to see him walking about, mother?"

"Yes, yes," said the old woman, but without conviction, "it is wonderful." She turned her near-sighted eyes to the clock and tried to read the time.

The old man was conducted by his daughter to the large leather chair. He sank into it heavily, as if he had been a load of stones.

"Your poor feet," she said, "are blue with cold."

After an anxious look at the clock she bent and commenced to chafe them briskly between her hands.

"You are both keeping something from me," said the old man. "When mother got up she thought I was asleep, but I wasn't. I knew when she left her bed. And I knew then that something was wrong. Is it about my boy?"

"No, father."

The old man removed the trumpet from his ear and laid it across his knees. By that action he cut himself off from the world of sounds and, blind and deaf, frowned terribly and worked his bushy eyebrows up and down. It was at this moment that the clock began to go through its usual throat clearing preamble to voicing the hour.

The women, white as death and trembling violently, sank to their knees and, as if by prearrangement, the same prayer came brokenly from their lips:

"Almighty and most merciful Father: We have erred, and strayed from Thy ways like lost sheep—"

The old man's terrible rumbling voice broke in upon them, and while he spoke, though they continued the prayer, it was in silence.

"As long as we are all up," the old man boomed and rumbled, "why doesn't somebody get breakfast ready?"

The clock had finished striking.

"A full stomach is the thing to keep the cold out," he said, and, seizing his ear-trumpet, thrust the small end of it into his left ear.

"What are you saying to mother?" he said.

"Nothing, father."

The old woman kept on praying.

"Why don't you tell me what is wrong? I'm not a log. I could tear this house down with my hands if I got angry. I'm not a child. Maybe you heard a noise and thought somebody had broken into the house. Was that it? Answer me."

He staggered heavily to his feet, and turned his empty sockets this way and that.

The two women rose from their knees and glanced at each other. Without speaking a word the daughter managed in that brief glance to ask a question and the mother to answer it. The daughter turned to her father. The mother sank once more to her knees. The fire roared in the chimney.

"Father," said the young woman, speaking into the mouth of the ear-trumpet, "it *was* a noise. Mother heard it and woke me. She thought she heard some one open a window and then close it. But she must have dreamed it, mustn't she? We ... we've been all through the house."

"I ought to have been called at once," said the old man. "Just because I'm deaf and blind you think I can't look after what belongs to me. Another time ... are you sure you've looked everywhere?"

"Mother must have been dreaming."

"You thought you heard steps, mother?" asked the old man.

"Yes, father." The old woman rose, tears pouring down her cheeks.

"Just think," said the old man, "it might have been somebody after my money."

"But it *wasn't,* father."

"And she thought she heard a window being opened?"

"I thought I heard it open and then close," said the old woman. "But I must have been dreaming."

The old man rose heavily and groped his way to the door, and fumbled till he had the knob in his hand.

"I'll just go about and make sure," he said. He passed out into the darkness and closed the door behind him. The two women heard the key turn in the lock.

"Father has locked us in," said the young woman.

"He doesn't like to be interfered with. Let him go. He'll soon find that there's nobody."

"Mother," said the young woman, "have we done right not to tell father?"

"Done right not to tell father about—about—"

"Yes, mother—*have* we?"

"Father's days are numbered in the land. His heart's threatened. That's what the doctor said. Any sudden shock would kill him. I think you'd best make a cup of hot coffee to give him when he comes back."

"It's terrible to think of him groping in those dark rooms."

"He couldn't see any better if there were lights in them. Besides, there's nothing to hurt him."

"How quietly he moves, mother; I can't hear a sound."

"Most likely he's standing still trying to listen with his old trumpet."

A curious change had come over the old woman. She seemed to take a kind of martial pride in the fact that her blind, half deaf, half crippled old husband had gone forth so boldly to hunt for a thief. She stood more erect; she had stopped trembling.

"Mother," said the young woman suddenly, "what are all these burnt matches doing on the floor?"

"Why, so there are," said the old woman. She picked one up and examined it. "It's not our kind," she said. The two women looked at each other in bewilderment; bewilderment that changed gradually to horror.

The old woman ran noiselessly to the door by which her husband had gone out, and tried to open it.

"There *is* somebody," she said. "We must get to father."

The young woman dragged her away from the door.

"If you make a noise," she said, "you will put them on their guard. Father must take his chances. We can't get to him without making a noise. We can't anyway; *we* can't break that door open. Maybe they've gone."

The two women leaned against the locked door listening with strained ears.

Suddenly, loudly and distinctly, footsteps sounded in the room above their heads, light, crisp, firm footsteps.

"They're in my boy's room," said the old woman.

"Mother—mother," said the young woman, her eyes blazing with excitement. "Don't you know that step—don't you know it?"

The old woman listened carefully. Her heart began to rise and fall rapidly. Her deep-set eyes seemed almost to protrude, so great was her wonder and fear.

"It *is*—it *is.*" Her voice dropped and broke in her throat.

"He has got away, mother—he must have got away."

"I wonder," said the old woman excitedly, "if your father hears him and knows who it is. Why *did* he lock this door. We've got to get it open. Your old—father—so deaf—blind—might get hold of him, and not realize who it was, and, and—God in heaven, girl—quick, get that poker."

The young woman flashed to the fireplace and back, bringing the long, solid, old-fashioned wrought-iron poker.

"Let *me,* mother." She tried to find a purchase between the door and the doorstep, but could not at first.

"Try higher up," said the old woman. "Stop—do you hear anything?"

They listened intently.

"Not a sound, mother. We must get it open."

They worked at the door frantically, but without success.

"Stop," said the old woman. "Why don't we warn him?" She began to beat a tattoo with the poker against the ceiling. "Boy!—boy!" she cried in a thin, piercing voice. "Answer me—it's mother."

There was no answer. The silence was leaden, horrible. "Boy!—boy!" screamed the old woman.

She listened. There was a sound of heavy steps descending the stair.

"It's all right—father's coming back," said the young woman. "Nothing can have happened."

"Then why didn't he answer me?"

There was a kind of fumbling sound upon the door, then the rasp of the key being turned. The old man stepped heavily into the room. His face had a high color, and he was breathing quickly, as an athlete flushes and breathes after putting out his full strength. He had removed the key of the door, and now, after much fumbling, reinserted it, gave it two rasping turns and dropped it into his overcoat pocket. Then he turned to the women, rolling his sockets from one to the other. He put his ear-trumpet to his ear.

"Daughter," he said, "when it gets to be really daylight you must go for the sheriff. In the meanwhile keep out of the room that is above this one—your brother's room. The man was coming out," he went on, "and he ran right into me."

Slowly and heavily the old man extended his right hand; the enormous thumb and fingers clawed into a trifle more than a semi-circumference—the circumference of a medium-sized man's neck. The thumb and fingers moved sharply inwards, became rigid, knotted, and began to tremble violently.

"A hangman," said the old man, "couldn't have done it better with a rope."

The hand fell nerveless, the tin ear-trumpet clattered hollowly on the floor. The color faded from the old man's face; his cheeks and chin took on a bluish tinge in the candle light. A kind of shuddering spasm passed through him from head to foot.

"Take me back to the fire," he said. "I am cold all over." He had never before spoken in such a quiet dependent voice.

The old woman, her face working with fear and horror, led him to his big chair. The young woman stood as if rooted, her face the color of salt; only her fingers moved. They kept picking at her skirt.

The old man fell, like a sack of stones, into his chair.

"I want to hear what you're saying," he said presently. His voice whined. "Give me back my ear-trumpet. I dropped it by the door."

The young woman, apathetic and numb, moved to, where the trumpet had fallen and picked it up. It fell twice from her jerking fingers.

The old woman, a black and white flash, crossed the room and seized her daughter's arm.

"Don't give him that," she cried. "Father mustn't know what he's done . . ."

The old man's voice once more, heavy and sonorous, broke over the old woman's words like a wave and drowned them.

"I can't hear what you say," he rumbled. "Give me my ear-trumpet."

"Not yet," said the old woman quickly; "father must never know what he's done."

The young woman's mouth opened and shut several times without uttering a sound. Her swallowing muscles worked violently and she kept licking her lower lip. Suddenly her half-palsied speaking machinery emitted a voice that was between a wail and a scream.

"He got out of prison"—the voice soared to its highest register—"and he came home."

"Quiet," said the old woman. Her voice was sharp and sudden, like a steel spring breaking. "Your father must not know of this." She seized the young woman by the shoulders and shook her.

"Can you be calm now?" she said. "Can you collect yourself? Can you speak in your natural voice?" The young woman could only gasp and mumble.

"Let me do the talking, then," said the old woman, with a sharp note of impatience. She snatched the ear-trumpet from her daughter and, flashing back to her husband, thrust it into his hands. They were lying open on his lap. The fingers did not close on the trumpet. His head had fallen forward as if in rumination.

The old woman, brisk and graceful—a young girl had not been more so—knelt and laid her ear to the old man's breast. Then she thrust her hand inside his overcoat and laid it on his heart. She felt rapidly of his hands, his feet, his legs. They were cold as ice.

She rose heavily, and began to stroke the dead man's streaming white hair.

"He knows all about it, my dear," she said. It was difficult to tell if she was addressing the dead man or his daughter. "He can hear and see now."

The young woman approached with halting, leaden steps.

"We must get him to his bed, somehow," said the old woman, "even if it breaks our backs. Nobody must know that he ever left it. Nobody must ever know what father has done."

There was not a trace of emotion now in the old woman's voice. It was the voice of a calm and zealous housekeeper, giving orders during a spring housecleaning.

"We must hide all the traces of what has happened," she said. "It wouldn't do to have people know what father has done. The snow will have covered all the tracks leading to the house. People must never know—"

"Mother—mother, if you talk so heartlessly I shall go mad."

"Help me now, we must get your father back to his bed, and then—"

The two women, the one calm, self-reliant and unmoved, the other hysterical, gasping and useless, were unable to stir the gigantic body of the old man.

The old woman stood for a long time in thought. Then she took the door-key from the dead man's overcoat pocket and thrust it into her daughter's hand.

"Get our bonnets and shawls," she said, "and the money."

"What—for—mother?"

"Do as I tell you."

The old woman occupied the moments of her daughter's absence by dragging the fire piecemeal from the fireplace and reconstructing it against the ancient tinder-dry wainscoting of the room.

The young woman returned to a room full of smoke, in which the candles made dim yellow halos.

"Mother—mother, what have you done?" she cried.

"My dear," said the old woman, "we couldn't have gone on living in this house. By the time we can fetch help there will be nothing left of it but ashes. Come."

The Bride's Dead

I

Only Farallone's face was untroubled. His big, bold eyes held a kind of grim humor, and he rolled them unblinkingly from the groom to the bride, and back again. His duck trousers, drenched and stained with sea-water, clung to the great muscles of his legs, particles of damp sand glistened upon his naked feet, and the hairless bronze of his chest and columnar throat glowed through the openings of his torn and buttonless shirt. Except for the life and vitality that literally sparkled from him, he was more like a statue of a shipwrecked sailor than the real article itself. Yet he had not the proper attributes of a shipwrecked sailor. There was neither despair upon his countenance nor hunger; instead a kind of enjoyment, and the expression of one who has been set free. Indeed, he must have secured a kind of liberty, for after the years of serving one master and another, he had, in our recent struggle with the sea, but served himself. His was the mind and his the hand that had brought us at length to that desert coast. He it was that had extended to us the ghost of a chance. He who so recently had been but one of forty in the groom's luxurious employ; a polisher of brass, a holy-stoner of decks, a wage-earning paragon who was not permitted to think, was now a thinker and a strategist, a wage-taker from no man, and the obvious master of us three.

The bride slept on the sand where Farallone had laid her. Her stained and draggled clothes were beginning to dry and her hair to blaze in the pulsing rays of the sun. Her breath came and went with the long-drawn placidity of deep sleep. One shoe had been torn from her by the surf, and through a tear in her left stocking blinked a pink and tiny toe. Her face lay upon her arm and was hidden by it, and by her blazing hair. In the loose-jointed abandon of exhaustion and sleep she had the effect of a flower that has wilted; the color and the fabric were still lovely, but the robust erectness and crispness were gone. The groom, almost unmanned and wholly forlorn, sat beside her in a kind of huddled attitude, as if he was very cold. He had drawn his knees close to his chest, and held them in that position with thin, clasped fingers. His hair, which he wore rather long, was in a wild tangle, and his neat eye-glasses with their black cord looked absurdly out of keeping with his general dishevelment. The groom, never strong or robust, looked as if he had shrunk. The bride, too, looked as if she had shrunk, and I certainly felt as if I had. But, however strong the contrast between us three small humans and the vast stretches of empty ocean and desert coast, there was no diminution about Farallone, but the contrary. I have never seen the presence of a man loom so strongly and so large. He sat upon his rock with a kind of vastness, so bold and strong he seemed, so utterly unperturbed.

Suddenly the groom, a kind of querulous shiver in his voice, spoke.

"The brandy, Farallone, the brandy."

The big sailor rolled his bold eyes from the groom to the bride, but returned no answer.

The groom's voice rose to a note of vexation.

"I said I wanted the brandy," he said.

Farallone's voice was large and free like a fresh breeze.

"I heard you," said he.

"Well," snapped the groom, "get it."

"Get it yourself," said Farallone quickly, and he fell to whistling in a major key.

The groom, born and accustomed to command, was on his feet shaking with fury.

"You damned insolent loafer—" he shouted.

"Cut it out—cut it out," said the big sailor, "you'll wake her."

The groom's voice sank to an angry whisper.

"Are you going to do what I tell you or not?"

"Not," said Farallone.

"I'll"—the groom's voice loudened—his eye sought an ally in mine. But I turned my face away and pretended that I had not seen or heard. There had been born in my breast suddenly a cold unreasoning fear of

Farallone and of what he might do to us weaklings. I heard no more words and, venturing a look, saw that the groom was seating himself once more by the bride.

"If you sit on the other side of her," said Farallone, "you'll keep the sun off her head."

He turned his bold eyes on me and winked one of them. And I was so taken by surprise that I winked back and could have kicked myself for doing so.

II

Farallone helped the bride to her feet. "That's right," he said with a kind of nursely playfulness, and he turned to the groom.

"Because I told you to help yourself," he said, "does not mean that I'm not going to do the lion's share of everything. I am. I'm fit. You and the writer man aren't. But you must do just a little more than you're able, and that's all we'll ask of you. Everybody works this voyage except the woman."

"I can work," said the bride.

"Rot!" said Farallone. "We'll ask you to walk ahead, like a kind of north star. Only we'll tell you which way to turn. Do you see that sugar-loaf? You head for that. Vamoose! We'll overhaul you."

The bride moved upon the desert alone, her face toward an easterly hill that had given Farallone his figure of the sugar-loaf. She had no longer the effect of a wilted flower, but walked with quick, considered steps. What the groom carried and what I carried is of little moment. Our packs united would not have made the half of the lumbersome weight that Farallone swung upon his giant shoulders.

"Follow the woman," said he, and we began to march upon the shoe-and-stocking track of the bride. Farallone, rolling like a ship (I had many a look at him over my shoulder) brought up the rear. From time to time he flung forward a phrase to us in explanation of his rebellious attitude.

"I take command because I'm fit; you're not. I give the orders because I can get 'em obeyed; you can't." And, again: "You don't know east from west; I do."

All the morning he kept firing disagreeable and very personal remarks at us. His proposition that we were not in any way fit for anything he enlarged upon and illustrated. He flung the groom's unemployed ancestry at him; he likened the groom to Rome at the time of the fall, which he attributed to luxury; he informed me that only men who were unable to work, or in any way help themselves, wrote books. "The woman's worth the two of you," he said. "Her people were workers. See it in her stride. She could milk a cow if she had one. If anything happens to me she'll give the orders. Mark my words. She's got a head on her shoulders, she has."

The bride halted suddenly in her tracks and, turning, faced the groom.

"Are you going to allow this man's insolence to run on forever?" she said.

The groom frowned at her and shook his head covertly.

"Pooh," said the bride, and I think I heard her call him *"my champion,"* in a bitter whisper. She walked straight back to Farallone and looked him fearlessly in the face.

"The bigger a man is, Mr. Farallone," she said, "and the stronger, the more he ought to mind his manners. We are grateful to you for all you have done, but if you cannot keep a civil tongue in your head, then the sooner we part company the better."

For a full minute the fearless eyes snapped at Farallone, then, suddenly abashed, softened, and turned away.

"There mustn't be any more mutiny," said Farallone. "But you've got sand, you have—I could love a woman like you. How did you come to hitch your wagon to little Nicodemus there? He's no star. You deserved a man. You've got sand, and when your poor feet go back on you, as they will in this swill (here he kicked the burning sand), I'll carry you. But if you hadn't spoken up so pert, I wouldn't. Now you walk ahead and pretend you're Christopher Columbus De Soto Peary leading a flock of sheep to the Fountain of Eternal Youth. . . . Bear to the left of the sage-brush, there's a tarantula under it. . . ."

We went forward a few steps, when suddenly I heard Farallone's voice in my ear. "Isn't she splendid?" he said, and at the same time he thumped me so violently between the shoulders that I stumbled and fell.

For a moment all fear of the man left me on the wings of rage, and I was for attacking him with my fists. But something in his steady eye brought me to my senses.

"Why did you do that?" I meant to speak sharply, but I think I whined.

"Because," said Farallone, "when the woman spoke up to me you began to brindle and act lion-like and bold. For a minute you looked dangerous—for a little feller. So I patted your back, in a friendly way—as a kind of reminder—a feeble reminder."

We had dropped behind the others. The groom had caught up with the bride, and from his nervous, irritable gestures I gathered that the poor soul was trying to explain and to ingratiate himself. But she walked on, steadily averted, you might say, her head very high, her shoulders drawn back. The groom, his eyes intent upon her averted face, kept stumbling with his feet.

"Just look," said Farallone in a friendly voice. "Those whom God hath joined together. What did the press say of it!"

"I don't remember," I said.

"You lie," said Farallone. "The press called it an ideal match. My God!" he cried—and so loudly that the bride and the groom must have heard—"think of being a woman like that and getting hitched to a little bit of a fuss with a few fine feathers"; and with a kind of sing-song he began to misquote and extemporize:

> "Just for a handful of silver she left me,
> Just for a yacht and a mansion of stone,
> Just for a little fool nest of fine feathers
> She wed Nicodemus and left me alone."

"But she'd never seen me," he went on, and mused for a moment. "Having seen me—do you guess what she's saying to herself? She's saying: 'Thank God I'm not too old to begin life over again,' or thinking it. Look at him! Even you wouldn't have been such a joke. I've a mind to kick the life out of him. One little kick with bare toes. Life? There's no life in him—nothing but a jenny-wren."

The groom, who must have heard at least the half of Farallone's speech, stopped suddenly and waited for us to come up. His face was red and white—blotchy with rage and vindictiveness. When we were within ten feet of him he suddenly drew a revolver and fired it point-blank at Farallone. He had no time for a second shot. Farallone caught his wrist and shook it till the revolver spun through the air and fell at a distance. Then Farallone seated himself and, drawing the groom across his knee, spanked him. Since the beginning of the world children have been punished by spankings, and the event is memorable, if at all, as a something rather comical and domestic. But to see a grown man spanked for the crime of attempted murder is horrible. Farallone's fury got the better of him, and the blows resounded in the desert. I grappled his arm, and the recoil of it flung me head over heels. When Farallone had finished, the groom could not stand. He rolled in the sands, moaning and hiding his face.

The bride was white as paper; but she had no eye for the groom.

"Did he miss you?" she said.

"No," said Farallone, "he hit me—Nicodemus hit me."

"Where?" said the bride.

"In the arm."

Indeed, the left sleeve of Farallone's shirt was glittering with blood.

"I will bandage it for you," she said, "if you will tell me how."

Farallone ripped open the sleeve of his shirt.

"What shall I bandage it with?" asked the bride.

"Anything," said Farallone.

The bride turned her back on us, stooped, and we heard a sound of tearing. When she had bandaged Farallone's wound (it was in the flesh and the bullet had been extracted by its own impetus) she looked him gravely in the face.

"What's the use of goading him?" she said gently.

"Look," said Farallone.

The groom was reaching for the fallen revolver.

"Drop it," bellowed Farallone.

The groom's hand, which had been on the point of grasping the revolver's stock, jerked away. The bride walked to the revolver and picked it up. She handed it to Farallone.

"Now," she said, "that all the power is with you, you will not go on abusing it."

"*You* carry it," said Farallone, "and any time *you* think I ought to be shot, why, you just shoot me. I won't say a word."

"Do you mean it?" said the bride.

"I cross my heart," said Farallone.

"I sha'n't forget," said the bride. She took the revolver and dropped it into the pocket of her jacket.

"Vamoose!" said Farallone. And we resumed our march.

III

The line between the desert and the blossoming hills was as distinctly drawn as that between a lake and its shore. The sage-brush, closer massed than any through which we had yet passed, seemed to have gathered itself for a serried assault upon the lovely verdure beyond. Outposts of the sage-brush, its unsung heroes, perhaps, showed here and there among ferns and wild roses—leafless, gaunt, and dead; one knotted specimen even had planted its banner of desolation in the shade of a wild lilac and there died. A twittering of birds gladdened our dusty ears, and from afar there came a splashing of water. Our feet, burned by the desert sands, torn by yucca and cactus, trod now upon a cool and delicious moss, above which nodded the delicate blossoms of the shooting-star, swung at the ends of strong and delicate stems. In the shadows the chocolate lilies and trilliums dully glinted, and flag flowers trooped in the sunlight. The resinous paradisiacal smell of tarweed and bay-tree refreshed us, and the wonder of life was a something strong and tangible like bread and wine.

The wine of it rushed in particular to Farallone's head; his brain became flooded with it; his feet cavorted upon the moss; his bellowed singing awoke the echoes, and the whole heavenly choir of the birds answered him.

"You, Nicodemus," he cried gayly, "thought that man was given a nose to be a tripod for his eye-glasses—but now—oh, smell—smell!"

His great bulk under its mighty pack tripped lightly, dancingly at the bride's elbow. Now his agile fingers nipped some tiny, scarce perceivable flower to delight her eye, and now his great hand scooped up whole sheaves of strong-growing columbine, and flung them where her feet must tread. He made her see great beauties and minute, and whatever had a look of smelling sweet he crushed in his hands for her to smell.

He was no longer that limb of Satan, that sardonic bully of the desert days, but a gay wood-god intent upon the gentle ways of wooing. At first the bride turned away her senses from his offerings to eye and nostril; for a time she made shift to turn aside from the flowers that he cast for her feet to tread. But after a time, like one in a trance, she began to yield up her indifference and aloofness. The magic of the riotous spring began to intoxicate her. I saw her turn to the sailor and smile a gracious smile. And after awhile she began to talk with him.

We came at length to a bright stream, fiom whose guileless superabundance Farallone, with a bent pin and a speck of red cloth, jerked a string of gaudy rainbow-trout. He made a fire and began to broil them; the bride searched the vicinal woods for dried branches to feed the fire. The groom knelt by the brook and washed the dust from his face and ears, snuffing the cool water into his dusty nose and blowing it out.

And I lay in the shade and wondered by what courses the brook found its way to what sea or lake; whether it touched in its wanderings only the virginal wilderness, or flowed at length among the habitations of men.

Farallone, of a sudden, jerked up his head from the broiling and answered my unspoken questions.

"A man," he said, "who followed this brook could come in a few days to the river Maria Cleofas, and following that, to the town of that name, in a matter of ten days more. I tell you," he went on, "because some day some of you may be going that voyage; no ill-found voyage either—spring-water and trout all the way to the river; and all the rest of the way river-water and trout; and at this season birds' eggs in the reeds and a turtlelike terrapin, and Brodeia roots and wild onion, and young sassafras—a child could do it. Eat that . . ." he tossed me with his fingers a split, sputtering, piping hot trout. . . .

We spent the rest of that day and the night following by the stream. Farallone was in a riotous good-humor, and the fear of him grew less in us until we felt at ease and could take an unmixed pleasure in the loafing.

Early the next morning he was astir, and began to prepare himself for further marching, but for the rest of us he said there would be one day more of rest.

"Who knows," he said, "but this is Sunday?"

"Where are you going?" asked the bride politely.

"Me?" said Farallone, and he laughed. "I'm going house-hunting—not for a house, of course, but for a site. It's not so easy to pick out just the place where you want to spend the balance of your days. The neighborhood's easy, but the exact spot's hard." He spoke now directly to the bride, and as if her opinion was law to him. "There must be sun and shade, mustn't there? Spring-water?—running water? A hill handy to take the view from? An easterly slope to be out of the trades? A big tree or two. . . . I'll find 'em all before dark. I'll be back by dark or at late moonrise, and you rest yourselves, because to-morrow or the next day we go at house-raising."

Had he left us then and there, I think that we would have waited for him. He had us, so to speak, abjectly under his thumbs. His word had come to be our law, since it was but child's play for him to enforce it. But it so happened that he now took a step which was to call into life and action that last vestige of manhood and independence that flickered in the groom and me. For suddenly, and not till after a moment of consideration, he took a step toward the bride, caught her around the waist, crushed her to his breast, and kissed her on the mouth.

But she must have bitten him, for the tender passion changed in him to an unmanly fury.

"You damned cat!" he cried; and he struck her heavily upon the face with his open palm. Not once only, but twice, three, four times, till she fell at his feet.

By that the groom and I, poor, helpless atoms, had made shift to grapple with him. I heard his giant laugh. I had one glimpse of the groom's face rushing at mine—and then it was as if showers of stars fell about me. What little strength I had was loosened from my joints, and more than half-senseless I fell full length upon my back. Farallone had foiled our attack by the simple method of catching us by the hair and knocking our heads together.

I could hear his great mocking laugh resounding through the forest.

"Let him go," I heard the groom moan.

The bride laughed. It was a very curious laugh. I could not make it out. There seemed to be no anger in it, and yet how, I wondered, could there be anything else?

IV

When distance had blotted from our ears the sound of Farallone's laughter, and when we had humbled ourselves to the bride for allowing her to be maltreated, I told the groom what Farallone had said about a man who should follow the stream by which we were encamped.

"See," I said, "we have a whole day's start of him. Even he can't make that up. We must go at once, and there mustn't be any letting up till we get somewhere."

The groom was all for running away, and the bride, silent and white, acquiesced with a nod. We made three light packs, and started—*bolted* is the better word.

For a mile or more, so thick was the underwood, we walked in the bed of the stream; now freely, where it was smooth-spread sand, and now where it narrowed and deepened among rocks, scramblingly and with many a splashing stumble. The bride met her various mishaps with a kind of silent disdain; she made no complaints, not even comments. She made me think of a sleep-walker. There was a set, far-off, cold expression upon her usually gentle and vivacious face, and once or twice it occurred to me that she went with us unwillingly. But when I remembered the humiliation that Farallone had put upon her and the blows that he had struck her, I could not well credit the recurrent doubt of her willingness. The groom, on the other hand, recovered his long-lost spirits with immeasurable rapidity. He talked gayly and bravely, and you would have said that he was a man who had never had occasion to be ashamed of himself. He went ahead, the bride following next, and he kept giving a constant string of advices and imperatives. "That stone's loose"; "keep to the left, there's a hole." "Splash—dash—damn, look out for that one." Branches that hung low across our course he bent and held back until the bride had passed. Now he turned and smiled in her face, and now he offered her the helping hand. But she met his courtesies, and the whole punctilious fabric of his behavior, with the utmost absence and nonchalance. He had, it seemed, been too long in contempt to recover soon his former position of husband and beloved. For long days she had contemplated his naked soul, limited, weak, incapable. He had shown a certain capacity for sudden, explosive temper, but not for courage of any kind, or force. Nor had he played the gentleman in his helplessness. Nor had I. We had not in us the stuff of heroes; at first sight of instruments of torture we were of those who would confess to anything, abjure, swear falsely, beg for mercy, change our so-called religions—anything. The bride had learned to despise us from the bottom of her heart. She despised us still. And I would have staked my last dollar, or, better, my hopes of escaping from Farallone, that as man and wife she and the groom would never live together again. I felt terribly sorry for the groom. He had, as had I, been utterly inefficient, helpless, babyish, and cowardly—yet the odds against us had seemed overwhelming. But now as we journeyed down the river, and the distance between us and Farallone grew more, I kept thinking of men whom I had known; men physically weaker than the groom and I, who, had Farallone offered to bully them, would have fought him and endured his torture till they died. In my immediate past, then, there was nothing of which I was not burningly ashamed, and in the not-too-distant future I hoped to separate from the bride and the groom, and never see them or hear of them in this world again. At that, I had a real affection for the bride, a real admiration. On the yacht, before trouble showed me up, we had bid fair to become fast and enduring friends. But that was all over—a bud, nipped by the frost of conduct and circumstance, or ever the fruit could so much as set. For many days now I had avoided her eye; I had avoided addressing her; I had exerted my ingenuity to keep out of her sight. It is a terrible thing for a man to be thrown daily into the society of a woman who has found him out, and who despises him, mind, soul, marrow, and bone.

The stream broke at length from the forest and, swelled by a sizable tributary, flowed broad and deep into a rolling, park-like landscape. Grass spread over the country's undulations and looked in the distance like well-kept lawns; and at wide intervals splendidly grown live-oaks lent an effect of calculated planting. Here our flight, for our muscles were hardened to walking, became easy and swift. I think there were hours when we must have covered our four miles, and even on long, upward slopes we must have made better than three. There is in swift walking, when the muscles are hard, the wind long, and the atmosphere exhilarating, a buoyant rhythm that more, perhaps, than merited success, or valorous conduct, smoothes out the creases in a man's soul. And so quick is a man to recover from his own baseness, and to ape outwardly his transient inner feelings, that I found myself presently, walking with a high head and a mind full of martial thoughts.

All that day, except for a short halt at noon, we followed the river across the great natural park; now paralleling its convolutions, and now cutting diagonals. Late in the afternoon we came to the end of the park land. A more or less precipitous formation of glistening quartz marked its boundary, and into a fissure of this the stream, now a small river, plunged with accelerated speed. The going became difficult. The walls of the fissure through which the river rushed were smooth and water-worn, impossible to ascend; and between the brink of the river and the base of the walls were congestions of boulders, jammed drift-wood, and tangled alder bushes. There were times when we had to crawl upon our hands and knees, under one log and over the next. To add to our diffi-culties darkness was swiftly falling, and we were glad, indeed, when the wall of the fissure leaned at length so far from the perpendicular that we were able to scramble up it. We found ourselves upon a levelish little meadow of grass. In the centre of it there grew a monstrous and gigantic live-oak, between two of whose roots there glittered a spring. On all sides of the meadow, except on that toward the river, were su-perimpending cliffs of quartz. Along the base of thew was a dense growth of bushes.

"We'll rest here," said the groom. "What a place. It's a natural for-tress. Only one way into it." He stood looking down at the noisy river and considering the steep slope we had just climbed. "See this boul-der?" he said. "It's wobbly. If that damned longshoreman tries to get us here, all we've got to do is to choose the psychological moment and push it over on him."

The groom looked quite bellicose and daring. Suddenly he flung his fragment of a cap high into the air and at the very top of his lungs cried: "Liberty!"

The echoes answered him, and the glorious, abused word was tossed from cliff to cliff, across the river and back, and presently died away.

At that, from the very branches of the great oak that stood in the centre of the meadow there burst a titanic clap of laughter, and Farallone, literally bursting with merriment, dropped lightly into our midst.

I can only speak for myself. I was frightened—I say it deliberately and truthfully—*almost* into a fit. And for fully five minutes I could not command either of my legs. The groom, I believe, screamed. The bride became whiter than paper—then suddenly the color rushed into her cheeks, and she laughed. She laughed until she had to sit down, until the tears literally gushed from her eyes. It was not hysterics either—could it have been amusement? After a while, and many prolonged gasps and relapses, she stopped.

"This," said Farallone, "is my building site. Do you like it?"

"Oh, oh," said the bride, "I think it's the m—most am—ma—musing site I ever saw," and she went into another uncontrollable burst of laughter.

"Oh—oh," she said at length, and her shining eyes were turned from the groom to me, and back and forth between us, "if you *could* have seen your faces!"

V

It seemed strange to us, an alteration in the logical and natural, but neither the groom nor I received corporal punishment for our attempt at escape. Farallone had read our minds like an open book; he had, as it were, put us up to the escapade in order to have the pure joy of thwarting us. That we should have been drawn to his exact waiting-place like needles to the magnet had a smack of the supernatural, but was in reality a simple and explicable happening. For if we had not ascended to the little meadow, Farallone, alertly watching, would have descended from it, and surprised us at some further point. That we should have caught no glimpse of his great bulk anywhere ahead of us in the day-long stretch of open, park-like country was also easily explained. For Farallone had made the most of the journey in the stream itself, drifting with a log.

And although, as I have said, we were not to receive corporal punishment, Farallone visited his power upon us in other ways. He would not at first admit that we had intended to escape, but kept praising us for having followed him so loyally and devotedly, for saving him the trouble of a return journey, and for thinking to bring along the bulk of our worldly possessions. Tiring at length of this, he switched to the opposite point of view. He goaded us nearly to madness with his criticisms of our inefficiency, and he mocked repeatedly the groom's ill-timed cry of Liberty.

"Liberty!" he said, "you never knew, you never will know, what that is—you miserable little pinhead. Liberty is for great natures.

> 'Stone walls do not a prison make,
>   Nor iron bars a cage.'

But the woman shall know what liberty is. If she had wanted to leave me there was nothing to stop her. Do you think she'd have followed the river, leaving a broad trail? Do you think she'd have walked right into this meadow—unless she hadn't cared? Not she. Did you ask her advice, you self-sufficiencies? Not you. You were the men-folk, you thought, and you were to have the ordering of everything. You make me sick, the pair of you. . . ."

He kept us awake until far into the night with his jibes and his laughter.

"Well," he said lastly, "good-night, girls. I'm about sick of you, and in the morning we part company. . . ."

At the break of dawn he waked us from heavy sleep—me with a cuff, the groom with a kick, the bride with a feline touch upon the hair.

"And now," said he, "be off."

He caught the bride by the shoulder.

"Not *you*," he said.

"I am to stay?" she asked, as if to settle some trivial and unimportant point.

"Do you ask?" said he; "Was man meant to live alone? This will be enough home for us." And he turned to the groom. "Get," he said savagely.

"Mr. Farallone," said the bride—she was very white, but calm, apparently, and collected—"you have had your joke. Let us go now, or better, come with us. We will forget our former differences, and you will never regret your future kindnesses."

"Don't you *want* to stay?" exclaimed Farallone in a tone of astonishment.

"If I did," said the bride gently, "I could not, and would not."

"What's to stop you?" asked Farallone.

"My place is with my husband," said the bride, "whom I have sworn to love, and to honor, and to obey."

"Woman," said Farallone, "do you love him, do you honor him?"

She pondered a moment, then held her head high.

"I do," she said.

"God bless you," cried the groom.

"Rats," said Farallone, and he laughed bitterly. "But you'll get over it," he went on. "Let's have no more words." He turned to the groom and to me.

"Will you climb down the cliff or shall I throw you?"

"Let us all go," said the bride, and she caught at his trembling arm, "and I will bless you, and wish you all good things—and kiss you good-by."

"If you go," said Farallone, and his great voice trembled, "I die. You are everything. You know that. Would I have hit you if I hadn't loved you so—poor little cheek!" His voice became a kind of mumble.

"Let us go," said the bride, "if you love me."

"Not *you*," said Farallone, "while I live. I would not be such a fool. Don't you know that in a little while you'll be glad?"

"Is that your final word?" said the bride.

"It must be," said Farallone. "Are you not a gift to me from God?"

"I think you must be mad," said the bride.

"I am unalterable," said Farallone, "as God made me—I *am*. And you are mine to take."

"Do you remember," said the bride, "what you said when you gave me the revolver? You said that if ever I thought it best to shoot you—you would let me do it."

"I remember," said Farallone, and he smiled.

"That was just talk, of course?" said the bride.

"It was not," said Farallone; "shoot me."

"Let us go," said the bride. Her voice faltered.

"Not you," said Farallone, "while I live."

His voice, low and gentle, had in it a kind of far-off sadness. He turned his eyes from the bride and looked the rising sun in the face. He turned back to her and smiled.

"You haven't the heart to shoot me," he said. "My darling."

"Let us go."

"*Let—you—go!*" He laughed. "*Send—away—my—mate!*"

His eyes clouded and became vacant. He blinked them rapidly and raised his hand to his brow. It seemed to me that in that instant, suddenly come and suddenly gone, I perceived a look of insanity in his face. The bride, too, perhaps, saw something of the kind, for like a flash she had the revolver out and cocked it.

"Splendid," cried Farallone, and his eyes blazed with a tremendous love and admiration. "This is something like," he cried. "Two forces face to face—a man and a bullet—love behind them both. Ah, you do love me—don't you?"

"Let us go," said the bride. Her voice shook violently.

"Not you," said Farallone, "while I live."

He took a step toward her, his eyes dancing and smiling. "Do you know," he said, "I don't know if you'll do it or not. By my soul, I don't know. This is living, this is. This is gambling. I'll do nothing violent," he said, "until my hands are touching you. I'll move toward you slowly one slow step at a time—with my arms open—like this—you'll have plenty of chance to shoot me—we'll see if you'll do it."

"We shall see," said the bride.

They faced each other motionless. Then Farallone, his eyes glorious with excitement and passion, his arms open, moved toward her one slow, deliberate step.

"Wait," he cried suddenly. "This is too good for *them*." He jerked his thumb toward the groom and me. "This is a sight for gods—not jackasses. Go down to the river," he said to us. "If you hear a shot come back. If you hear a scream—then as you value your miserable hides—get!"

We did not move.

The bride, her voice tense and high-pitched, turned to us.

"Do as you're told," she cried, "or I shall ask this man to throw you over the cliff." She stamped her foot.

"And this man," said Farallone, "will do as he's told."

There was nothing for it. We left them alone in the meadow and descended the cliff to the river. And there we stood for what seemed the ages of ages, listening and trembling.

A faint, far-off detonation, followed swiftly by louder and fainter echoes, broke suddenly upon the rushing noises of the river. We commenced feverishly to scramble back up the cliff. Half-way to the top we heard another shot, a second later a third, and after a longer interval, as if to put a quietus upon some final show of life—a fourth.

A nebulous drift of smoke hung above the meadow.

Farallone lay upon his face at the bride's feet. The groom sprang to her side and threw a trembling arm about her.

"Come away," he cried, "come away."

But the bride freed herself gently from his encircling arm, and her eyes still bent upon Farallone—

"Not till I have buried my dead," she said.

Back There in the Grass

It was spring in the South Seas when, for the first time, I went ashore at Batengo, which is the Polynesian village, and the only one on the big grass island of the same name. There is a cable station just up the beach from the village, and a good-natured young chap named Graves had charge of it. He was an upstanding, clean-cut fellow, as the fact that he had been among the islands for three years without falling into any of their ways proved. The interior of the corrugated iron house in which he lived, for instance, was bachelor from A to Z. And if that wasn't a sufficient alibi, my pointer dog, Don, who dislikes anything Polynesian or Melanesian, took to him at once. And they established a romping friendship. He gave us lunch on the porch, and because he had not seen a white man for two months, or a liver-and-white dog for two years, he told us the entire story of his young life, with reminiscences of early childhood and plans for the future thrown in.

The future was very simple. There was a girl coming out to him from the States by the next steamer but one; the captain of that steamer would join them together in holy wedlock, and after that the Lord would provide.

"My dear fellow," he said, "you think I'm asking her to share a very lonely sort of life, but if you could imagine all the—the affection and gentleness, and thoughtfulness that I've got stored up to pour out at her feet for the rest of our lives, you wouldn't be a bit afraid for her happiness. If a man spends his whole time and imagination thinking up ways to make a girl happy and occupied, he can think up a whole lot. . . . I'd like ever so much to show her to you."

He led the way to his bedroom, and stood in silent rapture before a large photograph that leaned against the wall over his dressing-table.

She didn't look to me like the sort of girl a cable agent would happen to marry. She looked like a swell—the real thing—beautiful and simple and unaffected.

"Yes," he said, "isn't she?"

I hadn't spoken a word. Now I said:

"It's easy to see why you aren't lonely with that wonderful girl to look at. Is she really coming out by the next steamer but one? It's hard to believe because she's so much too good to be true."

"Yes," he said, "isn't she?"

"The usual cable agent," I said, "keeps from going mad by having a dog or a cat or some pet or other to talk to. But I can understand a photograph like this being all-sufficient to any man—even if he had never seen the original. Allow me to shake hands with you."

Then I got him away from the girl, because my time was short and I wanted to find out about some things that were important to *me*.

"You haven't asked me my business in these parts," I said, "but I'll tell you. I'm collecting grasses for the Bronx Botanical Garden."

"Then, by Jove!" said Graves, "you have certainly come to the right place. There used to be a tree on this island, but the last man who saw it died in 1789— Grass! The place is all grass: there are fifty kinds right around my house here."

"I've noticed only eighteen," I said, "but that isn't the point. The point is: when do the Batengo Island grasses begin to go to seed?" And I smiled.

"You think you've got me stumped, don't you?" he said. "That a mere cable agent wouldn't notice such things. Well, that grass there," and he pointed—"beach nut we call it—is the first to ripen seed, and, as far as I know, it does it just six weeks from now."

"Are you just making things up to impress me?"

"No, sir, I am not. I know to the minute. You see, I'm a victim of hay-fever."

"In that case," I said, "expect me back about the time your nose begins to run."

"Really?" And his whole face lighted up. "I'm delighted. Only six weeks. Why, then, if you'll stay round for only five or six weeks *more* you'll be here for the wedding."

"I'll make it if I possibly can," I said. "I want to see if that girl's really true."

"Anything I can do to help you while you're gone? I've got loads of spare time—"

"If you knew anything about grasses—"

"I don't. But I'll blow back into the interior and look around. I've been meaning to right along, just for fun. But I can never get any of *them* to go with me."

"The natives?"

"Yes. Poor lot. They're committing race suicide as fast as they can. There are more wooden gods than people in Batengo village, and the superstitions so thick you could cut it with a knife. All the manly virtues have perished. . . . Aloiu!"

The boy who did Graves's chores for him came lazily out of the house.

"Aloiu," said Graves, "just run back into the island to the top of that hill—see?—that one over there—and fetch a handful of grass for this gentleman. He'll give you five dollars for it."

Aloiu grinned sheepishly and shook his head.

"Fifty dollars?"

Aloiu shook his head with even more firmness, and I whistled. Fifty dollars would have made him the Rockefeller-Carnegie-Morgan of those parts.

"All right, coward," said Graves cheerfully. "Run away and play with the other children. . . . Now, isn't that curious? Neither love, money, nor insult will drag one of them a mile from the beach. They say that if you go 'back there in the grass' something awful will happen to you."

"As what?" I asked.

"The last man to try it," said Graves, "in the memory of the oldest inhabitant was a woman. When they found her she was all black and swollen—at least that's what they say. Something had bitten her just above the ankle."

"Nonsense," I said, "there are no snakes in the whole Batengo group."

"They didn't say it was a snake," said Graves. "They said the marks of the bite were like those that would be made by the teeth of a very little—child."

Graves rose and stretched himself.

"What's the use of arguing with people that tell yarns like that! All the same, if you're bent on making expeditions back into the grass, you'll make 'em alone, unless the cable breaks and I'm free to make 'em with you."

Five weeks later I was once more coasting along the wavering hills of Batengo Island, with a sharp eye out for a first sight of the cable station and Graves. Five weeks with no company but Kanakas and a pointer dog makes one white man pretty keen for the society of another. Furthermore, at our one meeting I had taken a great shine to Graves and to the charming young lady who was to brave a life in the South Seas for his sake. If I was eager to get ashore, Don was more so. I had a shot-gun across my knees with which to salute the cable station, and the sight of that weapon, coupled with toothsome memories of a recent big hunt down on Forked Peak, had set the dog quivering from stem to stern, to crouching, wagging his tail till it disappeared, and beating sudden tattoos upon the deck with his forepaws. And when at last we rounded on the cable station and I let off both barrels, he began to bark and ram about the schooner like a thing possessed.

The salute brought Graves out of his house. He stood on the porch waving a handkerchief, and I called to him through a megaphone; hoped that he was well, said how glad I was to see him, and asked him to meet me in Batengo village.

Even at that distance I detected a something irresolute in his manner; and a few minutes later when he had fetched a hat out of the house, locked the door, and headed toward the village, he looked more like a soldier marching to battle than a man walking half a mile to greet a friend.

"That's funny," I said to Don. "He's coming to meet us in spite of the fact that he'd much rather not. Oh, well!"

I left the schooner while she was still under way, and reached the beach before Graves came up. There were too many strange brown men to suit Don, and he kept very close to my legs. When Graves arrived the natives fell away from him as if he had been a leper. He wore a sort of sickly smile, and when he spoke the dog stiffened his legs and growled menacingly.

"Don!" I exclaimed sternly, and the dog cowered, but the spines along his back bristled and he kept a menacing eye upon Graves. The man's face looked drawn and rather angry. The frank boyishness was clean out of it. He had been strained by something or other to the breaking-point—so much was evident.

"My dear fellow," I said, "what the devil is the matter?"

Graves looked to right and left, and the islanders shrank still farther away from him.

"You can see for yourself," he said curtly. "I'm taboo." And then, with a little break in his voice: "Even your dog feels it. Don, good boy! Come here, sir!"

Don growled quietly.

"You see!"

"Don," I said sharply, "this man is my friend and yours. Pat him, Graves."

Graves reached forward and patted Don's head and talked to him soothingly.

But although Don did not growl or menace, he shivered under the caress and was unhappy.

"So you're taboo!" I said cheerfully. "That's the result of anything, from stringing pink and yellow shells on the same string to murdering your uncle's grandmother-in-law. Which have *you* done?"

"I've been back there in the grass," he said, "and because—because nothing happened to me I'm taboo."

"Is that all?"

"As far as they know—yes."

"Well!" said I, "my business will take me back there for days at a time, so I'll be taboo, too. Then there'll be two of us. Did you find any curious grasses for me?"

"I don't know about grasses," he said, "but I found something very curious that I want to show you and ask your advice about. Are you going to share my house?"

"I think I'll keep head-quarters on the schooner," I said, "but if you'll put me up now and then for a meal or for the night—"

"I'll put you up for lunch right now," he said, "if you'll come. I'm my own cook and bottle-washer since the taboo, but I must say the change isn't for the worse so far as food goes."

He was looking and speaking more cheerfully.

"May I bring Don?"

He hesitated.

"Why—yes—of course."

"If you'd rather not?"

"No, bring him. I want to make friends again if I can."

So we stated for Graves's house, Don very close at my heels.

"Graves," I said, "surely a taboo by a lot of fool islanders hasn't upset you. There's something on your mind. Bad news?"

"Oh, no," he said. "She's coming. It's other things. I'll tell you by and by—everything. Don't mind me. I'm all right. Listen to the wind in the grass. That sound day and night is enough to put a man off his feed."

"You say you found something very curious back there in the grass?"

"I found, among other things, a stone monolith. It's fallen down, but it's almost as big as the Flatiron Building in New York. It's ancient as days—all carved—it's a sort of woman, I think. But we'll go back one day and have a look at it. Then, of course, I saw all the different kinds of grasses in the world—they'd interest you more—but I'm such a punk botanist that I gave up trying to tell 'em apart. I like the flowers best—there's millions of 'em—down among the grass. . . . I tell you, old man, this island is the greatest curiosity-shop in the whole world."

He unlocked the door of his house and stood aside for me to go in first.

"Shut up, Don!"

The dog growled savagely, but I banged him with my open hand across the snout, and he quieted down and followed into the house, all tense and watchful.

On the shelf where Graves kept his books, with its legs hanging over, was what I took to be an idol of some light brownish wood—say sandalwood, with a touch of pink. But it was the most lifelike and astounding piece of carving I ever saw in the islands or out of them. It was about a foot high, and represented a Polynesian woman in the prime of life, say, fifteen or sixteen years old, only the features were finer and cleaner carved. It was a nude, in an attitude of easy repose—the legs hanging, the toes dangling—the hands resting, palms downward, on the blotter, the trunk relaxed. The eyes, which were a kind of steely blue, seemed to have been made, depth upon depth, of some wonderful translucent enamel, and to make his work still more realistic the artist had planted the statuette's eyebrows, eyelashes, and scalp with real hair, very soft and silky, brown on the head and black for the lashes and eyebrows. The thing was so lifelike that it frightened me. And when Don began to growl like distant thunder I didn't blame him. But I leaned over and caught him by the collar, because it was evident that he wanted to get at that statuette and destroy it.

When I looked up the statuette's eyes had moved. They were turned downward upon the dog, with cool curiosity and indifference. A kind of shudder went through me. And then, lo and behold, the statuette's tiny brown breasts rose and fell slowly, and a long breath came out of its nostrils.

I backed violently into Graves, dragging Don with me and half-choking him. "My God Almighty!" I said. "It's alive!"

"Isn't she!" said he. "I caught her back there in the grass—the little minx. And when I heard your signal I put her up there to keep her out of mischief. It's too high for her to jump—and she's very sore about it."

"You found her in the grass," I said. "For God's sake!—are there more of them?"

"Thick as quail," said he, "but it's hard to get a sight of 'em. But you were overcome by curiosity, weren't you, old girl? You came out to have a look at the big white giant and he caught you with his thumb and forefinger by the scruff of the neck—so you couldn't bite him—and here you are."

The womankin's lips parted and I saw a flash of white teeth. She looked up into Graves's face and the steely eyes softened. It was evident that she was very fond of him.

"Rum sort of a pet," said Graves. "What?"

"Rum?" I said. "It's horrible—it isn't decent—it—it ought to be taboo. Don's got it sized up right. He—he wants to kill it."

"Please don't keep calling her It," said Graves. "She wouldn't like it—if she understood." Then he whispered words that were Greek to me, and the womankin laughed aloud. Her laugh was sweet and tinkly, like the upper notes of a spinet.

"You can speak her language?"

"A few words—Tog ma Lao?"

"Na!"

"Aba Ton sug ato."

"Nan Tane dom ud lon anea!"

It sounded like that—only all whispered and very soft. It sounded a little like the wind in the grass.

"She says she isn't afraid of the dog," said Graves, "and that he'd better let her alone."

"I almost hope he won't," said I. "Come outside. I don't like her. I think I've got a touch of the horrors."

Graves remained behind a moment to lift the womankin down from the shelf, and when he rejoined me I had made up my mind to talk to him like a father.

"Graves," I said, "although that creature in there is only a foot high, it isn't a pig or a monkey, it's a woman, and you're guilty of what's considered a pretty ugly crime at home—abduction. You've stolen this woman away from kith and kin, and the least you can do is to carry her back where you found her and turn her loose. Let me ask you one thing—what would Miss Chester think?"

"Oh, that doesn't worry me," said Graves. "But I *am* worried—worried sick. It's early—shall we talk now, or wait till after lunch?"

"Now," I said.

"Well," said he, "you left me pretty well enthused on the subject of botany—so I went back there twice to look up grasses for you. The second time I went I got to a deep sort of valley where the grass is waist-high—that, by the way, is where the big monolith is—and that place was alive with things that were frightened and ran. I could see the directions they took by the way the grass tops acted. There were lots of loose stones about and I began to throw 'em to see if I could knock one of the things over. Suddenly all at once I saw a pair of bright little eyes peering out of a bunch of grass—I let fly at them, and something gave a sort of moan and thrashed about in the grass—and then lay still. I went to look, and found that I'd stunned—*her*. She came to and tried to bite me, but I had her by the scruff of the neck and she couldn't. Further, she was sick with being hit in the chest with the stone, and first thing I knew she keeled over in the palm of my hand in a dead faint. I couldn't find any water or anything—and I didn't want her to die—so I brought her home. She was sick for a week—and I took care of her—as I would a sick pup— and she began to get well and want to play and romp and poke into everything. She'd get the lower drawer of my desk open and hide in it—or crawl into a rubber boot and play house. And she got to be right good company—same as any pet does—a cat or a dog—or a monkey—and naturally, she being so small, I couldn't think of her as anything but a sort of little beast that I'd caught and tamed. . . . You see how it all happened, don't you? Might have happened to anybody."

"Why, yes," I said. "If she didn't give a man the horrors right at the start—I can understand making a sort of pet of her—but, man, there's only one thing to do. Be persuaded. Take her back where you found her, and turn her loose."

"Well and good," said Graves. "I tried that, and next morning I found her at my door, sobbing—horrible, dry sobs—no tears. . . . You've said one thing that's full of sense: she isn't a pig—or a monkey—she's a woman."

"You don't mean to say," said I, "that that mite of a thing is in love with you?"

"I don't know what else you'd call it."

"Graves," I said, "Miss Chester arrives by the next steamer. In the meanwhile something has got to be done."

"What?" said he hopelessly.

"I don't know," I said. "Let me think."

The dog Don laid his head heavily on my knee, as if he wished to offer a solution of the difficulty.

A week before Miss Chester's steamer was due the situation had not changed. Graves's pet was as much a fixture of Graves's house as the front door. And a man was never confronted with a more serious problem. Twice he carried her back into the grass and deserted her, and each time she returned and was found sobbing—horrible, dry sobs—on the porch. And a number of times we took her, or Graves did, in the pocket of his jacket, upon systematic searches for her people. Doubtless she could have helped us to find them, but she wouldn't. She was very sullen on these expeditions and frightened. When Graves tried to put her down she would cling to him, and it took real force to pry her loose.

In the open she could run like a rat; and in open country it would have been impossible to desert her; she would have followed at Graves's heels as fast as he could move them. But forcing through the thick grass tired her after a few hundred yards, and she would gradually drop farther and farther behind—sobbing. There was a pathetic side to it.

She hated me; and made no bones about it; but there was an armed truce between us. She feared my influence over Graves, and I feared her—well, just as some people fear rats or snakes. Things utterly out of the normal always do worry me, and Bo, which was the name Graves had learned for her, was, so far as I know, unique in human experience. In appearance she was like an unusually good-looking island girl observed through the wrong end of an opera-glass, but in habit and action she was different. She would catch flies and little grasshoppers and eat them all alive and kicking, and if you teased her more than she liked her ears would flatten the way a cat's do, and she would hiss like a snapping-turtle, and show her teeth.

But one got accustomed to her. Even poor Don learned that it was not his duty to punish her with one bound and a snap. But he would never let her touch him, believing that in her case discretion was the better part of valor. If she approached him he withdrew, always with dignity, but equally with determination. He knew in his heart that something about her was horribly wrong and against nature. I knew it, too, and I think Graves began to suspect it.

Well, a day came when Graves, who had been up since dawn, saw the smoke of a steamer along the horizon, and began to fire off his revolver so that I, too, might wake and participate in his joy. I made tea and went ashore.

"It's *her* steamer," he said.

"Yes," said I, "and we've got to decide something."

"About Bo?"

"Suppose I take her off your hands—for a week or so—till you and Miss Chester have settled down and put your house in order. Then Miss Chester—Mrs. Graves, that is—can decide what is to be done. I admit that I'd rather wash my hands of the business—but I'm the only white man available, and I propose to stand by my race. Don't say a word to Bo—just bring her out to the schooner and leave her."

In the upshot Graves accepted my offer, and while Bo, fairly bristling with excitement and curiosity, was exploring the farther corners of my cabin, we slipped out and locked the door on her. The minute she knew what had happened she began to tear around and raise Cain. It sounded a little like a cat having a fit.

Graves was white and unhappy. "Let's get away quick," he said; "I feel like a skunk."

But Miss Chester was everything that her photograph said about her, and more too, so that the trick he had played Bo was very soon a negligible weight on Graves's mind.

If the wedding was quick and business-like, it was also jolly and romantic. The oldest passenger gave the bride away. All the crew came aft and sang "The Voice That Breathed O'er E-den That Earliest Wedding-Day"—to the tune called "Blairgowrie." They had worked it up in secret for a surprise. And the bride's dove-brown eyes got a little teary. I was best man. The captain read the service, and choked occasionally. As for Graves—I had never thought him handsome—well, with his brown face and white linen suit, he made me think, and I'm sure I don't know why, of St. Michael—that time he overcame Lucifer. The captain blew us to breakfast, with champagne and a cake, and then the happy pair went ashore in a boat full of the bride's trousseau, and the crew manned the bulwarks and gave three cheers, and then something like twenty-seven more, and last thing of all the brass cannon was fired, and the little square flags that spell G-o-o-d L-u-c-k were run up on the signal halyards.

As for me, I went back to my schooner feeling blue and lonely. I knew little about women and less about love. It didn't seem quite fair. For once I hated my profession—seed-gatherer to a body of scientific gentlemen whom I had never seen. Well, there's nothing so good for the blues as putting things in order.

I cleaned my rifle and revolver. I wrote up my notebook. I developed some plates; I studied a brand-new book on South Sea grasses that had been sent out to me, and I found some mistakes. I went ashore with Don, and had a long walk on the beach—in the opposite direction from Graves's house, of course—and I sent Don into the water after sticks, and he seemed to enjoy it, and so I stripped and went in with him. Then I dried in the sun, and had a match with my hands to see which could find the tiniest shell. Toward dusk we returned to the schooner and had dinner, and after that I went into my cabin to see how Bo was getting on.

She flew at me like a cat, and if I hadn't jerked my foot back she must have bitten me. As it was, her teeth tore a piece out of my trousers. I'm afraid I kicked her. Anyway, I heard her land with a crash in a far corner. I struck a match and lighted candles—they are cooler than lamps—very warily—one eye on Bo. She had retreated under a chair and looked out—very sullen and angry. I sat down and began to talk to her. "It's no use," I said, "you're trying to bite and scratch, because you're only as big as a minute. So come out here and make friends. I don't like you and you don't like me; but we're going to be thrown together for quite some time, so we'd better make the best of it. You come out here and behave pretty and I'll give you a bit of gingersnap."

The last word was intelligible to her, and she came a little way out from under the chair. I had a bit of gingersnap in my pocket, left over from treating Don, and I tossed it on the floor midway between us. She darted forward and ate it with quick bites.

Well, then, she looked up, and her eyes asked—just as plain as day: "Why are things thus? Why have I come to live with you? I don't like you. I want to go back to Graves."

I couldn't explain very well, and just shook my head and then went on trying to make friends—it was no use. She hated me, and after a time I got bored. I threw a pillow on the floor for her to sleep on, and left her. Well, the minute the door was shut and locked she began to sob. You could hear her for quite a distance, and I couldn't stand it. So I went back—and talked to her as nicely and soothingly as I could. But she wouldn't even look at me—just lay face down—heaving and sobbing.

Now I don't like little creatures that snap—so when I picked her up it was by the scruff of the neck. She had to face me then, and I saw that in spite of all the sobbing her eyes were perfectly dry. That struck me as curious. I examined them through a pocket magnifying-glass, and discovered that they had no tear-ducts. Of course she couldn't cry. Perhaps I squeezed the back of her neck harder than I meant to—anyway, her lips began to draw back and her teeth to show.

It was exactly at that second that I recalled the legend Graves had told me about the island woman being found dead, and all black and swollen, back there in the grass, with teeth marks on her that looked as if they had been made by a very little child.

I forced Bo's mouth wide open and looked in. Then I reached for a candle and held it steadily between her face and mine. She struggled furiously so that I had to put down the candle and catch her legs together in my free hand. But I had seen enough. I felt wet and cold all over. For if the swollen glands at the base of the deeply grooved canines meant anything, that which I held between my hands was not a woman— but a snake.

I put her in a wooden box that had contained soap and nailed slats over the top. And, personally, I was quite willing to put scrap-iron in the box with her and fling it overboard. But I did not feel quite justified without consulting Graves.

As an extra precaution in case of accidents, I overhauled my medicine-chest and made up a little package for the breast pocket—a lancet, a rubber bandage, and a pill-box full of permanganate crystals. I had still much collecting to do, "back there in the grass," and I did not propose to step on any of Bo's cousins or her sisters or her aunts—without having some of the elementary first-aids to the snake-bitten handy.

It was a lovely starry night, and I determined to sleep on deck. Before turning in I went to have a look at Bo. Having nailed her in a box securely, as I thought, I must have left my cabin door ajar. Anyhow she was gone. She must have braced her back one side of the box, her feet against the other, and burst it open. I had most certainly underestimated her strength and resources.

The crew, warned of peril, searched the whole schooner over, slowly and methodically, lighted by lanterns. We could not find her. Well, swimming comes natural to snakes.

I went ashore as quickly as I could get a boat manned and rowed. I took Don on a leash, a shot-gun loaded, and both pockets of my jacket full of cartridges. We ran swiftly along the beach, Don and I, and then turned into the grass to make a short cut for Graves's house. All of a sudden Don began to tremble with eagerness and nuzzle and sniff among the roots of the grass. He was "making game."

"Good Don," I said, "good boy—hunt her up! Find her!"

The moon had risen. I saw two figures standing in the porch of Graves's house. I was about to call to them and warn Graves that Bo was loose and dangerous—when a scream—shrill and frightful—rang in my ears. I saw Graves turn to his bride and catch her in his arms.

When I came up she had collected her senses and was behaving splendidly. While Graves fetched a lantern and water she sat down on the porch, her back against the house, and undid her garter, so that I could pull the stocking off her bitten foot. Her instep, into which Bo's venomous teeth had sunk, was already swollen and discolored. I slashed the teeth-marks this way and that with my lancet. And Mrs. Graves kept saying: "All right—all right—don't mind me—do what's best."

Don's leash had wedged between two of the porch planks, and all the time we were working over Mrs. Graves he whined and struggled to get loose.

"Graves," I said, when we had done what we could, "if your wife begins to seem faint, give her brandy—just a very little—at a time—and—I think we were in time—and for God's sake don't ever let her know *why* she was bitten—or by *what*—"

Then I turned and freed Don and took off his leash.

The moonlight was now very white and brilliant. In the sandy path that led from Graves's porch I saw the print of feet—shaped just like human feet—less than an inch long. I made Don smell them, and said:

"Hunt close, boy! Hunt close!"

Thus hunting, we moved slowly through the grass toward the interior of the island. The scent grew hotter—suddenly Don began to move more stiffly—as if he had the rheumatism—his eyes straight ahead saw something that I could not see—the tip of his tail vibrated furiously—he sank lower and lower—his legs worked more and more stiffly—his head was thrust forward to the full stretch of his neck toward a thick clump of grass. In the act of taking a wary step he came to a dead halt—his right forepaw just clear of the ground. The tip of his tail stopped vibrating. The tail itself stood straight out behind him and became rigid like a bar of iron. I never saw a stancher point.

"Steady, boy!"

I pushed forward the safety of my shot-gun and stood at attention.

"How is she?"

"Seems to be pulling through. I heard you fire both barrels. What luck?"

Derrick's Return

I

Derrick dreamed that Indians had captured him and had laid him face down in their camp fire and were slowly burning his head off. As a matter of fact a surgeon was working out a difficult problem in the back of Derrick's throat, and for a little while, toward the end of the operation, anesthesia had not been complete.

The operation was a success. Something that ought not to have been in Derrick's throat was now out of it, and an incorrect arrangement of this and that had been corrected. The only trouble was a slight, ever so slight bleeding which could not be stopped. The measures taken to stop it were worse than the dream about the Indians, and, still worse, they didn't stop it. The thin trickle of blood kept on trickling until the reservoirs from which it came were empty, and then the doctors—there were a good many of them now—told the woman who sobbed and carried on that her husband's sufferings were all over. They told her that Derrick was dead.

But Derrick wouldn't have admitted that. Even the bleeding and the pain of which he seemed to have died were now but vague and negligible nuisances. The great thing was to get out of that body which had already begun to decay, and making use of a new and perfectly delightful power of locomotion, to get as far away from it as possible. He caught up with sounds and passed them. And he discovered presently that he could move a little more quickly than light. In a crumb of time some unnerving intuition told him that he had come to the Place to which some other unerring intuition had directed him.

Among the beautiful lights and shadows and colors of that Place, he learned fast. There were voices which answered his questions just as fast

275

as he could think them. And something wonderful had happened to his memory, because it was never necessary to think the same question twice. Knowledge came to stay. To discover how very little he had ever really known about anything didn't humiliate him. It was funny. It made him laugh.

And now that he was able to perceive what insuperable obstacles there must always be between the man-mob and real knowledge of any kind, he developed a certain respect for the man-mob. It had taken them, for instance, so many millions of years to find out that the world in which they lived was not flat but round. The wonder was that they had made the discovery at all. And they had succeeded in prying into certain other secrets that they were not supposed to know—ever. As, for instance, the immortality of the soul, and how to commit race suicide.

To let the man-mob discover its own immortality had been a dreadful mistake. Everybody admitted that now. The discovery had made man take himself seriously and caused him to evolve the erroneous doctrine that the way to a happy immortality lay only through making his brief mortality and that of others as miserable as possible.

He thought a question and received this answer, only the answer was in terms of thought rather than in words:

"No, they were put on earth to be happy and to enjoy themselves. For no other reason. But for some reason or other nobody told them, and they got to taking themselves seriously. They were forced to invent all kinds of sins and bad habits so that they could gain favor by resisting them. . . . But with all respect to what you are now, you must perceive and admit what a perfect ass you were up to the time of your recent, and so-called, death."

He thought another question. The answer was a negative.

"No. They will not evolve into anything better. They have stood still too long and got themselves into much too dreadful a mess. As a pack they will never learn that they were meant only to be happy and to enjoy themselves. Individuals, of course, have from time to time had this knowledge and practiced it, and will, but the others won't let them practice it. But don't worry. Man will die out, and insects will step in and succeed where he failed. Souls will continue for millions of years to come to this place to learn what you are learning, and be happy to know that they have waked forever from the wretched little nightmare they made for themselves on earth. And since happiness is inseparable from laughter, it will make them laugh to look back and see how religiously they sidestepped and ducked out of everything that was really worth while."

II

In the first days of some novel, beautiful or merely exciting experience a man misses neither his friends nor his family. And it was a long time, as time is reckoned here on earth, before Derrick realized that he had parted from all his without so much as bidding any one of them good-by.

In time, of course, they would all come to the place where he now found himself, and share with him all that delicious wealth of knowledge and clear vision the lack of which now stood between them and happiness. Here the knowing how to be happy seemed the mere *a b c* of happiness. It was the first thing you learned. You not only learned how to be happy, but you applied your easily acquired knowledge and you actually *were* happy.

But how, the earth-dweller asks, can the spirit of a man, separated from his wife and children and from the friends he loves, and conscious of the separation, be happy? Very easily. It was one of Derrick's first questions, and the answer had been perfectly satisfactory.

He could always go back. He had learned that almost at once. There is no such thing as separation. If he chose to wait where he was, gathering the sweetest and delightfulest knowledge among the lovely lights and shadows and colors and perfumes, even as a man gathers flowers in a beautiful garden, in the course of time all those whom he had loved so greatly would come to him and be with him forever. But if waiting would make him unhappy, here where no one need be unhappy, he could always go back. When? Now. Soon. Whenever he liked. Oh, it took a little time to get back; but not much. If, for instance, his wife at a given moment were about to lift her hands to her hair, and at that same moment he made up his mind to go back to her and actually started, he would get to her before her hands had moved more than a thousandth of an inch from her lap.

How could he communicate with her? As of old, if he liked. He could be with her. She could hear his voice, on occasions, if the actinic and electrical conditions were just right. She might actually see him. And of course he would be able to see her and to hear her. There was never any trouble about that. If he wanted to be with his family *all* the time, until they in turn got ready to come here, there was nothing to prevent— absolutely nothing. But had he, in his earth life, ever wanted to be with his dear ones all the time? Probably not. One of these days he would probably run into Romeo and Juliet. Very likely he would find them together. They were often together; but not always. Probably, like other loving spirits, he would not wish to be with *his* family *all* the time. He would probably do as other spirits did—go and come, and go and come.

About communicating? He would probably find that plain, straight talk was too strong for earth-dwellers. It had been tried out on them often, and usually disastrously. It was like forcing champagne and brandy on men who had always been content with beer. Straight talk from the spirit world often produced epilepsy among earth-dwellers. It was too much for them to have all at once. And then such a very little was enough to content them, and he would find it far more satisfactory to furnish them with a little—a mysterious and nicely stage-managed *little*— than with a plain-spoken, straight from the shoulder *lot.* To the wise, and he was now beginning to be wise, a hint is sufficient. Suppose, his wife being at her dressing table, he were to plant himself beneath and rap out a few words in the Morse code? Let him keep on with these rappings until she called in someone to interpret them for her.

He could not only comfort her about his death and reassure her as to his general whereabouts and activities, but he could have a lot of fun with her. There is no harm in having harmless fun with those you love. It is the fear of fun, the suspicion with which it is regarded, more than any one single thing that has given the man-pack such a miserable run for its money. By means of the Morse code, he could persuade her to buy a ouija board. He would love that, and so would she and the children.

But Derrick kept putting off his return to the earth.

If a loving husband and father were turned loose in the finest jewelry store in the world and told to take his pick of the diamonds and rubies and pears, as many as he could carry, he would not at once rush off to tell his loved ones of the privilege that had been extended to him. He would stick to the store. He would hang about it possibly for days, taking mental stock of all its precious contents. Blurring the tops of the glass show cases with his breath and staring till his eyes ached.

Derrick was in somewhat the same case. He had the impulse to rush out at once to his family to tell them of the extraordinary wisdom and mental equilibrium which were being lavished upon him; but he was restrained by the very natural wish to remain where he was until the last vestiges of earth-marks had been rubbed from him.

He had been a very decent man as men go; but the amazing sense of purity which now pervaded his being was new in his experience. It was not so much a smug consciousness and conceit in personal purity as a happy negation of all that is not directly of the spirit in its most calm and lucid moments.

Here nothing soiled, and nothing tired. An immense and delicious mental activity swept one past all the earthly halting places. There was no eating or drinking or love-making. There was no sleeping, and the mere fact of existence among the lights and shadows and colors was more cleansing than the most refined species of Oriental bathing.

Life here was mental. Burning curiosities and instantaneous satisfactions thereof seemed at once the aim and the end of existence. And since there can be no limit to the number and extent of the spirit's curiosities, it was obvious that there could be no limit to existence itself. And Derrick together with those spirits which had passed into the Place at the same time with his own began to have a clear understanding of humanity.

Here, for instance, all that one learned about God was fact, but there was so much to learn that heaping fact on fact, with a speed unknown on earth—even in the heaping of falsehood upon falsehood—it would take from now until eternity to learn all about God. And this, of course, had to be the case. Since God is infinite, He can only be wholly revealed to those who, by pursuing knowledge to infinity, have acquired infinite knowledge.

The man-mob conception of God seemed very absurd to him. For man had formed it in the days when he still believed the earth to be flat, and had subsequently seen no good reason or obligation to change it. The man-mob had never gone beyond the idea that God was a definite person whom certain things like praise and toadying were infinitely agreeable, and to whom certain other things like being happy and not very serious were as a red rag to a bull. This conception was the work of certain men who, the moment they had conceived a God in their own narrow and intolerant image, became themselves godlike. To men of that stamp simple and practical discoveries in geography, mechanics or ceramics would have been utterly out of the question. But the greatest discovery of all with its precise descriptions and limitations lay to their credit. And from that time to this no very great number of men had ever taken the trouble to gainsay them, or ever would.

"I never did, for one," thought Derrick, and he recalled with a smile the religious phases through which he had passed in his earth-life. As he remembered that he had once, for a short period of his childhood, believed in the fiery, old-fashioned Hell of the Puritans, the smile broadened, and he burst into joyous and musical laughter.

III

There was one thing that he must be prepared to face. His wife and their three children would *look* just as they had looked when he last saw them, and as a matter of fact they would be just what they were; but to him, with all his new and accurate knowledge and his inconceivably clear vision, they would seem to have changed greatly.

He had always considered his wife an intelligent, well educated, even an advanced woman, and he had considered his children, especially the youngest, who was a girl, altogether brighter and more precocious than his neighbors' children. Well, along those lines he must be prepared for shocks and disillusionment.

It would not be possible, for instance, to sit down with his wife to a rational discussion of anything. She would seem like a moron to him; superstitious, backward, ignorant and stubborn as a mule. He would find her erroneous beliefs and convictions hard to change. It would be the same with the children, but in less degree. The oldest was twelve, and his brain was still capable of a little development. He would have some inclination to listen to his father and to believe what his father told him. With Sammy, aged ten, and Ethel, aged eight, much might be done.

He would begin by asking these young hopefuls to forget everything that had been taught them, with the exception of that one startling fact, that the world is round. He would then proceed to feed their eager young earth-minds on as many simple and helpful truths as would be good for them, and he would show them, what was now so clear to him, how to find happiness on earth with a minimum of labor and worry.

A question carelessly thought and instantly answered caused him to return to earth sooner than he had intended. The answer to his question had been in the nature of a hard jolt. It had to do with sin.

Sin, he learned, is not doing something which other people regard as sinful, but something which you yourself know to be sinful. Lying, theft, arson, murder, bigamy may on occasion be acts of light, charity and commiseration, no matter how the man-mob may execrate, judge and punish them. But the same things may be also the worst of crimes. And only the individual who commits them can possibly know. That individual doesn't even have to know. It is what he thinks that counts; not what he pretends to think, not what he swears in open court that he did think, but what, without self-deception, he actually did and does think.

And Derrick learned that if during his brief absence from them any of those earth-persons whom he loved so dearly had sinned, committed some act or other which they knew for themselves to be sinful, there would be an opaque veil which neither his eyes nor theirs could pierce, nor the words of their mouths.

But he was not *greatly* worried.

As men count time he had been absent from the earth and from his loved ones only for a very short time. They would still be in the depths of mourning for him. And even if they were evilly disposed persons, which they were not, they would hardly have had time to think of anything but their grief and their loss.

IV

As he left the Place of the wonderful lights and shades and colors and perfumes, he realized that he could not have been perfectly happy in it. He could not have been *perfectly* happy, because he now perceived that by the mere act of leaving it behind he had become still happier, and that perfect happiness could only be his when he reached "home" and beheld his loved ones.

When he had been taken from his home to the hospital the buds on the pear trees had been on the point of bursting. The pear trees would be in full bloom now. When he had been taken away the shutters of the house had been taken from their hinges, painted a pleasant applegreen and stood in the old carriage house to dry. They would be back on their hinges now, vying in smartness with the two new coats of white paint which the painters had been spreading over the low, rambling house itself. How sweet the house would look among the fresh young greens of spring! Perhaps the peewees who came every year had already begun to build in the veranda eaves.

He had no more than time to think these things before he had come to the end of his journey.

Home had never looked so sweet or inviting. The garden was bounded on the south by a little brook; and beyond this was a little hill planted with kalmia and many species of native ferns.

It was on the top of this hill that he alighted, and here he paused for a while and filled his eyes with the humble beauty of the home which his earth-mind had conceived and achieved.

From the hill he could see not only the house, but to the left the garage and beyond that the stable. It was about eleven o'clock in the morning, and it seemed queer to him that at that hour and at that season there should be no sign of life anywhere. Surely the gardener and his assistant ought to be at work. He turned a puzzled and indignant glance back upon the garden, and he observed a curious phenomenon.

A strip of soil in the upper left-hand corner of the garden was being turned and broken by a spade. Near-by a fork was taking manure from a wheelbarrow and spreading it over the roots of a handsome crabapple.

Both the spade and the fork appeared to be performing these meritorious acts without the aid of any human agency.

And Derrick knew at once that McIntyre, the gardener, and Chub, his assistant, must, since his departure, have sinned in their own eyes, so that they could now no longer show themselves to him, or he to them.

He started anxiously toward the house, but a familiar sound arrested him.

The blue roadster, hitting on all its cylinders, came slowly out of the garage and descended the hill and crossed the bridge and honked its horn for the mill corner and sped off along the county road toward Stamford *all by itself.*

There was nobody in the roadster. He could swear to that. And this meant, of course, that Britton, the chauffeur, had done something which he knew that he ought not to have done, and was forever separated from those who had gone beyond.

When Derrick reached the house he was in an exceedingly anxious state of mind. He stepped into the entrance hall and listened. And heard no sound. He passed rapidly through the master's rooms downstairs and upstairs. In the sewing-room a thread and needle was mending the heel of a silk stocking, but there did not seem to be anybody in the room.

He looked from the window and saw two fishing-poles and a tin pail moving eagerly toward the river. The boys, perhaps. Oh, what *could* they have done to separate themselves from him? The window was open and he called and shouted, but the fishing-poles and the tin pail kept on going.

He went downstairs, through the dining-room and into the pantry.

His heart stood still.

On tiptoe on the seat of a chair stood his little girl, Ethel. Her hair shone like spun gold. She looked like an angel. And his heart swelled with an exquisite bliss; but before he could speak to her and make himself known, she had reached down something from the next to the top shelf and put it in her mouth.

At that instant she vanished.

He lingered for a while about the house and gardens, but it was no use. He knew that. They had all sinned in some way or other, and therefore he was indeed dead to them, and they to him.

Back of the stables were woods. From these woods there came a sudden sound of barking. The sound was familiar to Derrick, and thrilled him.

"If I can hear Scoop," he thought, "Scoop can hear me."

He whistled long and shrill.

Not long after a little black dog came running, his stomach to the ground, his floppy silk ears flying. With a sob Derrick knelt and took the dog in his arms.

"Oh, Mumsey!" called Ethel. "Do come and look at Scoopie. He's doing all his tricks by himself."

The two looked from a window, and saw the little dog sit up and play dead and roll over—all very joyously—and jump as if through circled arms. Then they saw his tail droop and his head droop and his left hind leg begin to scratch furiously at his ribs. He always *had* to do that when anyone scratched his back in a particular spot.

When Derrick returned to the Place of the wonderful lights and shadows he was very unhappy and he knew that he must always be unhappy.

"Instead of coming to this Place," he said to himself, "knowing what I know now, I might just as well have gone to Hell."

A voice, sardonic and on the verge of laughter, answered him.

"That's just what you did."

Bibliography

Irvin S. Cobb

"The Belled Buzzard." *Saturday Evening Post* (28 September 1912). In *The Escape of Mr. Trimm: His Plight and Other Plights.* New York: George H. Doran, 1913.

"Fishhead." *All-Story Cavalier* (11 January 1913). In *The Escape of Mr. Trimm: His Plight and Other Plights.* New York: George H. Doran, 1913.

"The Gallowsmith." *All-Story Weekly* (9 February 1918). In *From Place to Place.* New York: George H. Doran, 1920.

"Darkness." *Saturday Evening Post* (20 August 1921). In *Sundry Accounts.* New York: George H. Doran, 1922.

"Snake Doctor." *Cosmopolitan* (November 1922). In *Snake Doctor and Other Stories.* New York: George H. Doran, 1923.

"The Second Coming of a First Husband." In *Snake Doctor and Other Stories.* New York: George H. Doran, 1923.

"The Unbroken Chain." *Cosmopolitan* (September 1923). In *On an Island that Cost $24.00.* New York: George H. Doran, 1926.

"Faith, Hope and Charity." *Cosmopolitan* (April 1930). In *Faith, Hope and Charity.* Indianapolis: Bobbs-Merrill, 1934.

Gouverneur Morris

"The Crocodile." *Collier's* (25 November 1905). In *The Footprint and Other Stories*. New York: Scribner's, 1908.

"The Footprint." *Collier's* (14 December 1907). In *The Footprint and Other Stories*. New York: Scribner's, 1908.

"The Execution." In *The Footprint and Other Stories*. New York: Scribner's, 1908.

"The Bride's Dead." *Collier's* (28 November 1908). In *It and Other Stories*. New York: Scribner's, 1912.

"Back There in the Grass." *Collier's* (16 December 1911). In *It and Other Stories*. New York: Scribner's, 1912.

"Derrick's Return." *Cosmopolitan* (December 1923). *Current Opinion* (January 1924).

About S. T. Joshi

S. T. JOSHI is the author of *The Weird Tale* (1990), *H. P. Lovecraft: The Decline of the West* (1990), and *Unutterable Horror: A History of Supernatural Fiction* (2012). He has prepared corrected editions of H. P. Lovecraft's work for Arkham House and annotated editions of Lovecraft's stories for Penguin Classics. He has also prepared editions of Lovecraft's collected essays and poetry. His exhaustive biography, *H. P. Lovecraft: A Life* (1996), was expanded as *I Am Providence: The Life and Times of H. P. Lovecraft* (2010). He is the editor of the anthologies *American Supernatural Tales* (Penguin, 2007), *Black Wings* I-VI (PS Publishing, 2010, 2012, 2013), *A Mountain Walked: Great Tales of the Cthulhu Mythos* (Centipede Press, 2014), *The Madness of Cthulhu* (Titan Books, 2014-15), and *Searchers After Horror: New Tales of the Weird and Fantastic* (Fedogan & Bremer, 2014). He is the editor of the *Lovecraft Annual, Spectral Realms,* and *Penumbra* (all published by Hippocampus Press). Among his works of fiction are *The Recurring Doom: Tales of Mystery and Horror* (Sarnath Press, 2019) and *Something from Below* (PS Publishing, 2019).

www.ingramcontent.com/pod-product-compliance
Lightning Source LLC
Chambersburg PA
CBHW050926030726
47503CB00007BB/2482